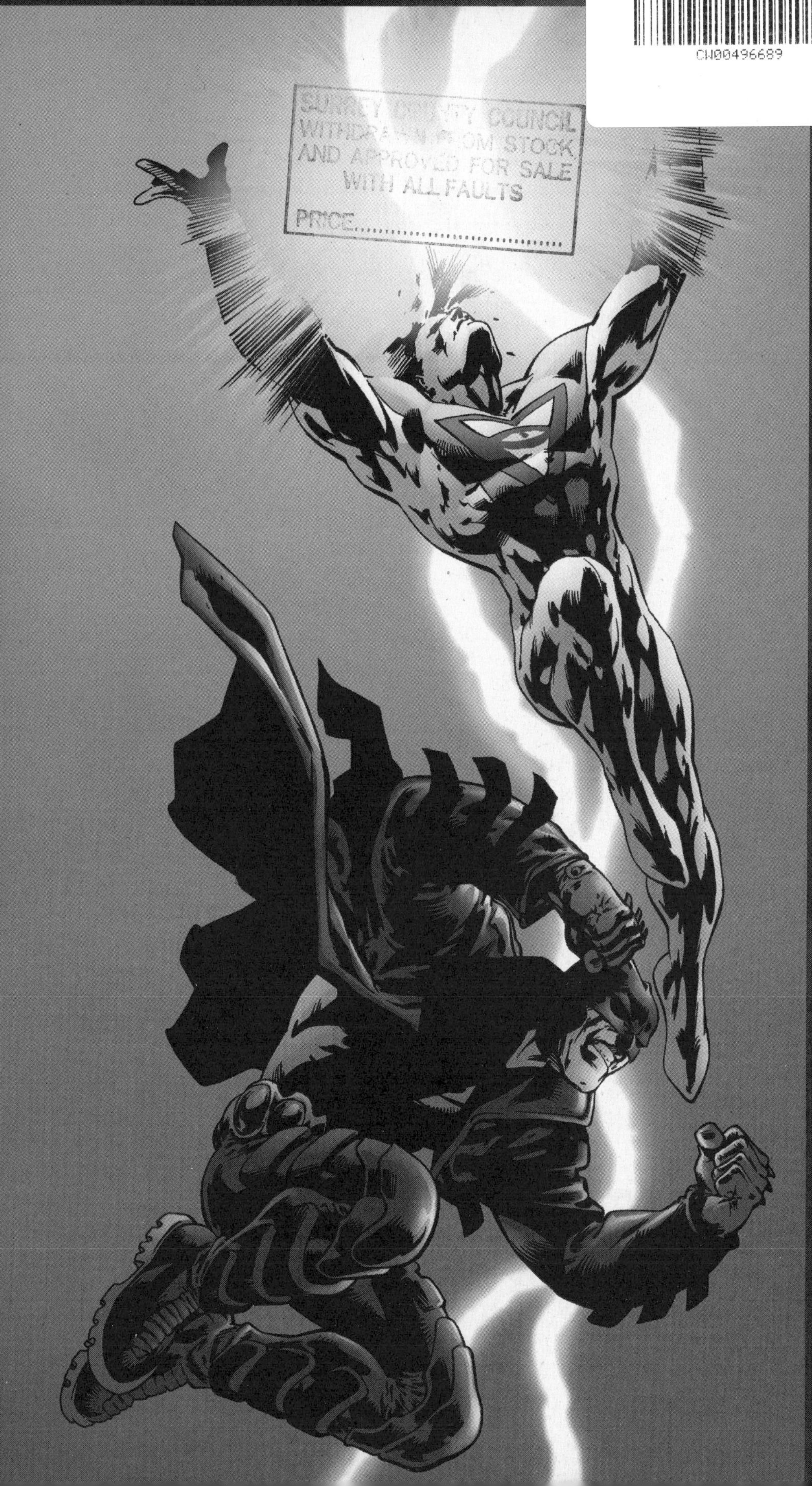

A FINER WORLD

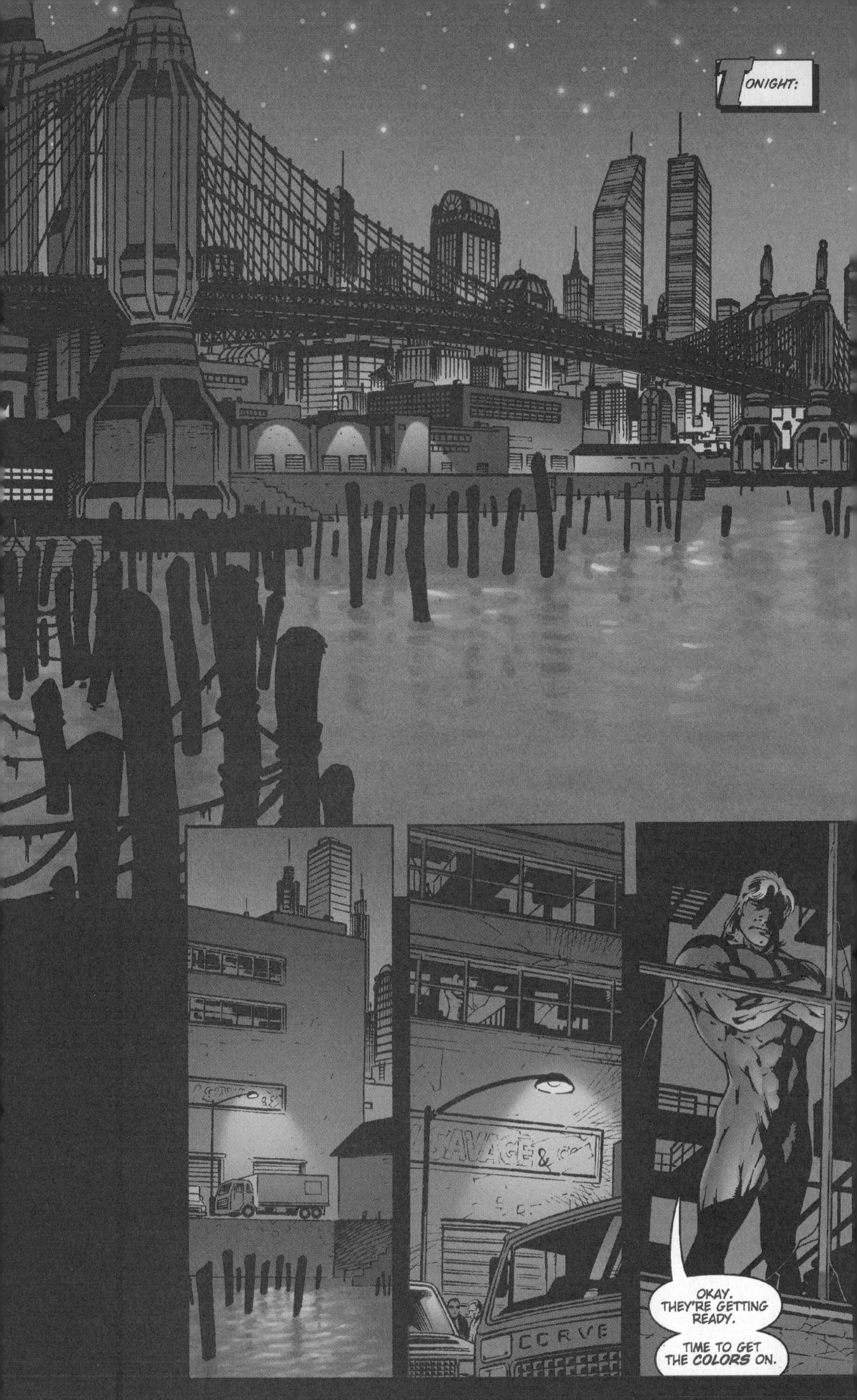
TONIGHT:
SAVAGE &
OKAY. THEY'RE GETTING READY.
TIME TO GET THE COLORS ON.

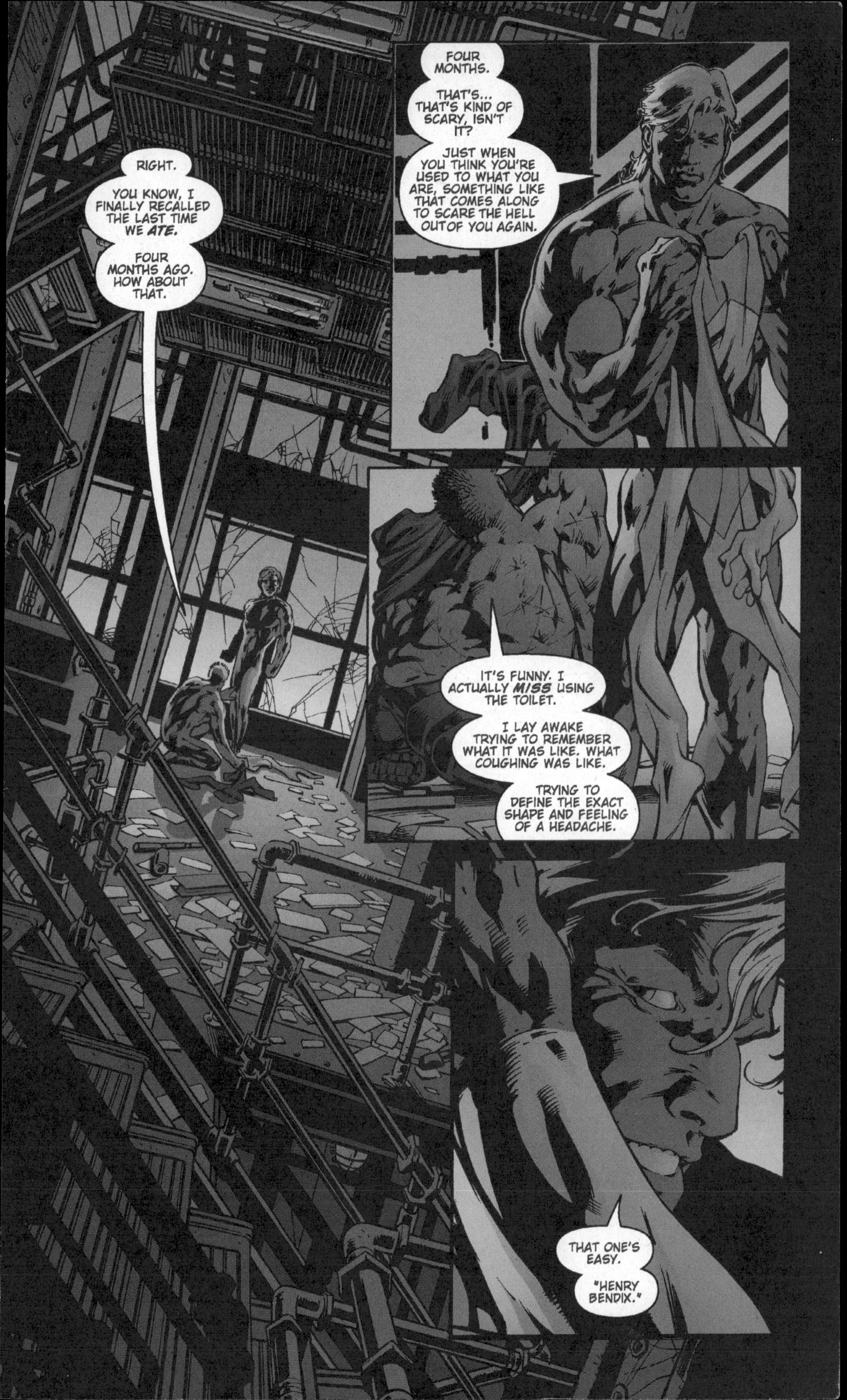
RIGHT.
YOU KNOW, I FINALLY RECALLED THE LAST TIME WE *ATE.*
FOUR MONTHS AGO. HOW ABOUT THAT.
FOUR MONTHS.
THAT'S... THAT'S KIND OF SCARY, ISN'T IT?
JUST WHEN YOU THINK YOU'RE USED TO WHAT YOU ARE, SOMETHING LIKE THAT COMES ALONG TO SCARE THE HELL OUT OF YOU AGAIN.
IT'S FUNNY. I ACTUALLY *MISS* USING THE TOILET.
I LAY AWAKE TRYING TO REMEMBER WHAT IT WAS LIKE. WHAT COUGHING WAS LIKE.
TRYING TO DEFINE THE EXACT SHAPE AND FEELING OF A HEADACHE.
THAT ONE'S EASY.
"HENRY BENDIX."

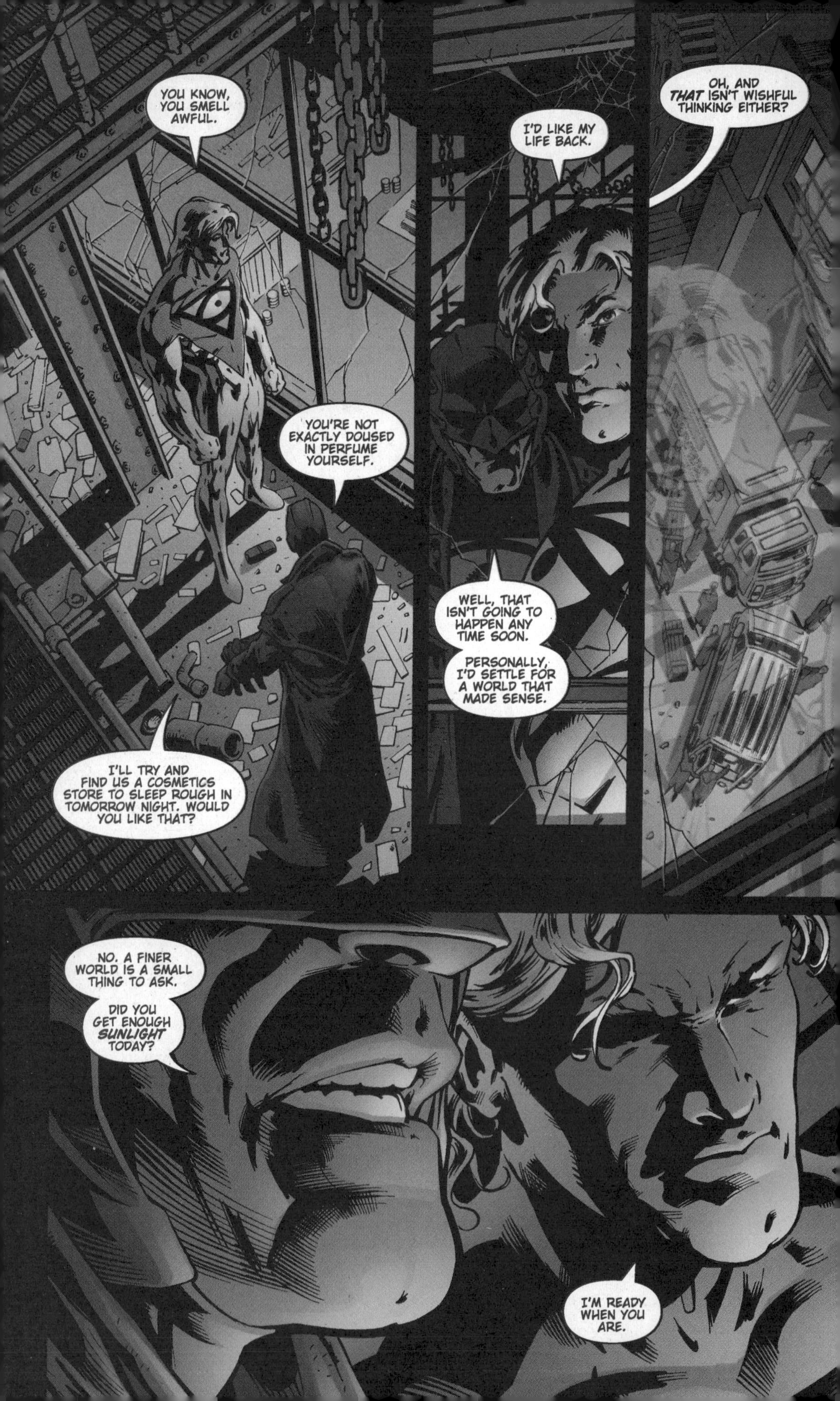
YOU KNOW, YOU SMELL AWFUL.
YOU'RE NOT EXACTLY DOUSED IN PERFUME YOURSELF.
I'LL TRY AND FIND US A COSMETICS STORE TO SLEEP ROUGH IN TOMORROW NIGHT. WOULD YOU LIKE THAT?
I'D LIKE MY LIFE BACK.
WELL, THAT ISN'T GOING TO HAPPEN ANY TIME SOON.
PERSONALLY, I'D SETTLE FOR A WORLD THAT MADE SENSE.
OH, AND *THAT* ISN'T WISHFUL THINKING EITHER?
NO. A FINER WORLD IS A SMALL THING TO ASK.
DID YOU GET ENOUGH *SUNLIGHT* TODAY?
I'M READY WHEN YOU ARE.

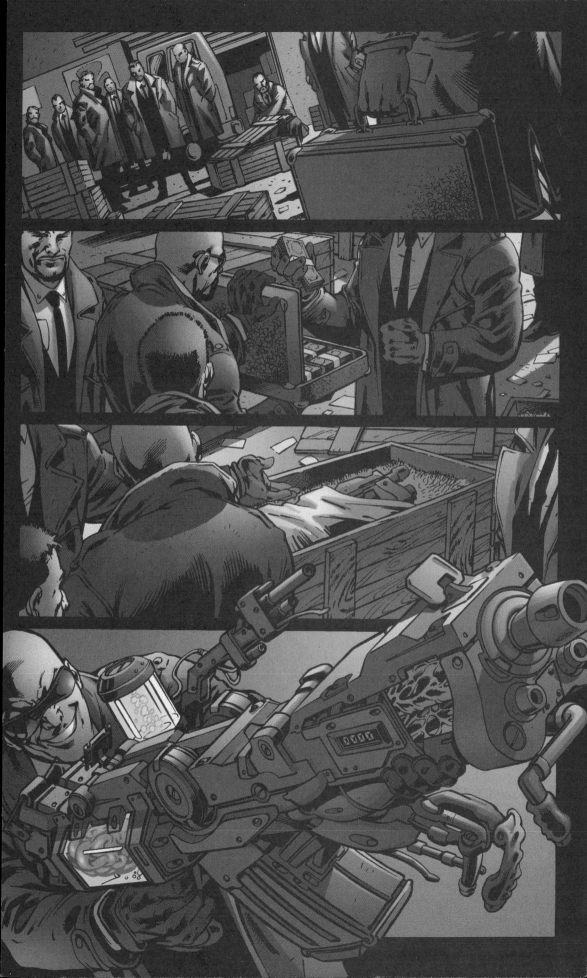

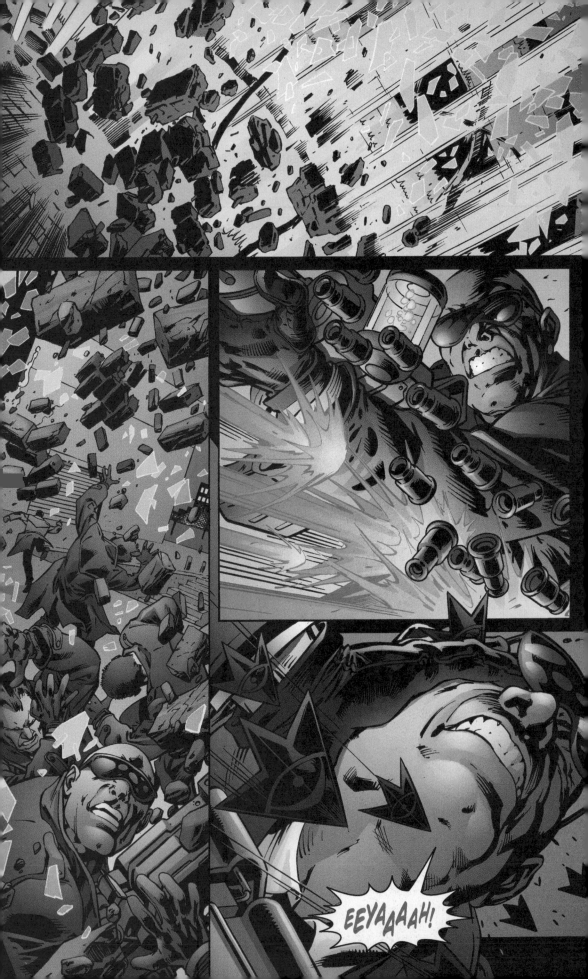

EEYAAAAH!

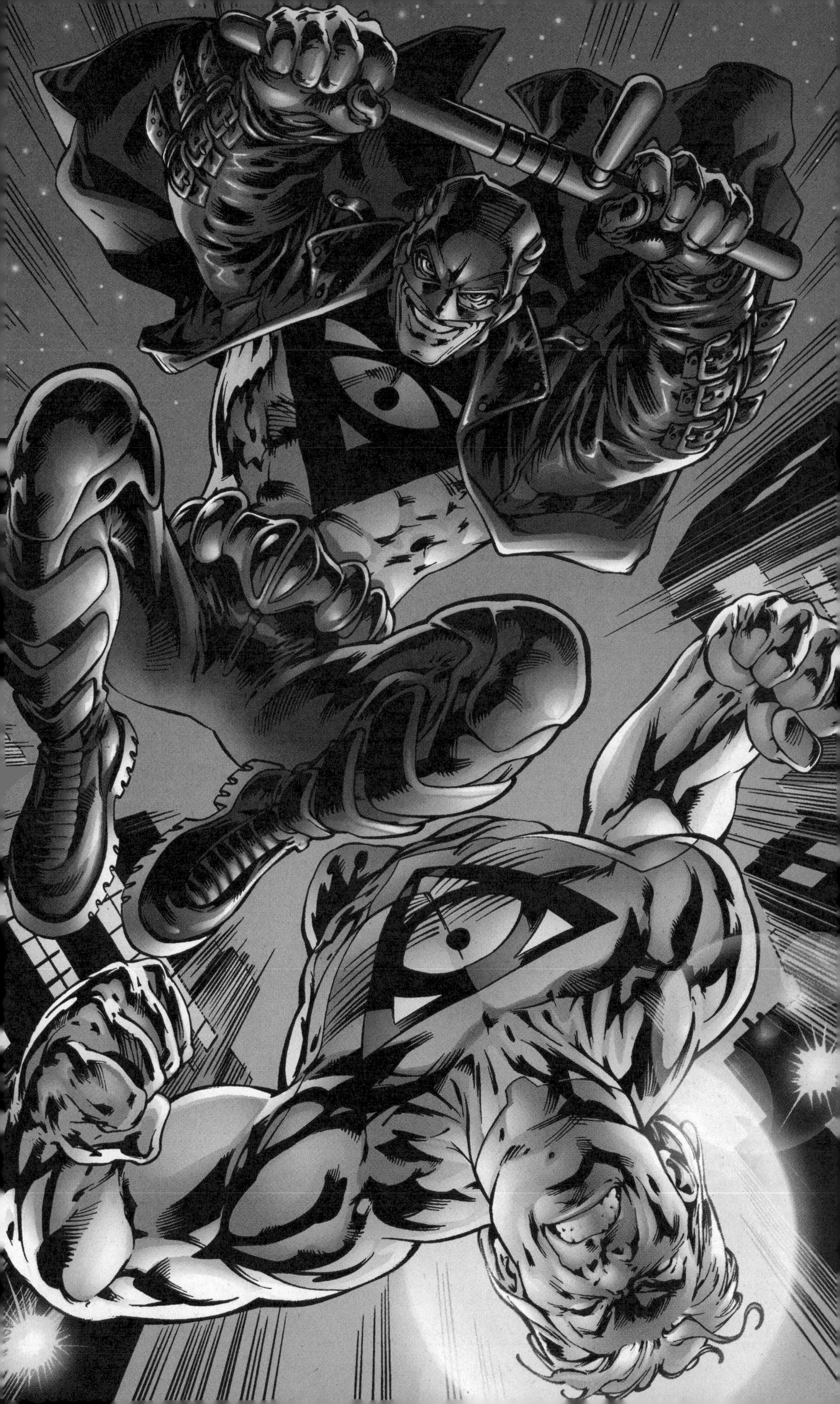

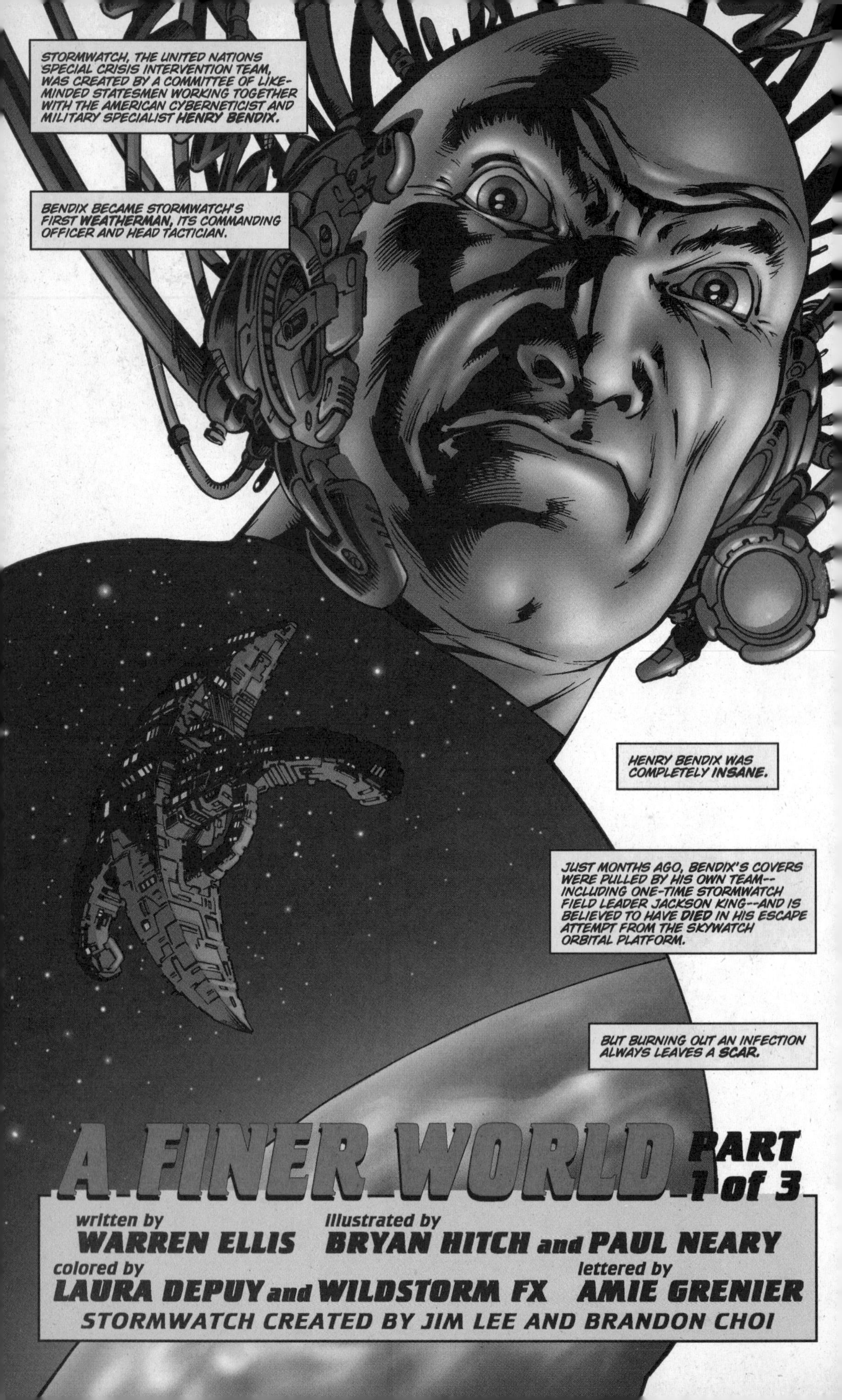
STORMWATCH, THE UNITED NATIONS SPECIAL CRISIS INTERVENTION TEAM, WAS CREATED BY A COMMITTEE OF LIKE-MINDED STATESMEN WORKING TOGETHER WITH THE AMERICAN CYBERNETICIST AND MILITARY SPECIALIST HENRY BENDIX.
BENDIX BECAME STORMWATCH'S FIRST WEATHERMAN, ITS COMMANDING OFFICER AND HEAD TACTICIAN.
HENRY BENDIX WAS COMPLETELY INSANE.
JUST MONTHS AGO, BENDIX'S COVERS WERE PULLED BY HIS OWN TEAM--INCLUDING ONE-TIME STORMWATCH FIELD LEADER JACKSON KING--AND IS BELIEVED TO HAVE DIED IN HIS ESCAPE ATTEMPT FROM THE SKYWATCH ORBITAL PLATFORM.
BUT BURNING OUT AN INFECTION ALWAYS LEAVES A SCAR.
A FINER WORLD PART 1 of 3
written by WARREN ELLIS
illustrated by BRYAN HITCH and PAUL NEARY
colored by LAURA DEPUY and WILDSTORM FX
lettered by AMIE GRENIER
STORMWATCH CREATED BY JIM LEE AND BRANDON CHOI

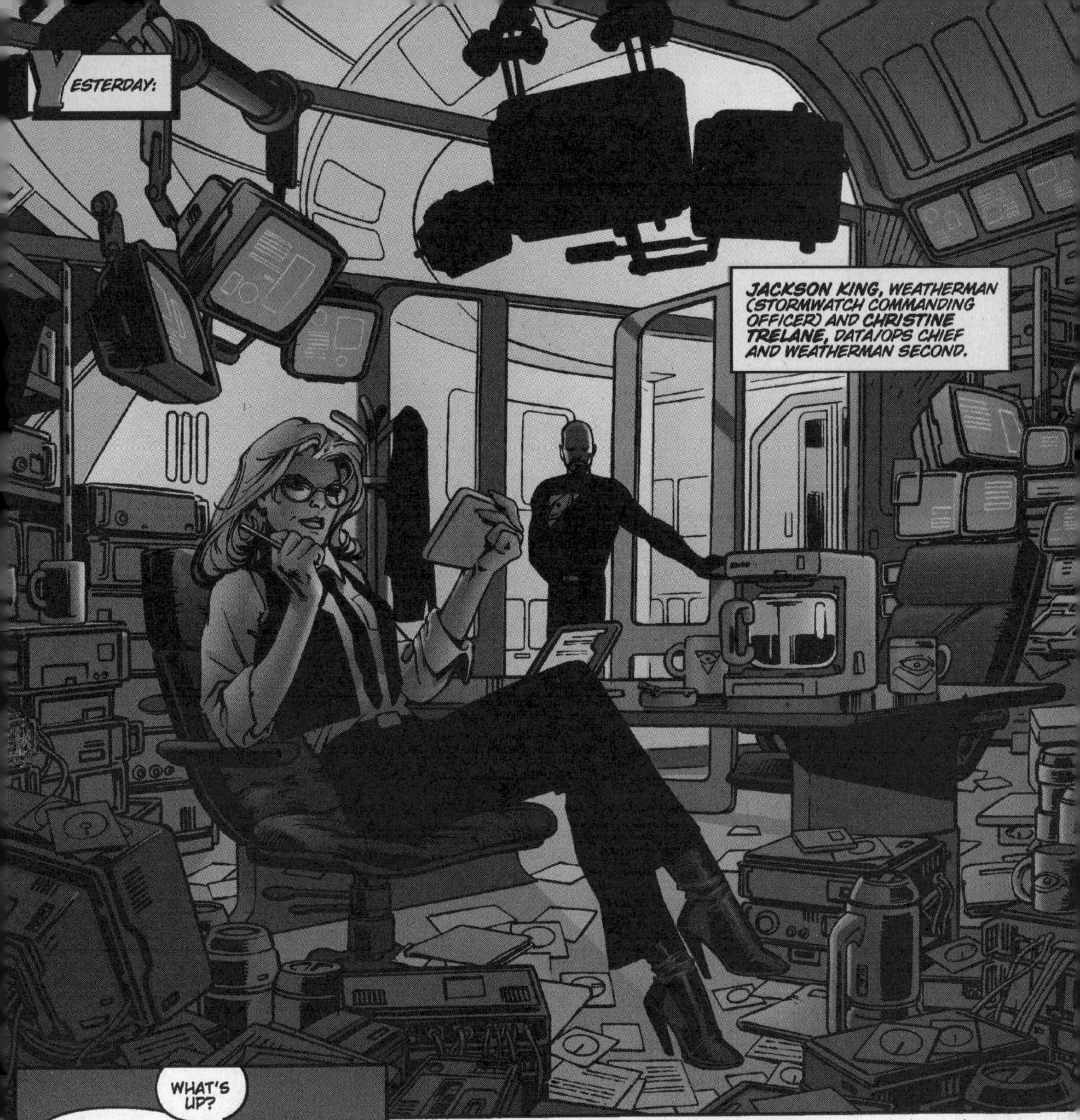
YESTERDAY:
JACKSON KING, WEATHERMAN (STORMWATCH COMMANDING OFFICER) AND CHRISTINE TRELANE, DATA/OPS CHIEF AND WEATHERMAN SECOND.

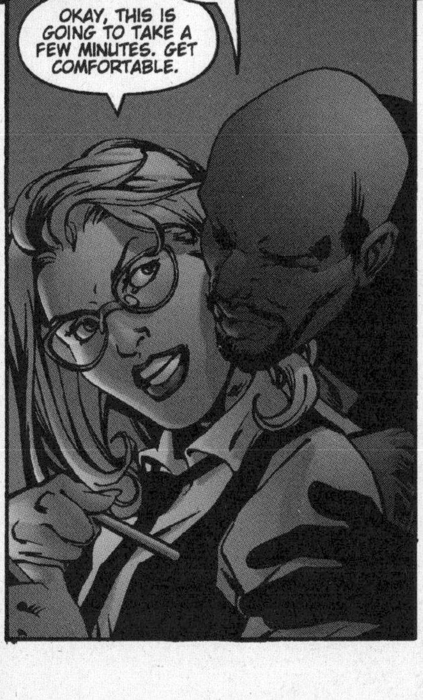
WHAT'S UP?
OKAY, THIS IS GOING TO TAKE A FEW MINUTES. GET COMFORTABLE.

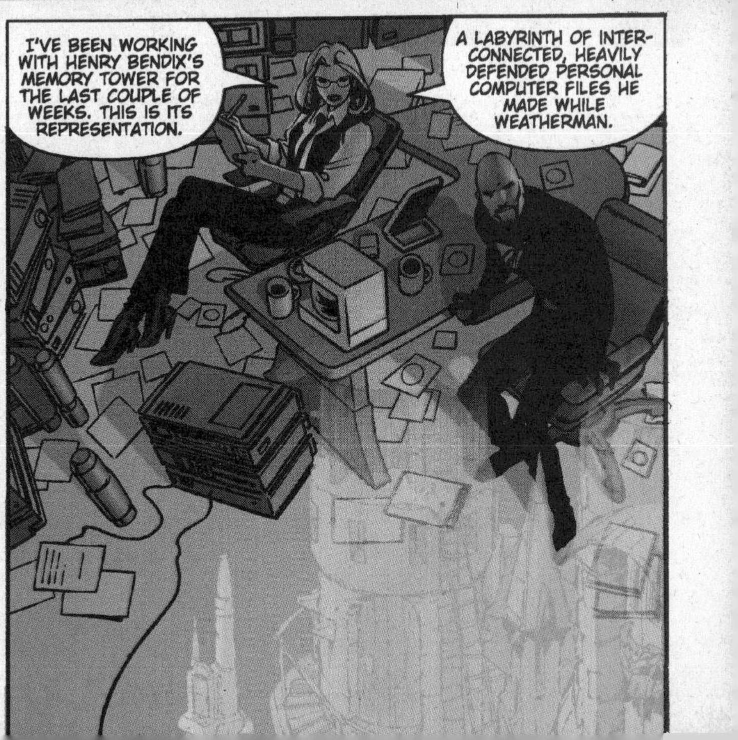
I'VE BEEN WORKING WITH HENRY BENDIX'S MEMORY TOWER FOR THE LAST COUPLE OF WEEKS. THIS IS ITS REPRESENTATION.
A LABYRINTH OF INTER-CONNECTED, HEAVILY DEFENDED PERSONAL COMPUTER FILES HE MADE WHILE WEATHERMAN.

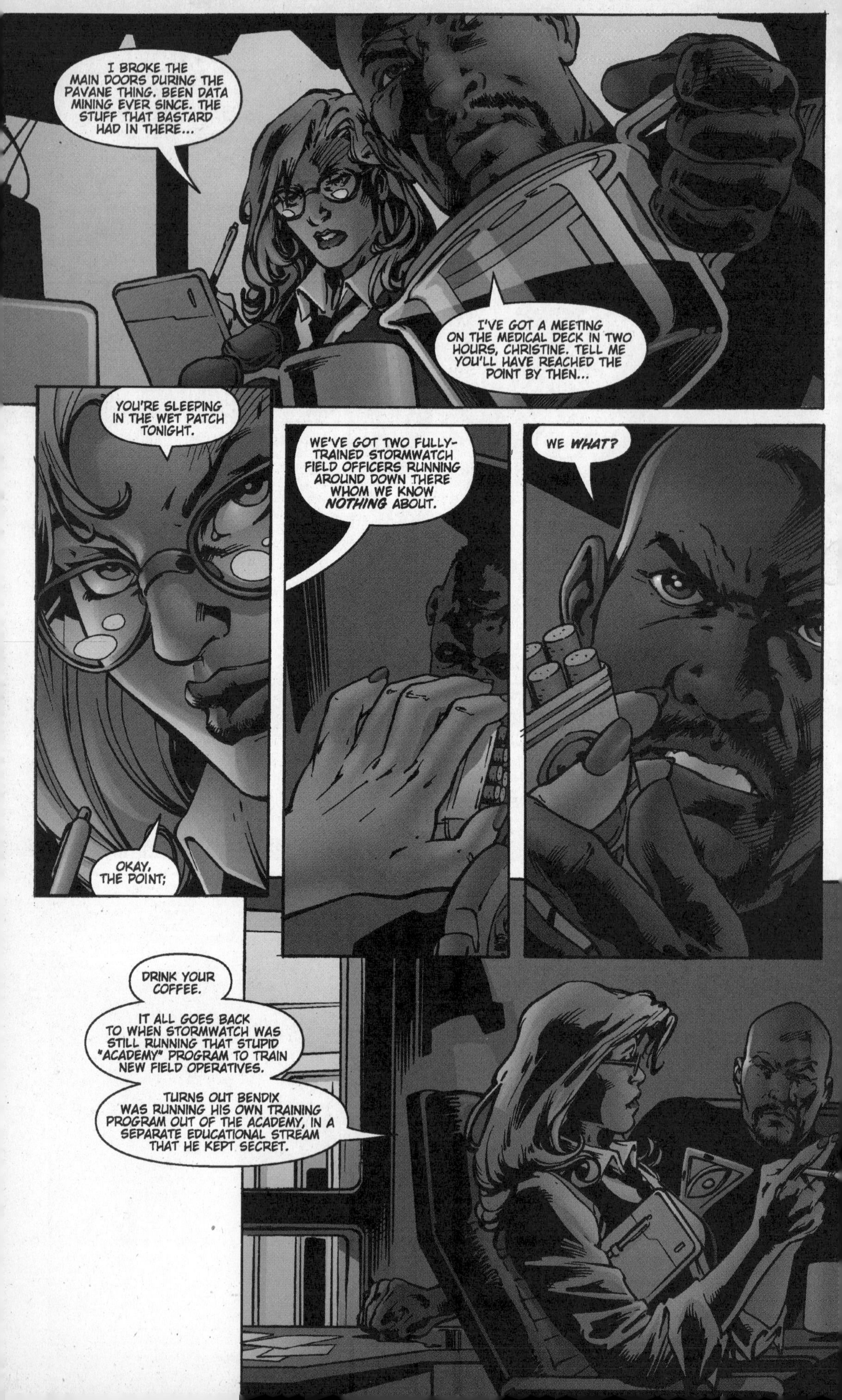
I BROKE THE MAIN DOORS DURING THE PAVANE THING. BEEN DATA MINING EVER SINCE. THE STUFF THAT BASTARD HAD IN THERE...
I'VE GOT A MEETING ON THE MEDICAL DECK IN TWO HOURS, CHRISTINE. TELL ME YOU'LL HAVE REACHED THE POINT BY THEN...
YOU'RE SLEEPING IN THE WET PATCH TONIGHT.
OKAY, THE POINT;
WE'VE GOT TWO FULLY-TRAINED STORMWATCH FIELD OFFICERS RUNNING AROUND DOWN THERE WHOM WE KNOW *NOTHING* ABOUT.
WE *WHAT?*
DRINK YOUR COFFEE.
IT ALL GOES BACK TO WHEN STORMWATCH WAS STILL RUNNING THAT STUPID "ACADEMY" PROGRAM TO TRAIN NEW FIELD OPERATIVES.
TURNS OUT BENDIX WAS RUNNING HIS OWN TRAINING PROGRAM OUT OF THE ACADEMY, IN A SEPARATE EDUCATIONAL STREAM THAT HE KEPT SECRET.

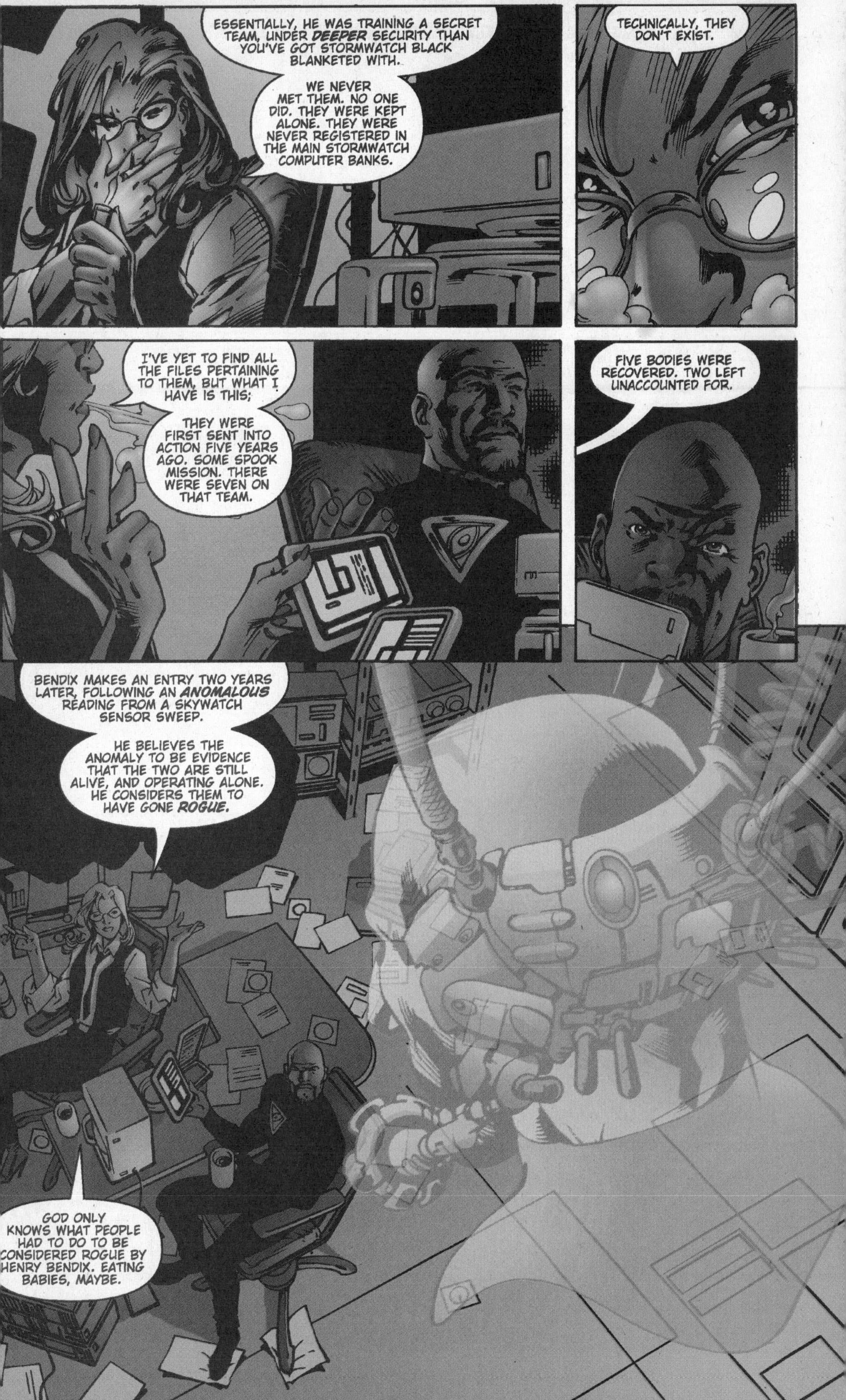
ESSENTIALLY, HE WAS TRAINING A SECRET TEAM, UNDER DEEPER SECURITY THAN YOU'VE GOT STORMWATCH BLACK BLANKETED WITH.
WE NEVER MET THEM. NO ONE DID. THEY WERE KEPT ALONE. THEY WERE NEVER REGISTERED IN THE MAIN STORMWATCH COMPUTER BANKS.
TECHNICALLY, THEY DON'T EXIST.
I'VE YET TO FIND ALL THE FILES PERTAINING TO THEM, BUT WHAT I HAVE IS THIS;
THEY WERE FIRST SENT INTO ACTION FIVE YEARS AGO. SOME SPOOK MISSION. THERE WERE SEVEN ON THAT TEAM.
FIVE BODIES WERE RECOVERED. TWO LEFT UNACCOUNTED FOR.
BENDIX MAKES AN ENTRY TWO YEARS LATER, FOLLOWING AN ANOMALOUS READING FROM A SKYWATCH SENSOR SWEEP.
HE BELIEVES THE ANOMALY TO BE EVIDENCE THAT THE TWO ARE STILL ALIVE, AND OPERATING ALONE. HE CONSIDERS THEM TO HAVE GONE ROGUE.
GOD ONLY KNOWS WHAT PEOPLE HAD TO DO TO BE CONSIDERED ROGUE BY HENRY BENDIX. EATING BABIES, MAYBE.

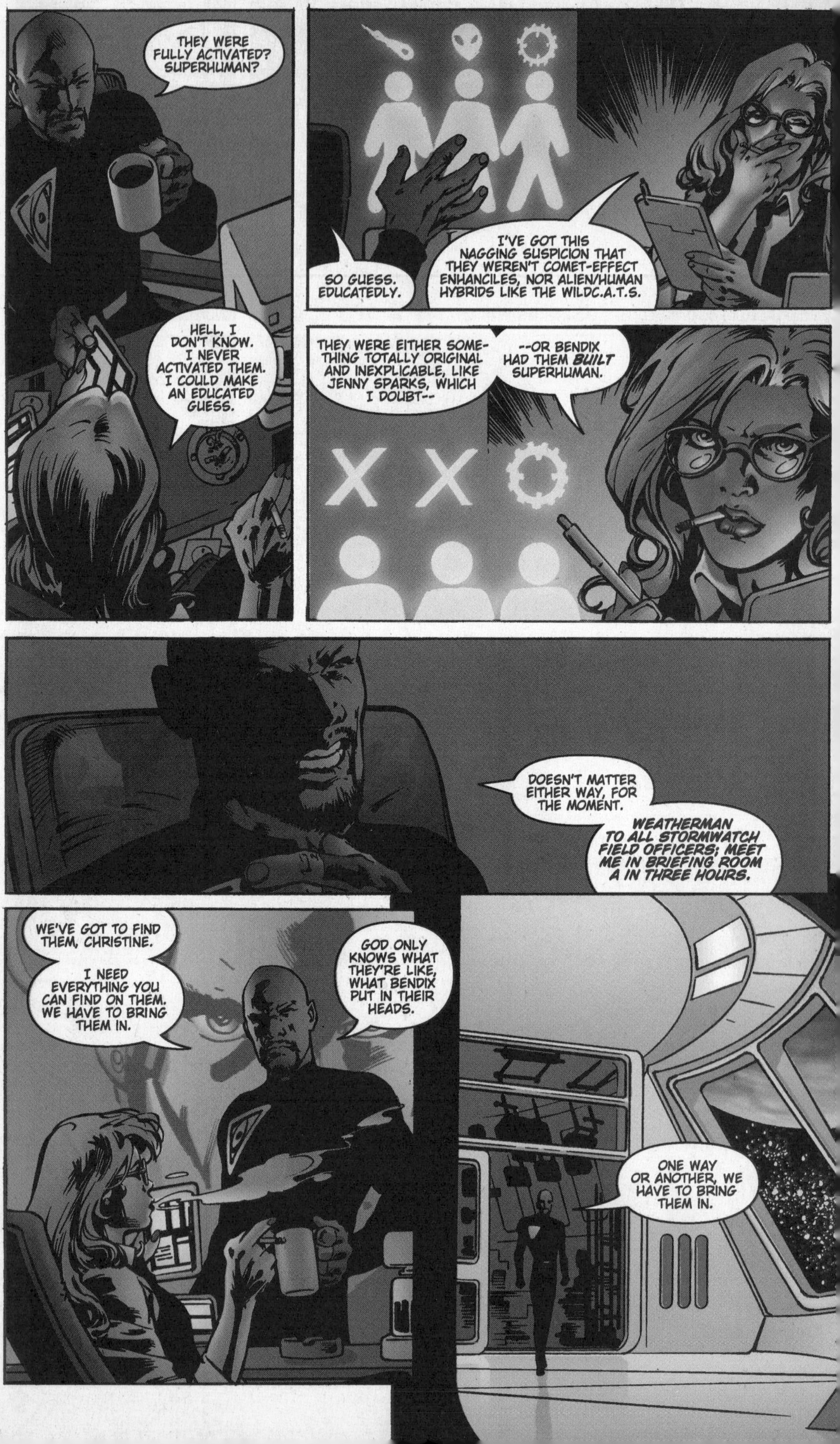
THEY WERE FULLY ACTIVATED? SUPERHUMAN?
HELL, I DON'T KNOW. I NEVER ACTIVATED THEM. I COULD MAKE AN EDUCATED GUESS.
SO GUESS. EDUCATEDLY.
I'VE GOT THIS NAGGING SUSPICION THAT THEY WEREN'T COMET-EFFECT ENHANCILES, NOR ALIEN/HUMAN HYBRIDS LIKE THE WILDC.A.T.S.
THEY WERE EITHER SOME-THING TOTALLY ORIGINAL AND INEXPLICABLE, LIKE JENNY SPARKS, WHICH I DOUBT--
--OR BENDIX HAD THEM BUILT SUPERHUMAN.
DOESN'T MATTER EITHER WAY, FOR THE MOMENT.
WEATHERMAN TO ALL STORMWATCH FIELD OFFICERS; MEET ME IN BRIEFING ROOM A IN THREE HOURS.
WE'VE GOT TO FIND THEM, CHRISTINE.
I NEED EVERYTHING YOU CAN FIND ON THEM. WE HAVE TO BRING THEM IN.
GOD ONLY KNOWS WHAT THEY'RE LIKE, WHAT BENDIX PUT IN THEIR HEADS.
ONE WAY OR ANOTHER, WE HAVE TO BRING THEM IN.

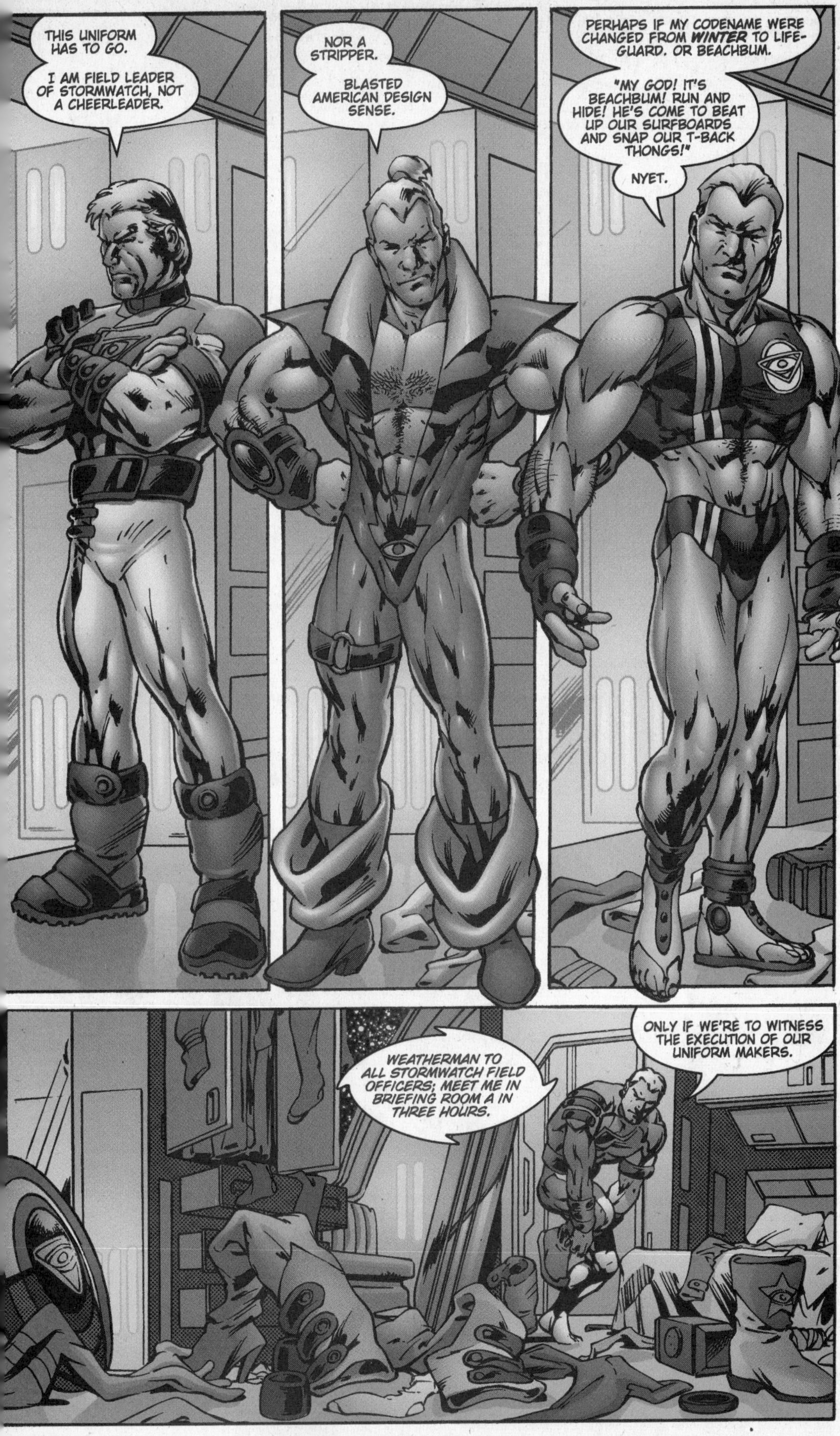
THIS UNIFORM HAS TO GO.
I AM FIELD LEADER OF STORMWATCH, NOT A CHEERLEADER.
NOR A STRIPPER.
BLASTED AMERICAN DESIGN SENSE.
PERHAPS IF MY CODENAME WERE CHANGED FROM WINTER TO LIFE-GUARD. OR BEACHBUM.
"MY GOD! IT'S BEACHBUM! RUN AND HIDE! HE'S COME TO BEAT UP OUR SURFBOARDS AND SNAP OUR T-BACK THONGS!"
NYET.
WEATHERMAN TO ALL STORMWATCH FIELD OFFICERS; MEET ME IN BRIEFING ROOM A IN THREE HOURS.
ONLY IF WE'RE TO WITNESS THE EXECUTION OF OUR UNIFORM MAKERS.

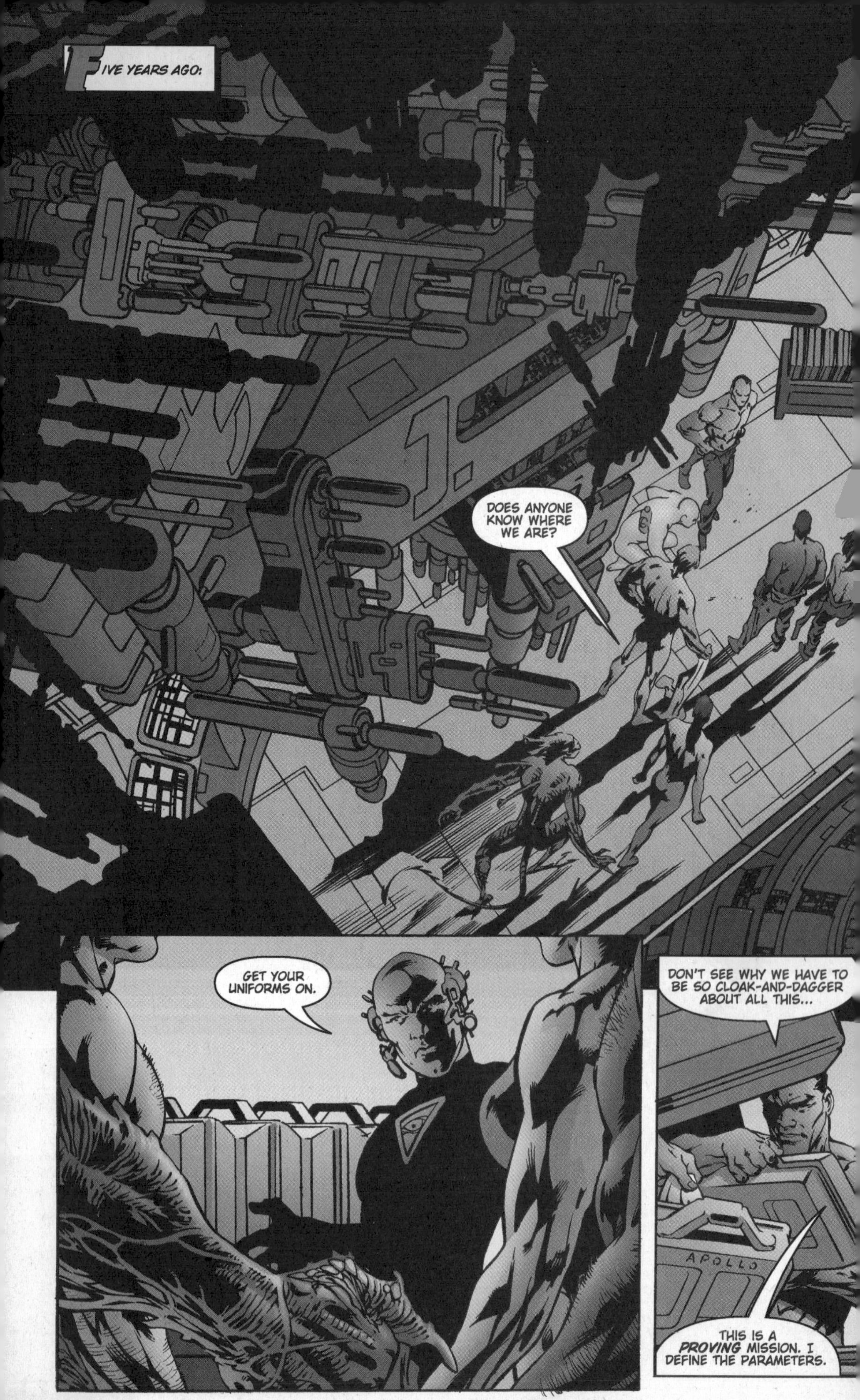
FIVE YEARS AGO:
DOES ANYONE KNOW WHERE WE ARE?
GET YOUR UNIFORMS ON.
DON'T SEE WHY WE HAVE TO BE SO CLOAK-AND-DAGGER ABOUT ALL THIS...
APOLLO
THIS IS A PROVING MISSION. I DEFINE THE PARAMETERS.

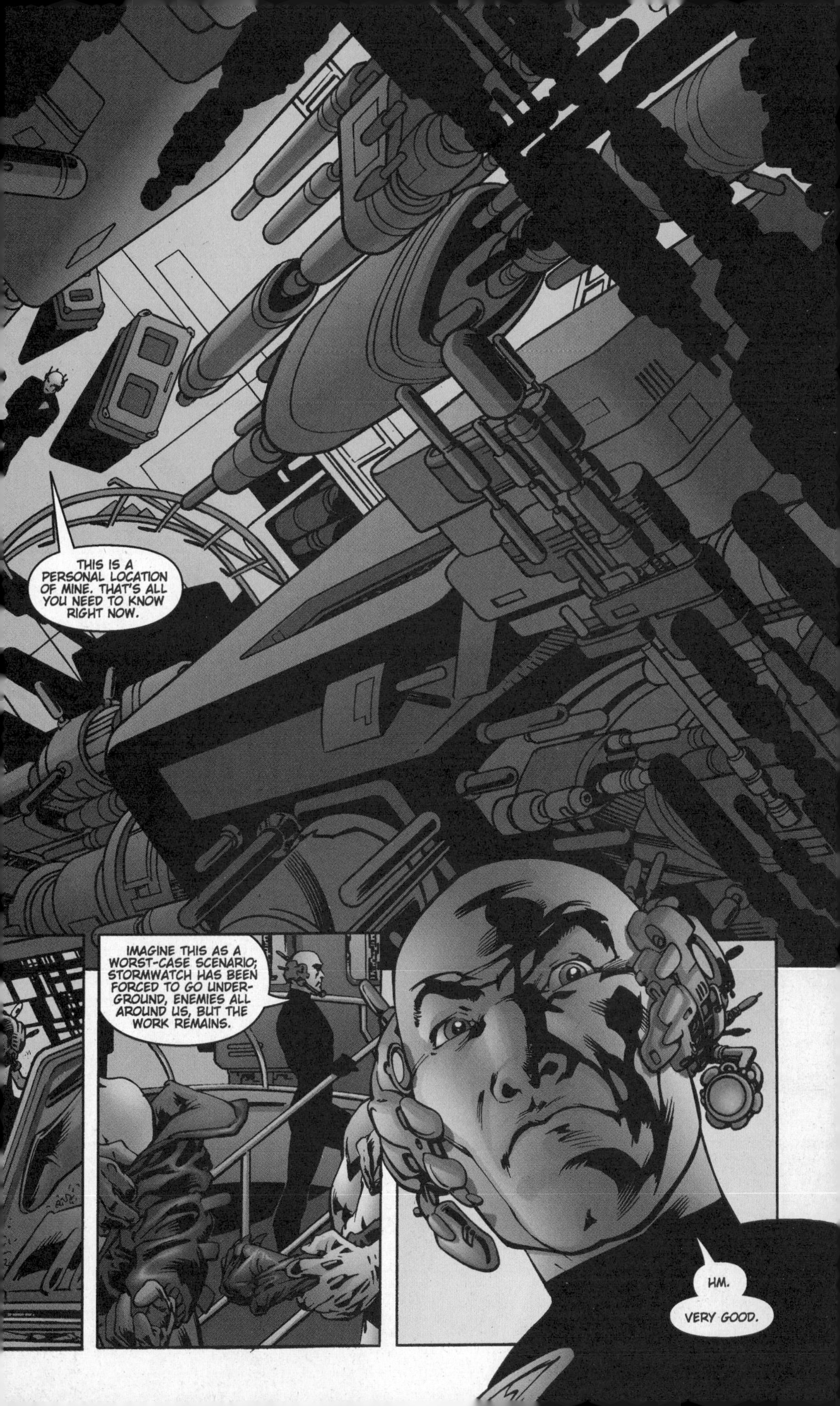

THIS IS A PERSONAL LOCATION OF MINE. THAT'S ALL YOU NEED TO KNOW RIGHT NOW.
IMAGINE THIS AS A WORST-CASE SCENARIO; STORMWATCH HAS BEEN FORCED TO GO UNDER-GROUND, ENEMIES ALL AROUND US, BUT THE WORK REMAINS.
HM.
VERY GOOD.

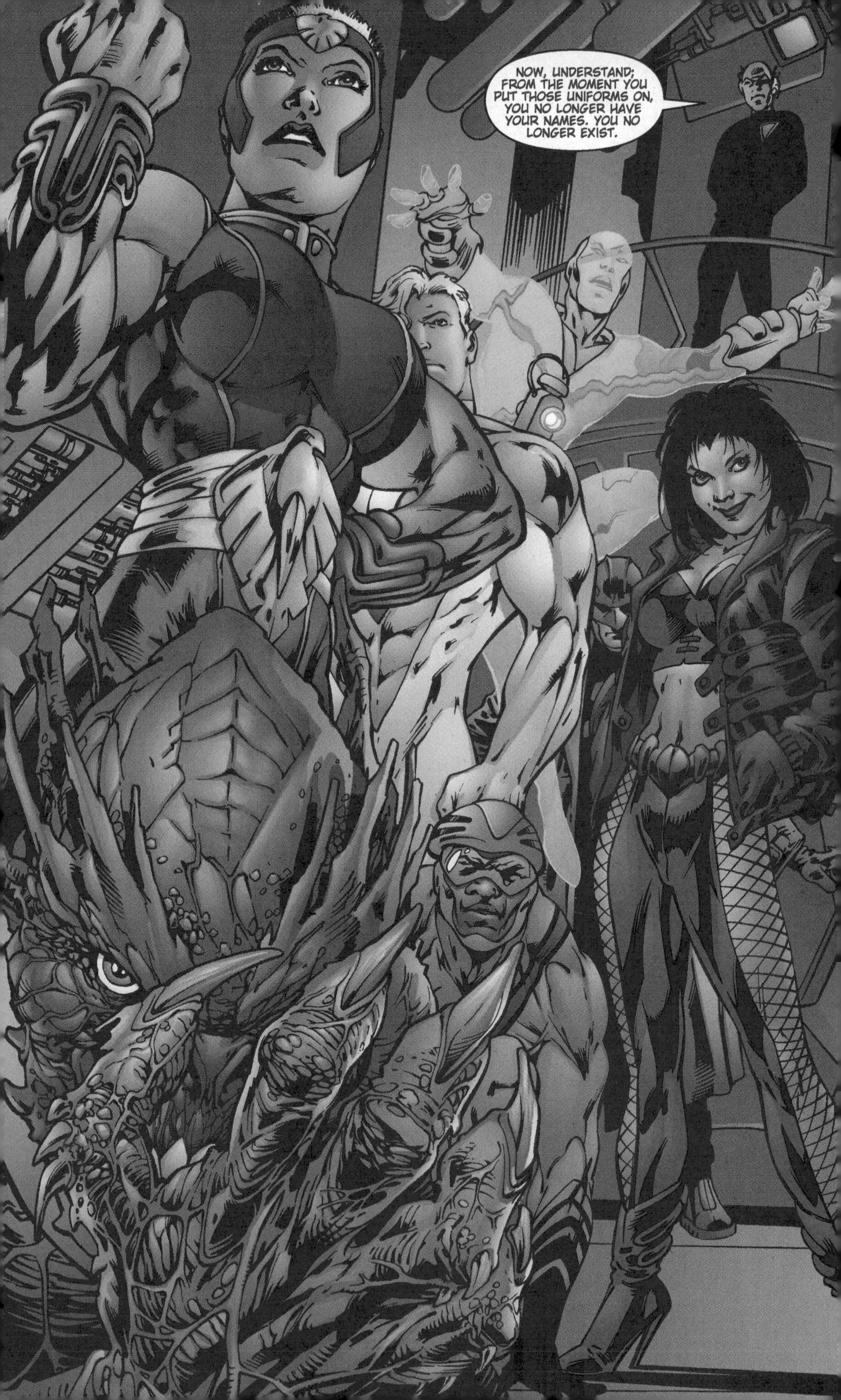
NOW, UNDERSTAND; FROM THE MOMENT YOU PUT THOSE UNIFORMS ON, YOU NO LONGER HAVE YOUR NAMES. YOU NO LONGER EXIST.

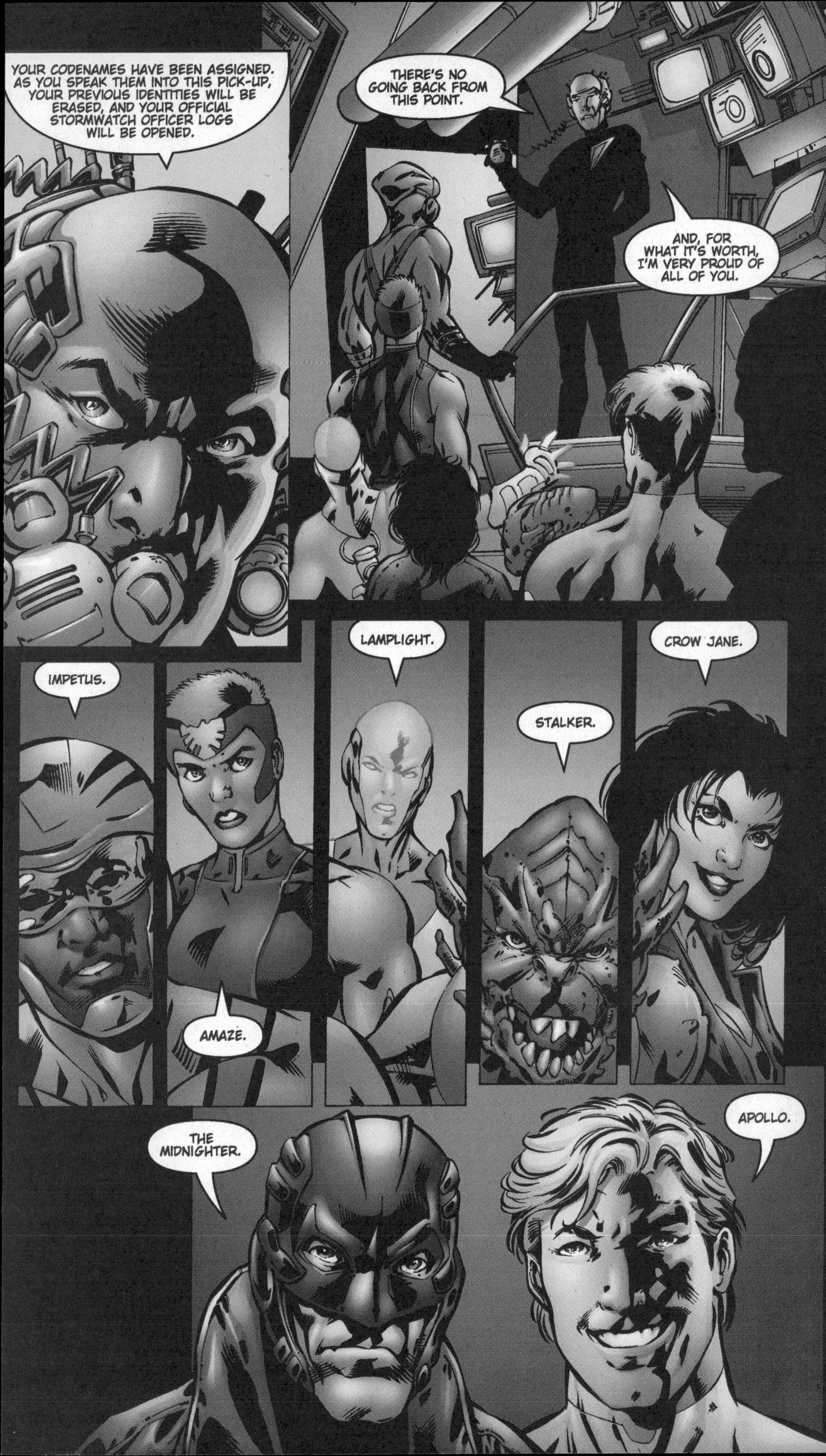
YOUR CODENAMES HAVE BEEN ASSIGNED. AS YOU SPEAK THEM INTO THIS PICK-UP, YOUR PREVIOUS IDENTITIES WILL BE ERASED, AND YOUR OFFICIAL STORMWATCH OFFICER LOGS WILL BE OPENED.
THERE'S NO GOING BACK FROM THIS POINT.
AND, FOR WHAT IT'S WORTH, I'M VERY PROUD OF ALL OF YOU.
IMPETUS.
AMAZE.
LAMPLIGHT.
STALKER.
CROW JANE.
THE MIDNIGHTER.
APOLLO.

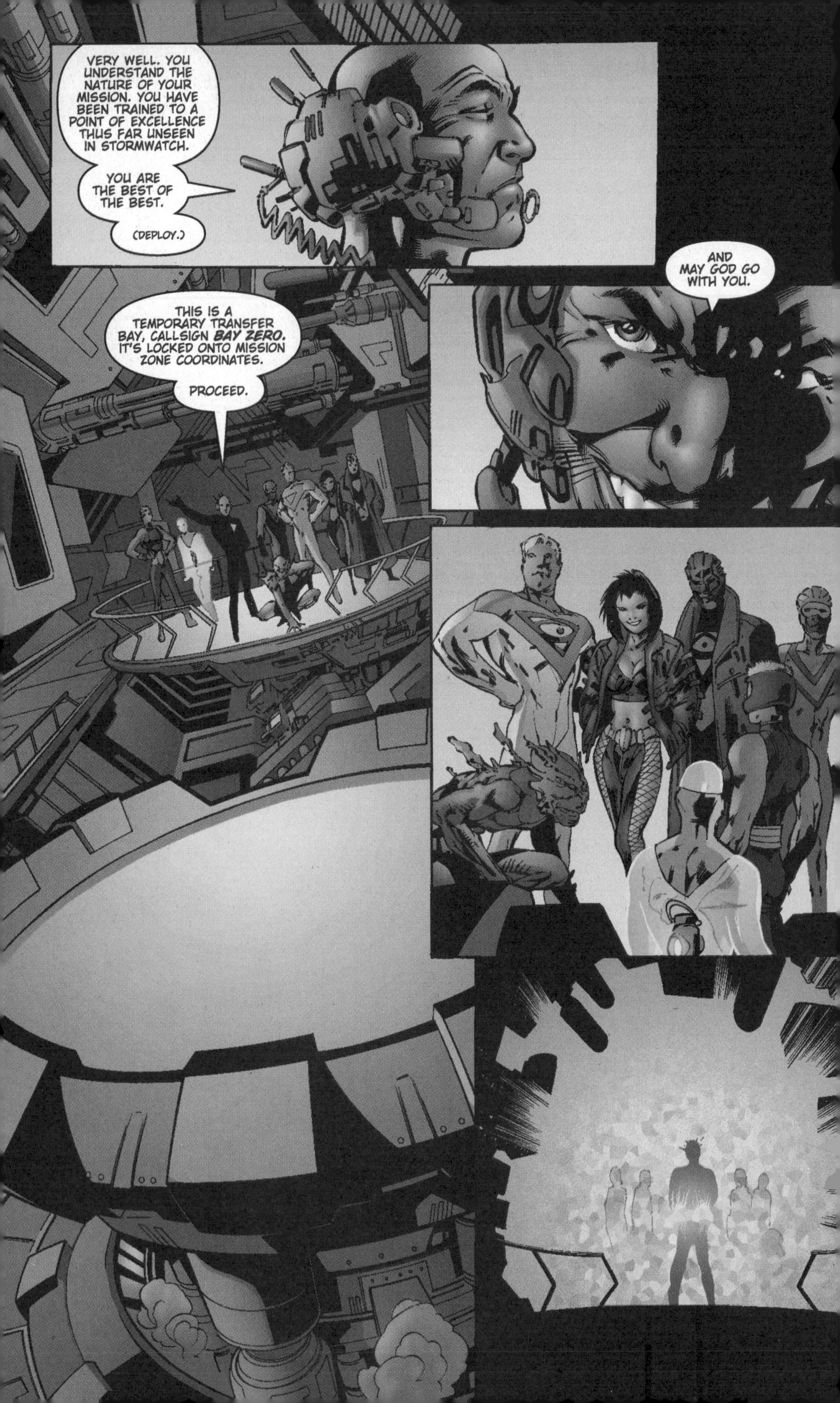
VERY WELL. YOU UNDERSTAND THE NATURE OF YOUR MISSION. YOU HAVE BEEN TRAINED TO A POINT OF EXCELLENCE THUS FAR UNSEEN IN STORMWATCH.
YOU ARE THE BEST OF THE BEST.
(DEPLOY.)
THIS IS A TEMPORARY TRANSFER BAY, CALLSIGN BAY ZERO. IT'S LOCKED ONTO MISSION ZONE COORDINATES.
PROCEED.
AND MAY GOD GO WITH YOU.

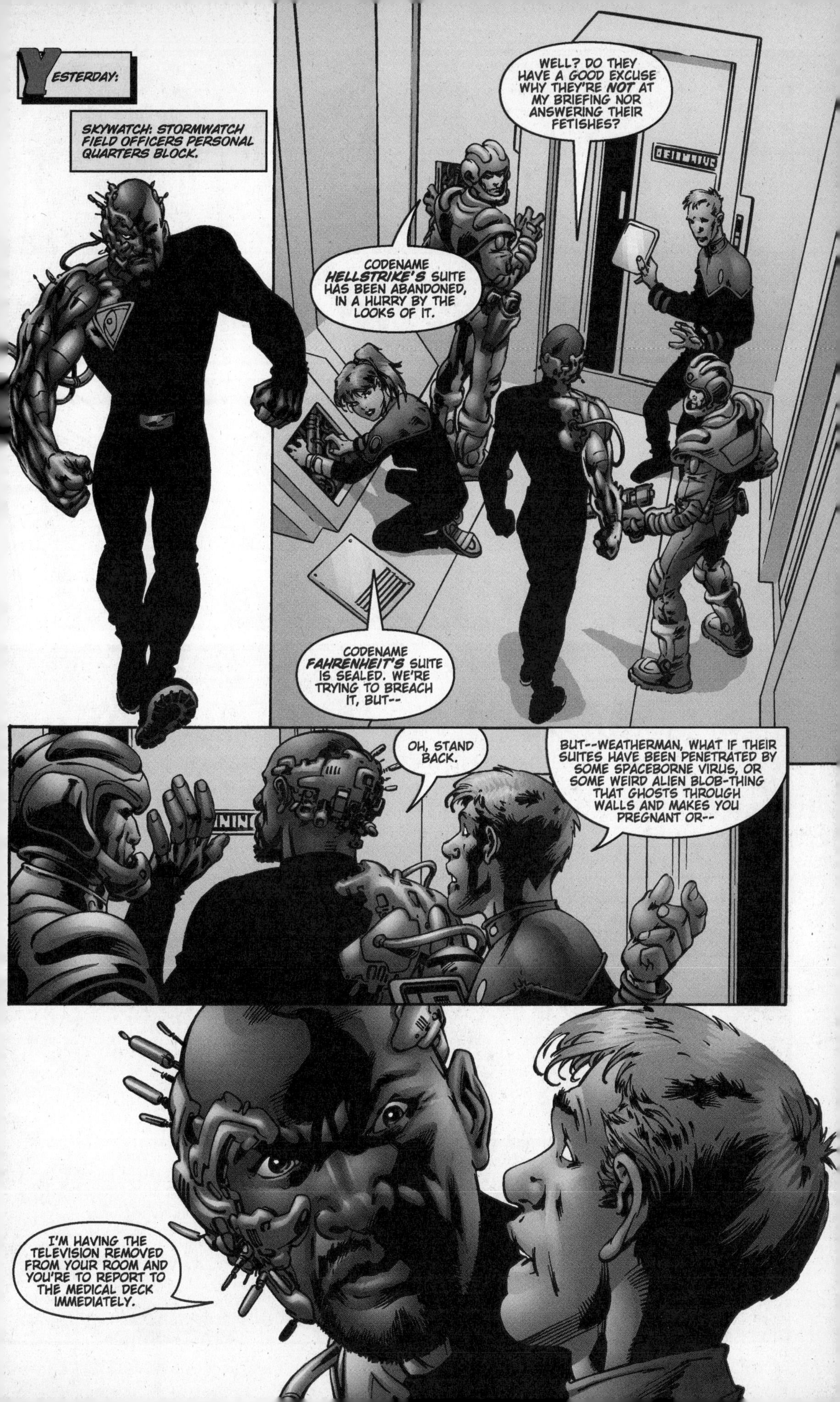
YESTERDAY:
SKYWATCH: STORMWATCH FIELD OFFICERS PERSONAL QUARTERS BLOCK.
WELL? DO THEY HAVE A GOOD EXCUSE WHY THEY'RE NOT AT MY BRIEFING NOR ANSWERING THEIR FETISHES?
CODENAME HELLSTRIKE'S SUITE HAS BEEN ABANDONED, IN A HURRY BY THE LOOKS OF IT.
CODENAME FAHRENHEIT'S SUITE IS SEALED. WE'RE TRYING TO BREACH IT, BUT--
OH, STAND BACK.
BUT--WEATHERMAN, WHAT IF THEIR SUITES HAVE BEEN PENETRATED BY SOME SPACEBORNE VIRUS, OR SOME WEIRD ALIEN BLOB-THING THAT GHOSTS THROUGH WALLS AND MAKES YOU PREGNANT OR--
I'M HAVING THE TELEVISION REMOVED FROM YOUR ROOM AND YOU'RE TO REPORT TO THE MEDICAL DECK IMMEDIATELY.

...MAKING ME USE MY GODDAMN POWERS AGAIN...I'LL KICK THEIR BUTTS INTO RE-ENTRY...

FIRE!

LOCK OFF THE BLOCK! SHUT DOWN THE OXYGEN FEED--

BELAY THAT. JUST RAMP UP THE AIR SCRUBBERS' INTAKE.

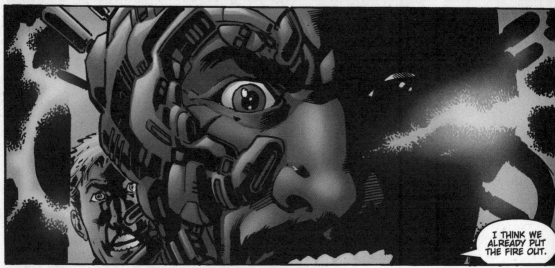

I THINK WE ALREADY PUT THE FIRE OUT.

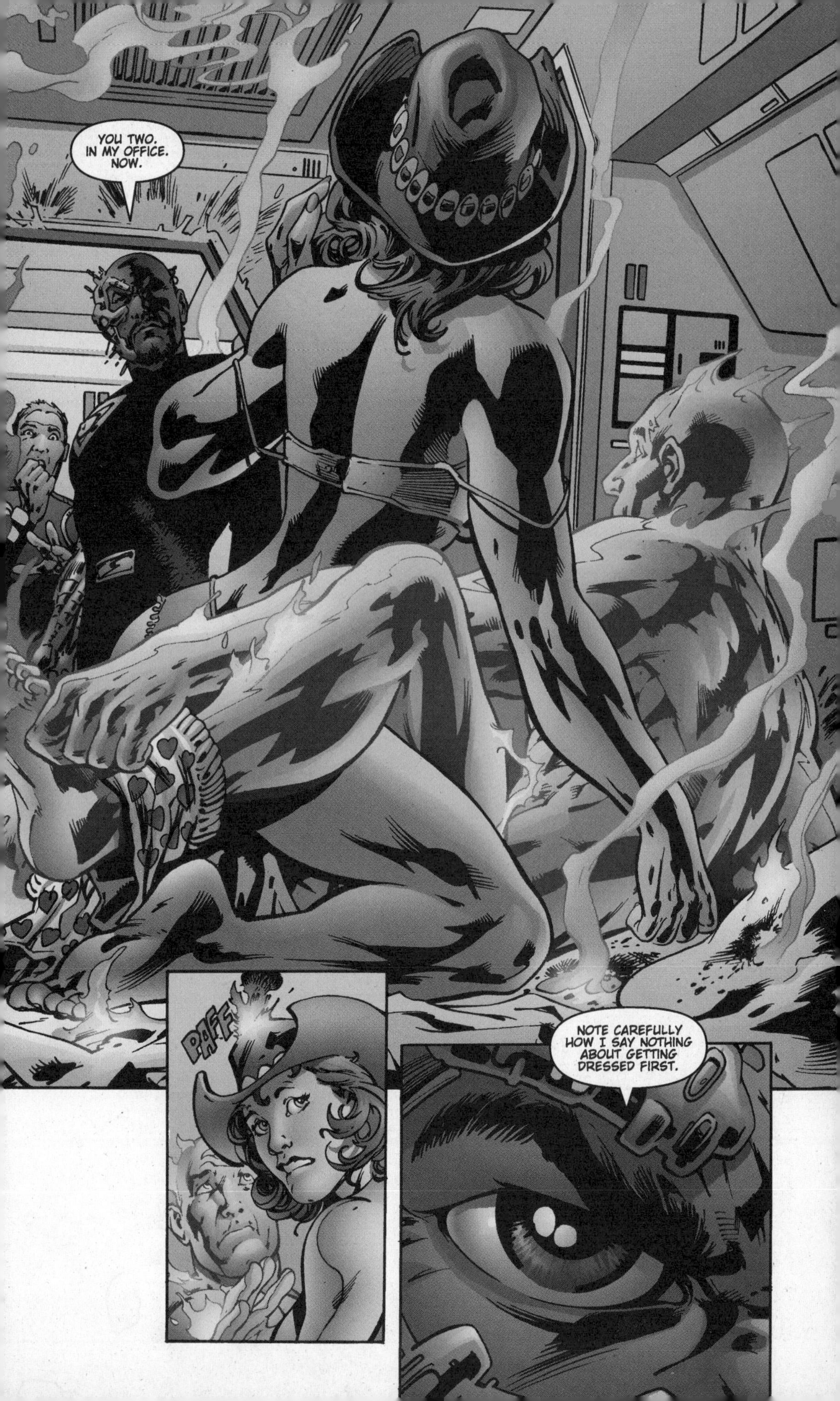
YOU TWO. IN MY OFFICE. NOW.
PAFF
NOTE CAREFULLY HOW I SAY NOTHING ABOUT GETTING DRESSED FIRST.

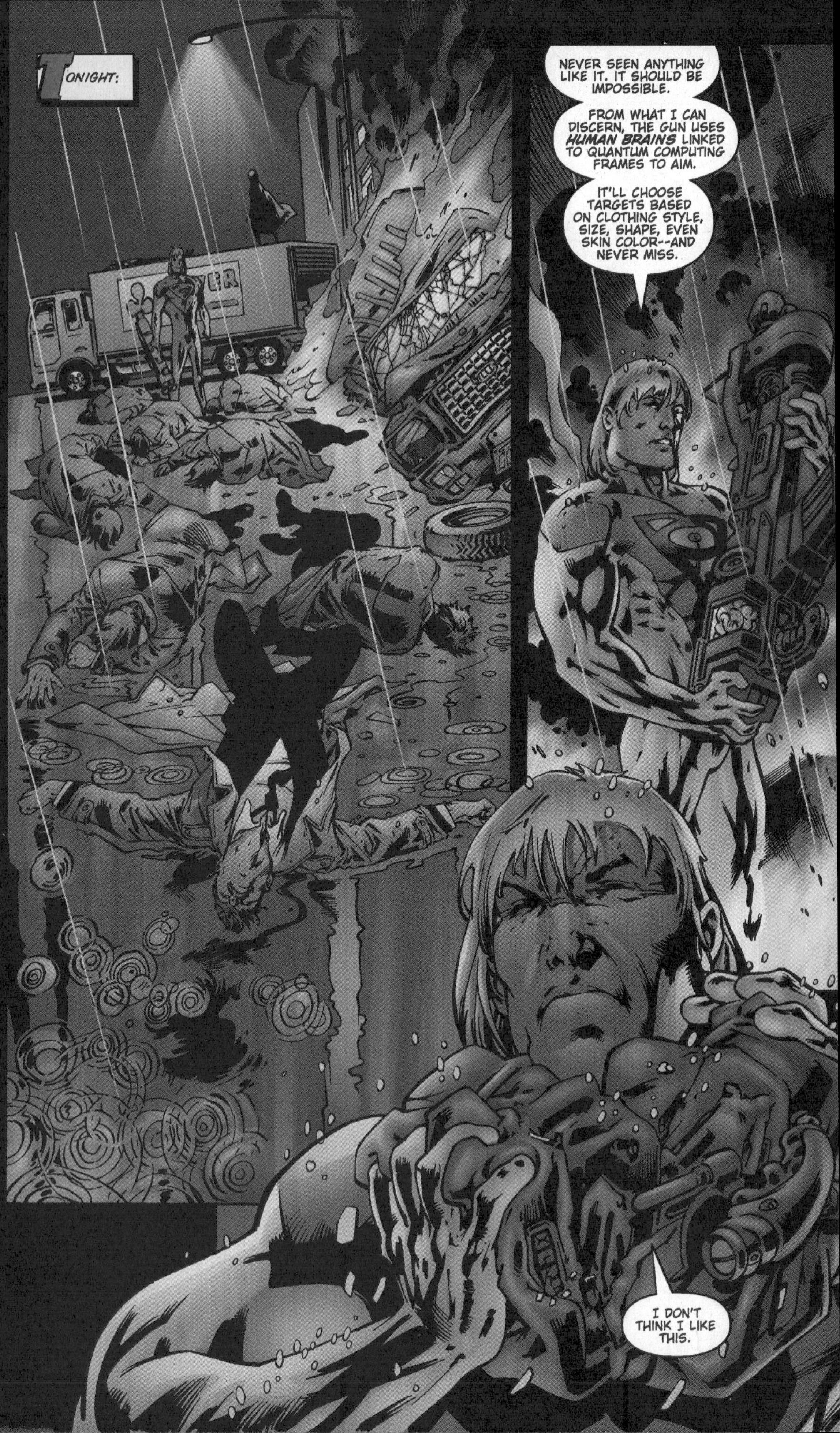
TONIGHT:
NEVER SEEN ANYTHING LIKE IT. IT SHOULD BE IMPOSSIBLE.
FROM WHAT I CAN DISCERN, THE GUN USES ***HUMAN BRAINS*** LINKED TO QUANTUM COMPUTING FRAMES TO AIM.
IT'LL CHOOSE TARGETS BASED ON CLOTHING STYLE, SIZE, SHAPE, EVEN SKIN COLOR--AND NEVER MISS.
I DON'T THINK I LIKE THIS.

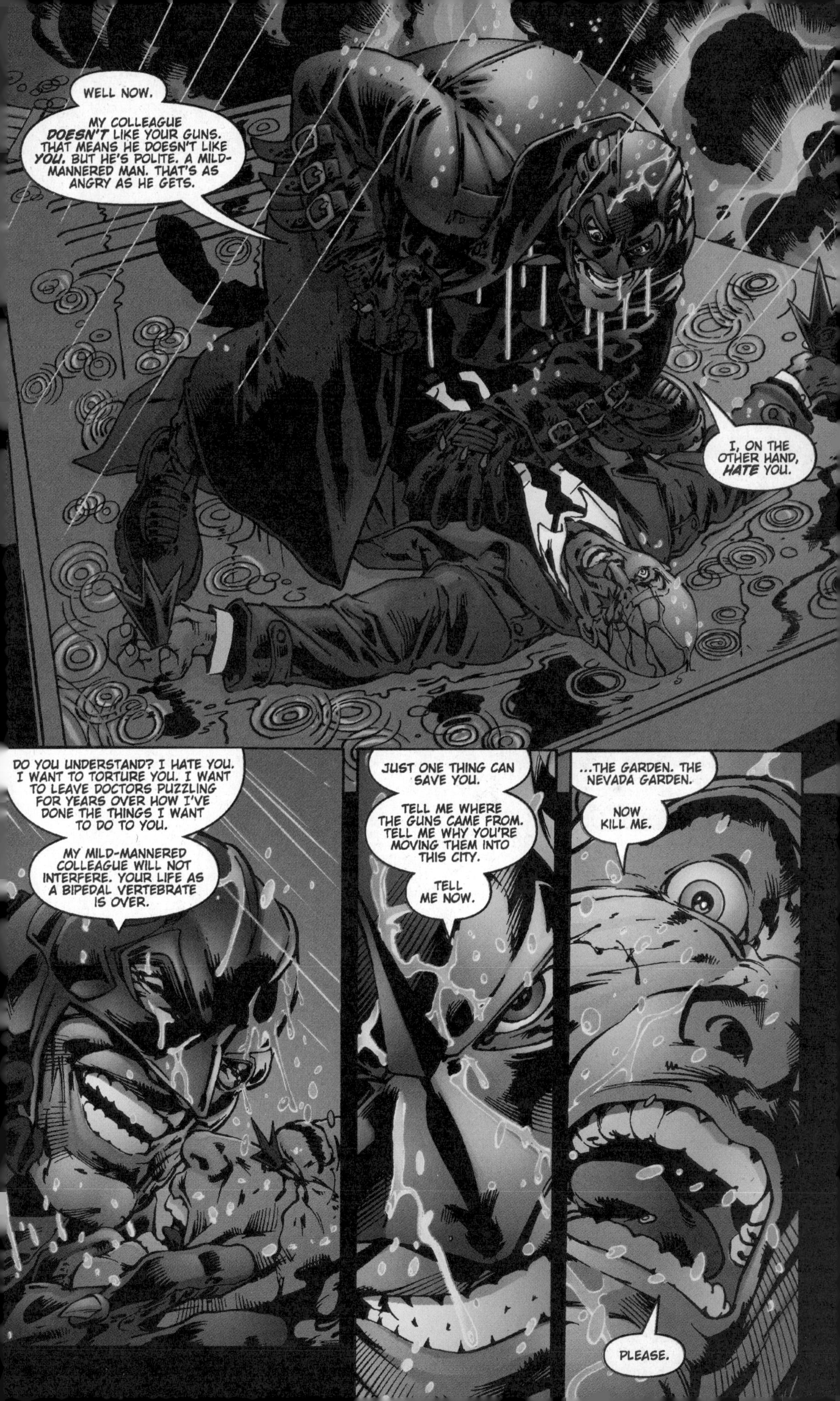
WELL NOW.
MY COLLEAGUE DOESN'T LIKE YOUR GUNS. THAT MEANS HE DOESN'T LIKE YOU. BUT HE'S POLITE. A MILD-MANNERED MAN. THAT'S AS ANGRY AS HE GETS.
I, ON THE OTHER HAND, HATE YOU.
DO YOU UNDERSTAND? I HATE YOU. I WANT TO TORTURE YOU. I WANT TO LEAVE DOCTORS PUZZLING FOR YEARS OVER HOW I'VE DONE THE THINGS I WANT TO DO TO YOU.
MY MILD-MANNERED COLLEAGUE WILL NOT INTERFERE. YOUR LIFE AS A BIPEDAL VERTEBRATE IS OVER.
JUST ONE THING CAN SAVE YOU.
TELL ME WHERE THE GUNS CAME FROM. TELL ME WHY YOU'RE MOVING THEM INTO THIS CITY.
TELL ME NOW.
...THE GARDEN. THE NEVADA GARDEN.
NOW KILL ME.
PLEASE.

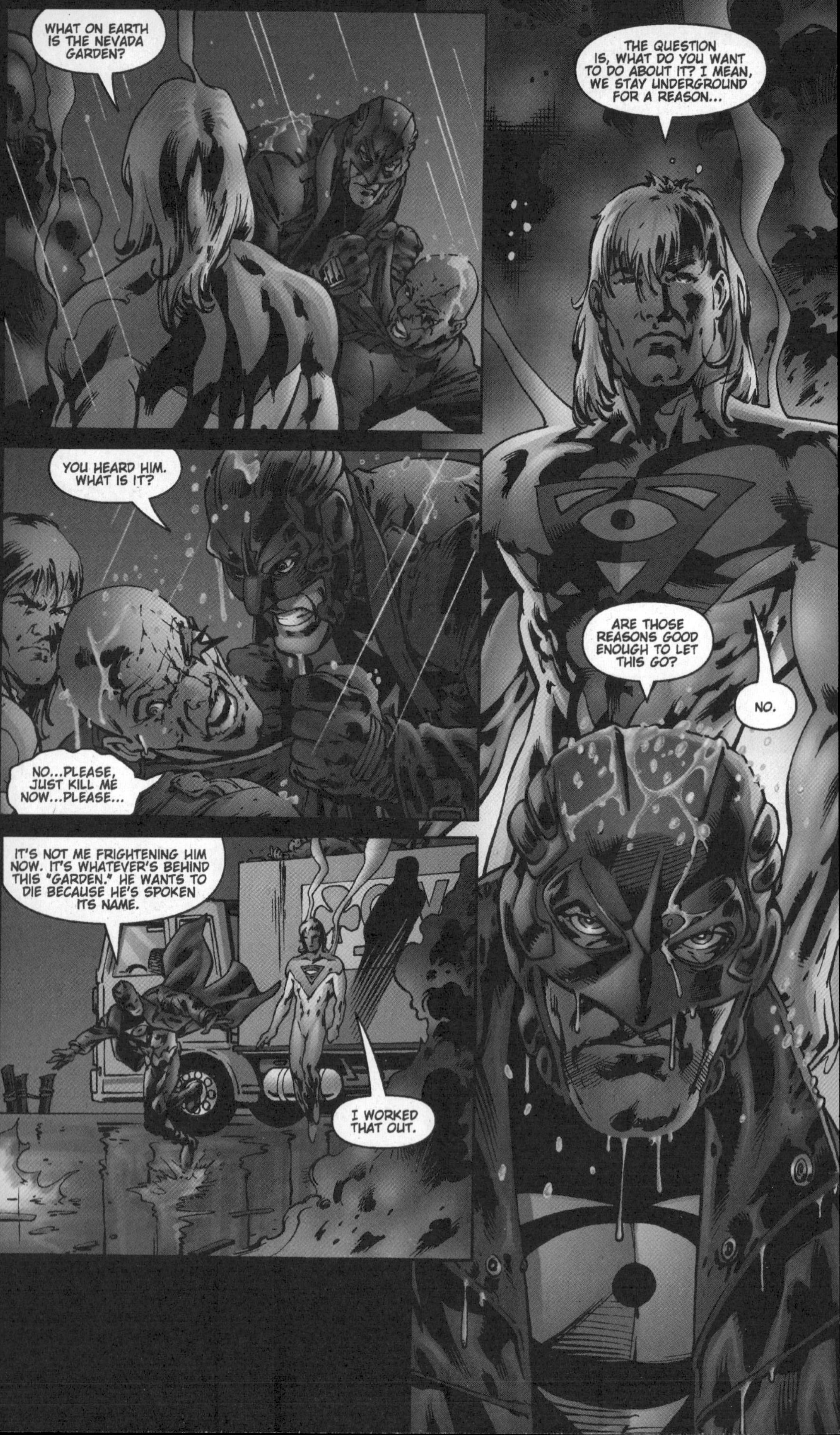
WHAT ON EARTH IS THE NEVADA GARDEN?
YOU HEARD HIM. WHAT IS IT?
NO...PLEASE, JUST KILL ME NOW...PLEASE...
IT'S NOT ME FRIGHTENING HIM NOW. IT'S WHATEVER'S BEHIND THIS "GARDEN." HE WANTS TO DIE BECAUSE HE'S SPOKEN ITS NAME.
I WORKED THAT OUT.
THE QUESTION IS, WHAT DO YOU WANT TO DO ABOUT IT? I MEAN, WE STAY UNDERGROUND FOR A REASON...
ARE THOSE REASONS GOOD ENOUGH TO LET THIS GO?
NO.

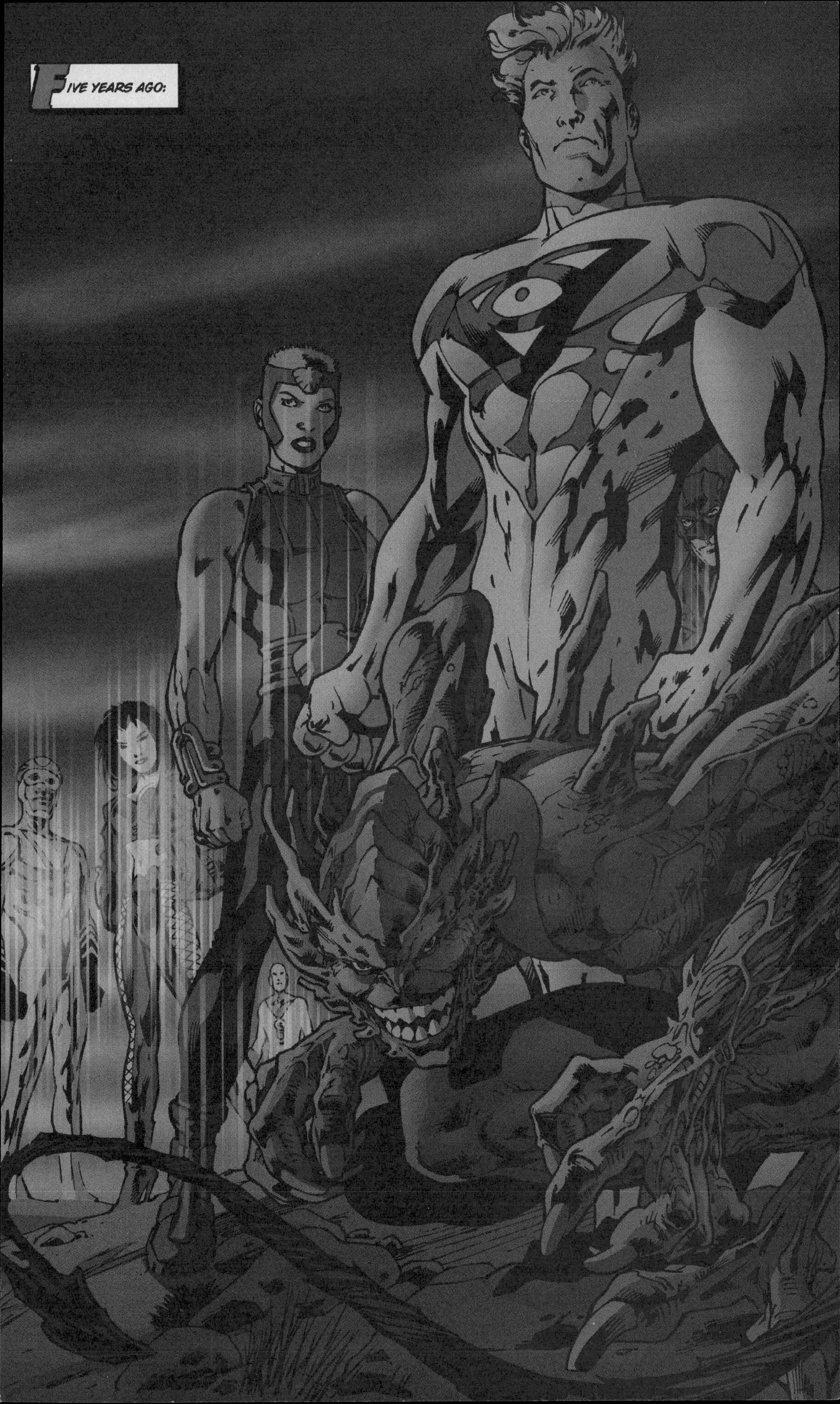
FIVE YEARS AGO:

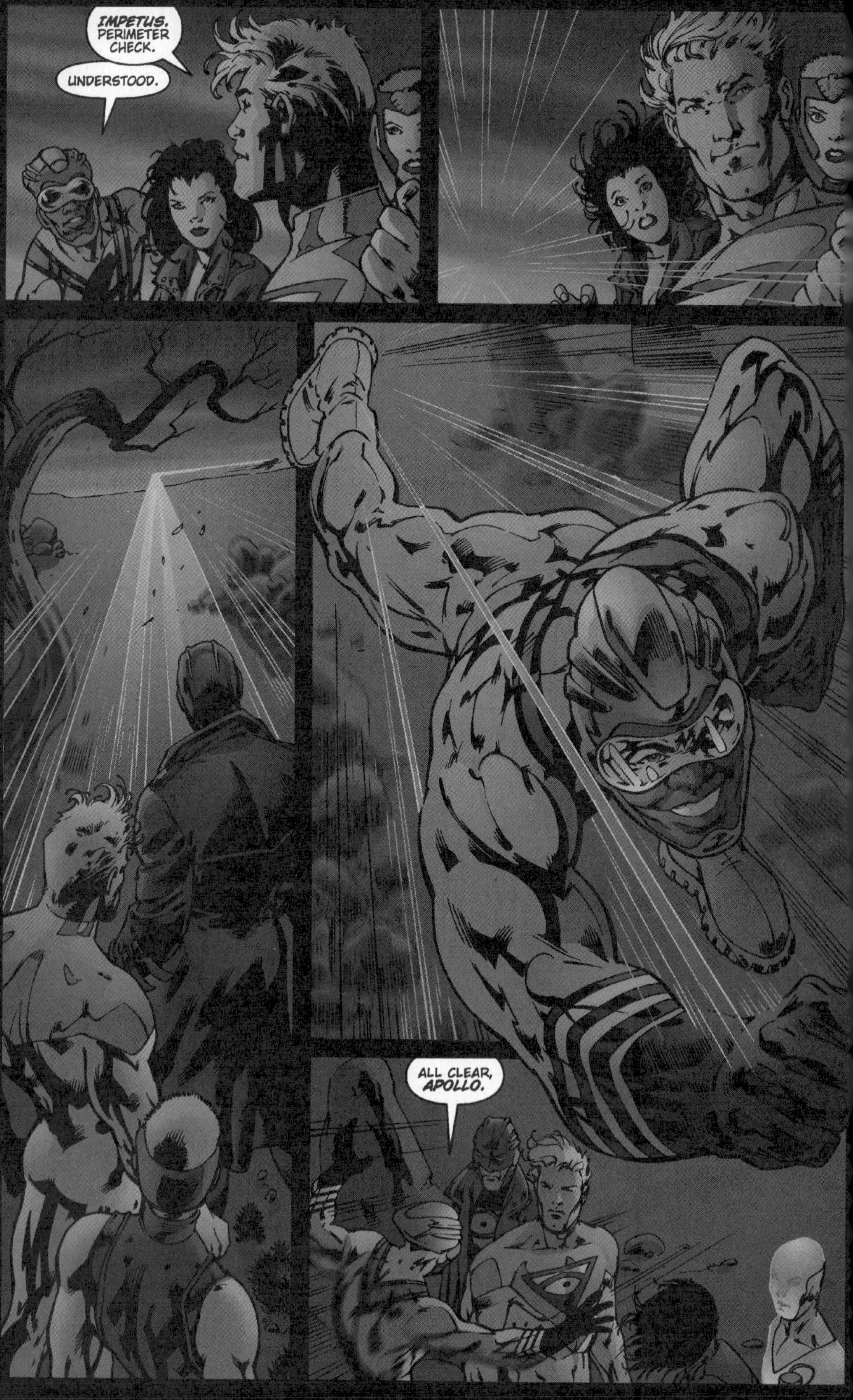
IMPETUS. PERIMETER CHECK.
UNDERSTOOD.
ALL CLEAR, APOLLO.

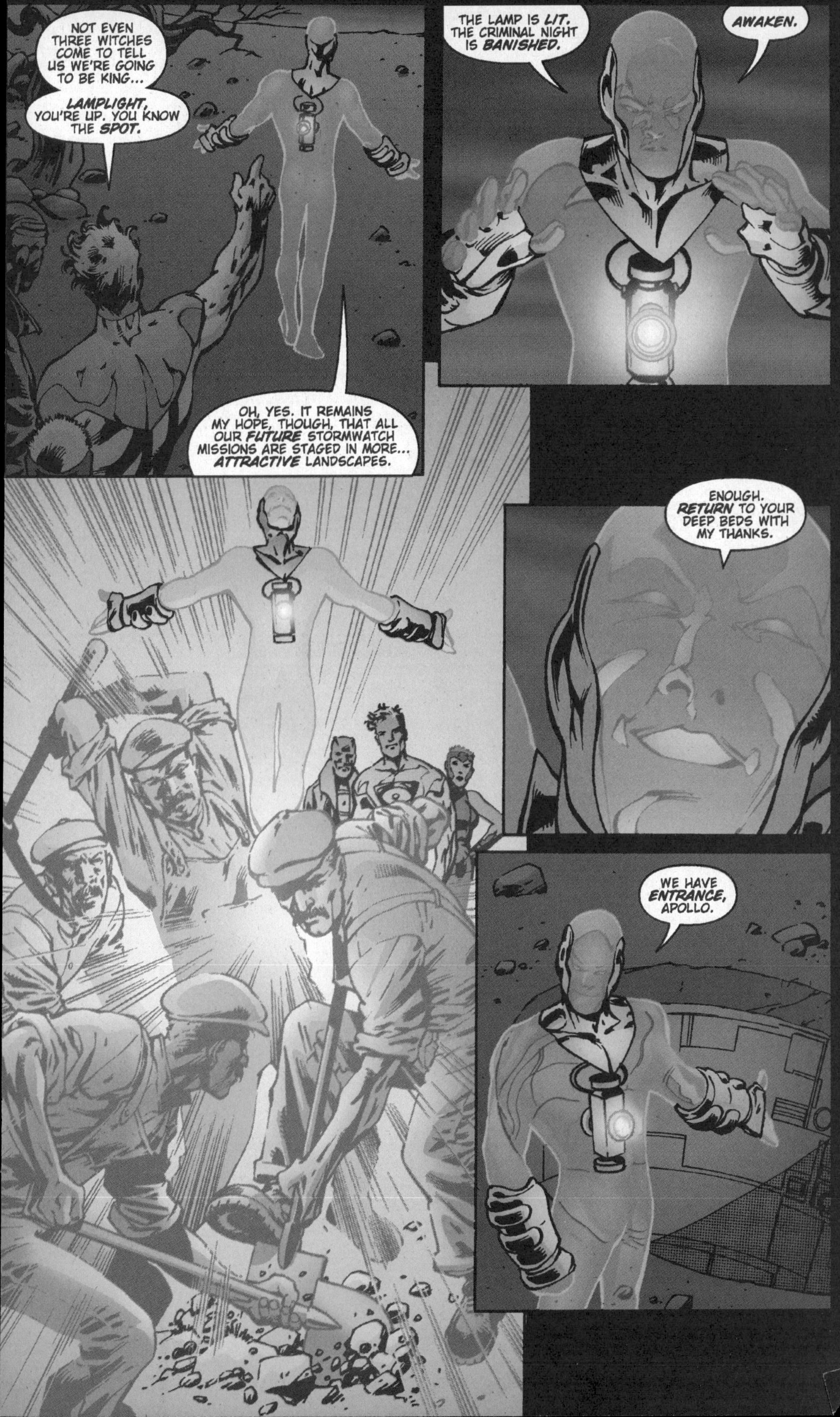
NOT EVEN THREE WITCHES COME TO TELL US WE'RE GOING TO BE KING...
LAMPLIGHT, YOU'RE UP. YOU KNOW THE SPOT.
OH, YES. IT REMAINS MY HOPE, THOUGH, THAT ALL OUR FUTURE STORMWATCH MISSIONS ARE STAGED IN MORE... ATTRACTIVE LANDSCAPES.
THE LAMP IS LIT. THE CRIMINAL NIGHT IS BANISHED.
AWAKEN.
ENOUGH. RETURN TO YOUR DEEP BEDS WITH MY THANKS.
WE HAVE ENTRANCE, APOLLO.

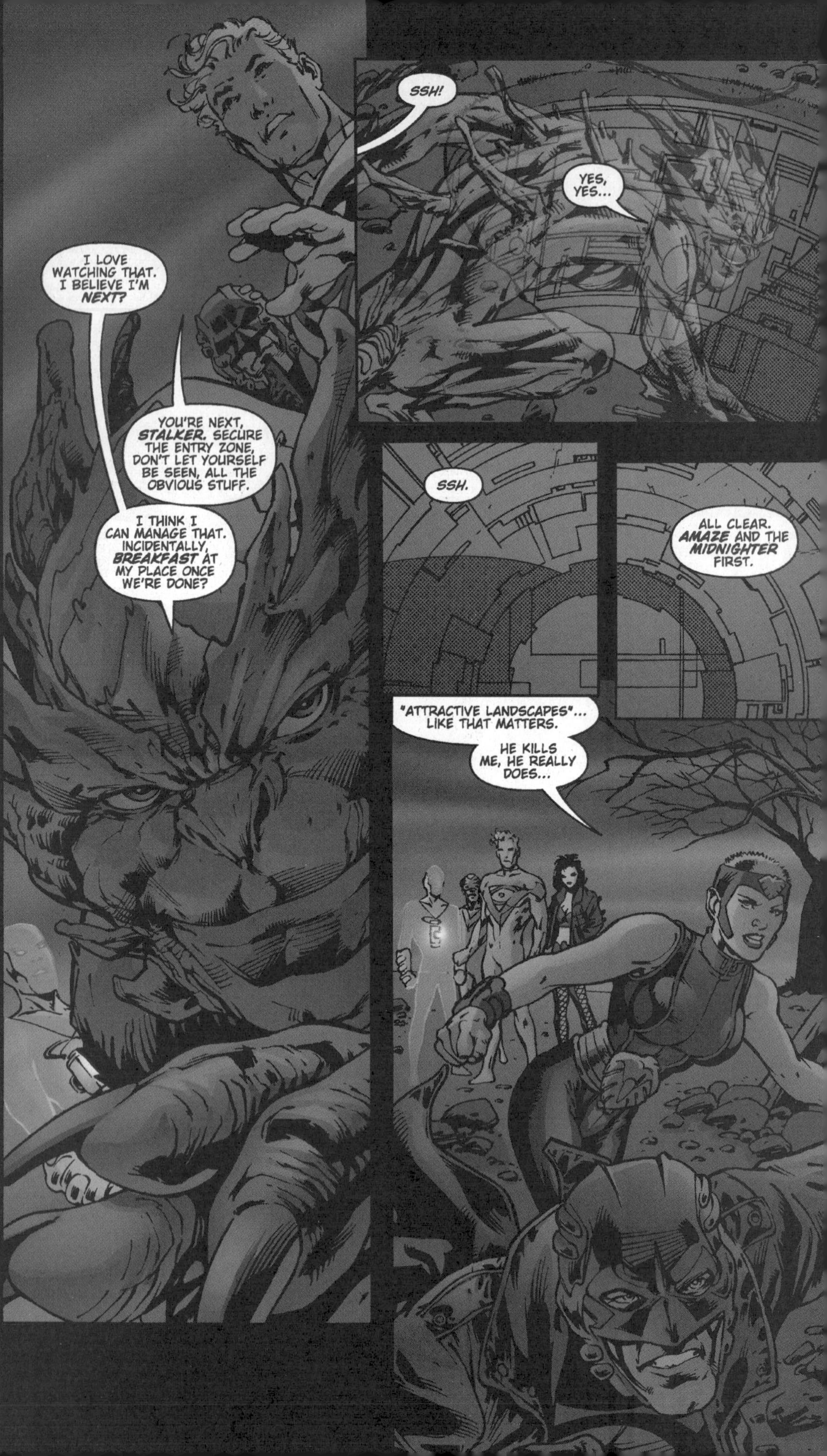
I LOVE WATCHING THAT. I BELIEVE I'M *NEXT?*
YOU'RE NEXT, **STALKER.** SECURE THE ENTRY ZONE, DON'T LET YOURSELF BE SEEN, ALL THE OBVIOUS STUFF.
I THINK I CAN MANAGE THAT. INCIDENTALLY, ***BREAKFAST*** AT MY PLACE ONCE WE'RE DONE?
SSH!
YES, YES...
SSH.
ALL CLEAR. ***AMAZE*** AND THE ***MIDNIGHTER*** FIRST.
"ATTRACTIVE LANDSCAPES"... LIKE THAT MATTERS.
HE KILLS ME, HE REALLY DOES...

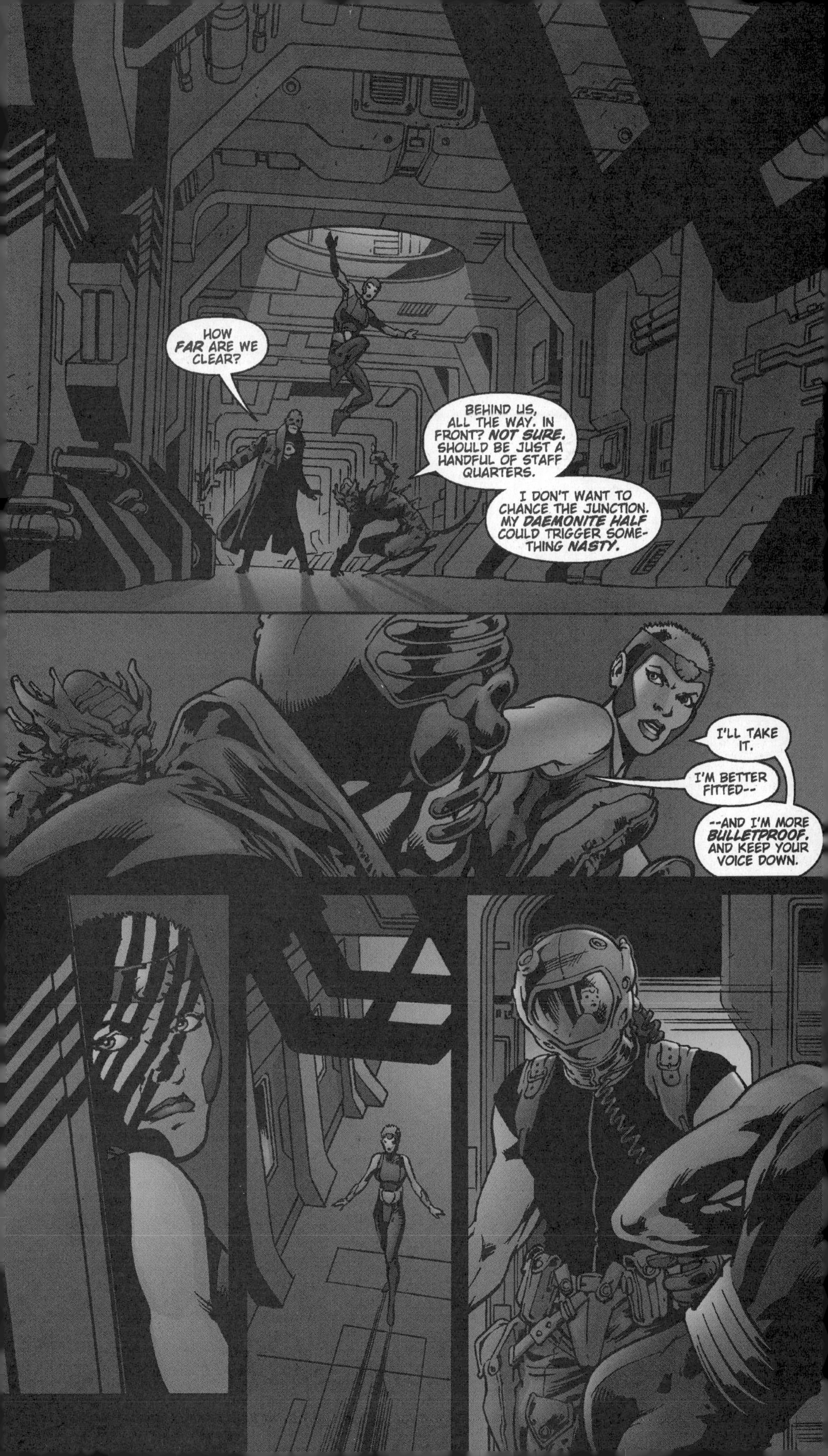
HOW FAR ARE WE CLEAR?
BEHIND US, ALL THE WAY. IN FRONT? NOT SURE. SHOULD BE JUST A HANDFUL OF STAFF QUARTERS.
I DON'T WANT TO CHANCE THE JUNCTION. MY DAEMONITE HALF COULD TRIGGER SOMETHING NASTY.
I'LL TAKE IT.
I'M BETTER FITTED--
--AND I'M MORE BULLETPROOF. AND KEEP YOUR VOICE DOWN.

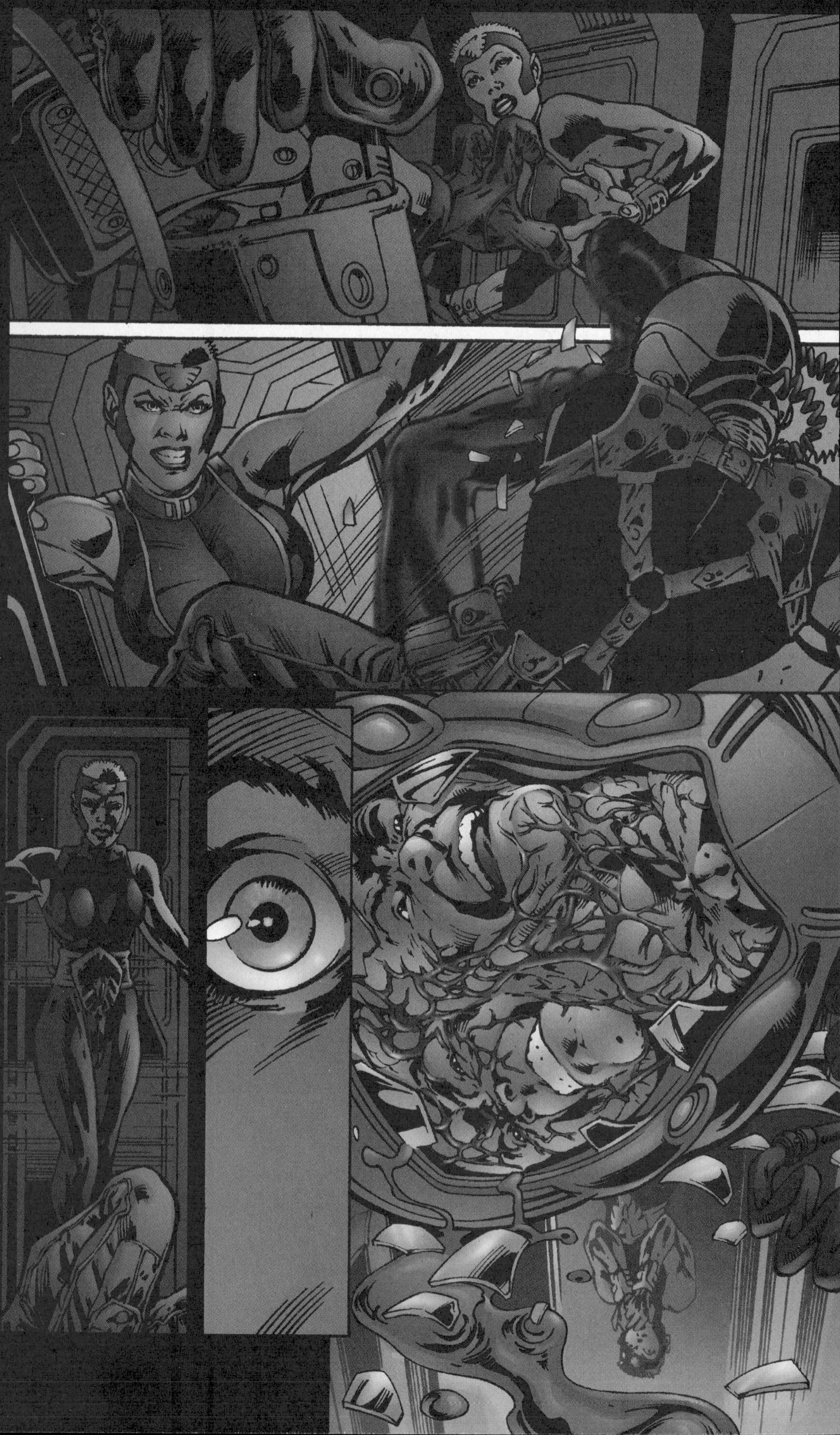

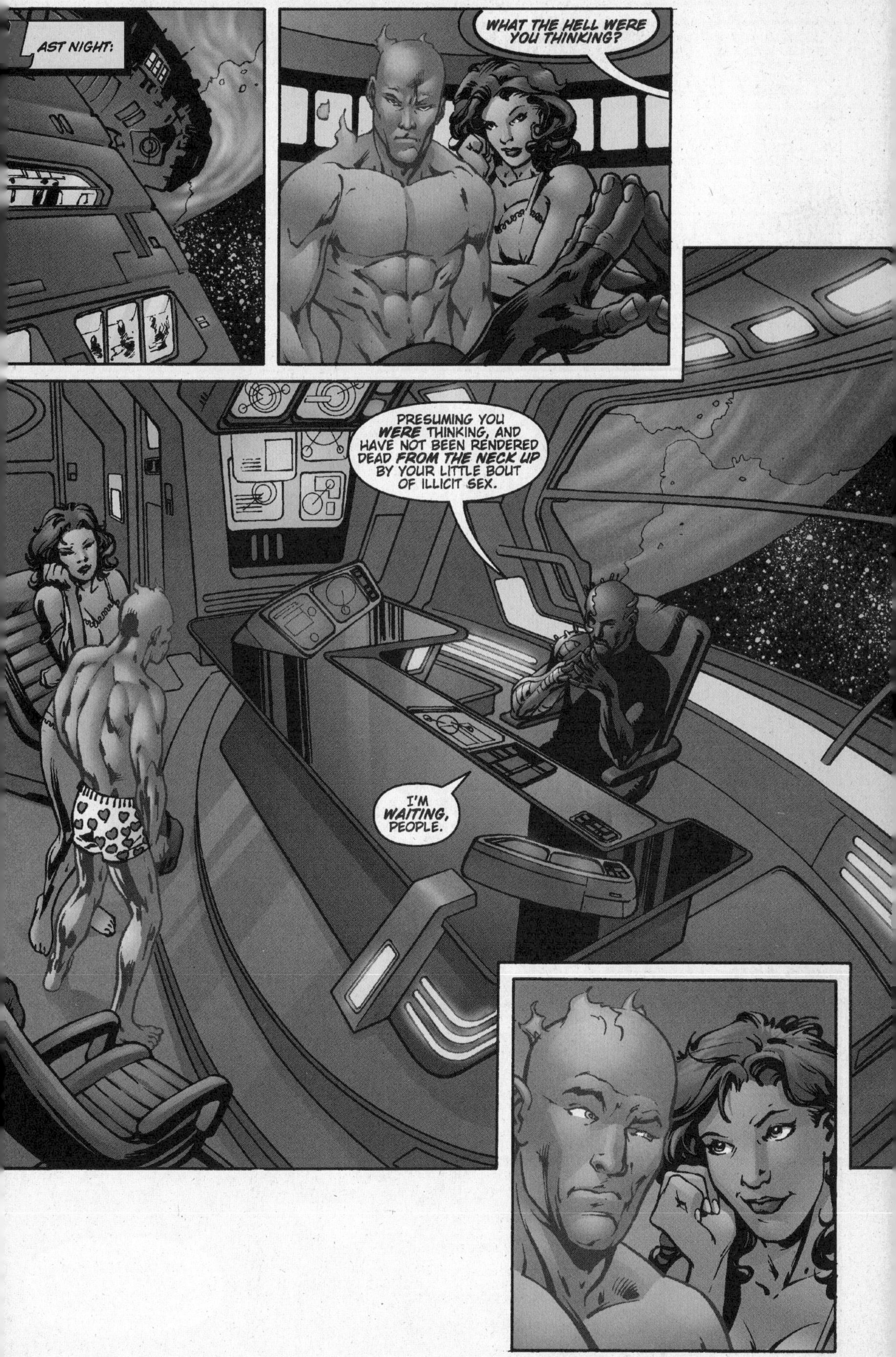
LAST NIGHT:
WHAT THE HELL WERE YOU THINKING?
PRESUMING YOU WERE THINKING, AND HAVE NOT BEEN RENDERED DEAD FROM THE NECK UP BY YOUR LITTLE BOUT OF ILLICIT SEX.
I'M WAITING, PEOPLE.

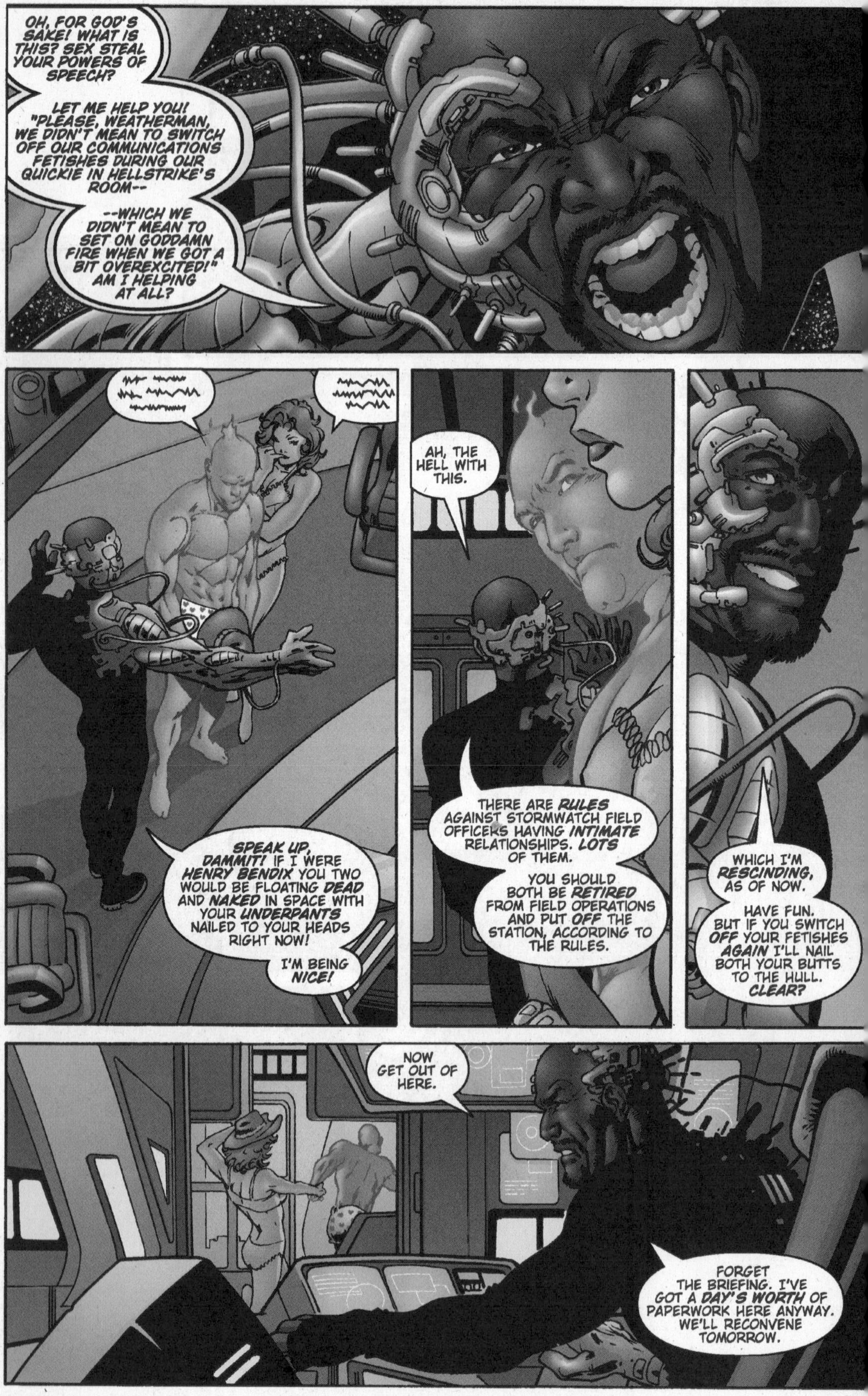
OH, FOR GOD'S SAKE! WHAT IS THIS? SEX STEAL YOUR POWERS OF SPEECH?
LET ME HELP YOU! "PLEASE, WEATHERMAN, WE DIDN'T MEAN TO SWITCH OFF OUR COMMUNICATIONS FETISHES DURING OUR QUICKIE IN HELLSTRIKE'S ROOM--
--WHICH WE DIDN'T MEAN TO SET ON GODDAMN FIRE WHEN WE GOT A BIT OVEREXCITED!" AM I HELPING AT ALL?
SPEAK UP, DAMMIT! IF I WERE HENRY BENDIX YOU TWO WOULD BE FLOATING DEAD AND NAKED IN SPACE WITH YOUR UNDERPANTS NAILED TO YOUR HEADS RIGHT NOW!
I'M BEING NICE!
AH, THE HELL WITH THIS.
THERE ARE RULES AGAINST STORMWATCH FIELD OFFICERS HAVING INTIMATE RELATIONSHIPS. LOTS OF THEM.
YOU SHOULD BOTH BE RETIRED FROM FIELD OPERATIONS AND PUT OFF THE STATION, ACCORDING TO THE RULES.
WHICH I'M RESCINDING, AS OF NOW.
HAVE FUN. BUT IF YOU SWITCH OFF YOUR FETISHES AGAIN I'LL NAIL BOTH YOUR BUTTS TO THE HULL. CLEAR?
NOW GET OUT OF HERE.
FORGET THE BRIEFING. I'VE GOT A DAY'S WORTH OF PAPERWORK HERE ANYWAY. WE'LL RECONVENE TOMORROW.

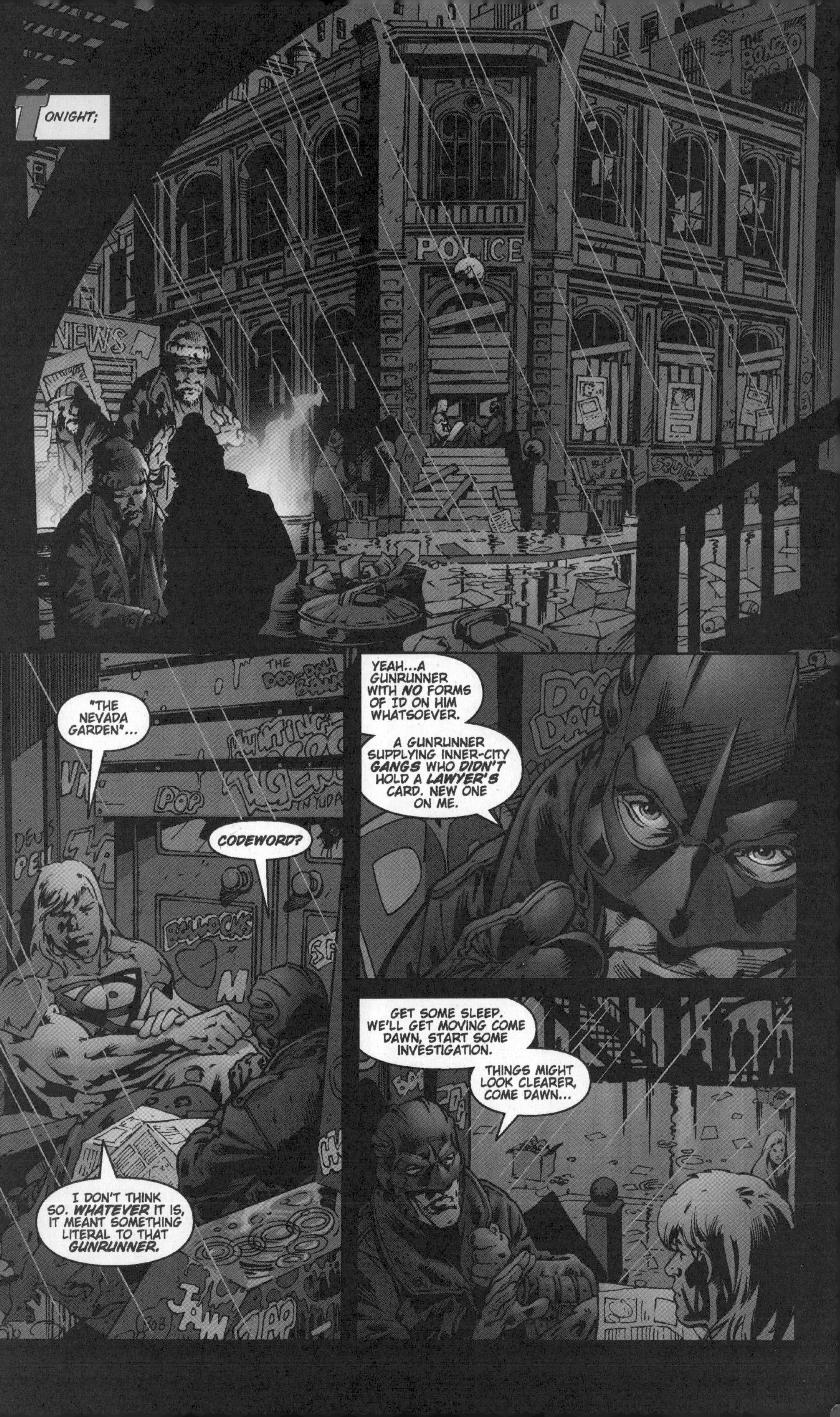
TONIGHT;
POLICE
NEWS
"THE NEVADA GARDEN"...
CODEWORD?
I DON'T THINK SO. WHATEVER IT IS, IT MEANT SOMETHING LITERAL TO THAT GUNRUNNER.
YEAH...A GUNRUNNER WITH NO FORMS OF ID ON HIM WHATSOEVER.
A GUNRUNNER SUPPLYING INNER-CITY GANGS WHO DIDN'T HOLD A LAWYER'S CARD. NEW ONE ON ME.
GET SOME SLEEP. WE'LL GET MOVING COME DAWN, START SOME INVESTIGATION.
THINGS MIGHT LOOK CLEARER, COME DAWN...

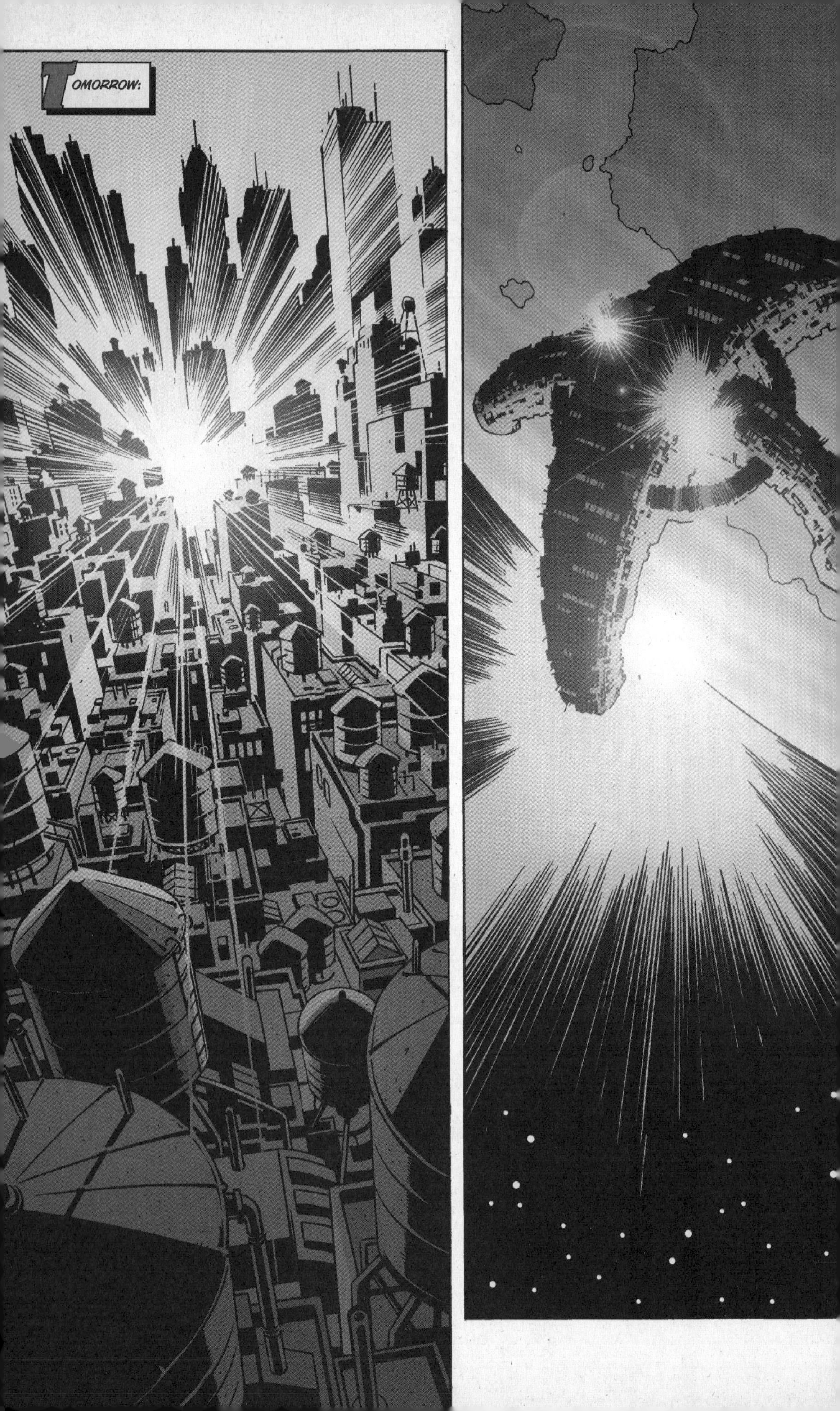
TOMORROW:

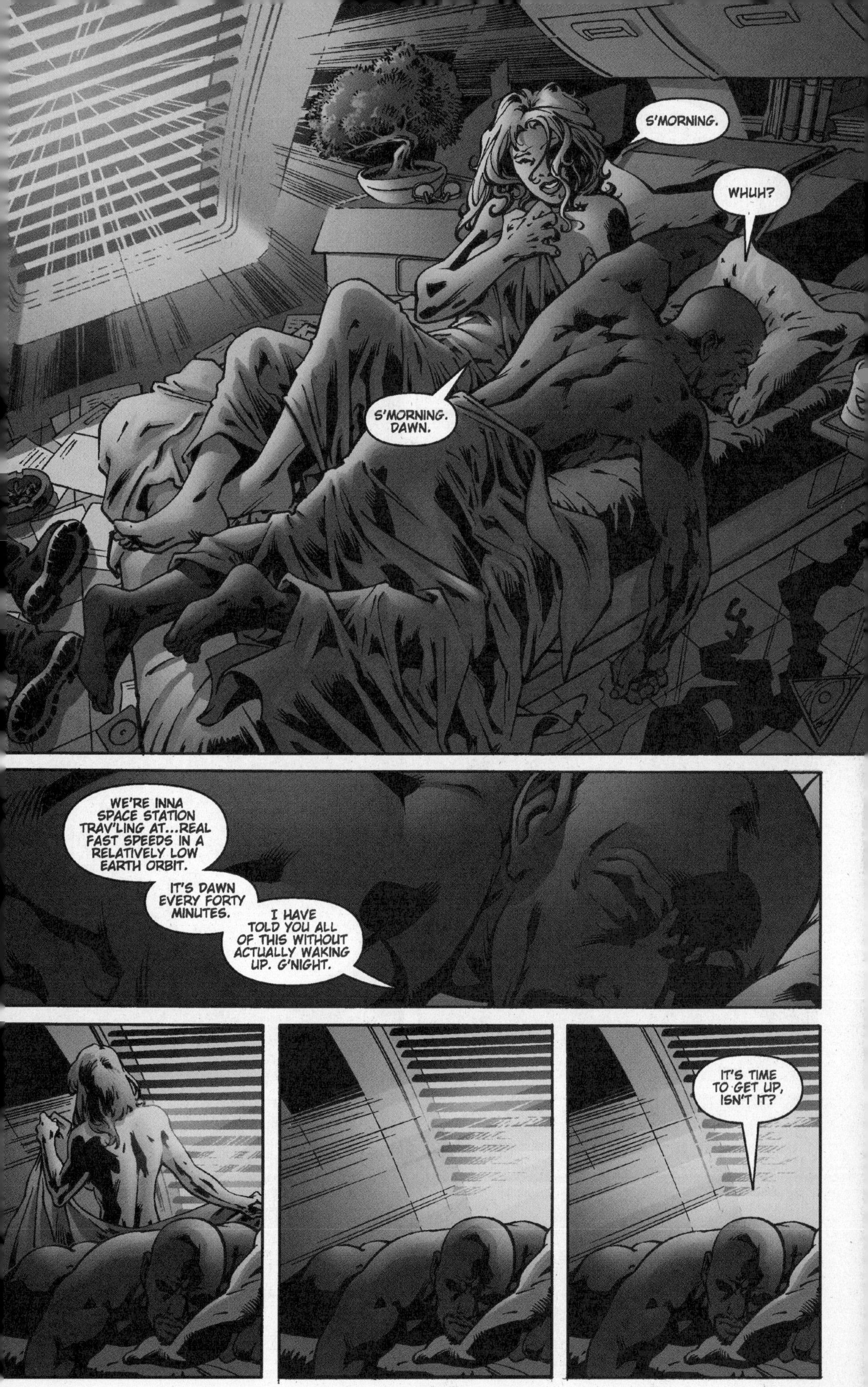
S'MORNING.
WHUH?
S'MORNING. DAWN.
WE'RE INNA SPACE STATION TRAV'LING AT...REAL FAST SPEEDS IN A RELATIVELY LOW EARTH ORBIT.
IT'S DAWN EVERY FORTY MINUTES.
I HAVE TOLD YOU ALL OF THIS WITHOUT ACTUALLY WAKING UP. G'NIGHT.
IT'S TIME TO GET UP, ISN'T IT?

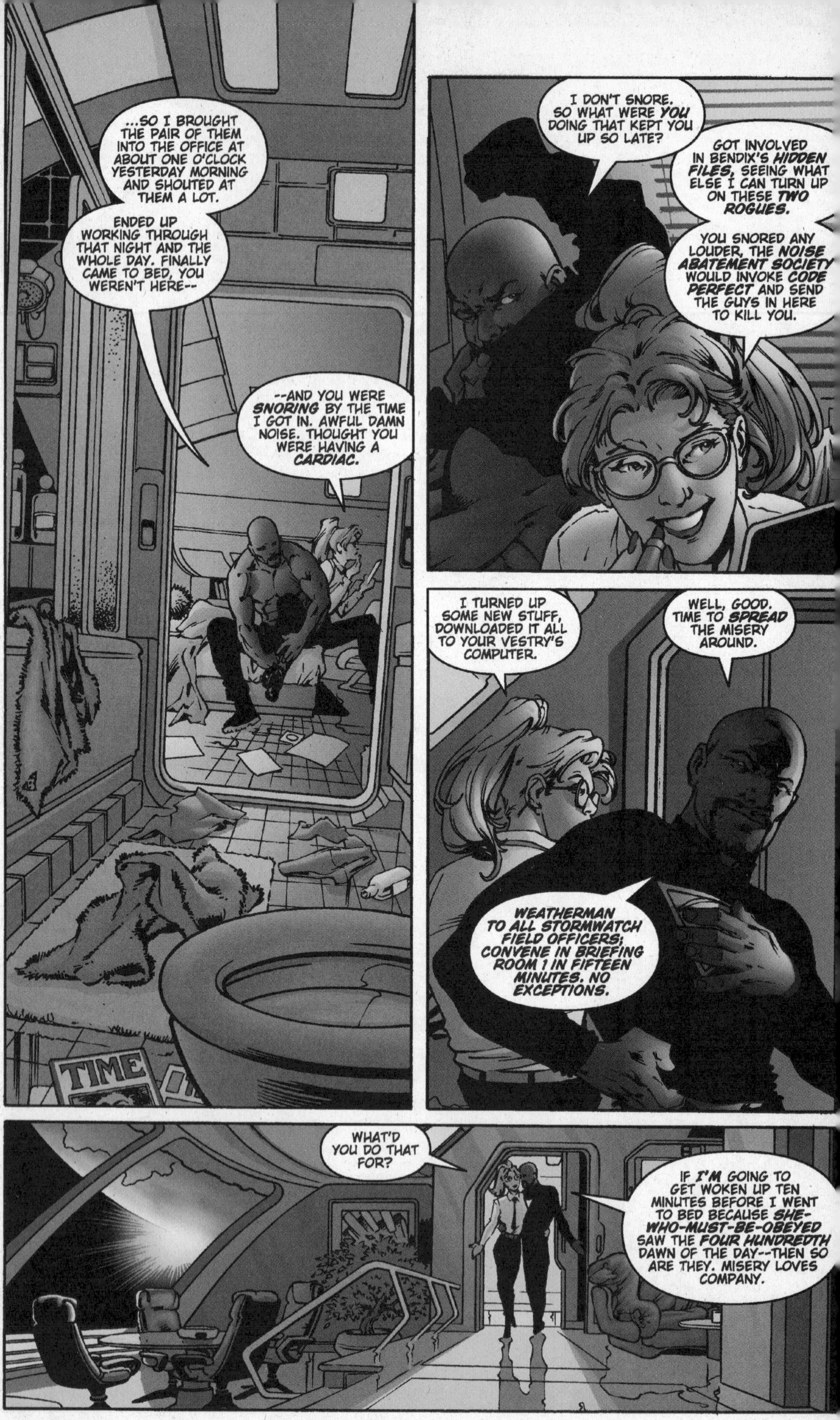
...SO I BROUGHT THE PAIR OF THEM INTO THE OFFICE AT ABOUT ONE O'CLOCK YESTERDAY MORNING AND SHOUTED AT THEM A LOT.
ENDED UP WORKING THROUGH THAT NIGHT AND THE WHOLE DAY. FINALLY CAME TO BED, YOU WEREN'T HERE--
--AND YOU WERE SNORING BY THE TIME I GOT IN. AWFUL DAMN NOISE. THOUGHT YOU WERE HAVING A CARDIAC.
TIME
I DON'T SNORE. SO WHAT WERE YOU DOING THAT KEPT YOU UP SO LATE?
GOT INVOLVED IN BENDIX'S HIDDEN FILES, SEEING WHAT ELSE I CAN TURN UP ON THESE TWO ROGUES.
YOU SNORED ANY LOUDER, THE NOISE ABATEMENT SOCIETY WOULD INVOKE CODE PERFECT AND SEND THE GUYS IN HERE TO KILL YOU.
I TURNED UP SOME NEW STUFF, DOWNLOADED IT ALL TO YOUR VESTRY'S COMPUTER.
WELL, GOOD. TIME TO SPREAD THE MISERY AROUND.
WEATHERMAN TO ALL STORMWATCH FIELD OFFICERS; CONVENE IN BRIEFING ROOM 1 IN FIFTEEN MINUTES. NO EXCEPTIONS.
WHAT'D YOU DO THAT FOR?
IF I'M GOING TO GET WOKEN UP TEN MINUTES BEFORE I WENT TO BED BECAUSE SHE-WHO-MUST-BE-OBEYED SAW THE FOUR HUNDREDTH DAWN OF THE DAY--THEN SO ARE THEY. MISERY LOVES COMPANY.

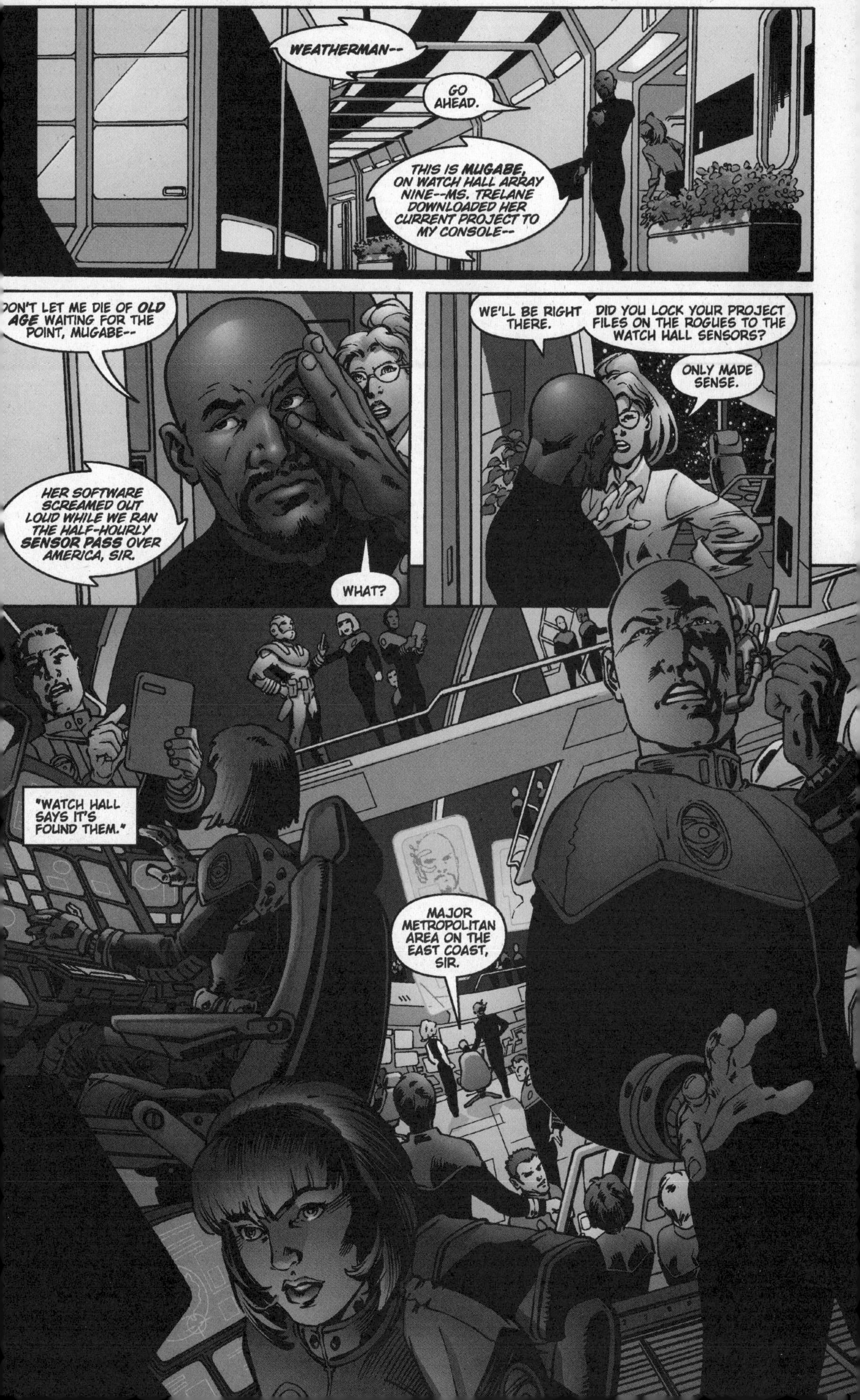
WEATHERMAN--
GO AHEAD.
THIS IS MUGABE, ON WATCH HALL ARRAY NINE--MS. TRELANE DOWNLOADED HER CURRENT PROJECT TO MY CONSOLE--
DON'T LET ME DIE OF OLD AGE WAITING FOR THE POINT, MUGABE--
HER SOFTWARE SCREAMED OUT LOUD WHILE WE RAN THE HALF-HOURLY SENSOR PASS OVER AMERICA, SIR.
WHAT?
WE'LL BE RIGHT THERE.
DID YOU LOCK YOUR PROJECT FILES ON THE ROGUES TO THE WATCH HALL SENSORS?
ONLY MADE SENSE.
"WATCH HALL SAYS IT'S FOUND THEM."
MAJOR METROPOLITAN AREA ON THE EAST COAST, SIR.

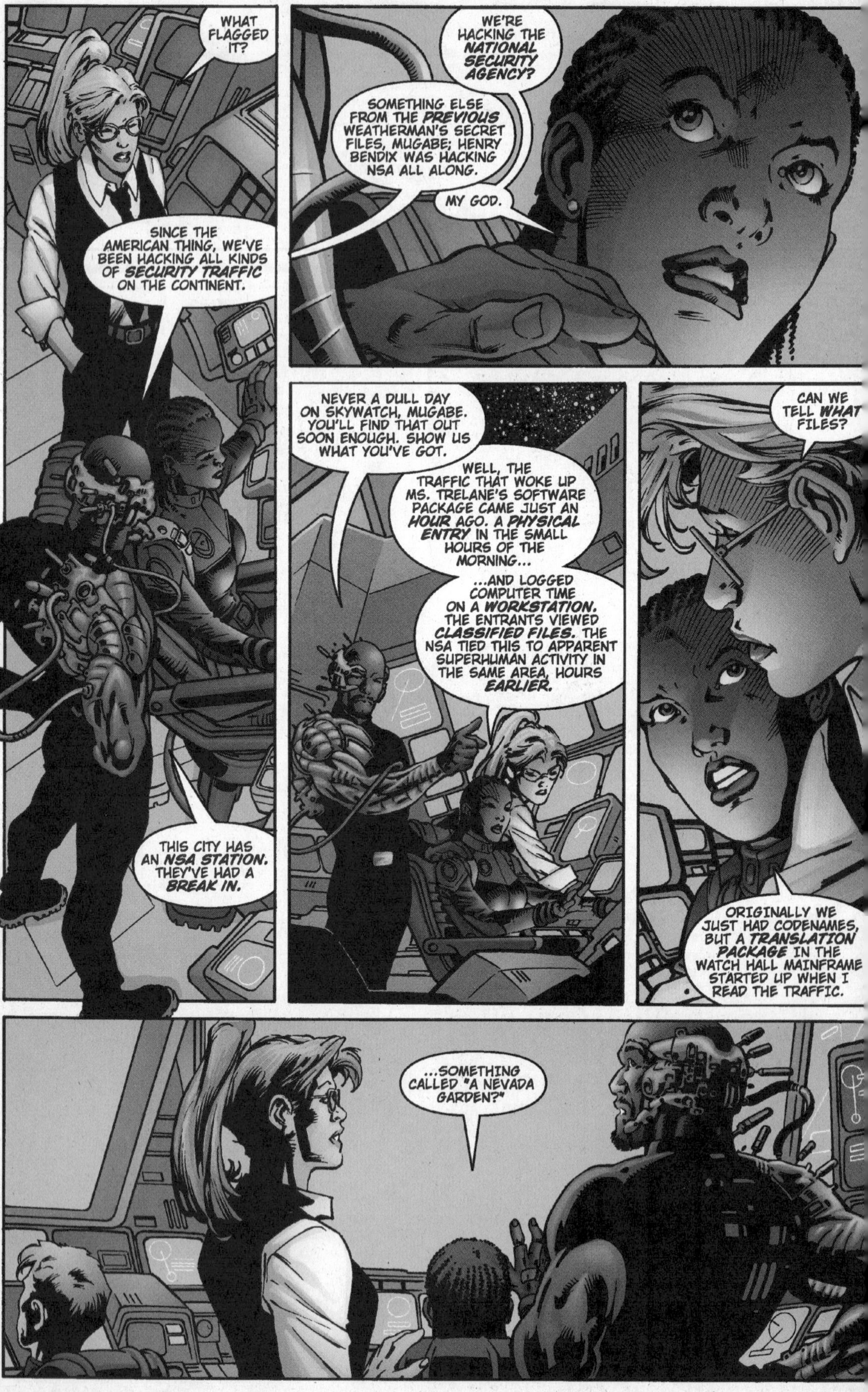

WHAT FLAGGED IT?
SINCE THE AMERICAN THING, WE'VE BEEN HACKING ALL KINDS OF SECURITY TRAFFIC ON THE CONTINENT.
THIS CITY HAS AN NSA STATION. THEY'VE HAD A BREAK IN.
WE'RE HACKING THE NATIONAL SECURITY AGENCY?
SOMETHING ELSE FROM THE PREVIOUS WEATHERMAN'S SECRET FILES, MUGABE; HENRY BENDIX WAS HACKING NSA ALL ALONG.
MY GOD.
NEVER A DULL DAY ON SKYWATCH, MUGABE. YOU'LL FIND THAT OUT SOON ENOUGH. SHOW US WHAT YOU'VE GOT.
WELL, THE TRAFFIC THAT WOKE UP MS. TRELANE'S SOFTWARE PACKAGE CAME JUST AN HOUR AGO. A PHYSICAL ENTRY IN THE SMALL HOURS OF THE MORNING...
...AND LOGGED COMPUTER TIME ON A WORKSTATION. THE ENTRANTS VIEWED CLASSIFIED FILES. THE NSA TIED THIS TO APPARENT SUPERHUMAN ACTIVITY IN THE SAME AREA, HOURS EARLIER.
CAN WE TELL WHAT FILES?
ORIGINALLY WE JUST HAD CODENAMES, BUT A TRANSLATION PACKAGE IN THE WATCH HALL MAINFRAME STARTED UP WHEN I READ THE TRAFFIC.
...SOMETHING CALLED "A NEVADA GARDEN?"

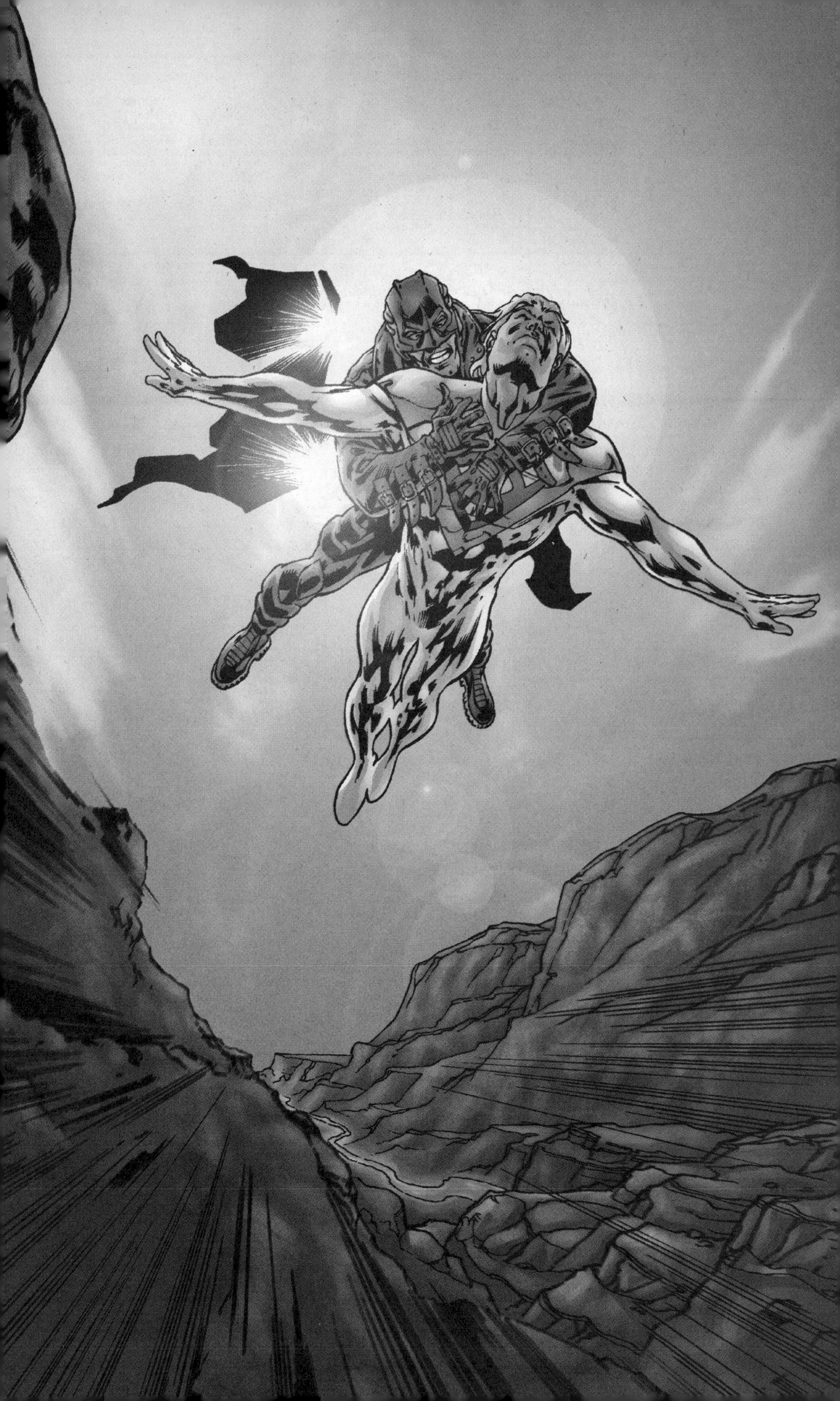

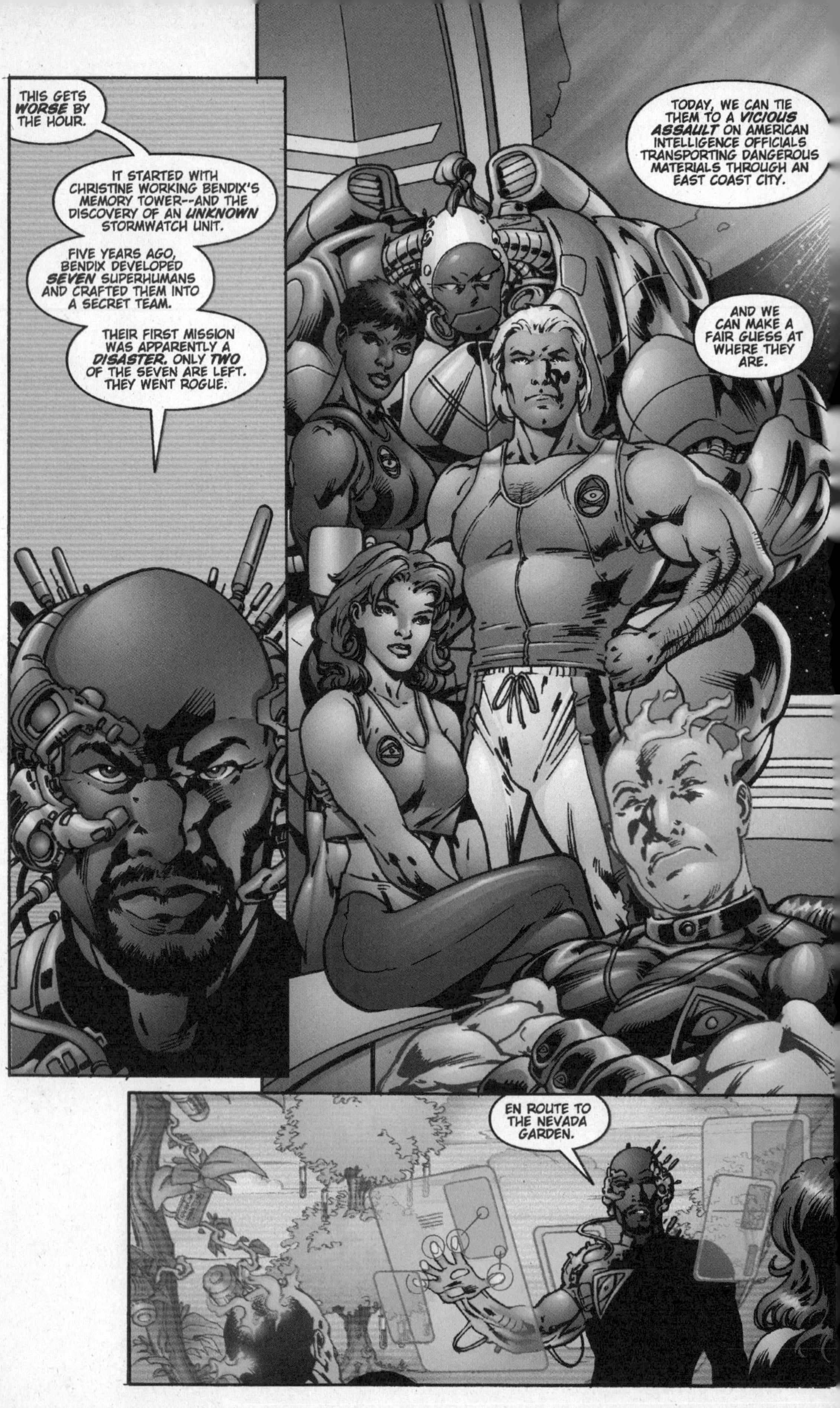
THIS GETS *WORSE* BY THE HOUR.
IT STARTED WITH CHRISTINE WORKING BENDIX'S MEMORY TOWER--AND THE DISCOVERY OF AN *UNKNOWN* STORMWATCH UNIT.
FIVE YEARS AGO, BENDIX DEVELOPED *SEVEN* SUPERHUMANS AND CRAFTED THEM INTO A SECRET TEAM.
THEIR FIRST MISSION WAS APPARENTLY A *DISASTER.* ONLY *TWO* OF THE SEVEN ARE LEFT. THEY WENT ROGUE.
TODAY, WE CAN TIE THEM TO A *VICIOUS ASSAULT* ON AMERICAN INTELLIGENCE OFFICIALS TRANSPORTING DANGEROUS MATERIALS THROUGH AN EAST COAST CITY.
AND WE CAN MAKE A FAIR GUESS AT WHERE THEY ARE.
EN ROUTE TO THE NEVADA GARDEN.

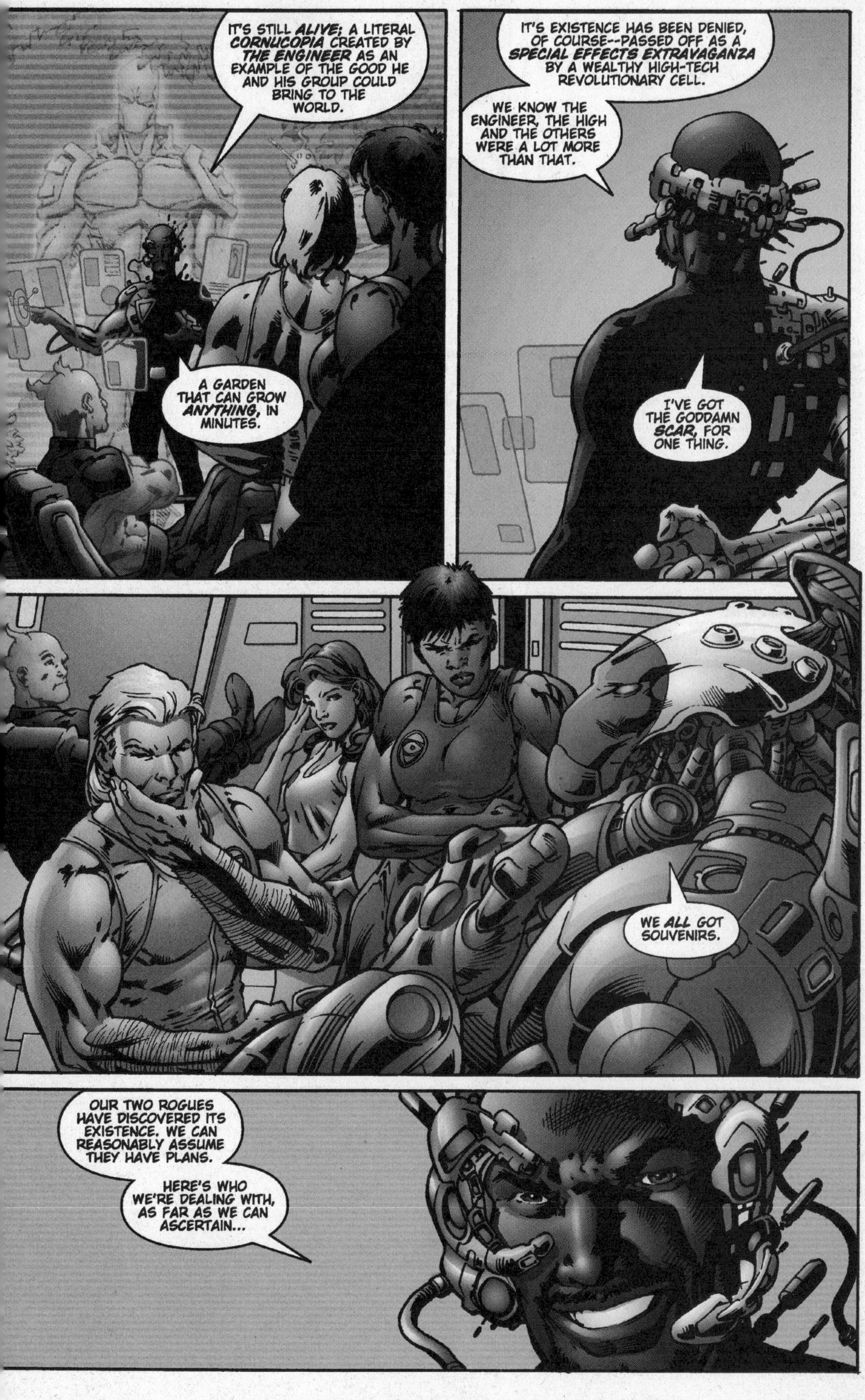
IT'S STILL ALIVE; A LITERAL CORNUCOPIA CREATED BY THE ENGINEER AS AN EXAMPLE OF THE GOOD HE AND HIS GROUP COULD BRING TO THE WORLD.
A GARDEN THAT CAN GROW ANYTHING, IN MINUTES.
IT'S EXISTENCE HAS BEEN DENIED, OF COURSE--PASSED OFF AS A SPECIAL EFFECTS EXTRAVAGANZA BY A WEALTHY HIGH-TECH REVOLUTIONARY CELL.
WE KNOW THE ENGINEER, THE HIGH AND THE OTHERS WERE A LOT MORE THAN THAT.
I'VE GOT THE GODDAMN SCAR, FOR ONE THING.
WE ALL GOT SOUVENIRS.
OUR TWO ROGUES HAVE DISCOVERED ITS EXISTENCE. WE CAN REASONABLY ASSUME THEY HAVE PLANS.
HERE'S WHO WE'RE DEALING WITH, AS FAR AS WE CAN ASCERTAIN...

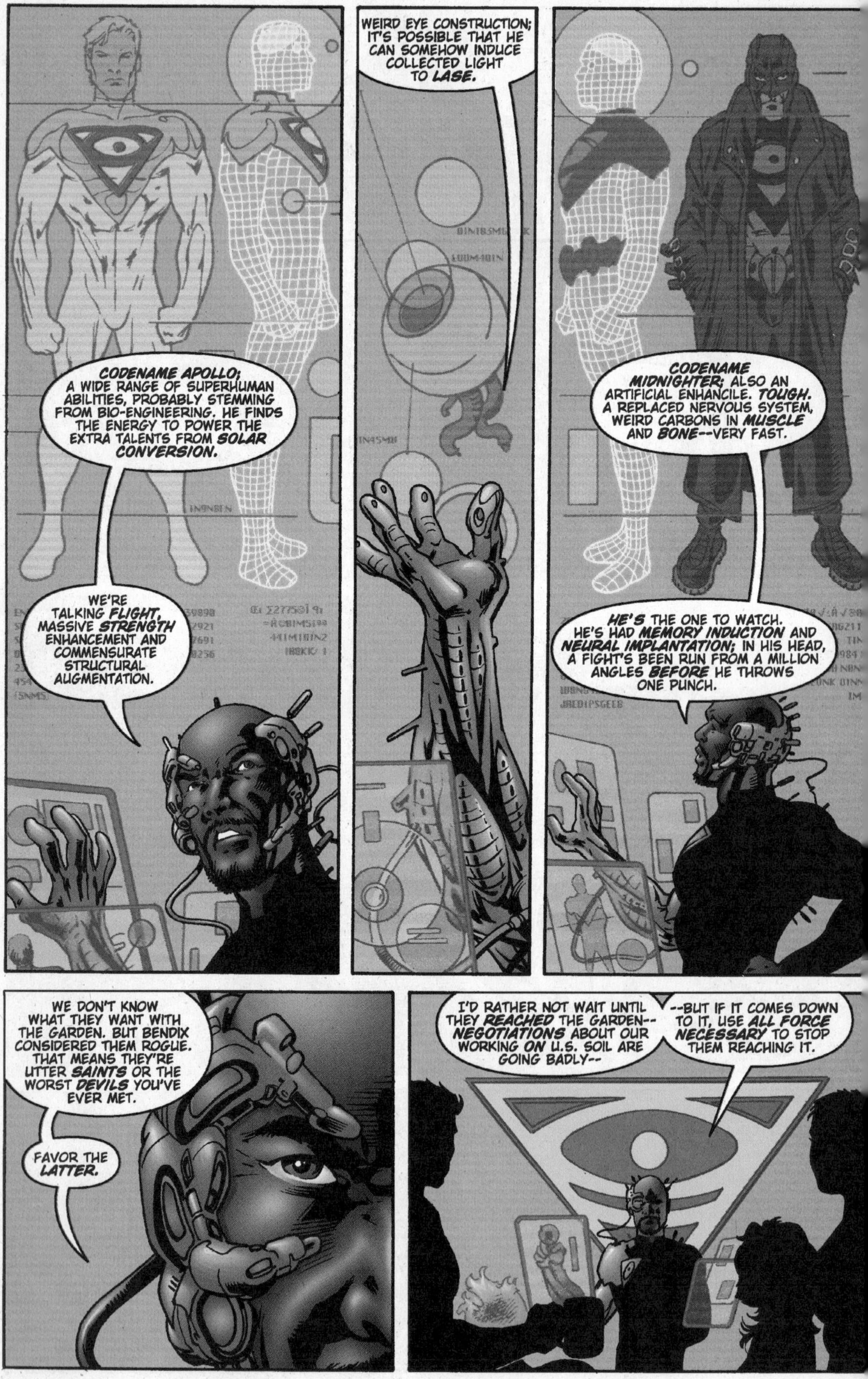
CODENAME APOLLO; A WIDE RANGE OF SUPERHUMAN ABILITIES, PROBABLY STEMMING FROM BIO-ENGINEERING. HE FINDS THE ENERGY TO POWER THE EXTRA TALENTS FROM SOLAR CONVERSION.
WE'RE TALKING FLIGHT, MASSIVE STRENGTH ENHANCEMENT AND COMMENSURATE STRUCTURAL AUGMENTATION.
WEIRD EYE CONSTRUCTION; IT'S POSSIBLE THAT HE CAN SOMEHOW INDUCE COLLECTED LIGHT TO LASE.
CODENAME MIDNIGHTER; ALSO AN ARTIFICIAL ENHANCILE. TOUGH. A REPLACED NERVOUS SYSTEM, WEIRD CARBONS IN MUSCLE AND BONE--VERY FAST.
HE'S THE ONE TO WATCH. HE'S HAD MEMORY INDUCTION AND NEURAL IMPLANTATION; IN HIS HEAD, A FIGHT'S BEEN RUN FROM A MILLION ANGLES BEFORE HE THROWS ONE PUNCH.
WE DON'T KNOW WHAT THEY WANT WITH THE GARDEN. BUT BENDIX CONSIDERED THEM ROGUE. THAT MEANS THEY'RE UTTER SAINTS OR THE WORST DEVILS YOU'VE EVER MET.
FAVOR THE LATTER.
I'D RATHER NOT WAIT UNTIL THEY REACHED THE GARDEN-- NEGOTIATIONS ABOUT OUR WORKING ON U.S. SOIL ARE GOING BADLY--
--BUT IF IT COMES DOWN TO IT, USE ALL FORCE NECESSARY TO STOP THEM REACHING IT.

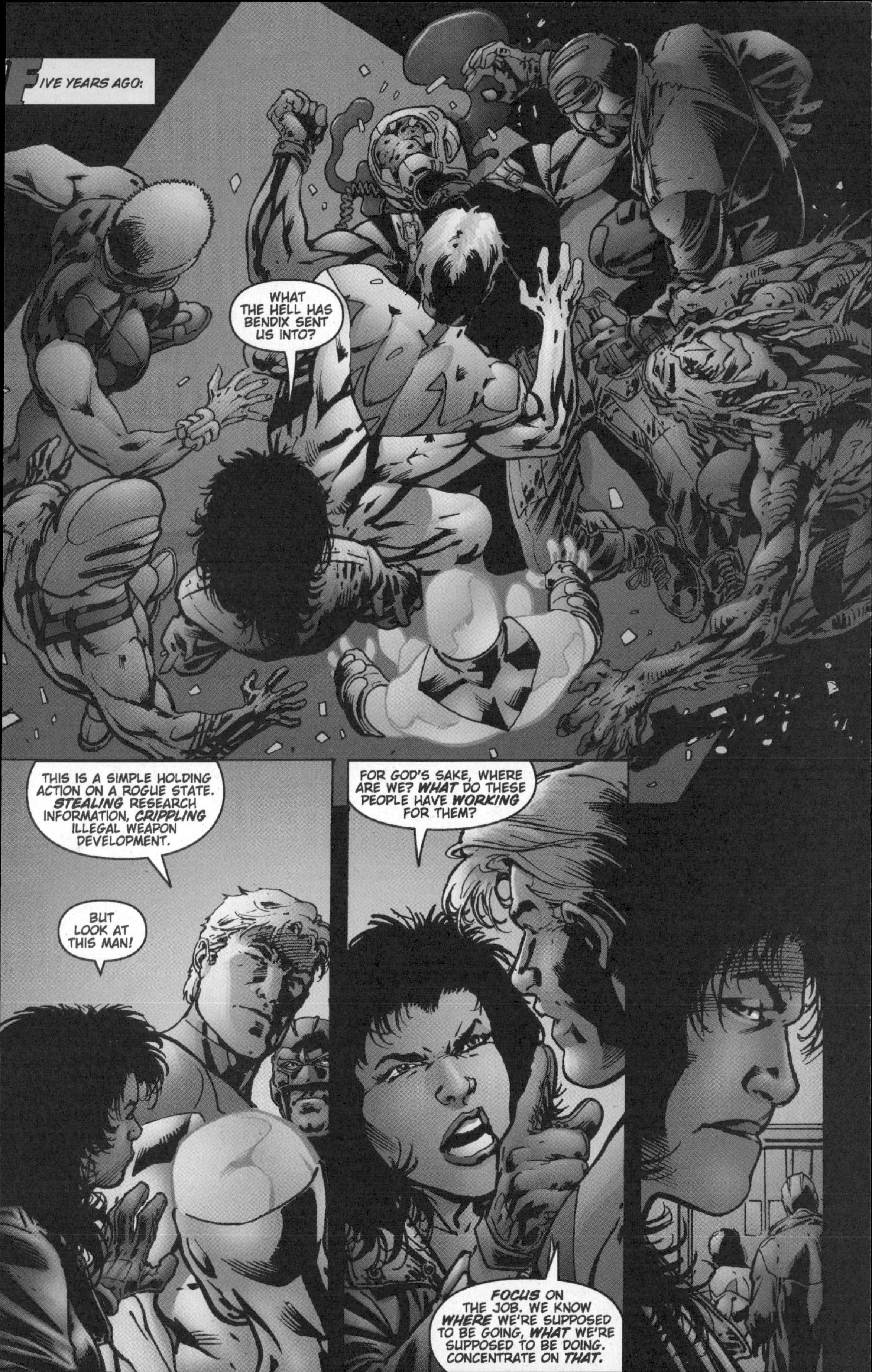
FIVE YEARS AGO:
WHAT THE HELL HAS BENDIX SENT US INTO?
THIS IS A SIMPLE HOLDING ACTION ON A ROGUE STATE. STEALING RESEARCH INFORMATION, CRIPPLING ILLEGAL WEAPON DEVELOPMENT.
BUT LOOK AT THIS MAN!
FOR GOD'S SAKE, WHERE ARE WE? WHAT DO THESE PEOPLE HAVE WORKING FOR THEM?
FOCUS ON THE JOB. WE KNOW WHERE WE'RE SUPPOSED TO BE GOING, WHAT WE'RE SUPPOSED TO BE DOING. CONCENTRATE ON THAT.

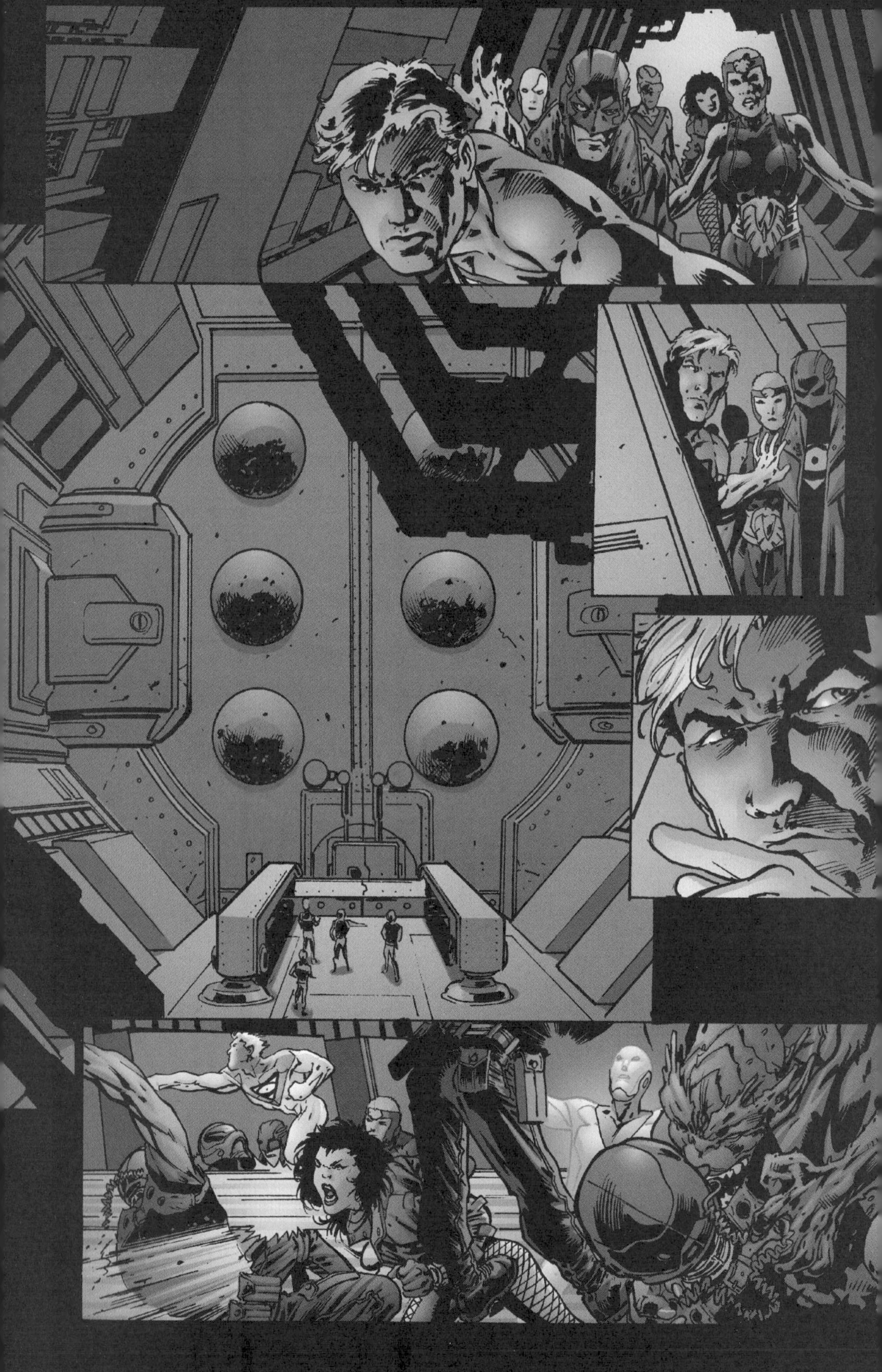

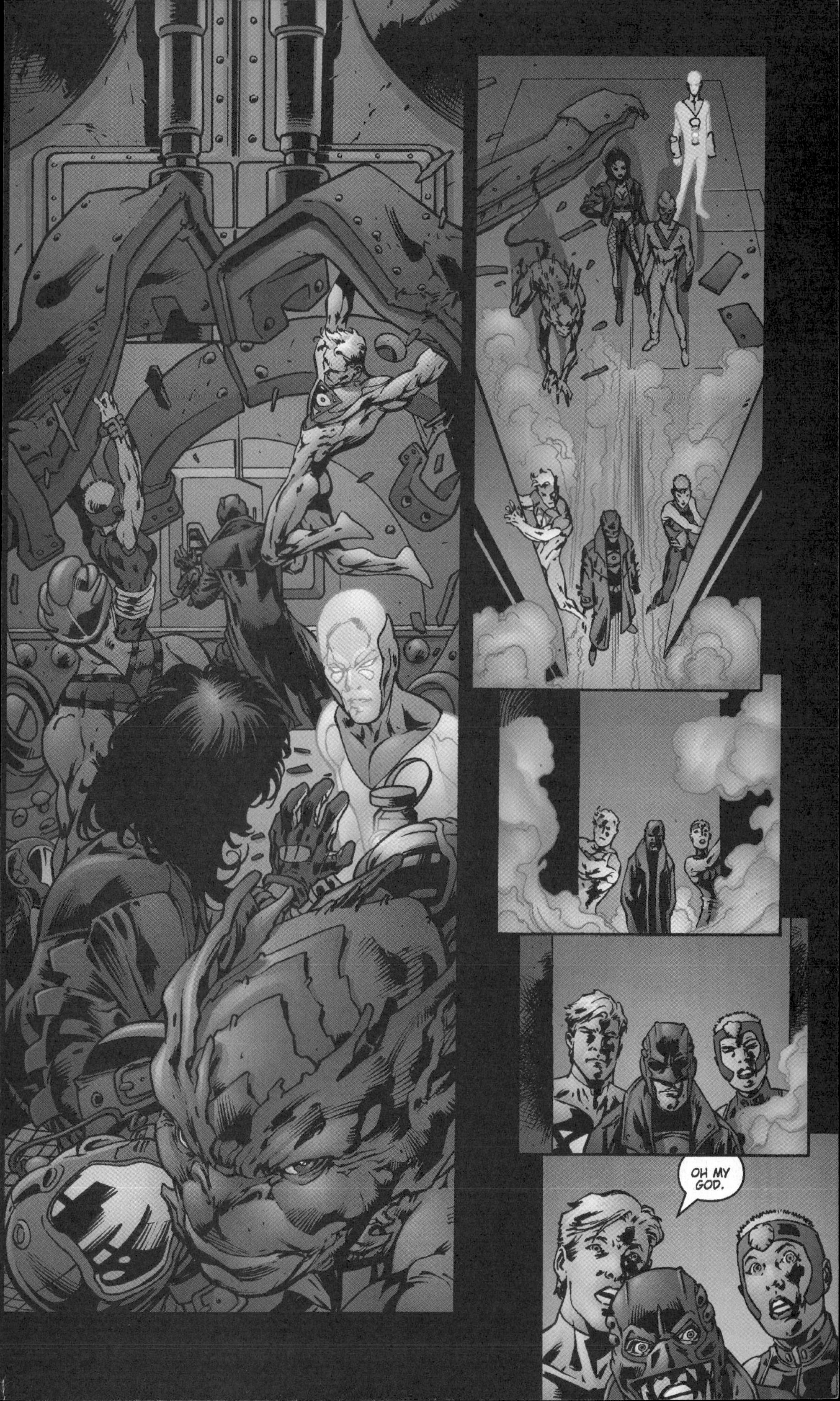
OH MY GOD.

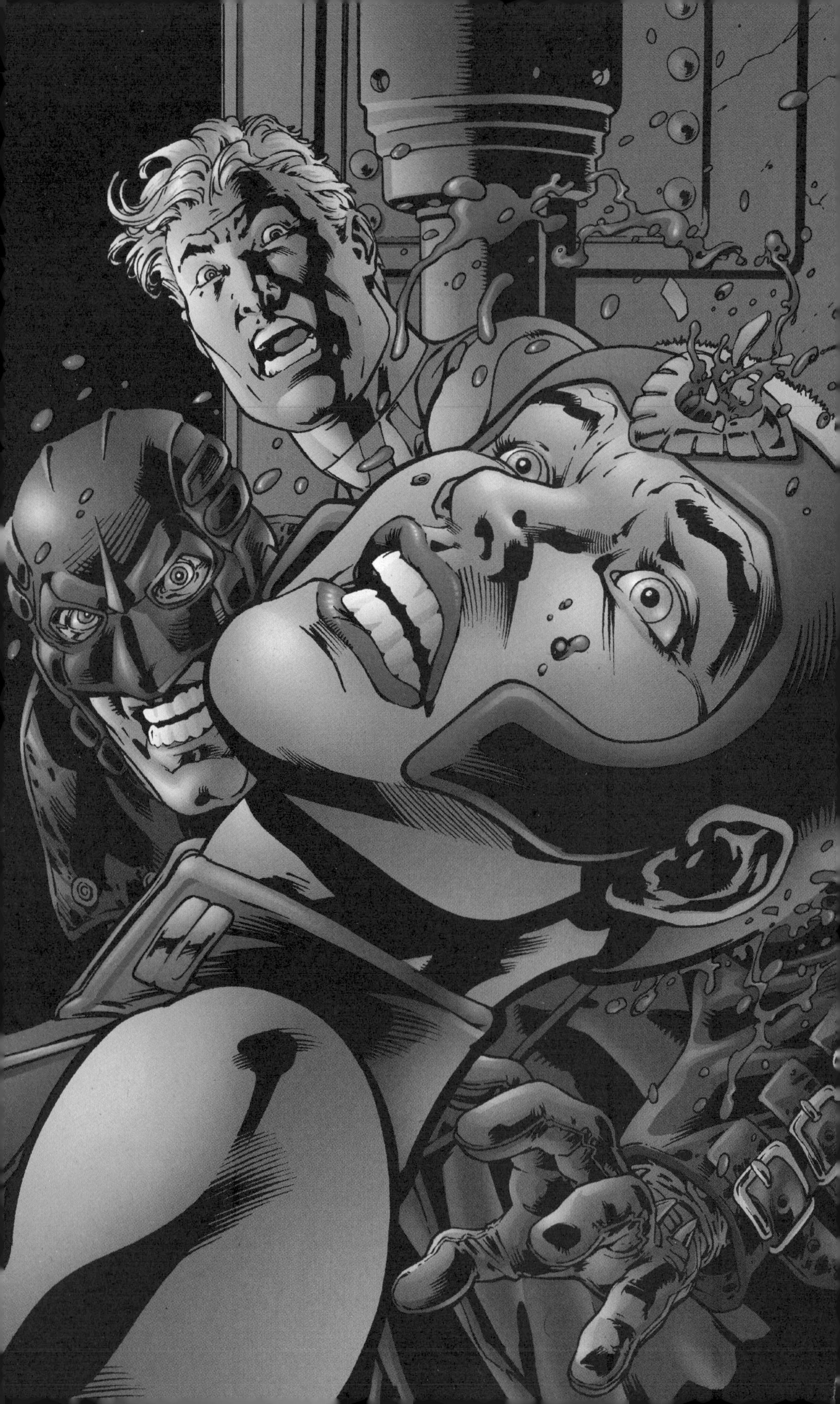

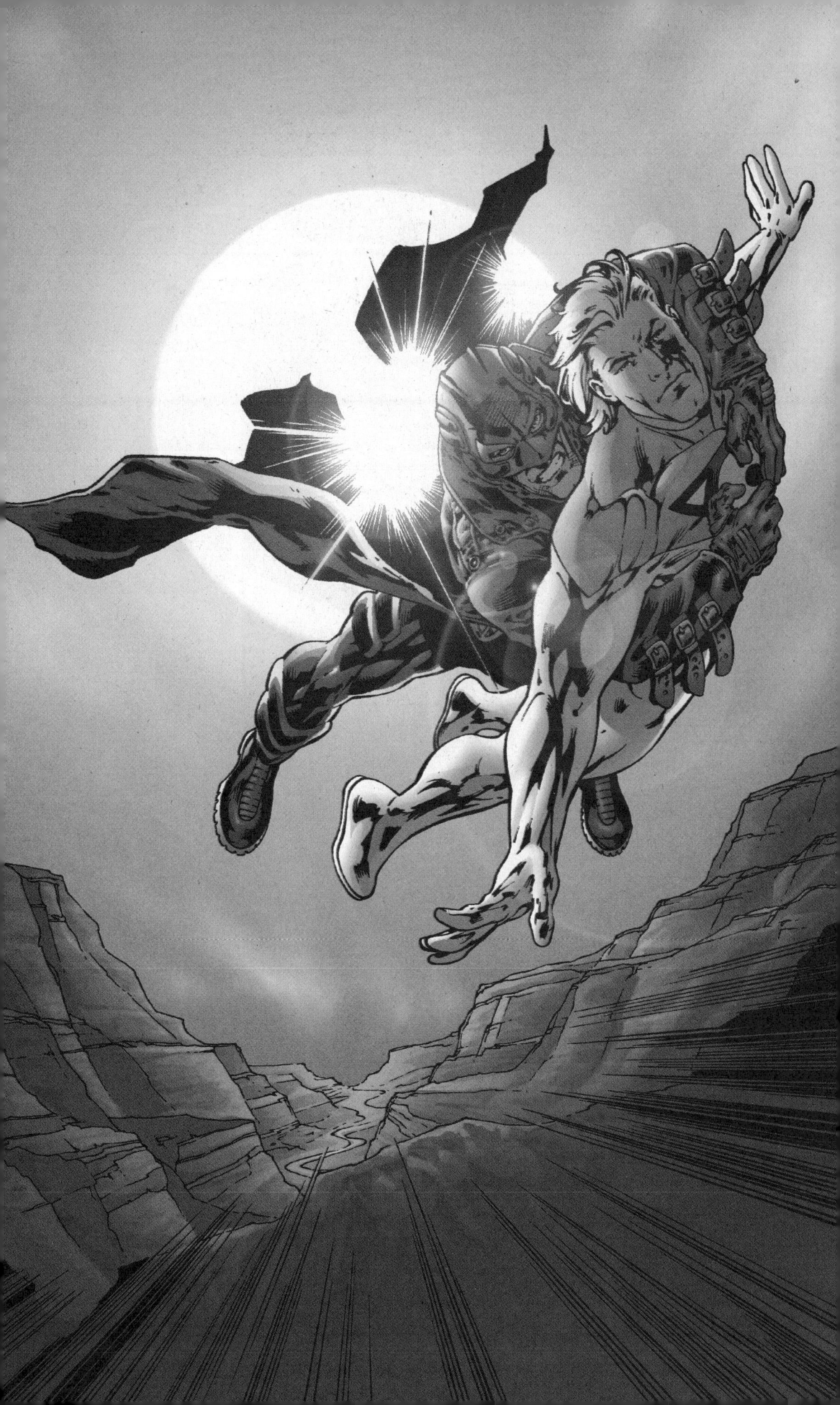

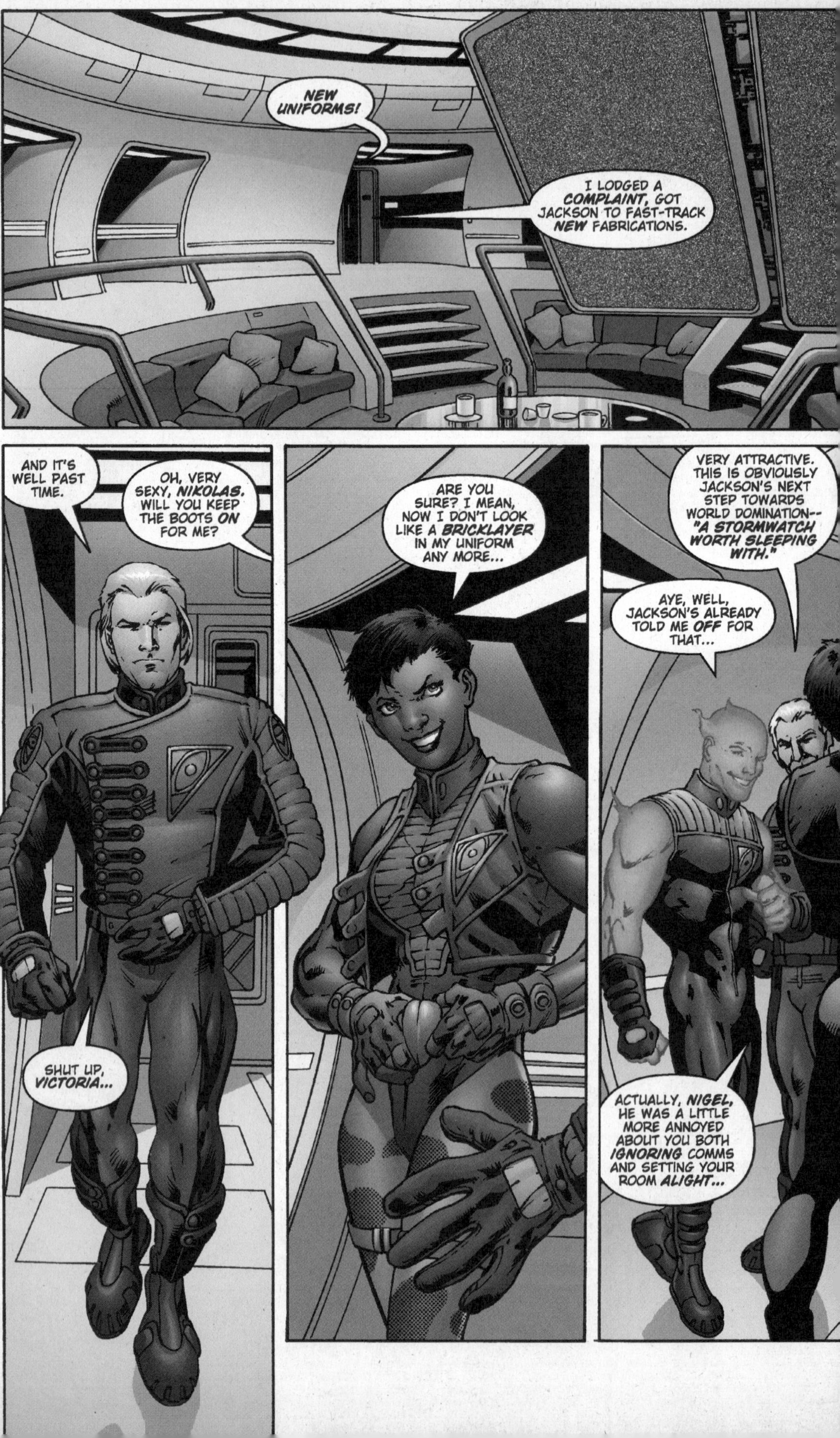
NEW UNIFORMS!
I LODGED A COMPLAINT, GOT JACKSON TO FAST-TRACK NEW FABRICATIONS.
AND IT'S WELL PAST TIME.
OH, VERY SEXY, NIKOLAS. WILL YOU KEEP THE BOOTS ON FOR ME?
SHUT UP, VICTORIA...
ARE YOU SURE? I MEAN, NOW I DON'T LOOK LIKE A BRICKLAYER IN MY UNIFORM ANY MORE...
VERY ATTRACTIVE. THIS IS OBVIOUSLY JACKSON'S NEXT STEP TOWARDS WORLD DOMINATION-- "A STORMWATCH WORTH SLEEPING WITH."
AYE, WELL, JACKSON'S ALREADY TOLD ME OFF FOR THAT...
ACTUALLY, NIGEL, HE WAS A LITTLE MORE ANNOYED ABOUT YOU BOTH IGNORING COMMS AND SETTING YOUR ROOM ALIGHT...

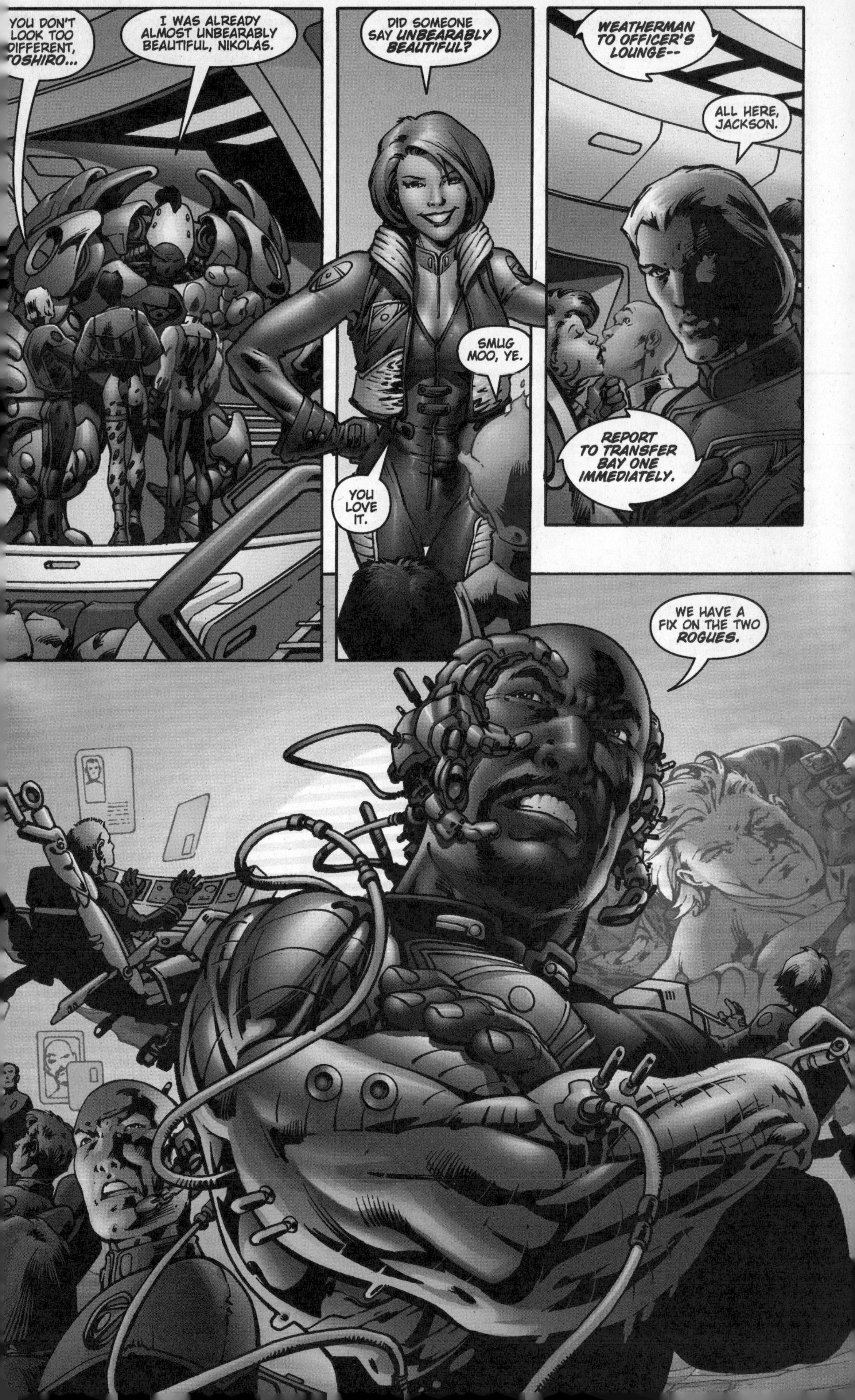

YOU DON'T LOOK TOO DIFFERENT, TOSHIRO...
I WAS ALREADY ALMOST UNBEARABLY BEAUTIFUL, NIKOLAS.
DID SOMEONE SAY UNBEARABLY BEAUTIFUL?
SMUG MOO, YE.
YOU LOVE IT.
WEATHERMAN TO OFFICER'S LOUNGE--
ALL HERE, JACKSON.
REPORT TO TRANSFER BAY ONE IMMEDIATELY.
WE HAVE A FIX ON THE TWO ROGUES.

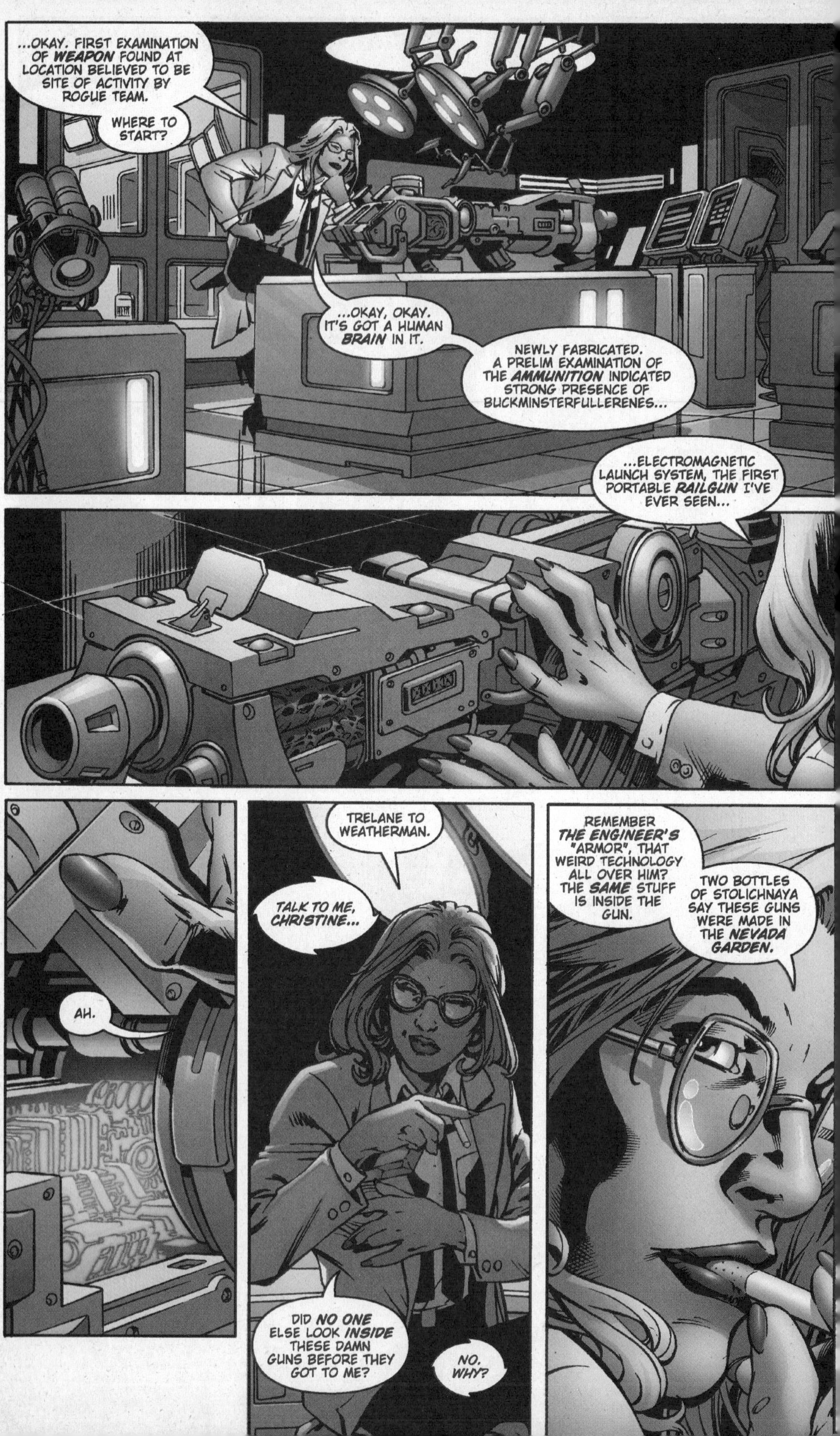
...OKAY. FIRST EXAMINATION OF WEAPON FOUND AT LOCATION BELIEVED TO BE SITE OF ACTIVITY BY ROGUE TEAM.
WHERE TO START?
...OKAY, OKAY. IT'S GOT A HUMAN BRAIN IN IT.
NEWLY FABRICATED. A PRELIM EXAMINATION OF THE AMMUNITION INDICATED STRONG PRESENCE OF BUCKMINSTERFULLERENES...
...ELECTROMAGNETIC LAUNCH SYSTEM, THE FIRST PORTABLE RAILGUN I'VE EVER SEEN...
AH.
TRELANE TO WEATHERMAN.
TALK TO ME, CHRISTINE...
DID NO ONE ELSE LOOK INSIDE THESE DAMN GUNS BEFORE THEY GOT TO ME?
NO. WHY?
REMEMBER THE ENGINEER'S "ARMOR", THAT WEIRD TECHNOLOGY ALL OVER HIM? THE SAME STUFF IS INSIDE THE GUN.
TWO BOTTLES OF STOLICHNAYA SAY THESE GUNS WERE MADE IN THE NEVADA GARDEN.

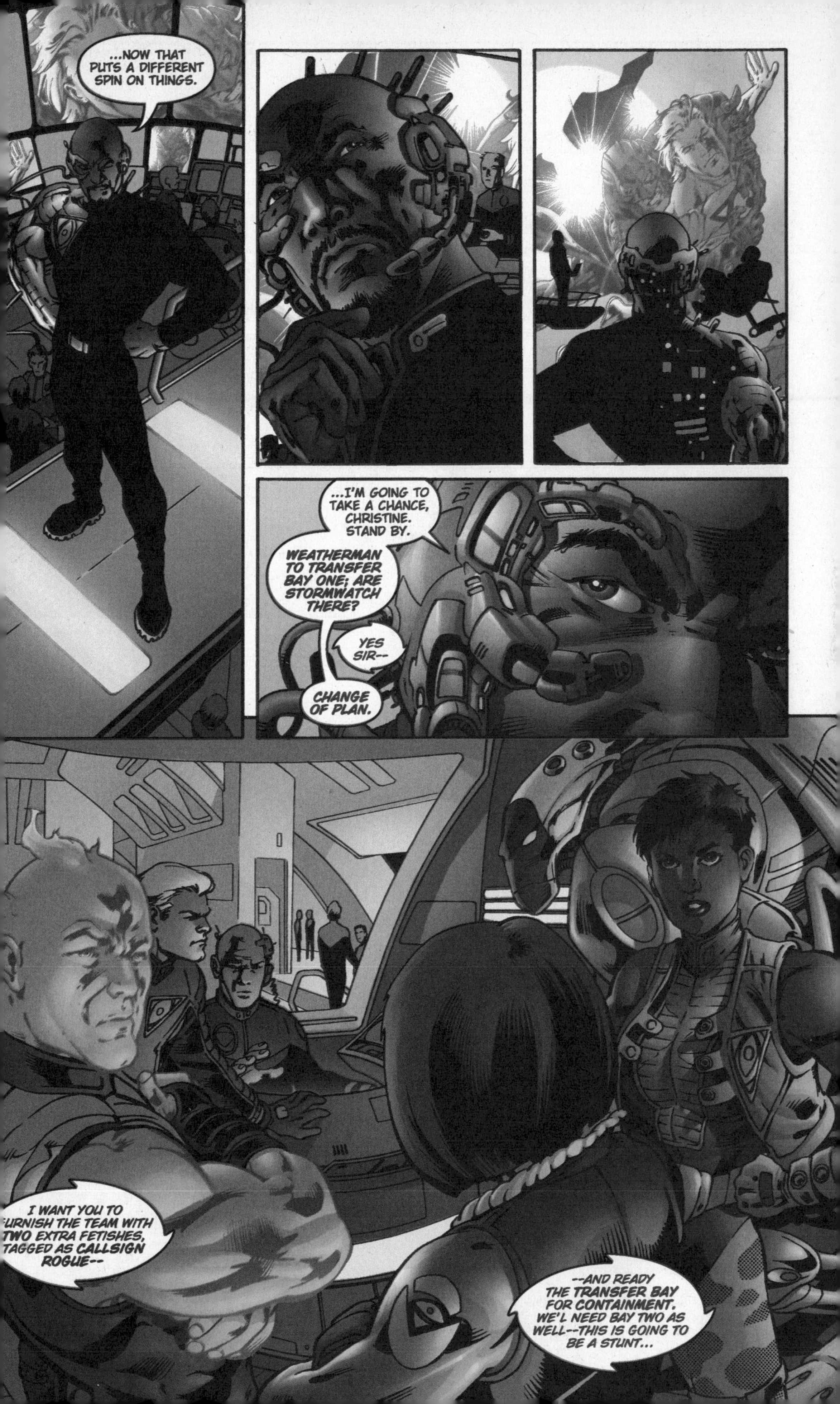
...NOW THAT PUTS A DIFFERENT SPIN ON THINGS.
...I'M GOING TO TAKE A CHANCE, CHRISTINE. STAND BY.
WEATHERMAN TO TRANSFER BAY ONE; ARE STORMWATCH THERE?
YES SIR--
CHANGE OF PLAN.
I WANT YOU TO FURNISH THE TEAM WITH TWO EXTRA FETISHES, TAGGED AS CALLSIGN ROGUE--
--AND READY THE TRANSFER BAY FOR CONTAINMENT. WE'L NEED BAY TWO AS WELL--THIS IS GOING TO BE A STUNT...

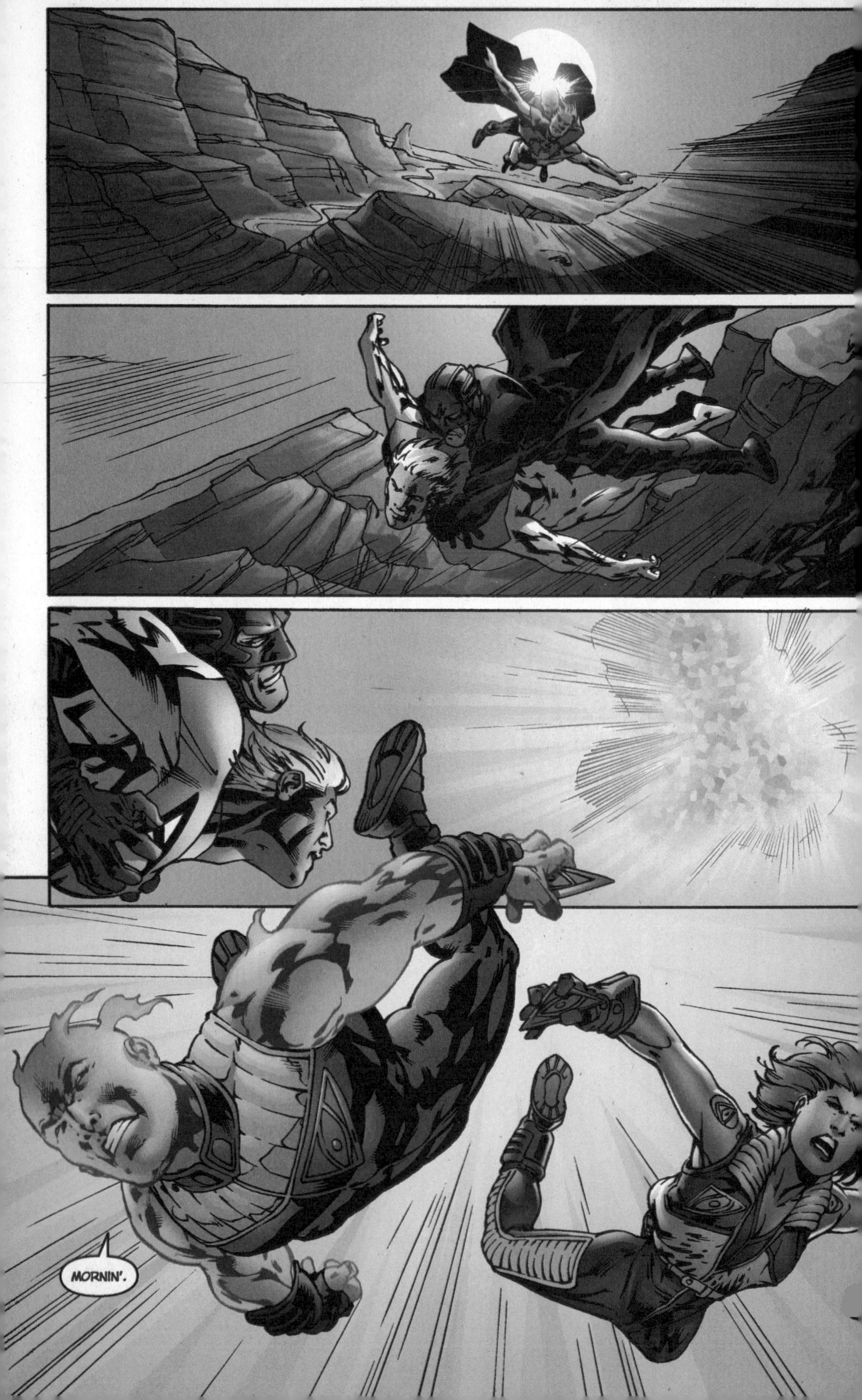
MORNIN'.

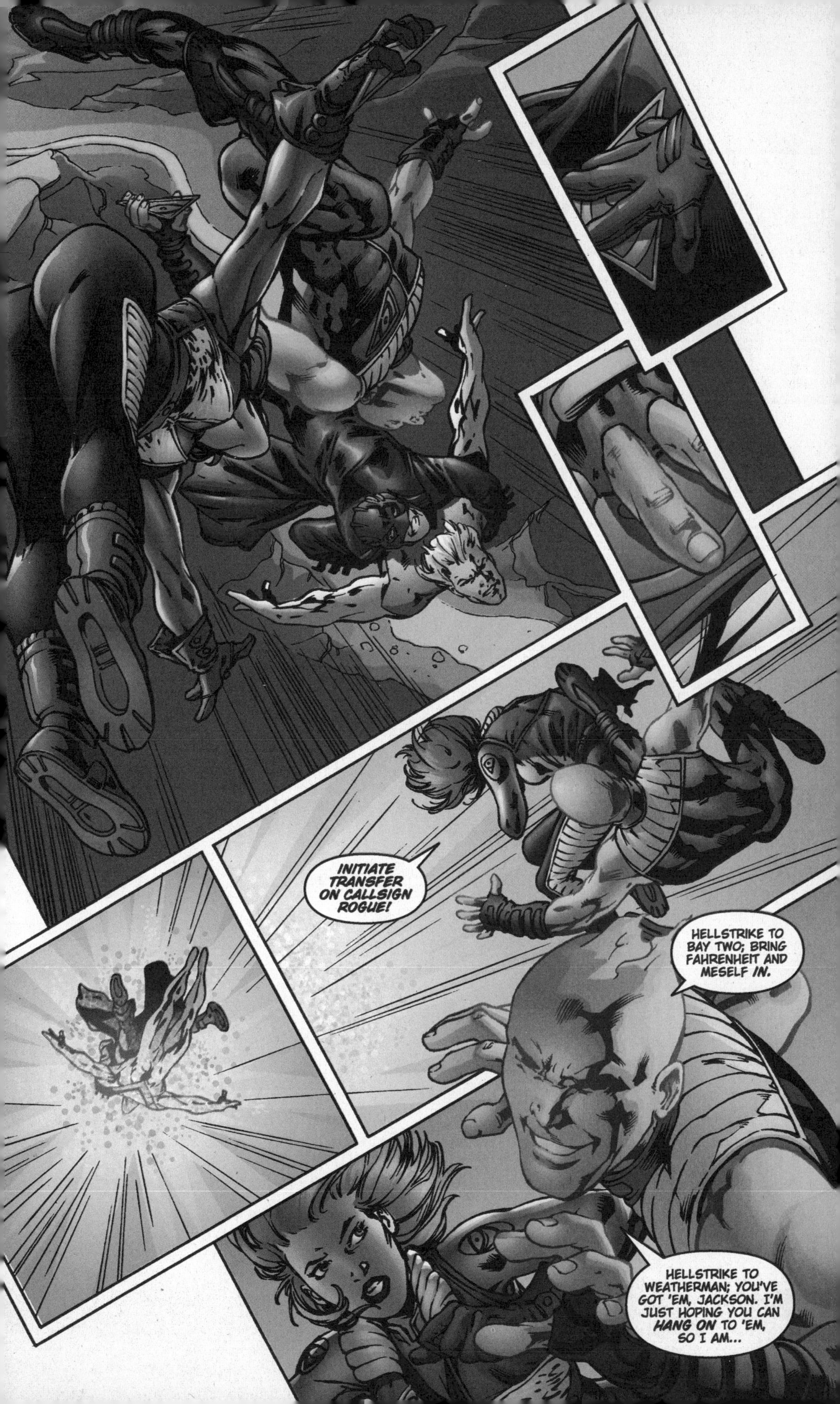
INITIATE TRANSFER ON CALLSIGN ROGUE!
HELLSTRIKE TO BAY TWO; BRING FAHRENHEIT AND MESELF IN.
HELLSTRIKE TO WEATHERMAN; YOU'VE GOT 'EM, JACKSON. I'M JUST HOPING YOU CAN HANG ON TO 'EM, SO I AM...

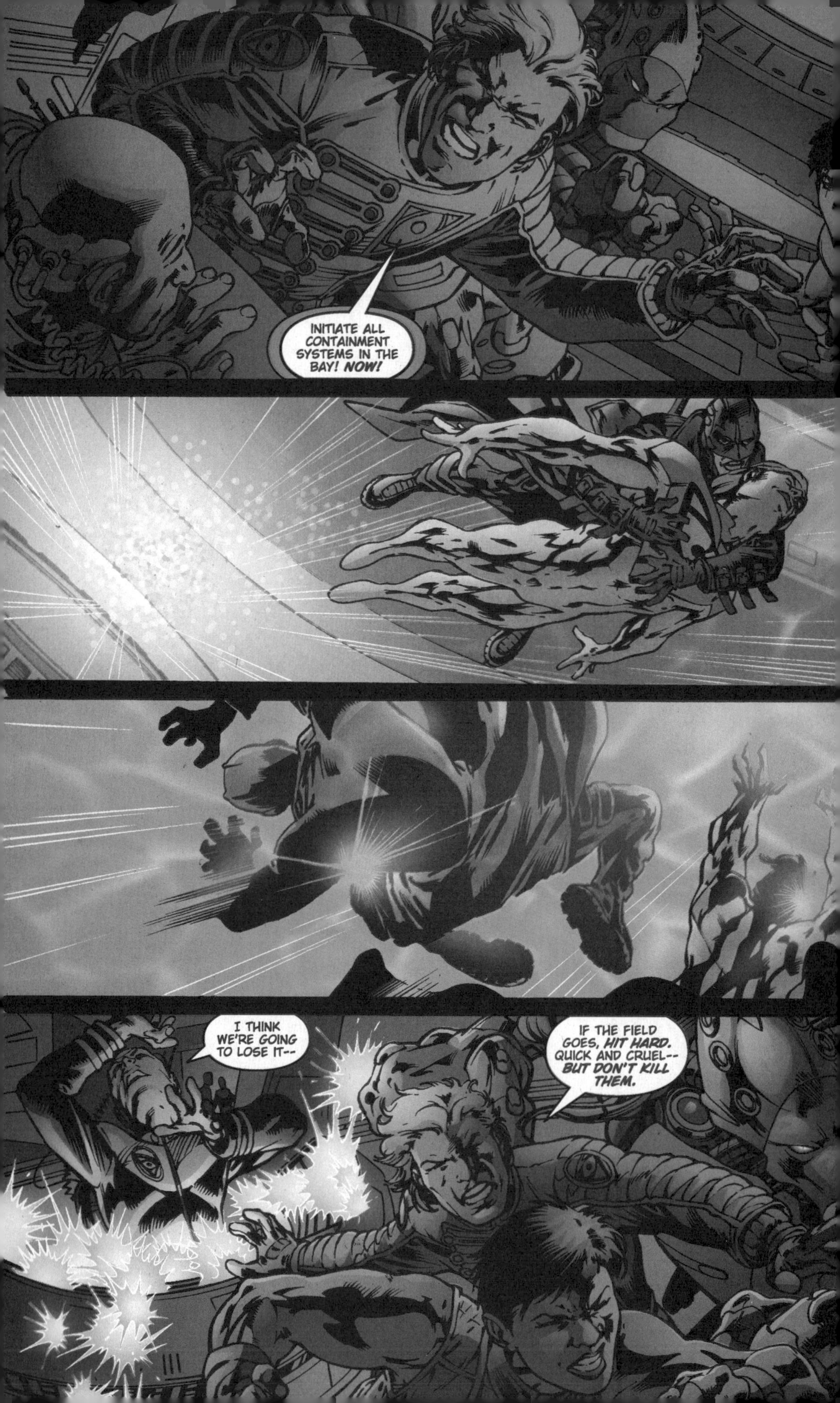
INITIATE ALL CONTAINMENT SYSTEMS IN THE BAY! NOW!
I THINK WE'RE GOING TO LOSE IT--
IF THE FIELD GOES, HIT HARD. QUICK AND CRUEL-- BUT DON'T KILL THEM.

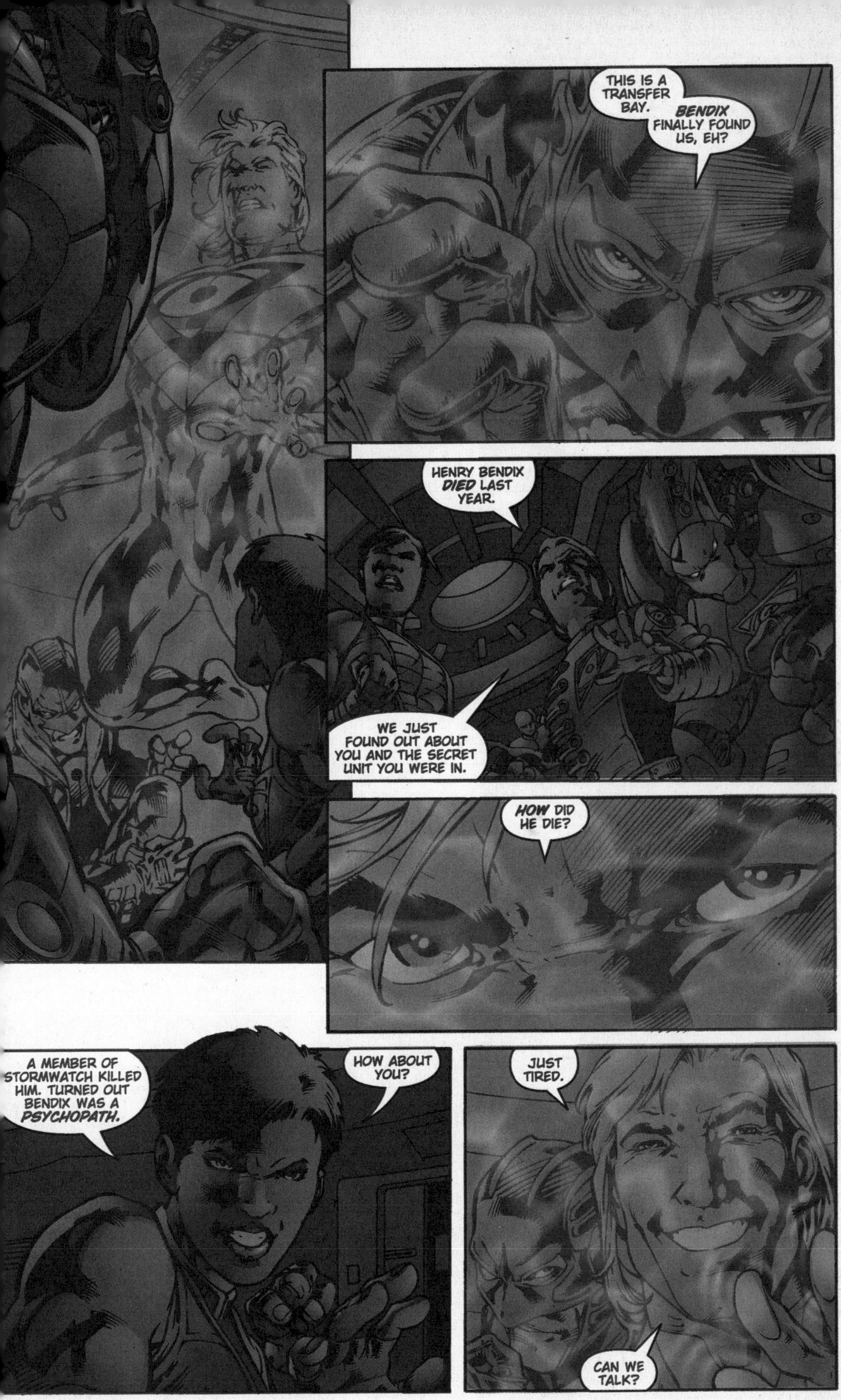
THIS IS A TRANSFER BAY. BENDIX FINALLY FOUND US, EH?
HENRY BENDIX DIED LAST YEAR.
WE JUST FOUND OUT ABOUT YOU AND THE SECRET UNIT YOU WERE IN.
HOW DID HE DIE?
A MEMBER OF STORMWATCH KILLED HIM. TURNED OUT BENDIX WAS A PSYCHOPATH.
HOW ABOUT YOU?
JUST TIRED.
CAN WE TALK?

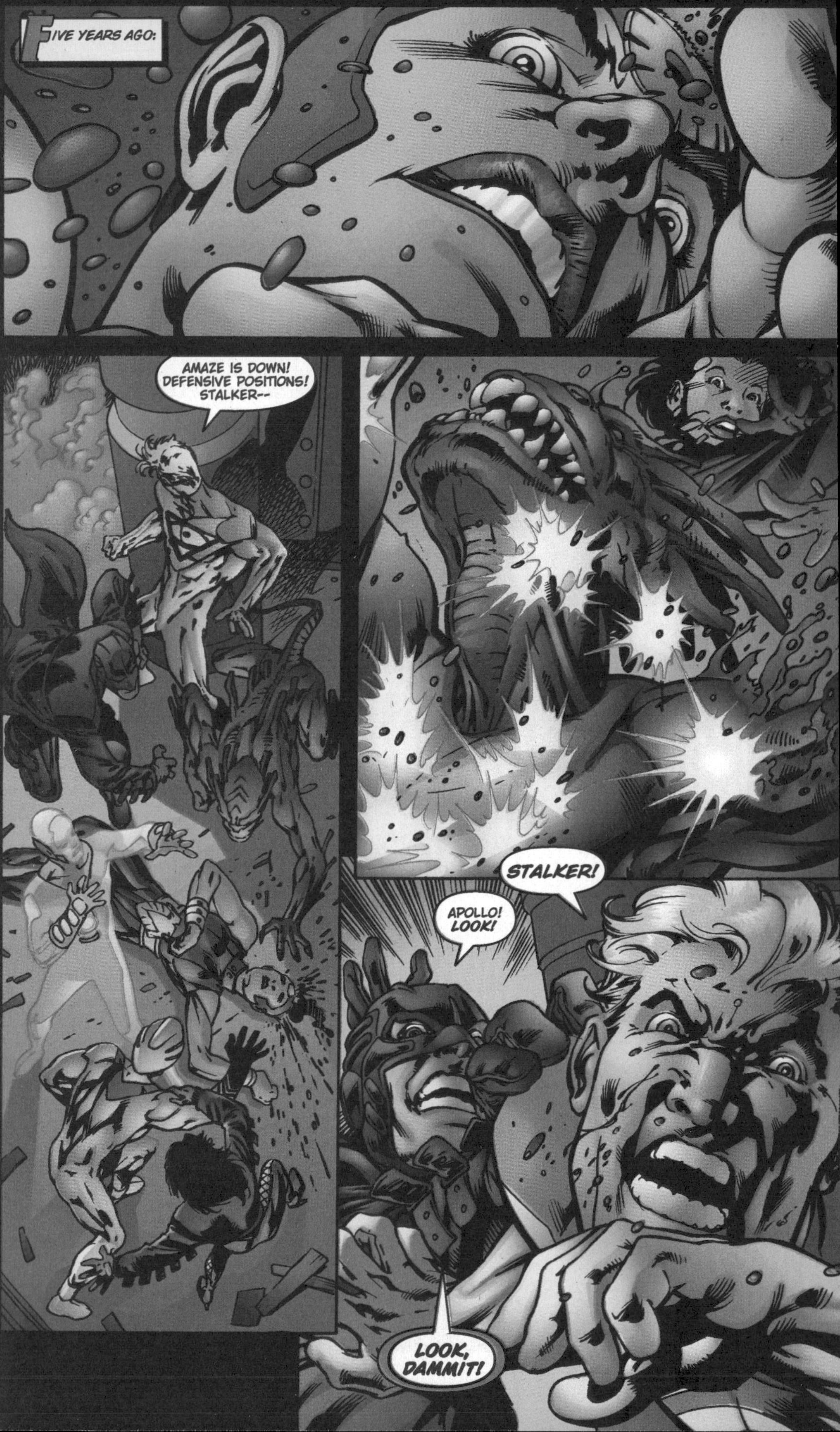
FIVE YEARS AGO:
AMAZE IS DOWN! DEFENSIVE POSITIONS! STALKER--
STALKER!
APOLLO! LOOK!
LOOK, DAMMIT!

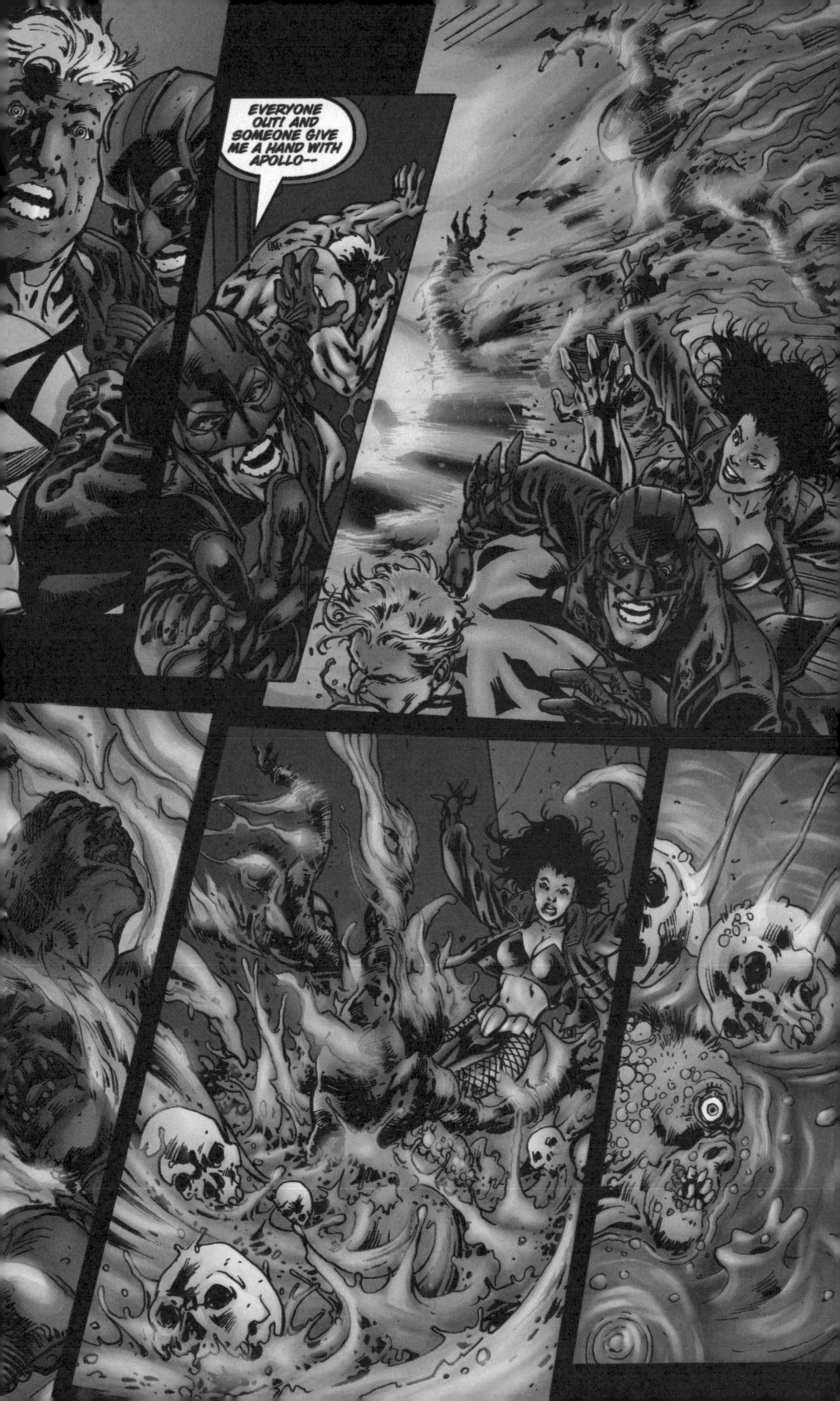
EVERYONE OUT! AND SOMEONE GIVE ME A HAND WITH APOLLO--

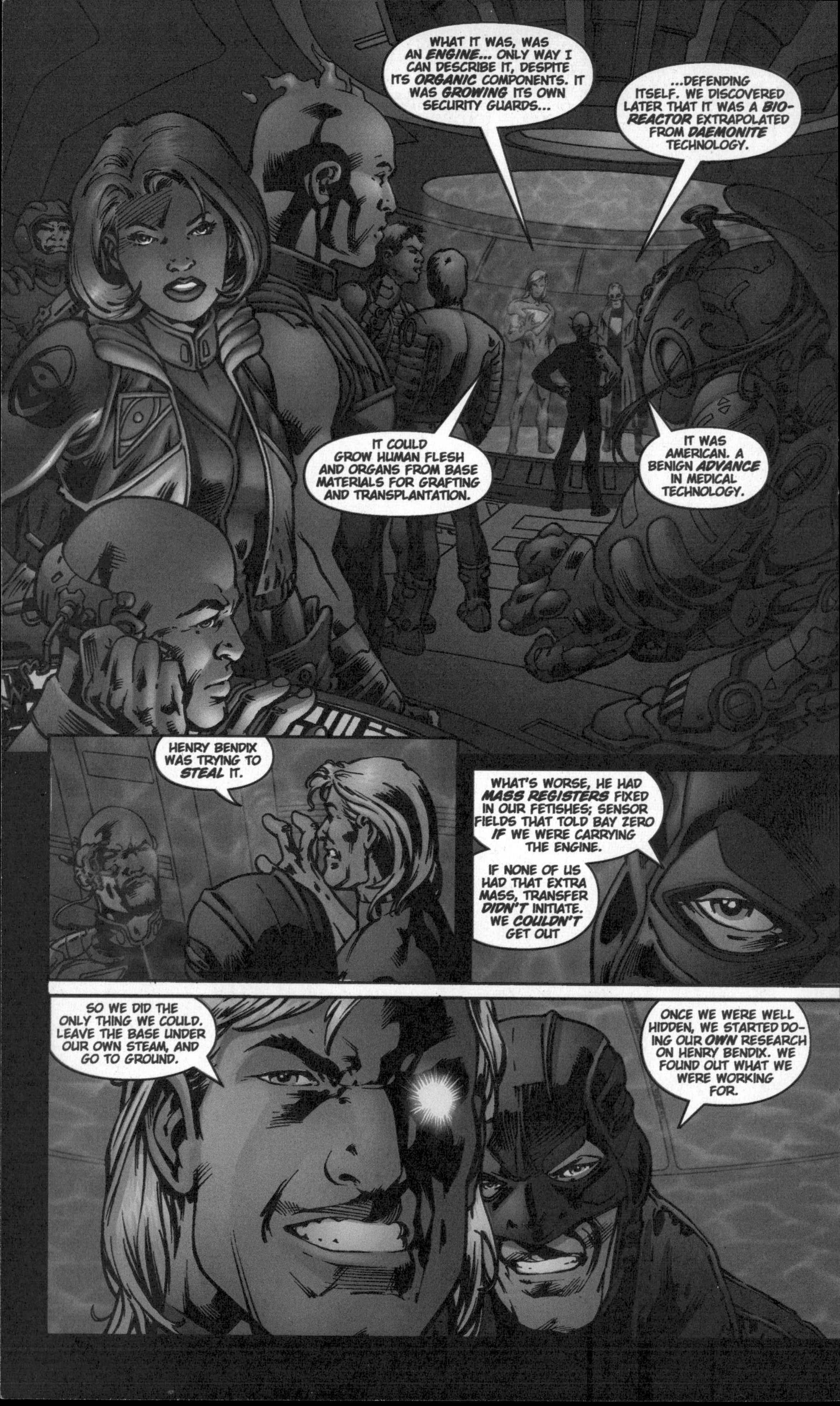
WHAT IT WAS, WAS AN ENGINE... ONLY WAY I CAN DESCRIBE IT, DESPITE ITS ORGANIC COMPONENTS. IT WAS GROWING ITS OWN SECURITY GUARDS...
...DEFENDING ITSELF. WE DISCOVERED LATER THAT IT WAS A BIO-REACTOR EXTRAPOLATED FROM DAEMONITE TECHNOLOGY.
IT COULD GROW HUMAN FLESH AND ORGANS FROM BASE MATERIALS FOR GRAFTING AND TRANSPLANTATION.
IT WAS AMERICAN. A BENIGN ADVANCE IN MEDICAL TECHNOLOGY.
HENRY BENDIX WAS TRYING TO STEAL IT.
WHAT'S WORSE, HE HAD MASS REGISTERS FIXED IN OUR FETISHES; SENSOR FIELDS THAT TOLD BAY ZERO IF WE WERE CARRYING THE ENGINE.
IF NONE OF US HAD THAT EXTRA MASS, TRANSFER DIDN'T INITIATE. WE COULDN'T GET OUT
SO WE DID THE ONLY THING WE COULD. LEAVE THE BASE UNDER OUR OWN STEAM, AND GO TO GROUND.
ONCE WE WERE WELL HIDDEN, WE STARTED DOING OUR OWN RESEARCH ON HENRY BENDIX. WE FOUND OUT WHAT WE WERE WORKING FOR.

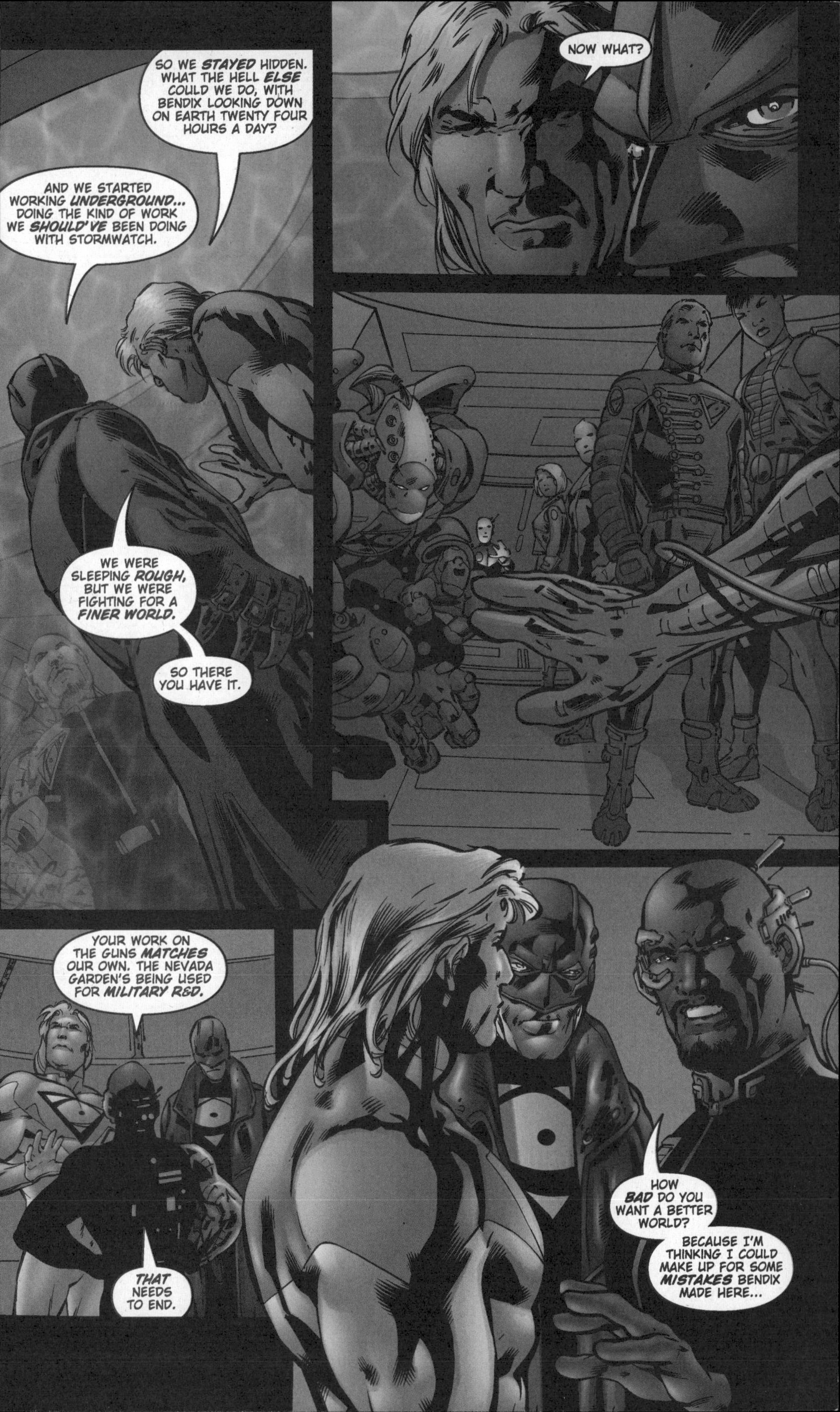
SO WE STAYED HIDDEN. WHAT THE HELL ELSE COULD WE DO, WITH BENDIX LOOKING DOWN ON EARTH TWENTY FOUR HOURS A DAY?
AND WE STARTED WORKING UNDERGROUND... DOING THE KIND OF WORK WE SHOULD'VE BEEN DOING WITH STORMWATCH.
WE WERE SLEEPING ROUGH, BUT WE WERE FIGHTING FOR A FINER WORLD.
SO THERE YOU HAVE IT.
NOW WHAT?
YOUR WORK ON THE GUNS MATCHES OUR OWN. THE NEVADA GARDEN'S BEING USED FOR MILITARY R&D.
THAT NEEDS TO END.
HOW BAD DO YOU WANT A BETTER WORLD?
BECAUSE I'M THINKING I COULD MAKE UP FOR SOME MISTAKES BENDIX MADE HERE...

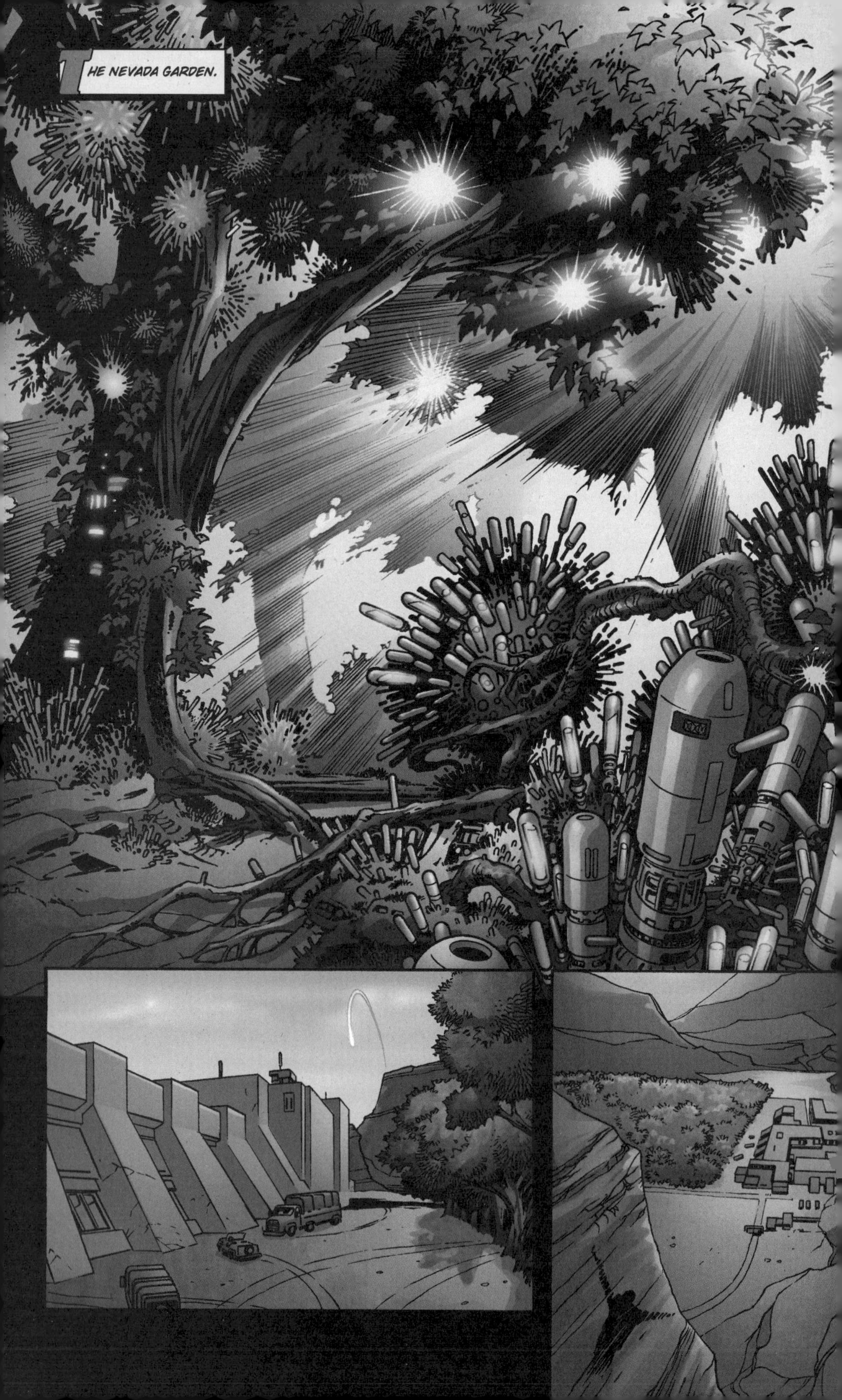
THE NEVADA GARDEN.

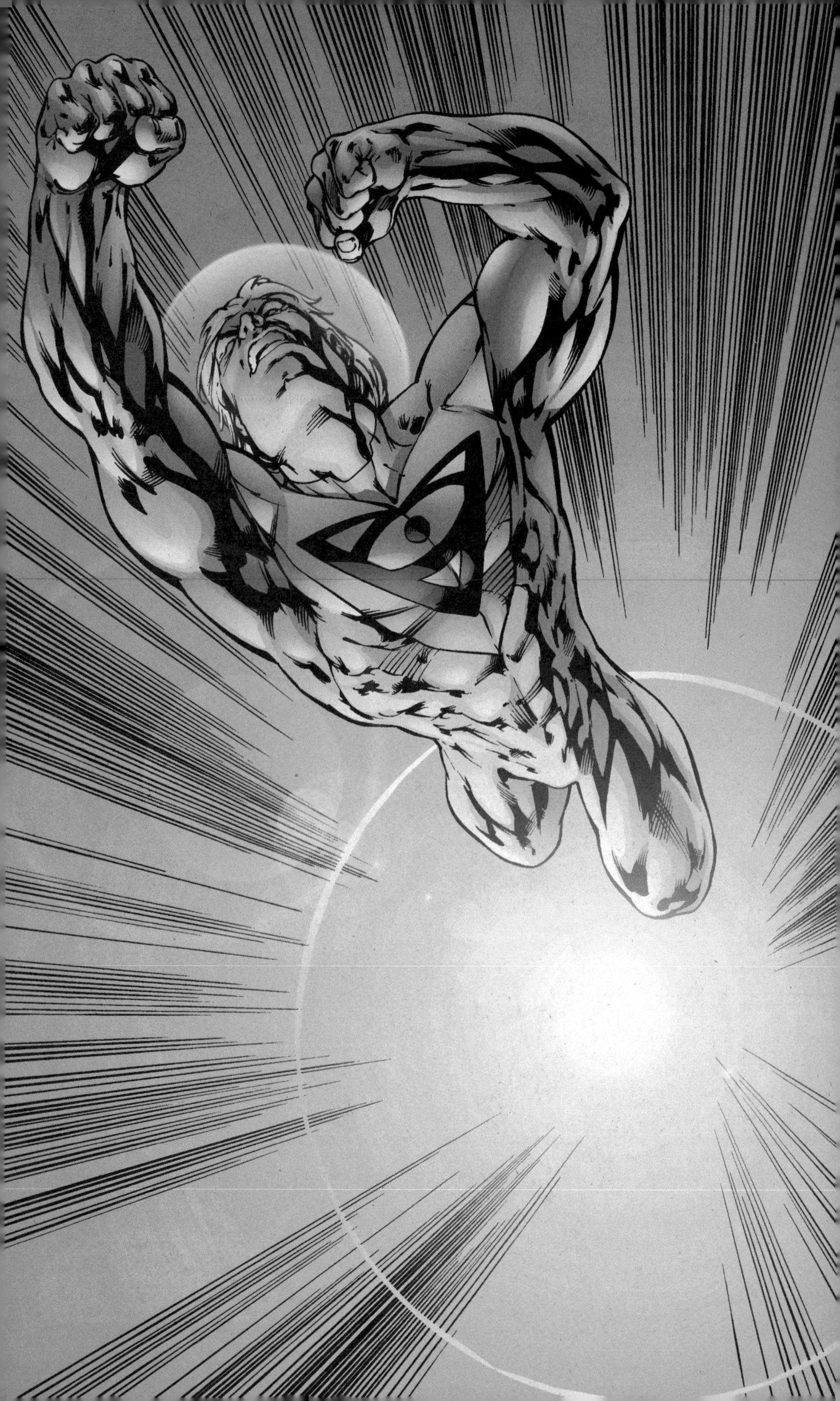

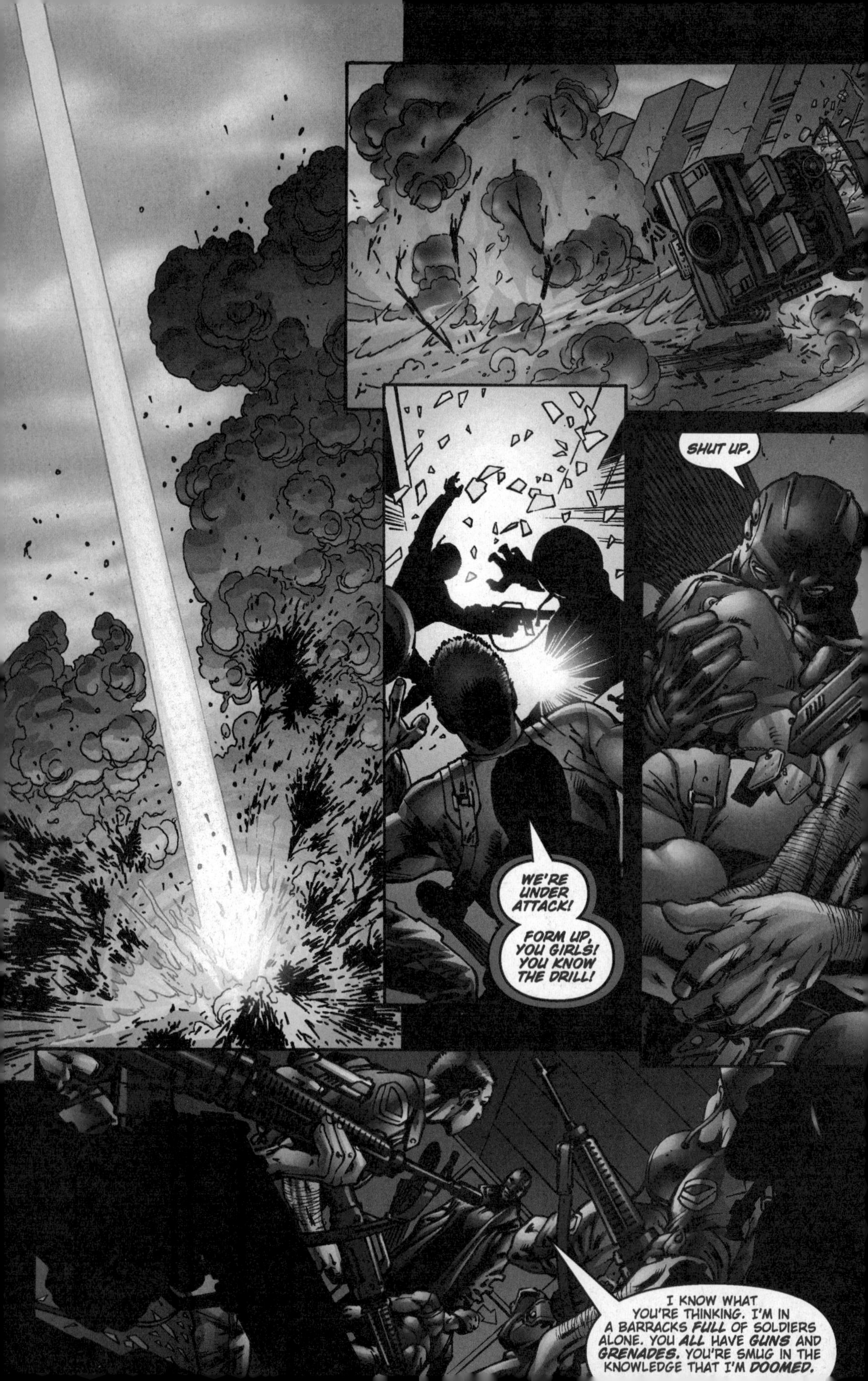
WE'RE UNDER ATTACK!
FORM UP, YOU GIRLS! YOU KNOW THE DRILL!
SHUT UP.
I KNOW WHAT YOU'RE THINKING. I'M IN A BARRACKS FULL OF SOLDIERS ALONE. YOU ALL HAVE GUNS AND GRENADES. YOU'RE SMUG IN THE KNOWLEDGE THAT I'M DOOMED.

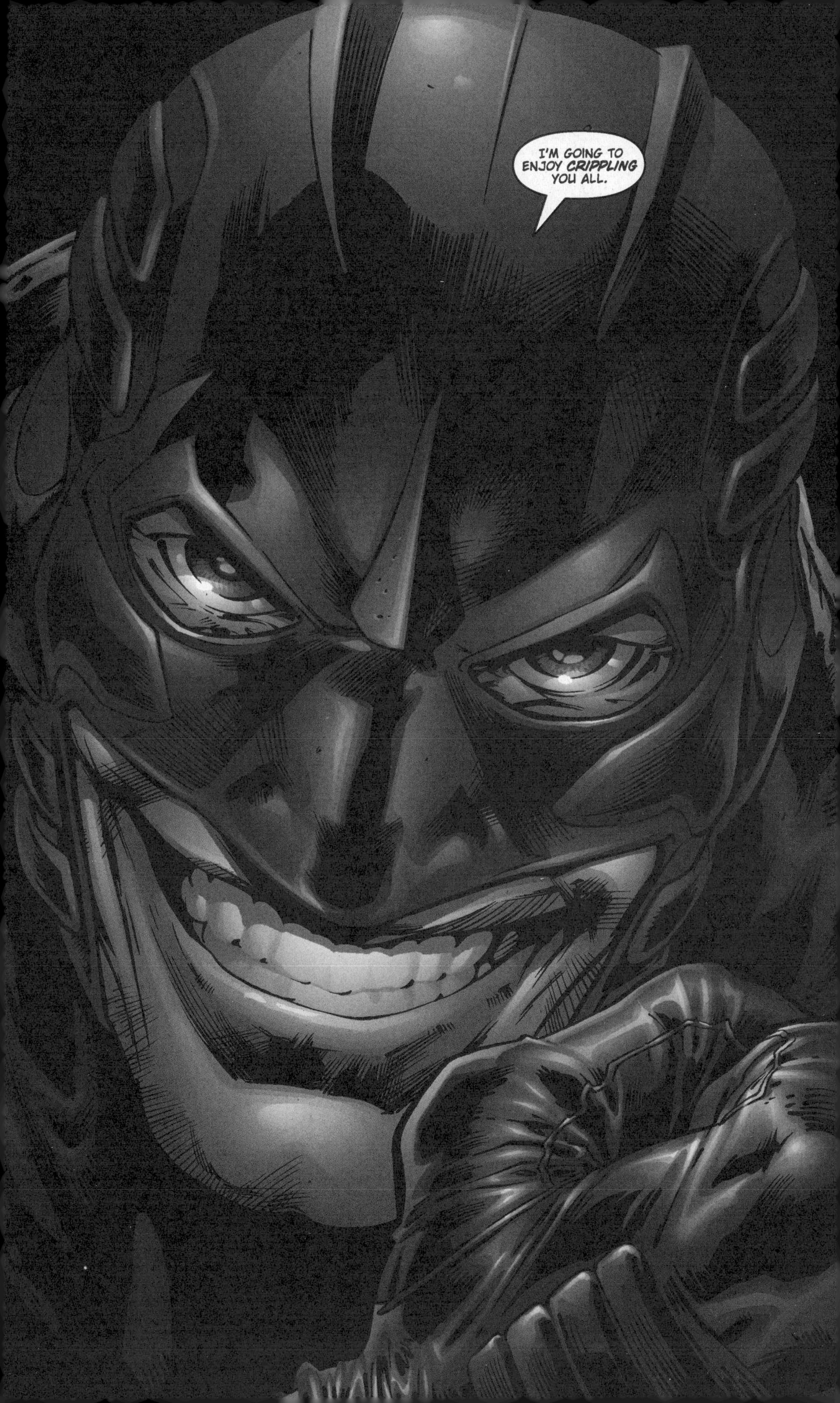
I'M GOING TO ENJOY CRIPPLING YOU ALL.

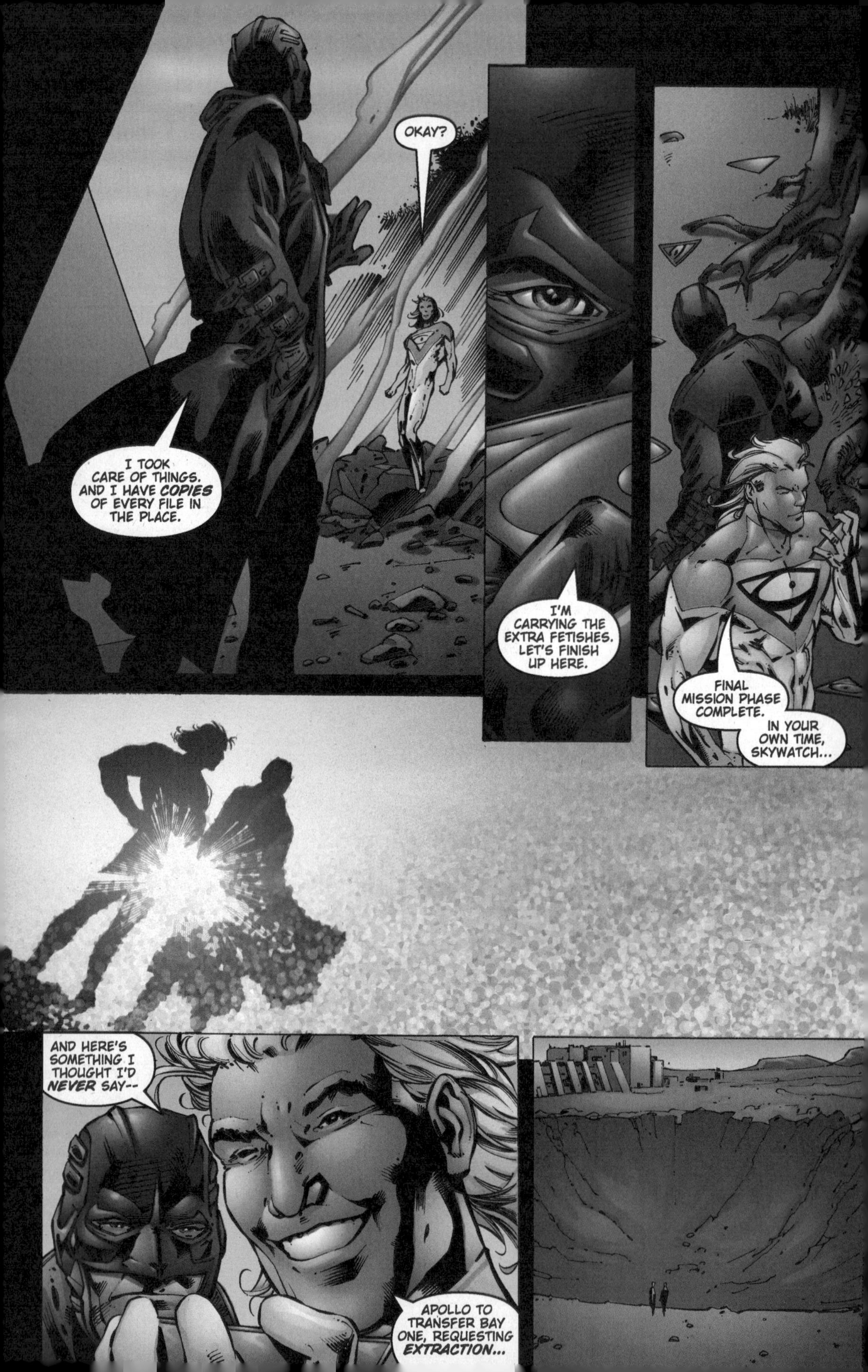
I TOOK CARE OF THINGS. AND I HAVE COPIES OF EVERY FILE IN THE PLACE.
OKAY?
I'M CARRYING THE EXTRA FETISHES. LET'S FINISH UP HERE.
FINAL MISSION PHASE COMPLETE.
IN YOUR OWN TIME, SKYWATCH...
AND HERE'S SOMETHING I THOUGHT I'D NEVER SAY--
APOLLO TO TRANSFER BAY ONE, REQUESTING EXTRACTION...

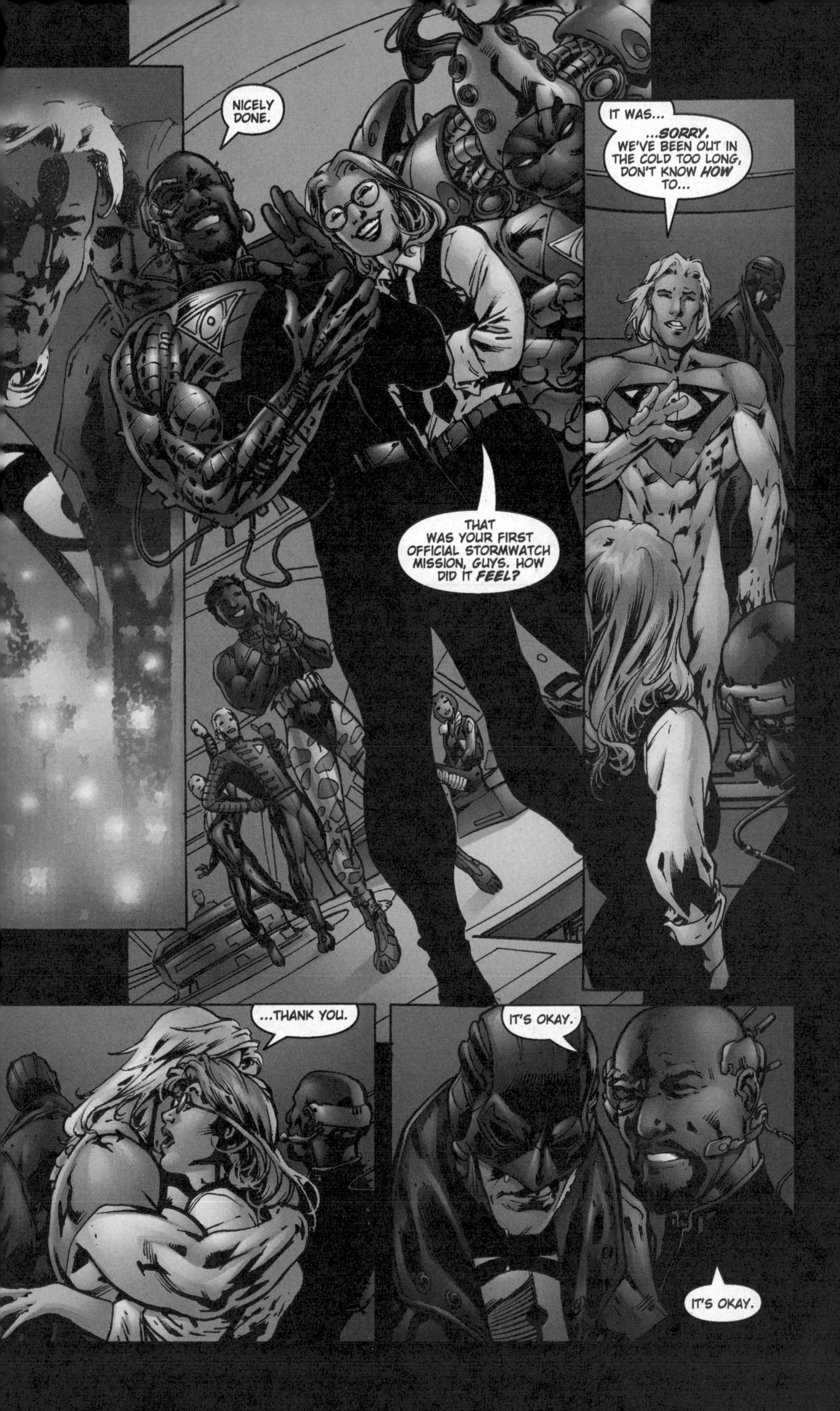
NICELY DONE.
THAT WAS YOUR FIRST OFFICIAL STORMWATCH MISSION, GUYS. HOW DID IT FEEL?
IT WAS...
...SORRY. WE'VE BEEN OUT IN THE COLD TOO LONG, DON'T KNOW HOW TO...
...THANK YOU.
IT'S OKAY.
IT'S OKAY.

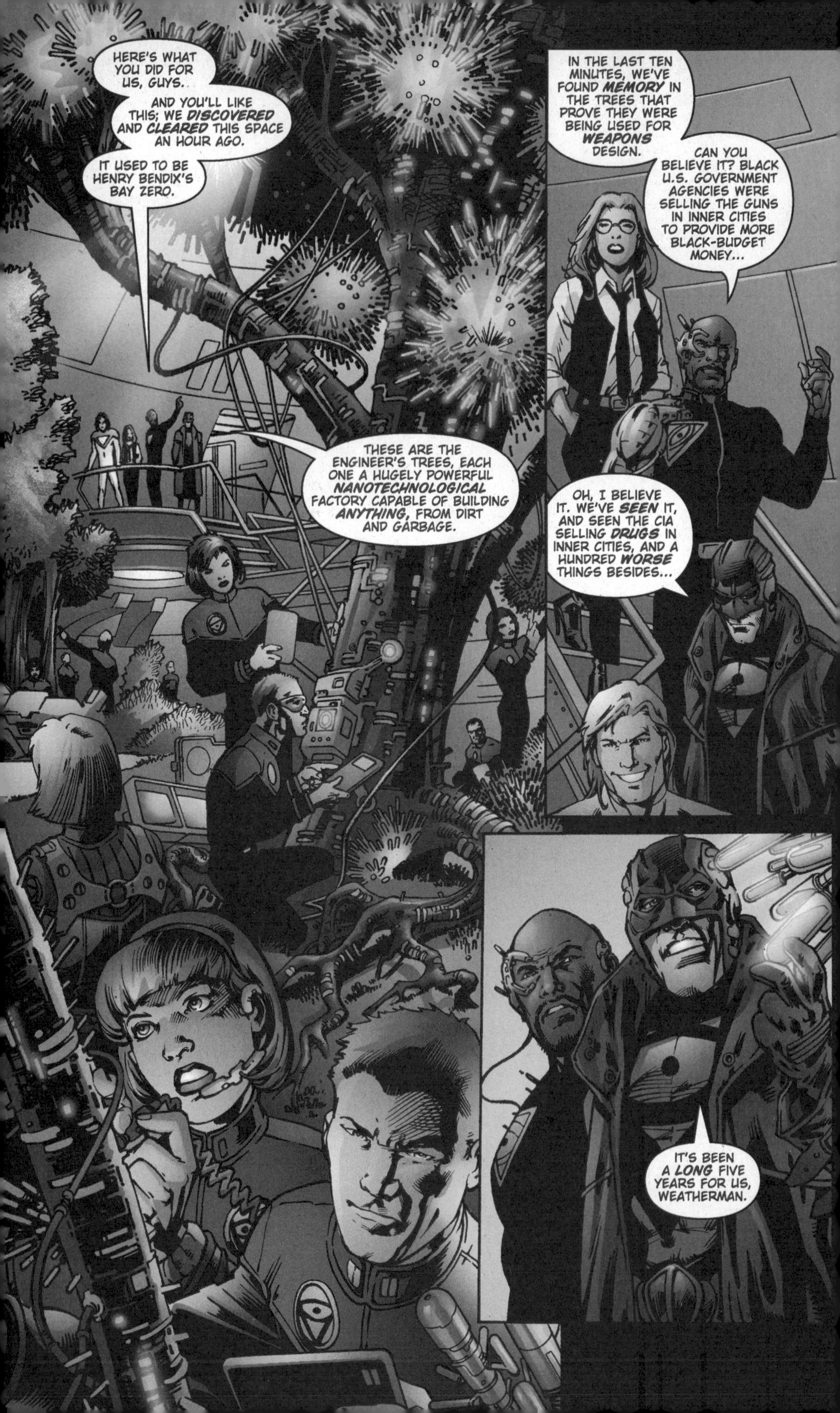

HERE'S WHAT YOU DID FOR US, GUYS.
AND YOU'LL LIKE THIS; WE DISCOVERED AND CLEARED THIS SPACE AN HOUR AGO.
IT USED TO BE HENRY BENDIX'S BAY ZERO.
THESE ARE THE ENGINEER'S TREES, EACH ONE A HUGELY POWERFUL NANOTECHNOLOGICAL FACTORY CAPABLE OF BUILDING ANYTHING, FROM DIRT AND GARBAGE.
IN THE LAST TEN MINUTES, WE'VE FOUND MEMORY IN THE TREES THAT PROVE THEY WERE BEING USED FOR WEAPONS DESIGN.
CAN YOU BELIEVE IT? BLACK U.S. GOVERNMENT AGENCIES WERE SELLING THE GUNS IN INNER CITIES TO PROVIDE MORE BLACK-BUDGET MONEY...
OH, I BELIEVE IT. WE'VE SEEN IT, AND SEEN THE CIA SELLING DRUGS IN INNER CITIES, AND A HUNDRED WORSE THINGS BESIDES...
IT'S BEEN A LONG FIVE YEARS FOR US, WEATHERMAN.

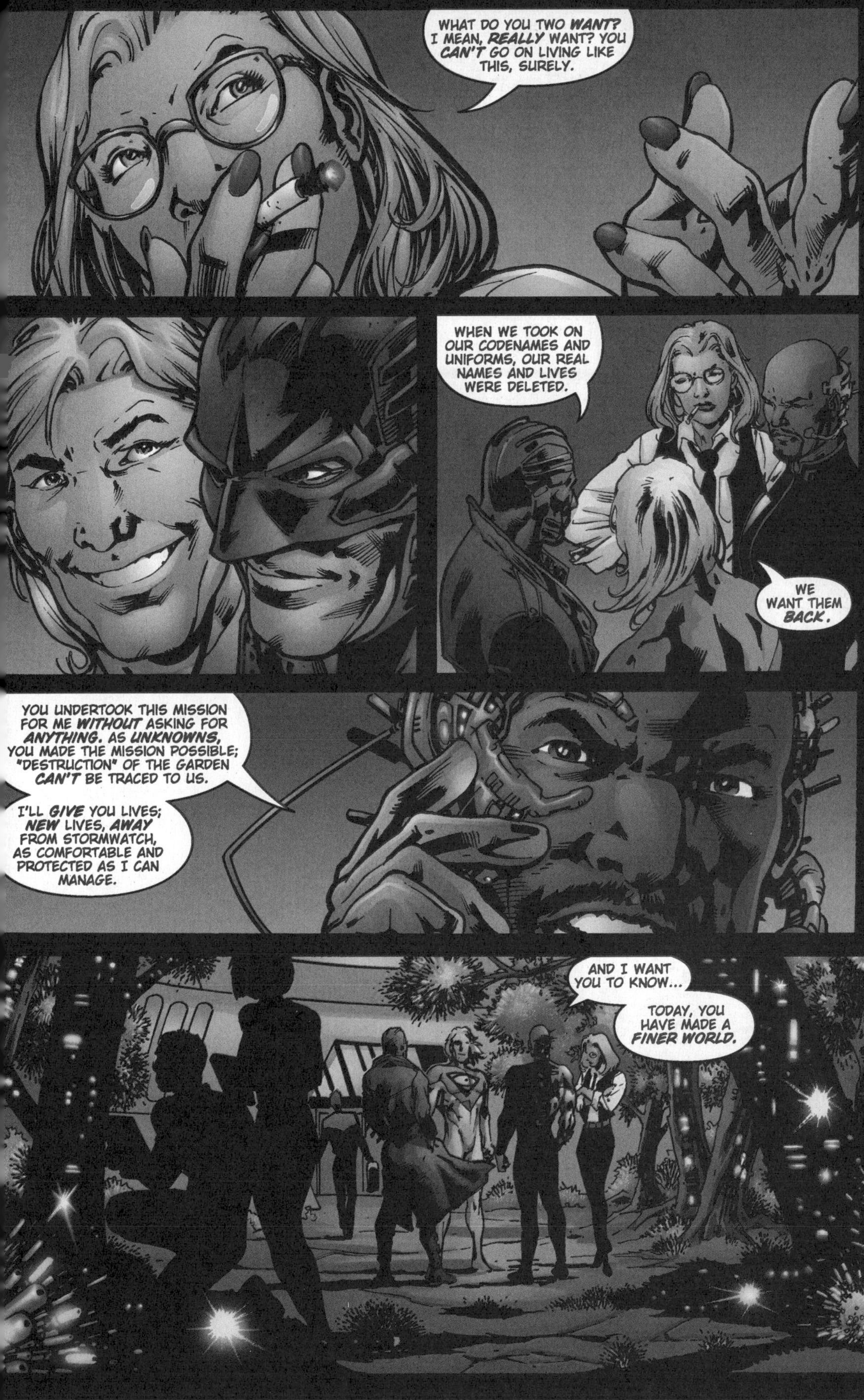
WHAT DO YOU TWO WANT? I MEAN, REALLY WANT? YOU CAN'T GO ON LIVING LIKE THIS, SURELY.
WHEN WE TOOK ON OUR CODENAMES AND UNIFORMS, OUR REAL NAMES AND LIVES WERE DELETED.
WE WANT THEM BACK.
YOU UNDERTOOK THIS MISSION FOR ME WITHOUT ASKING FOR ANYTHING. AS UNKNOWNS, YOU MADE THE MISSION POSSIBLE; "DESTRUCTION" OF THE GARDEN CAN'T BE TRACED TO US.
I'LL GIVE YOU LIVES; NEW LIVES, AWAY FROM STORMWATCH, AS COMFORTABLE AND PROTECTED AS I CAN MANAGE.
AND I WANT YOU TO KNOW...
TODAY, YOU HAVE MADE A FINER WORLD.

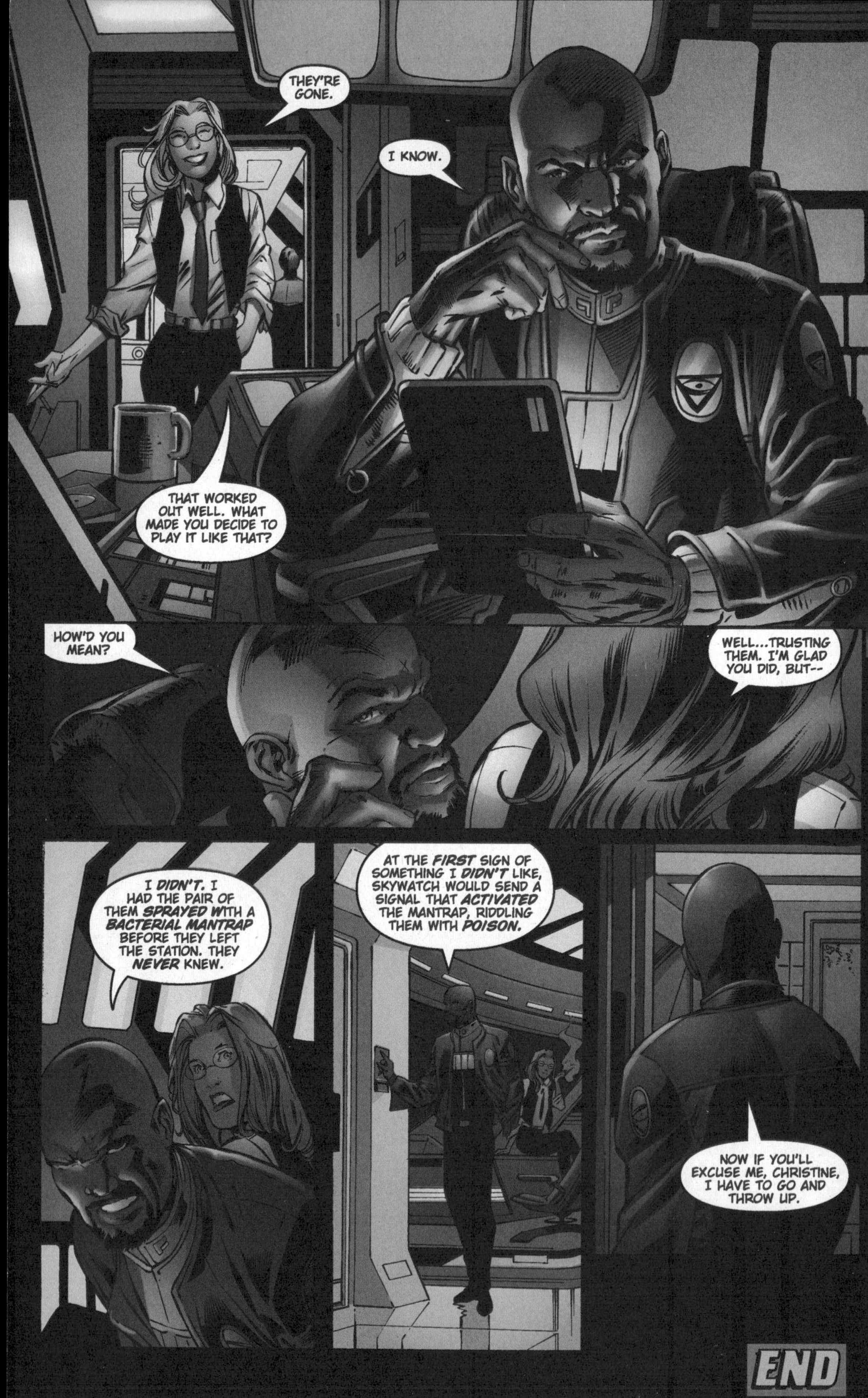
THEY'RE GONE.
I KNOW.
THAT WORKED OUT WELL. WHAT MADE YOU DECIDE TO PLAY IT LIKE THAT?
HOW'D YOU MEAN?
WELL...TRUSTING THEM. I'M GLAD YOU DID, BUT--
I DIDN'T. I HAD THE PAIR OF THEM SPRAYED WITH A BACTERIAL MANTRAP BEFORE THEY LEFT THE STATION. THEY NEVER KNEW.
AT THE FIRST SIGN OF SOMETHING I DIDN'T LIKE, SKYWATCH WOULD SEND A SIGNAL THAT ACTIVATED THE MANTRAP, RIDDLING THEM WITH POISON.
NOW IF YOU'LL EXCUSE ME, CHRISTINE, I HAVE TO GO AND THROW UP.
END

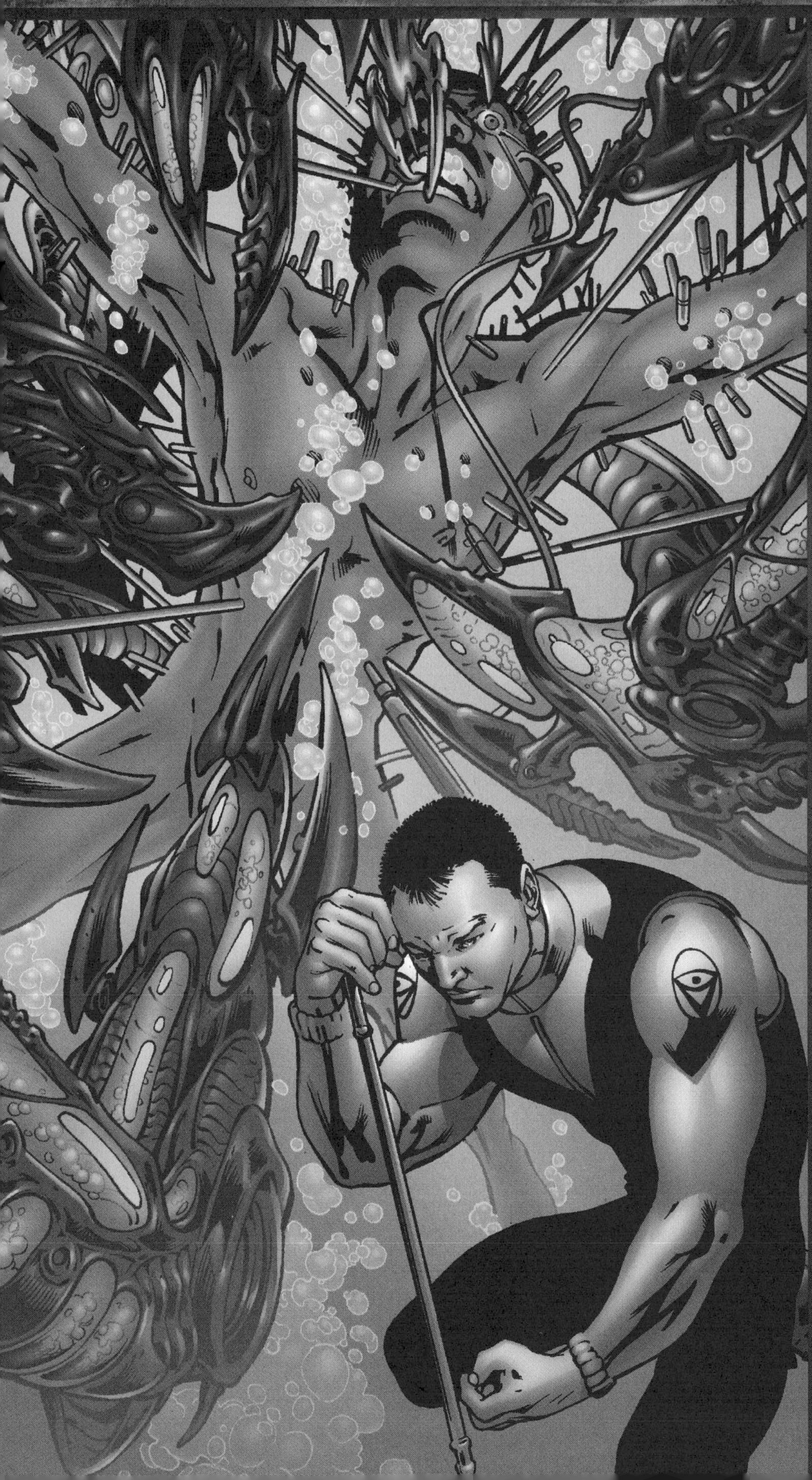

BLEED

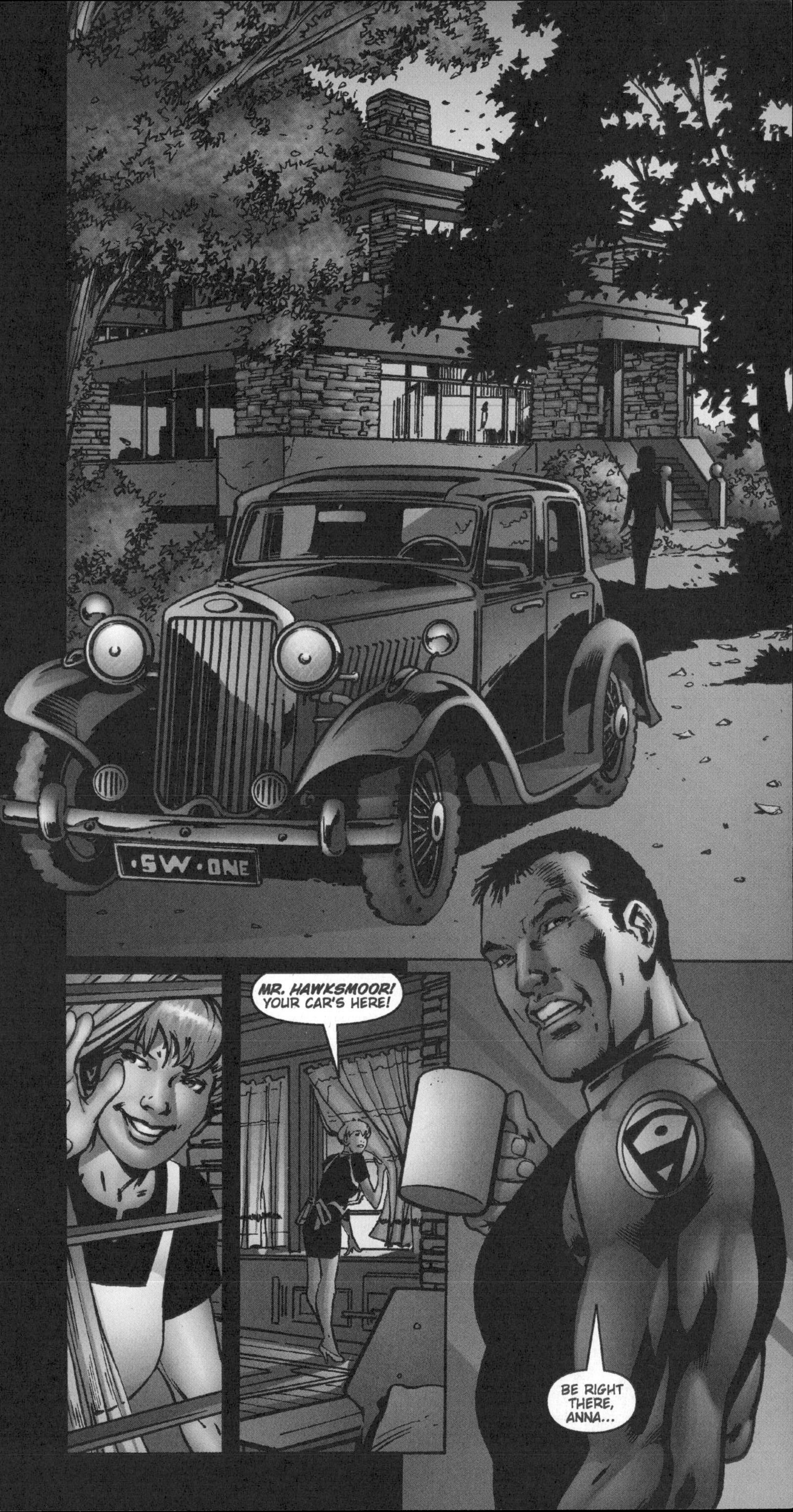
·SW·ONE
MR. HAWKSMOOR! YOUR CAR'S HERE!
BE RIGHT THERE, ANNA...

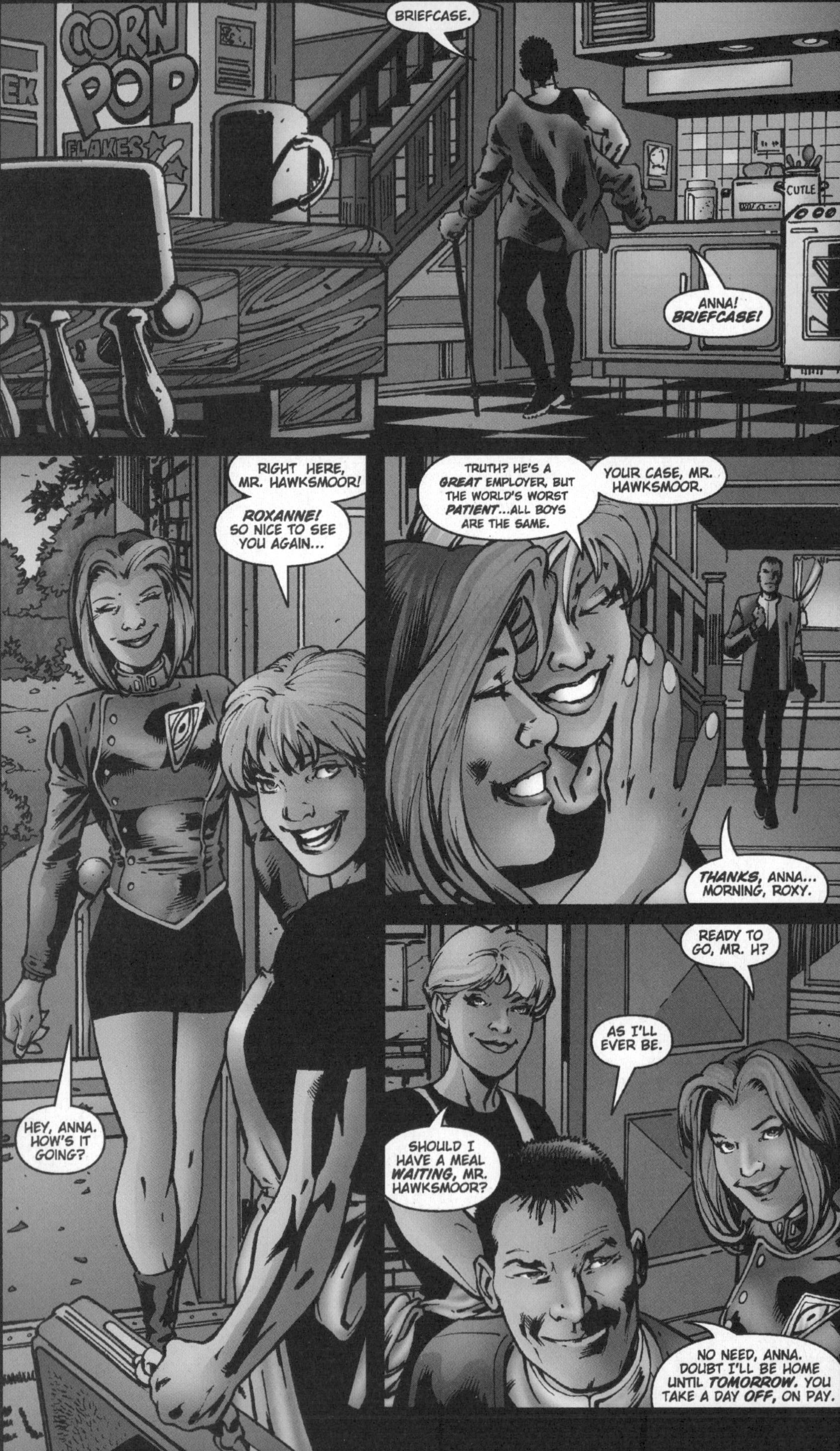
CORN POP
FLAKES
BRIEFCASE.
CUTLE
ANNA! BRIEFCASE!
RIGHT HERE, MR. HAWKSMOOR!
ROXANNE! SO NICE TO SEE YOU AGAIN...
HEY, ANNA. HOW'S IT GOING?
TRUTH? HE'S A GREAT EMPLOYER, BUT THE WORLD'S WORST PATIENT...ALL BOYS ARE THE SAME.
YOUR CASE, MR. HAWKSMOOR.
THANKS, ANNA... MORNING, ROXY.
READY TO GO, MR. H?
AS I'LL EVER BE.
SHOULD I HAVE A MEAL WAITING, MR. HAWKSMOOR?
NO NEED, ANNA. DOUBT I'LL BE HOME UNTIL TOMORROW. YOU TAKE A DAY OFF, ON PAY.

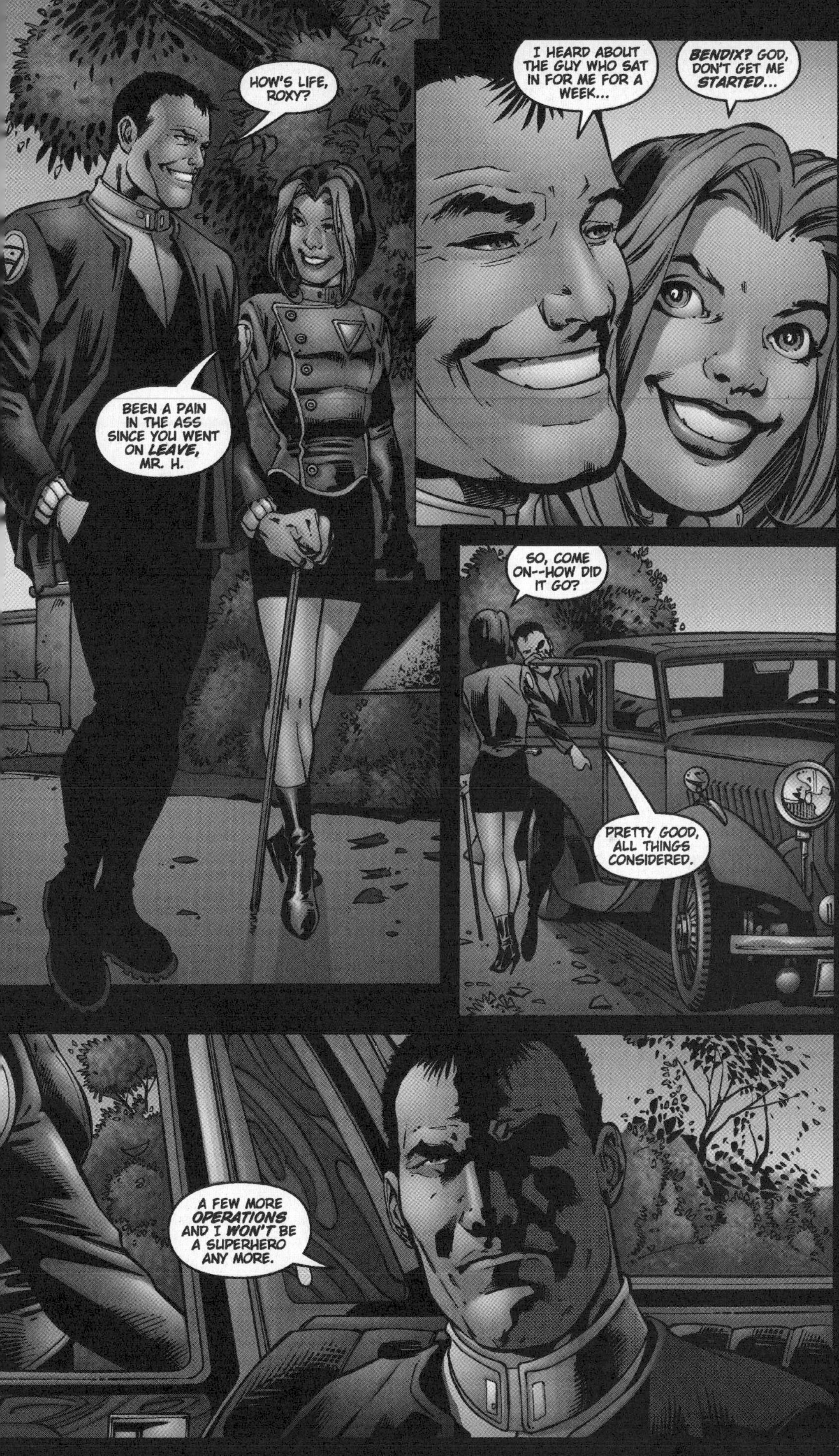
HOW'S LIFE, ROXY?
BEEN A PAIN IN THE ASS SINCE YOU WENT ON *LEAVE,* MR. H.
I HEARD ABOUT THE GUY WHO SAT IN FOR ME FOR A WEEK...
BENDIX? GOD, DON'T GET ME *STARTED...*
SO, COME ON--HOW DID IT GO?
PRETTY GOOD, ALL THINGS CONSIDERED.
A FEW MORE *OPERATIONS* AND I *WON'T* BE A SUPERHERO ANY MORE.

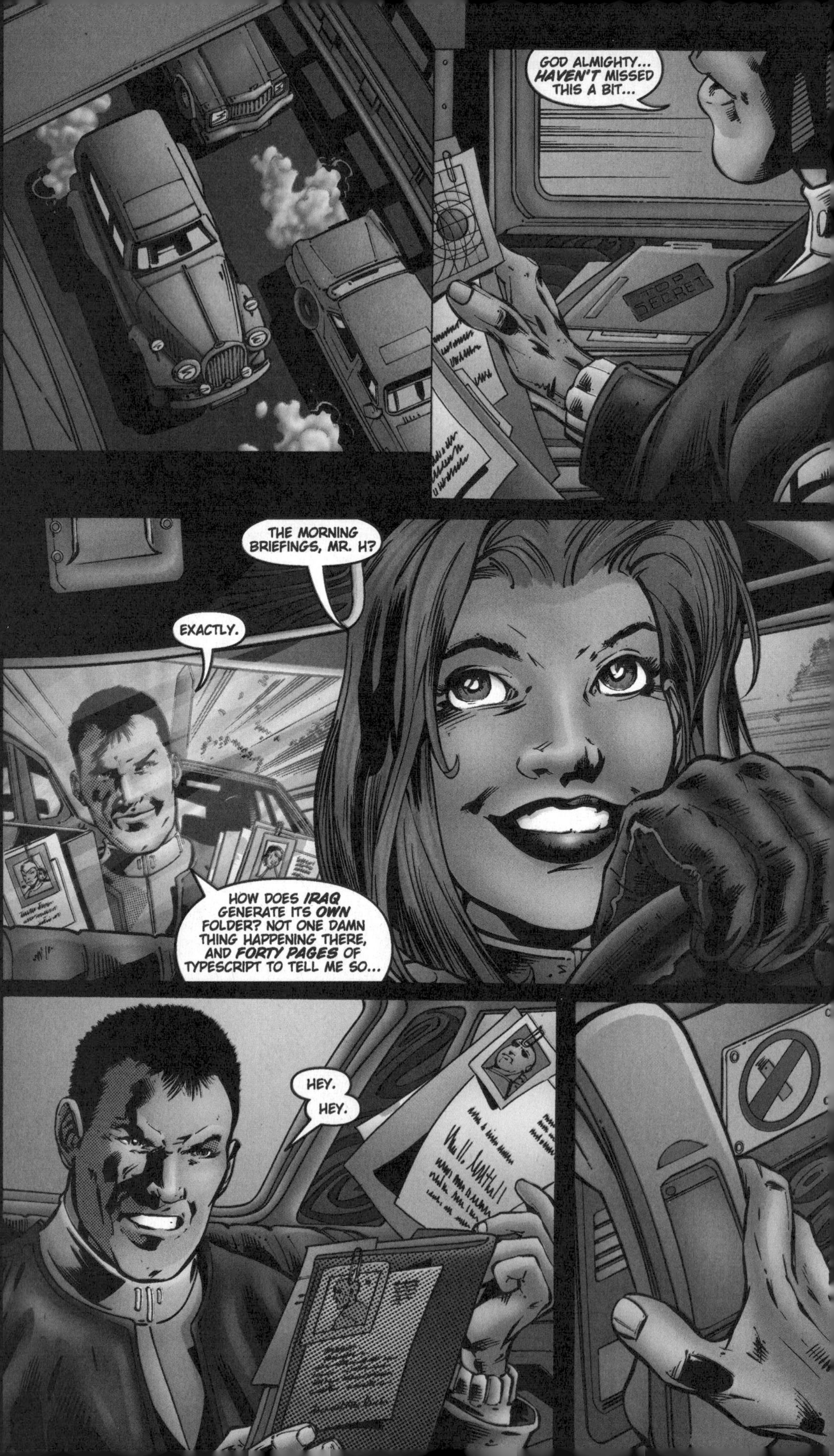
GOD ALMIGHTY... HAVEN'T MISSED THIS A BIT...
TOP SECRET
THE MORNING BRIEFINGS, MR. H?
EXACTLY.
HOW DOES IRAQ GENERATE ITS OWN FOLDER? NOT ONE DAMN THING HAPPENING THERE, AND FORTY PAGES OF TYPESCRIPT TO TELL ME SO...
HEY.
HEY.

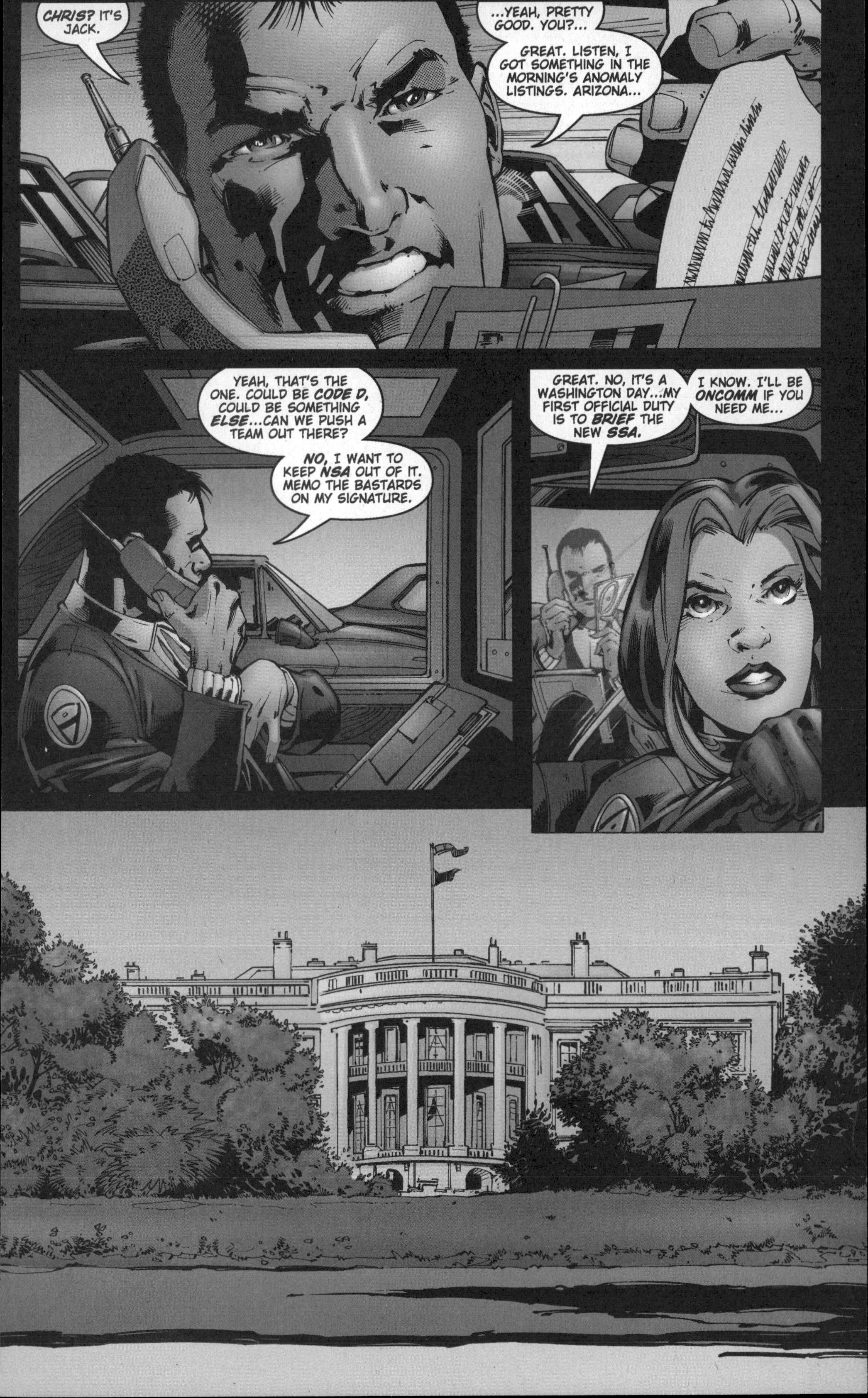
CHRIS? IT'S JACK.
...YEAH, PRETTY GOOD. YOU?...
GREAT. LISTEN, I GOT SOMETHING IN THE MORNING'S ANOMALY LISTINGS. ARIZONA...
YEAH, THAT'S THE ONE. COULD BE CODE D, COULD BE SOMETHING ELSE...CAN WE PUSH A TEAM OUT THERE?
NO, I WANT TO KEEP NSA OUT OF IT. MEMO THE BASTARDS ON MY SIGNATURE.
GREAT. NO, IT'S A WASHINGTON DAY...MY FIRST OFFICIAL DUTY IS TO BRIEF THE NEW SSA.
I KNOW. I'LL BE ONCOMM IF YOU NEED ME...

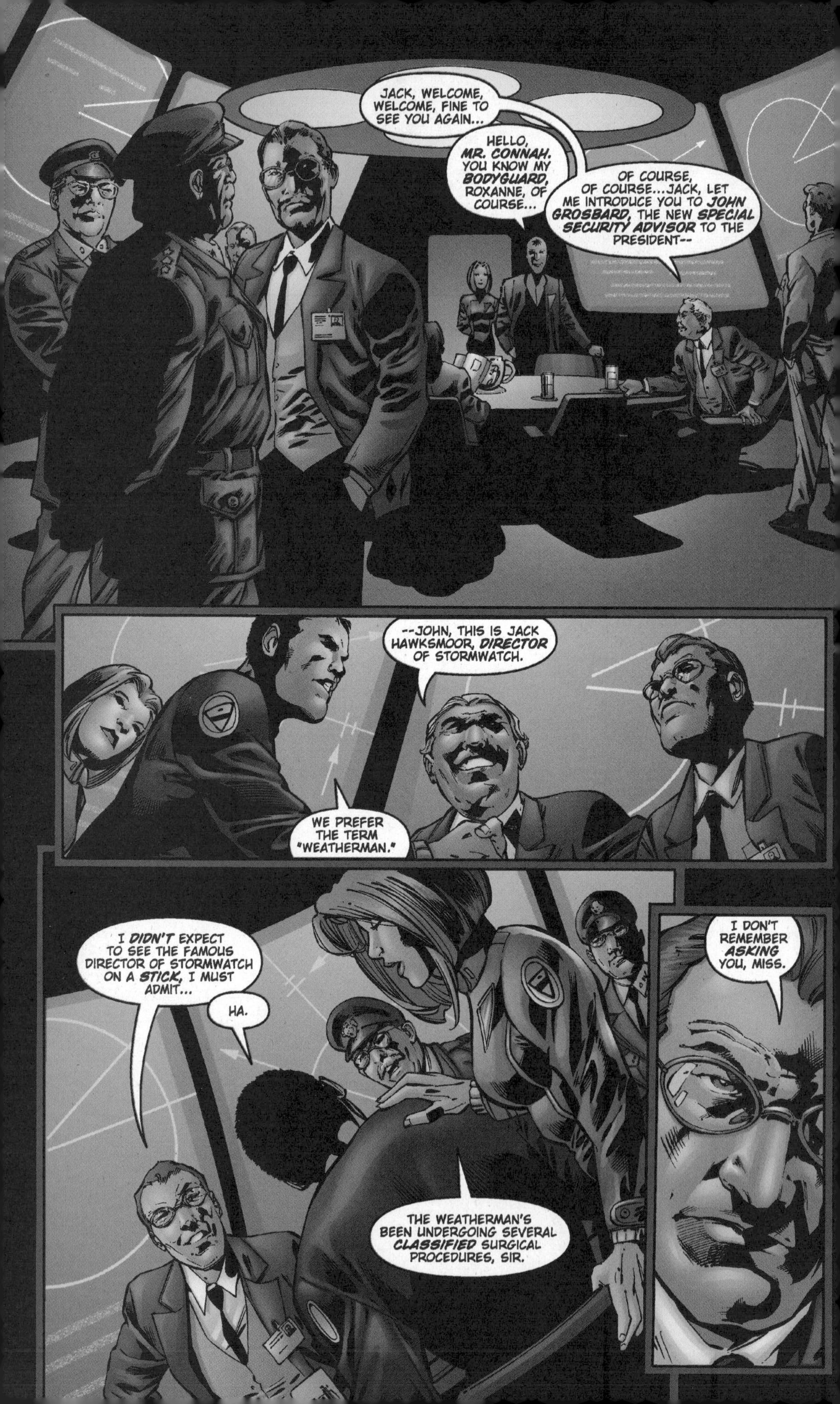
JACK, WELCOME, WELCOME, FINE TO SEE YOU AGAIN...
HELLO, MR. CONNAH. YOU KNOW MY BODYGUARD, ROXANNE, OF COURSE...
OF COURSE, OF COURSE...JACK, LET ME INTRODUCE YOU TO JOHN GROSBARD, THE NEW SPECIAL SECURITY ADVISOR TO THE PRESIDENT--
--JOHN, THIS IS JACK HAWKSMOOR, DIRECTOR OF STORMWATCH.
WE PREFER THE TERM "WEATHERMAN."
I DIDN'T EXPECT TO SEE THE FAMOUS DIRECTOR OF STORMWATCH ON A STICK, I MUST ADMIT...
HA.
THE WEATHERMAN'S BEEN UNDERGOING SEVERAL CLASSIFIED SURGICAL PROCEDURES, SIR.
I DON'T REMEMBER ASKING YOU, MISS.

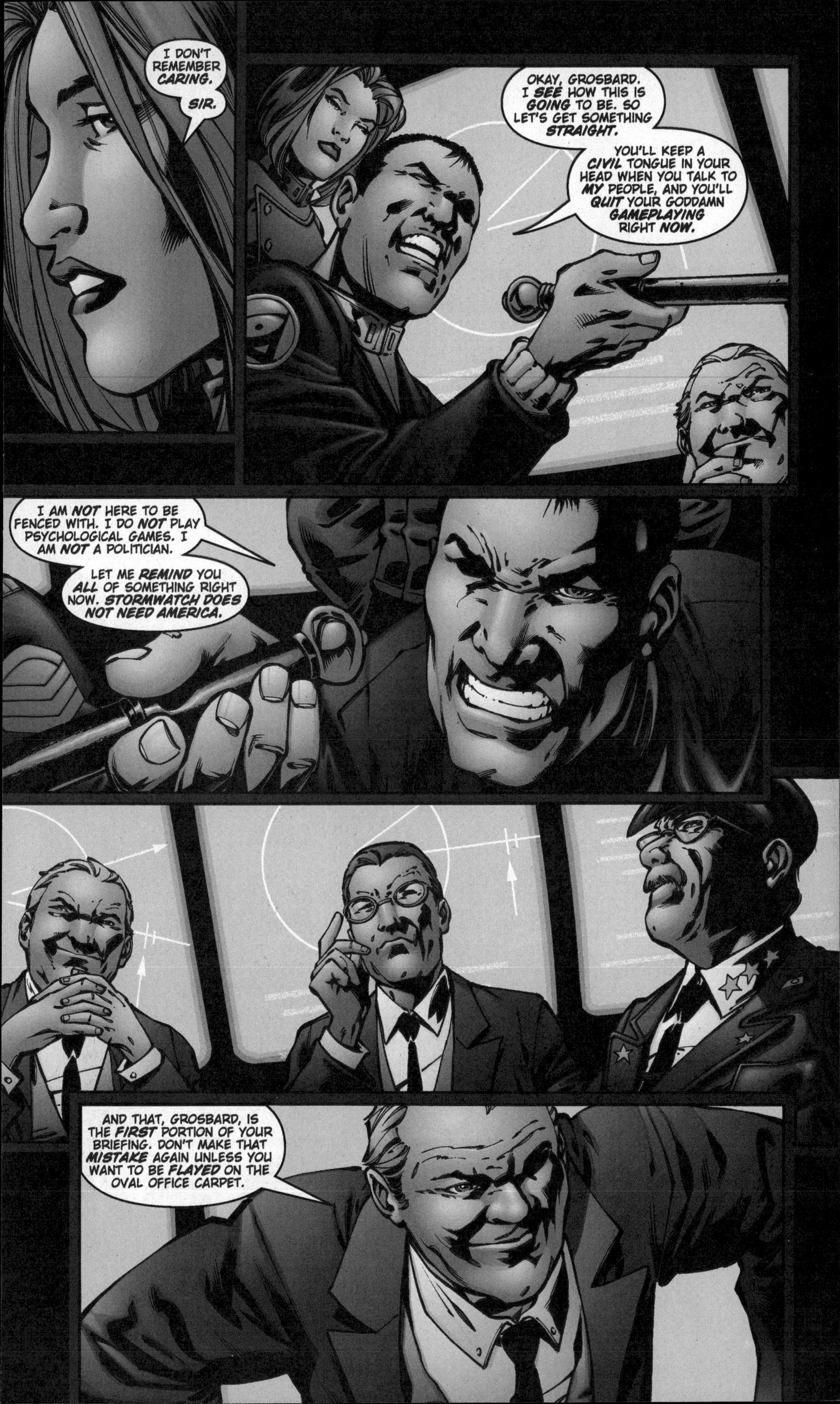
I DON'T REMEMBER CARING.
SIR.
OKAY, GROSBARD. I SEE HOW THIS IS GOING TO BE. SO LET'S GET SOMETHING STRAIGHT.
YOU'LL KEEP A CIVIL TONGUE IN YOUR HEAD WHEN YOU TALK TO MY PEOPLE, AND YOU'LL QUIT YOUR GODDAMN GAMEPLAYING RIGHT NOW.
I AM NOT HERE TO BE FENCED WITH. I DO NOT PLAY PSYCHOLOGICAL GAMES. I AM NOT A POLITICIAN.
LET ME REMIND YOU ALL OF SOMETHING RIGHT NOW. STORMWATCH DOES NOT NEED AMERICA.
AND THAT, GROSBARD, IS THE FIRST PORTION OF YOUR BRIEFING. DON'T MAKE THAT MISTAKE AGAIN UNLESS YOU WANT TO BE FLAYED ON THE OVAL OFFICE CARPET.

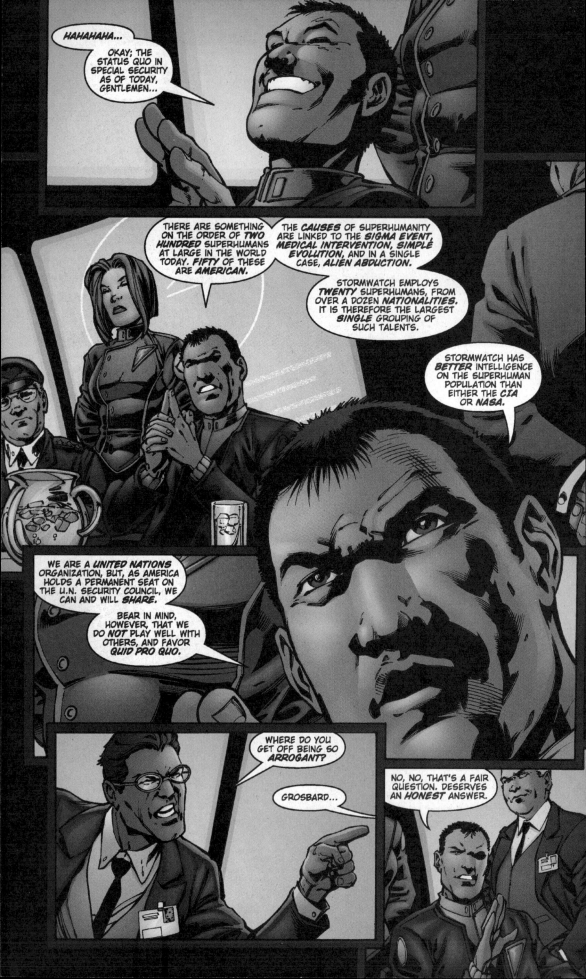

HAHAHAHA...

OKAY; THE STATUS QUO IN SPECIAL SECURITY AS OF TODAY, GENTLEMEN...

THERE ARE SOMETHING ON THE ORDER OF TWO HUNDRED SUPERHUMANS AT LARGE IN THE WORLD TODAY. FIFTY OF THESE ARE AMERICAN.

THE CAUSES OF SUPERHUMANITY ARE LINKED TO THE SIGMA EVENT, MEDICAL INTERVENTION, SIMPLE EVOLUTION, AND IN A SINGLE CASE, ALIEN ABDUCTION.

STORMWATCH EMPLOYS TWENTY SUPERHUMANS, FROM OVER A DOZEN NATIONALITIES. IT IS THEREFORE THE LARGEST SINGLE GROUPING OF SUCH TALENTS.

STORMWATCH HAS BETTER INTELLIGENCE ON THE SUPERHUMAN POPULATION THAN EITHER THE CIA OR NASA.

WE ARE A UNITED NATIONS ORGANIZATION, BUT, AS AMERICA HOLDS A PERMANENT SEAT ON THE U.N. SECURITY COUNCIL, WE CAN AND WILL SHARE.

BEAR IN MIND, HOWEVER, THAT WE DO NOT PLAY WELL WITH OTHERS, AND FAVOR QUID PRO QUO.

WHERE DO YOU GET OFF BEING SO ARROGANT?

GROSBARD...

NO, NO, THAT'S A FAIR QUESTION. DESERVES AN HONEST ANSWER.

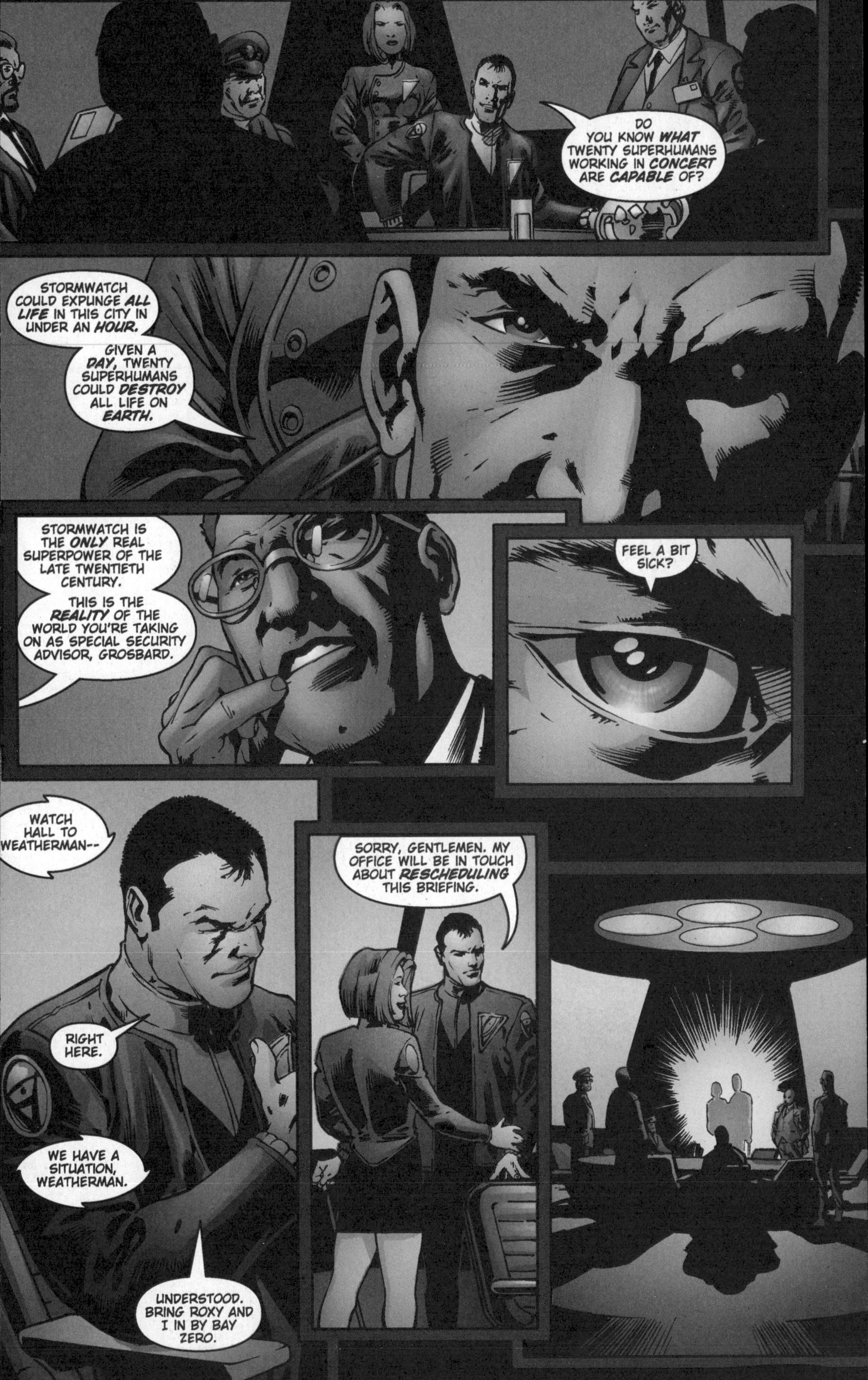
DO YOU KNOW WHAT TWENTY SUPERHUMANS WORKING IN CONCERT ARE CAPABLE OF?
STORMWATCH COULD EXPUNGE ALL LIFE IN THIS CITY IN UNDER AN HOUR.
GIVEN A DAY, TWENTY SUPERHUMANS COULD DESTROY ALL LIFE ON EARTH.
STORMWATCH IS THE ONLY REAL SUPERPOWER OF THE LATE TWENTIETH CENTURY.
THIS IS THE REALITY OF THE WORLD YOU'RE TAKING ON AS SPECIAL SECURITY ADVISOR, GROSBARD.
FEEL A BIT SICK?
WATCH HALL TO WEATHERMAN--
RIGHT HERE.
WE HAVE A SITUATION, WEATHERMAN.
UNDERSTOOD. BRING ROXY AND I IN BY BAY ZERO.
SORRY, GENTLEMEN. MY OFFICE WILL BE IN TOUCH ABOUT RESCHEDULING THIS BRIEFING.

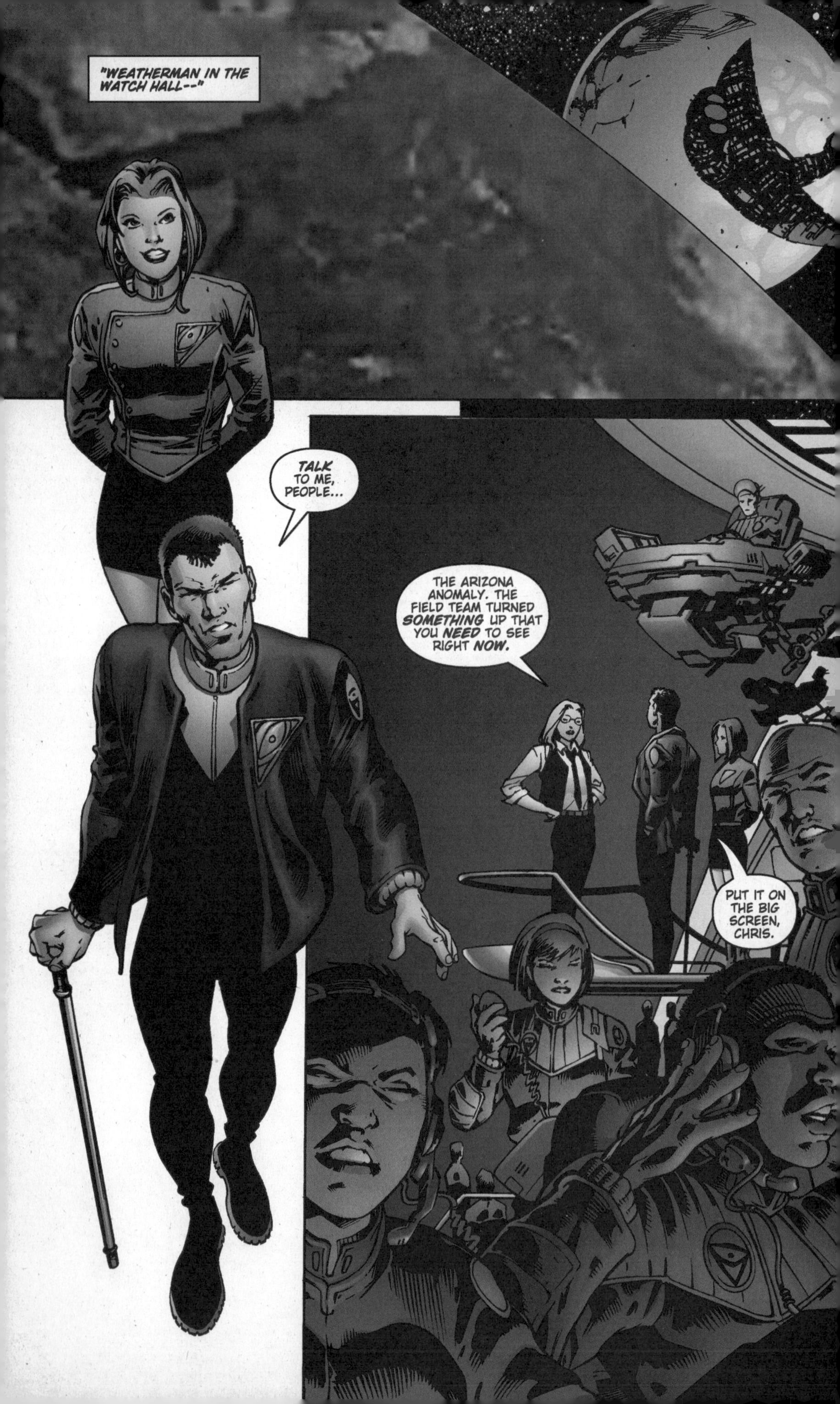
"WEATHERMAN IN THE WATCH HALL--"
TALK TO ME, PEOPLE...
THE ARIZONA ANOMALY. THE FIELD TEAM TURNED SOMETHING UP THAT YOU NEED TO SEE RIGHT NOW.
PUT IT ON THE BIG SCREEN, CHRIS.

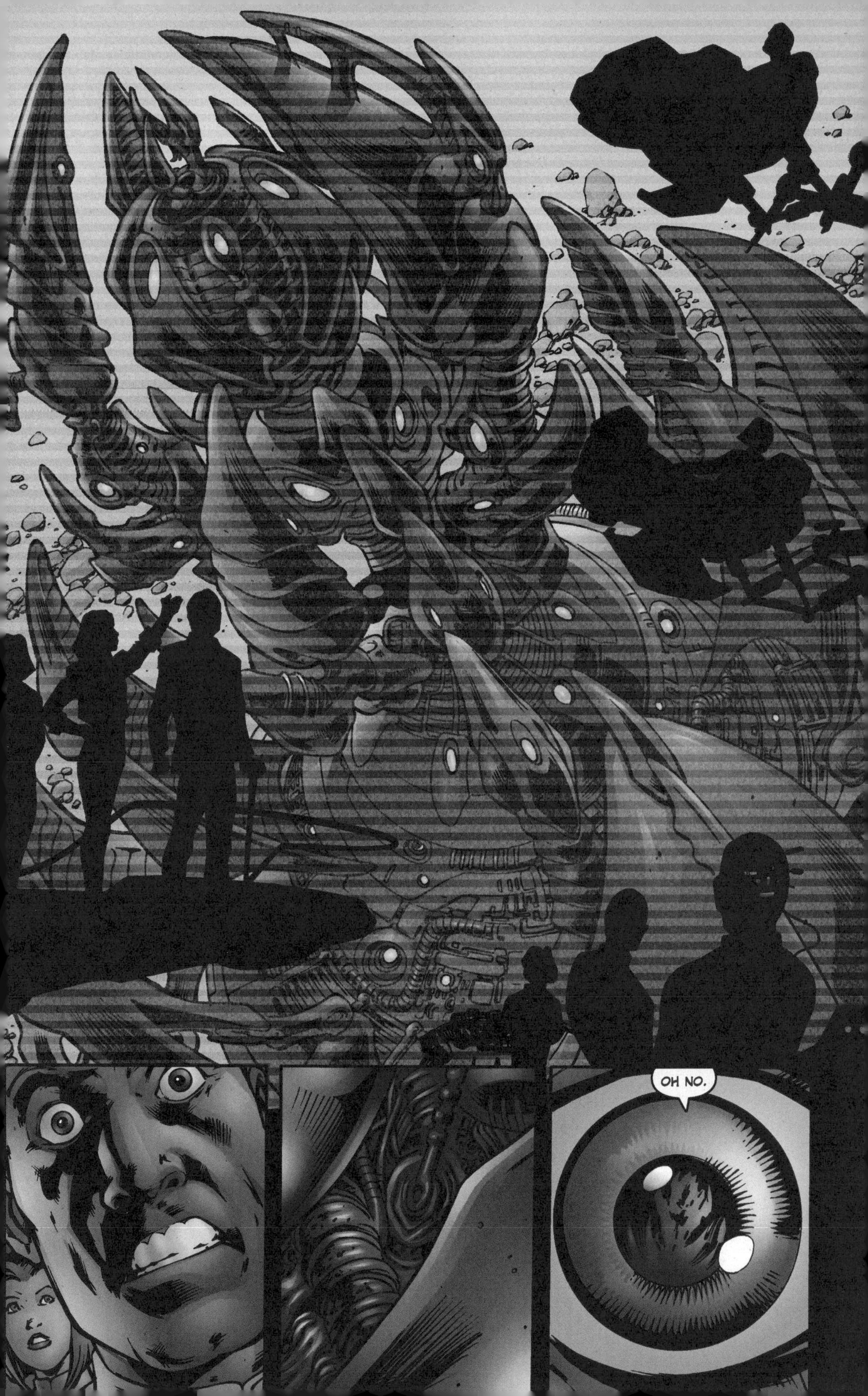
OH NO.

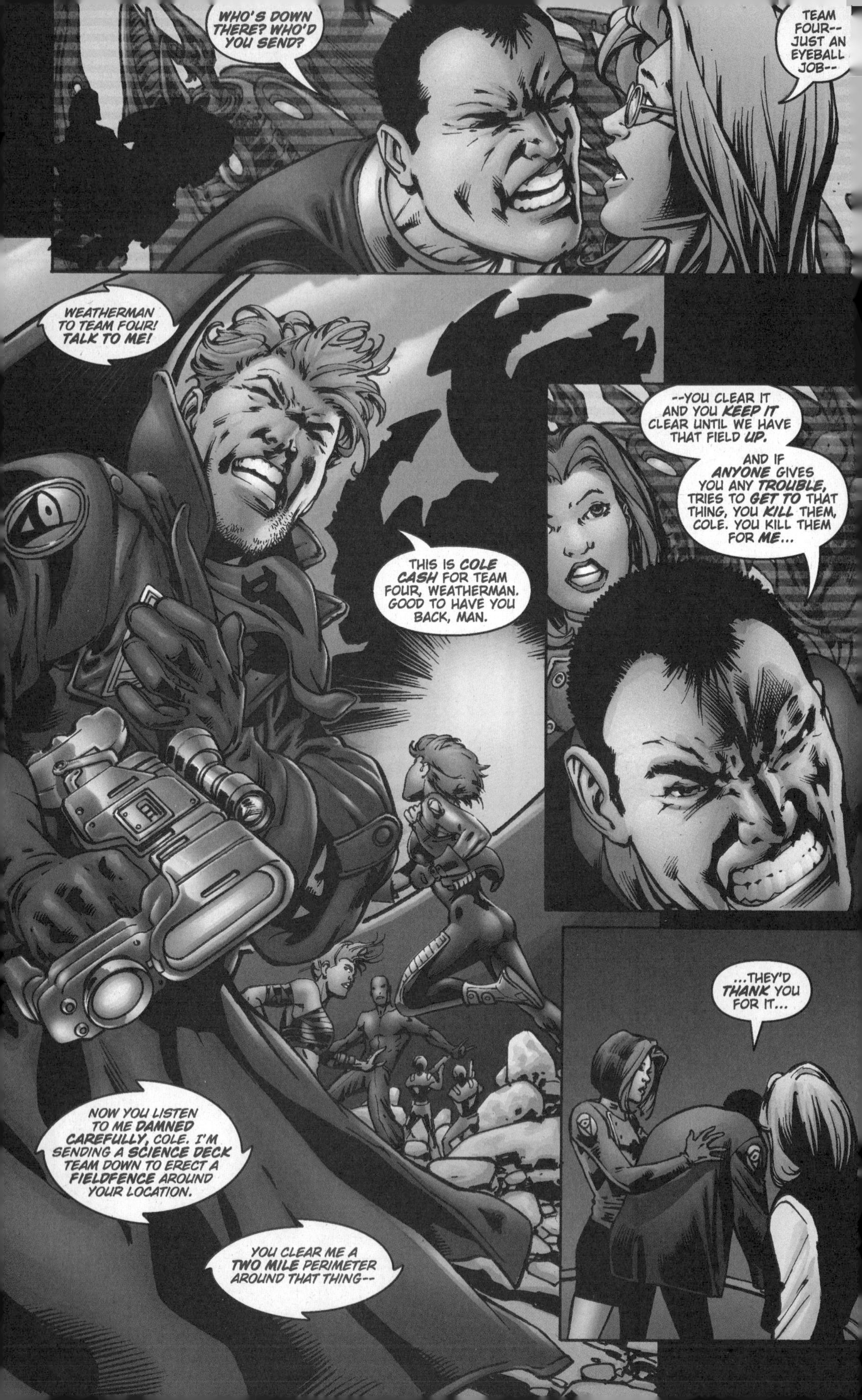
WHO'S DOWN THERE? WHO'D YOU SEND?
TEAM FOUR--JUST AN EYEBALL JOB--
WEATHERMAN TO TEAM FOUR! TALK TO ME!
THIS IS COLE CASH FOR TEAM FOUR, WEATHERMAN. GOOD TO HAVE YOU BACK, MAN.
NOW YOU LISTEN TO ME DAMNED CAREFULLY, COLE. I'M SENDING A SCIENCE DECK TEAM DOWN TO ERECT A FIELDFENCE AROUND YOUR LOCATION.
YOU CLEAR ME A TWO MILE PERIMETER AROUND THAT THING--
--YOU CLEAR IT AND YOU KEEP IT CLEAR UNTIL WE HAVE THAT FIELD UP.
AND IF ANYONE GIVES YOU ANY TROUBLE, TRIES TO GET TO THAT THING, YOU KILL THEM, COLE. YOU KILL THEM FOR ME...
...THEY'D THANK YOU FOR IT...

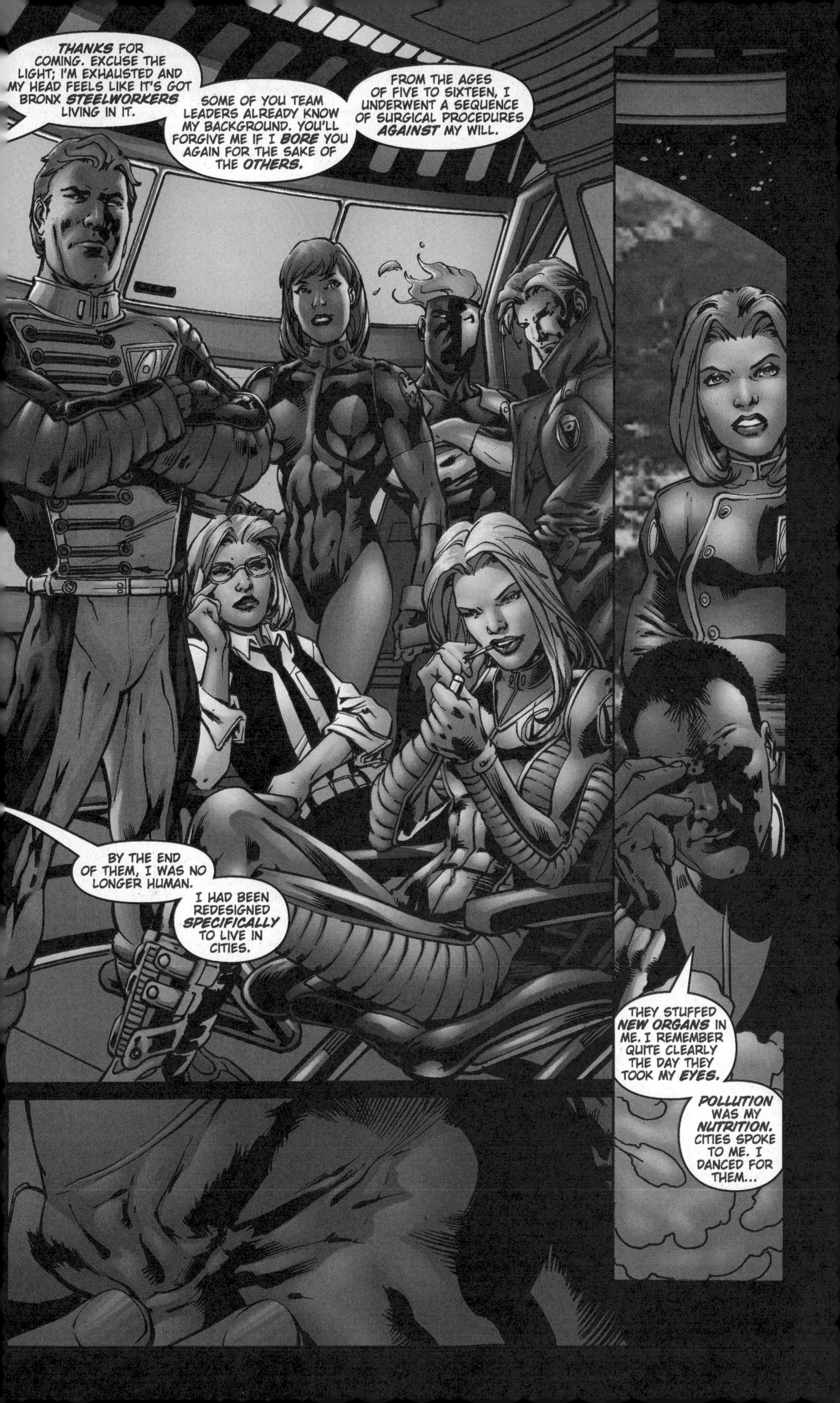
THANKS FOR COMING. EXCUSE THE LIGHT; I'M EXHAUSTED AND MY HEAD FEELS LIKE IT'S GOT BRONX STEELWORKERS LIVING IN IT.
SOME OF YOU TEAM LEADERS ALREADY KNOW MY BACKGROUND. YOU'LL FORGIVE ME IF I BORE YOU AGAIN FOR THE SAKE OF THE OTHERS.
FROM THE AGES OF FIVE TO SIXTEEN, I UNDERWENT A SEQUENCE OF SURGICAL PROCEDURES AGAINST MY WILL.
BY THE END OF THEM, I WAS NO LONGER HUMAN.
I HAD BEEN REDESIGNED SPECIFICALLY TO LIVE IN CITIES.
THEY STUFFED NEW ORGANS IN ME. I REMEMBER QUITE CLEARLY THE DAY THEY TOOK MY EYES.
POLLUTION WAS MY NUTRITION. CITIES SPOKE TO ME. I DANCED FOR THEM...

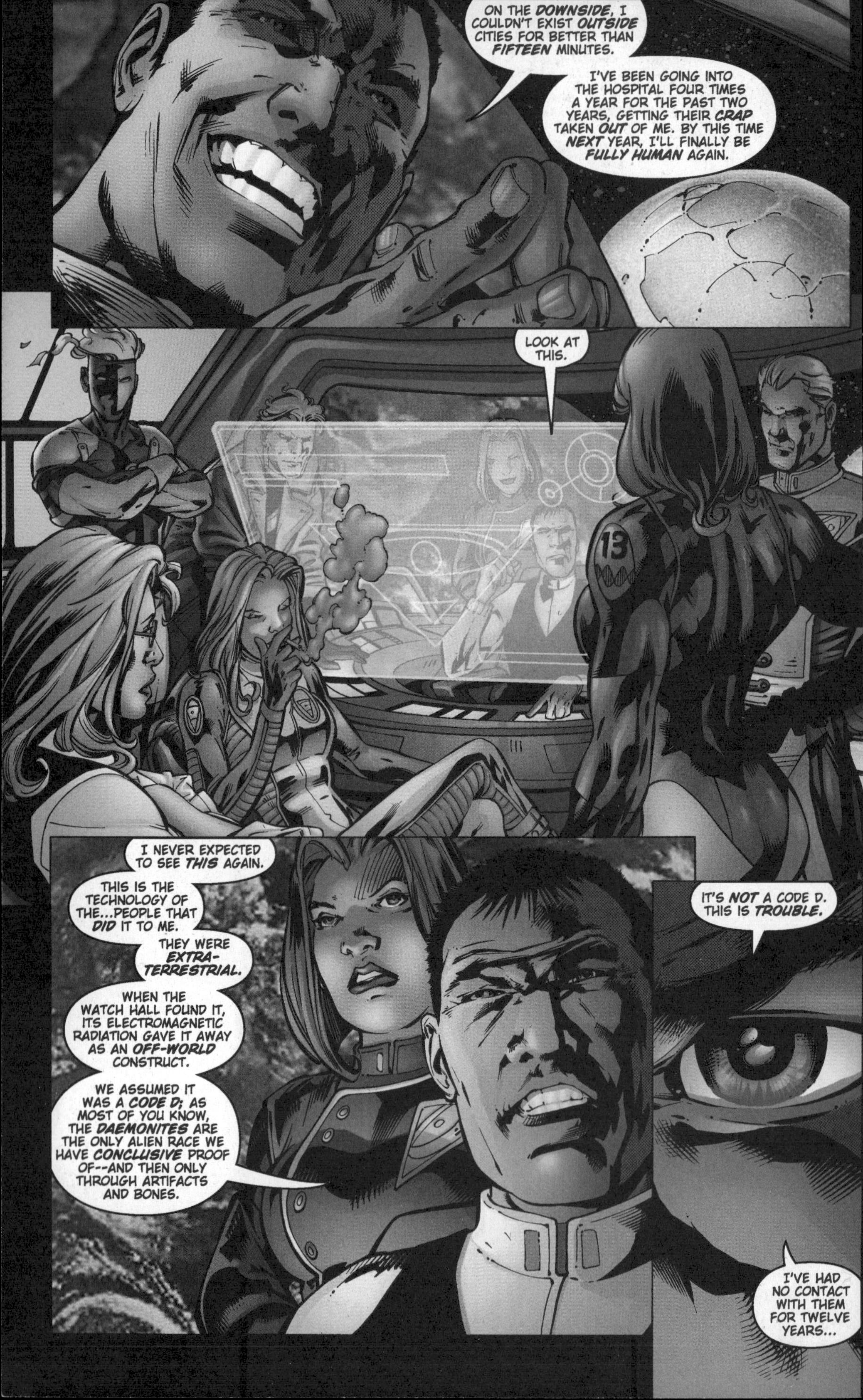
ON THE DOWNSIDE, I COULDN'T EXIST OUTSIDE CITIES FOR BETTER THAN FIFTEEN MINUTES.
I'VE BEEN GOING INTO THE HOSPITAL FOUR TIMES A YEAR FOR THE PAST TWO YEARS, GETTING THEIR CRAP TAKEN OUT OF ME. BY THIS TIME NEXT YEAR, I'LL FINALLY BE FULLY HUMAN AGAIN.
LOOK AT THIS.
I NEVER EXPECTED TO SEE THIS AGAIN.
THIS IS THE TECHNOLOGY OF THE...PEOPLE THAT DID IT TO ME.
THEY WERE EXTRA-TERRESTRIAL.
WHEN THE WATCH HALL FOUND IT, ITS ELECTROMAGNETIC RADIATION GAVE IT AWAY AS AN OFF-WORLD CONSTRUCT.
WE ASSUMED IT WAS A CODE D; AS MOST OF YOU KNOW, THE DAEMONITES ARE THE ONLY ALIEN RACE WE HAVE CONCLUSIVE PROOF OF--AND THEN ONLY THROUGH ARTIFACTS AND BONES.
IT'S NOT A CODE D. THIS IS TROUBLE.
I'VE HAD NO CONTACT WITH THEM FOR TWELVE YEARS...

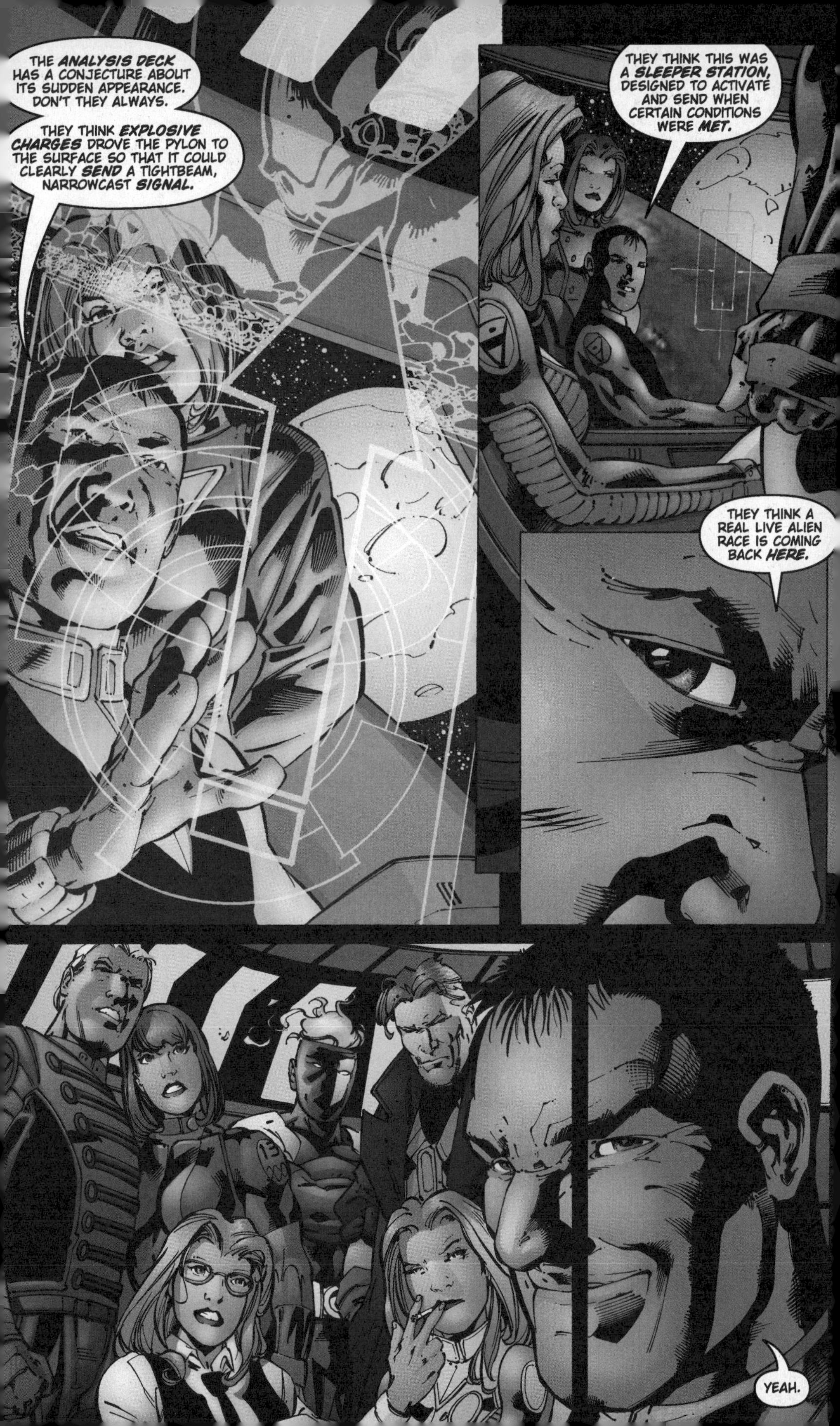
THE ANALYSIS DECK HAS A CONJECTURE ABOUT ITS SUDDEN APPEARANCE. DON'T THEY ALWAYS.
THEY THINK EXPLOSIVE CHARGES DROVE THE PYLON TO THE SURFACE SO THAT IT COULD CLEARLY SEND A TIGHTBEAM, NARROWCAST SIGNAL.
THEY THINK THIS WAS A SLEEPER STATION, DESIGNED TO ACTIVATE AND SEND WHEN CERTAIN CONDITIONS WERE MET.
THEY THINK A REAL LIVE ALIEN RACE IS COMING BACK HERE.
YEAH.

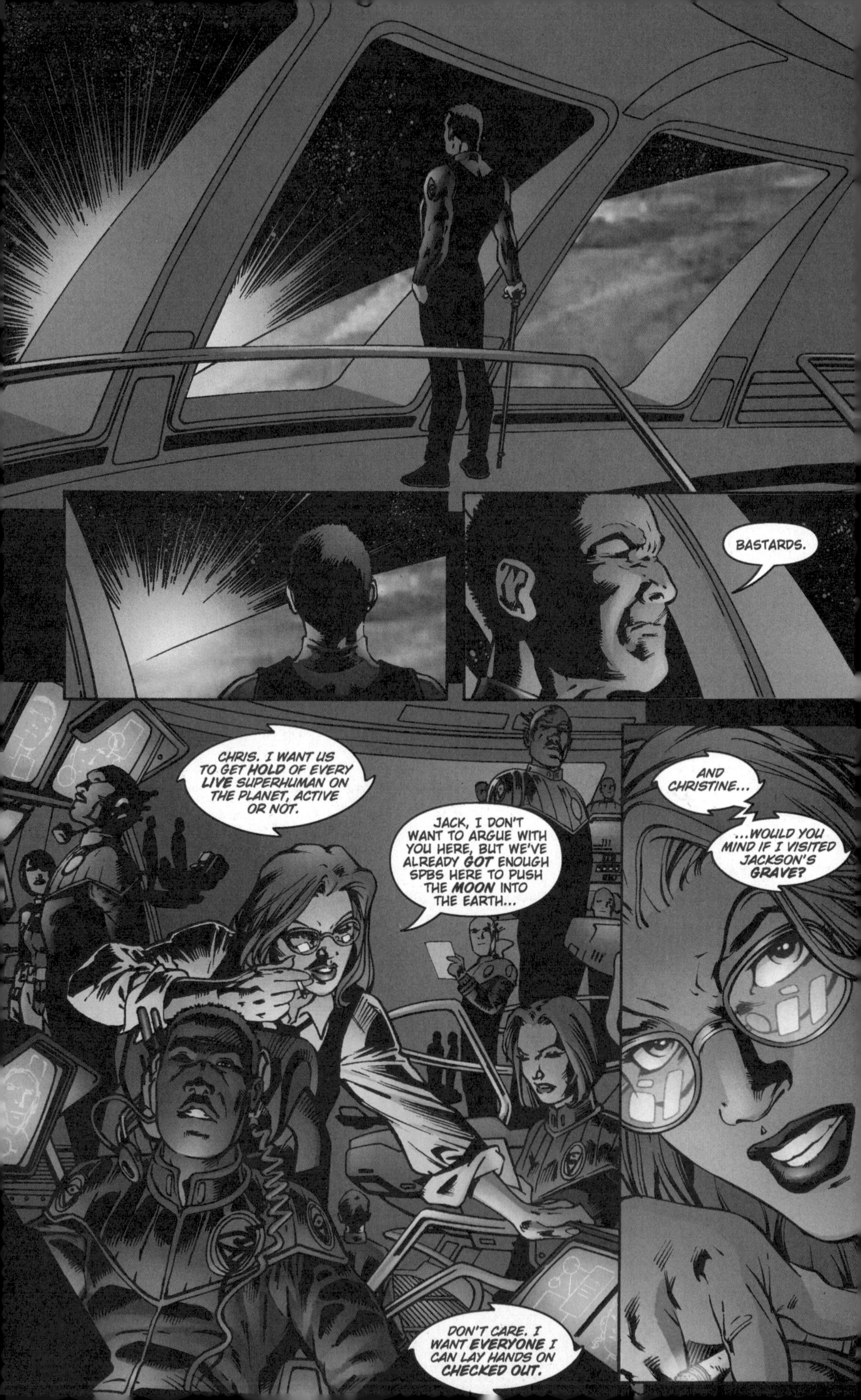
BASTARDS.
CHRIS. I WANT US TO GET HOLD OF EVERY LIVE SUPERHUMAN ON THE PLANET, ACTIVE OR NOT.
JACK, I DON'T WANT TO ARGUE WITH YOU HERE, BUT WE'VE ALREADY GOT ENOUGH SPBS HERE TO PUSH THE MOON INTO THE EARTH...
DON'T CARE. I WANT EVERYONE I CAN LAY HANDS ON CHECKED OUT.
AND CHRISTINE...
...WOULD YOU MIND IF I VISITED JACKSON'S GRAVE?

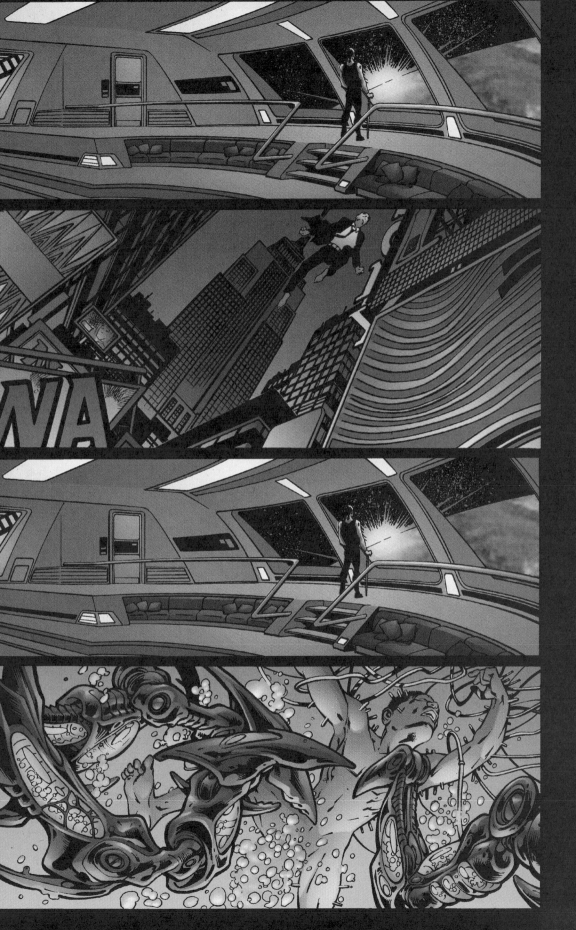

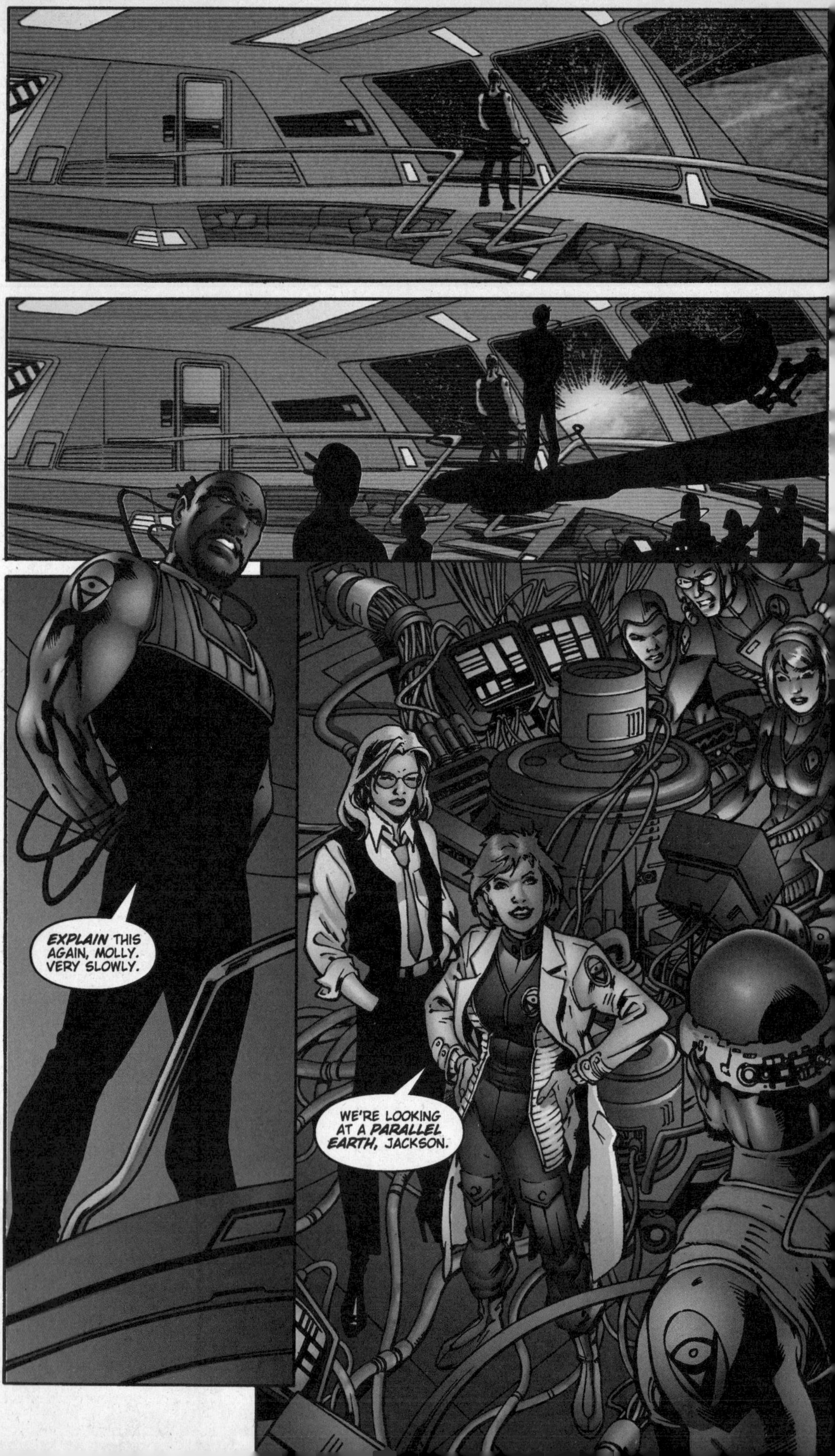
EXPLAIN THIS AGAIN, MOLLY. VERY SLOWLY.
WE'RE LOOKING AT A PARALLEL EARTH, JACKSON.

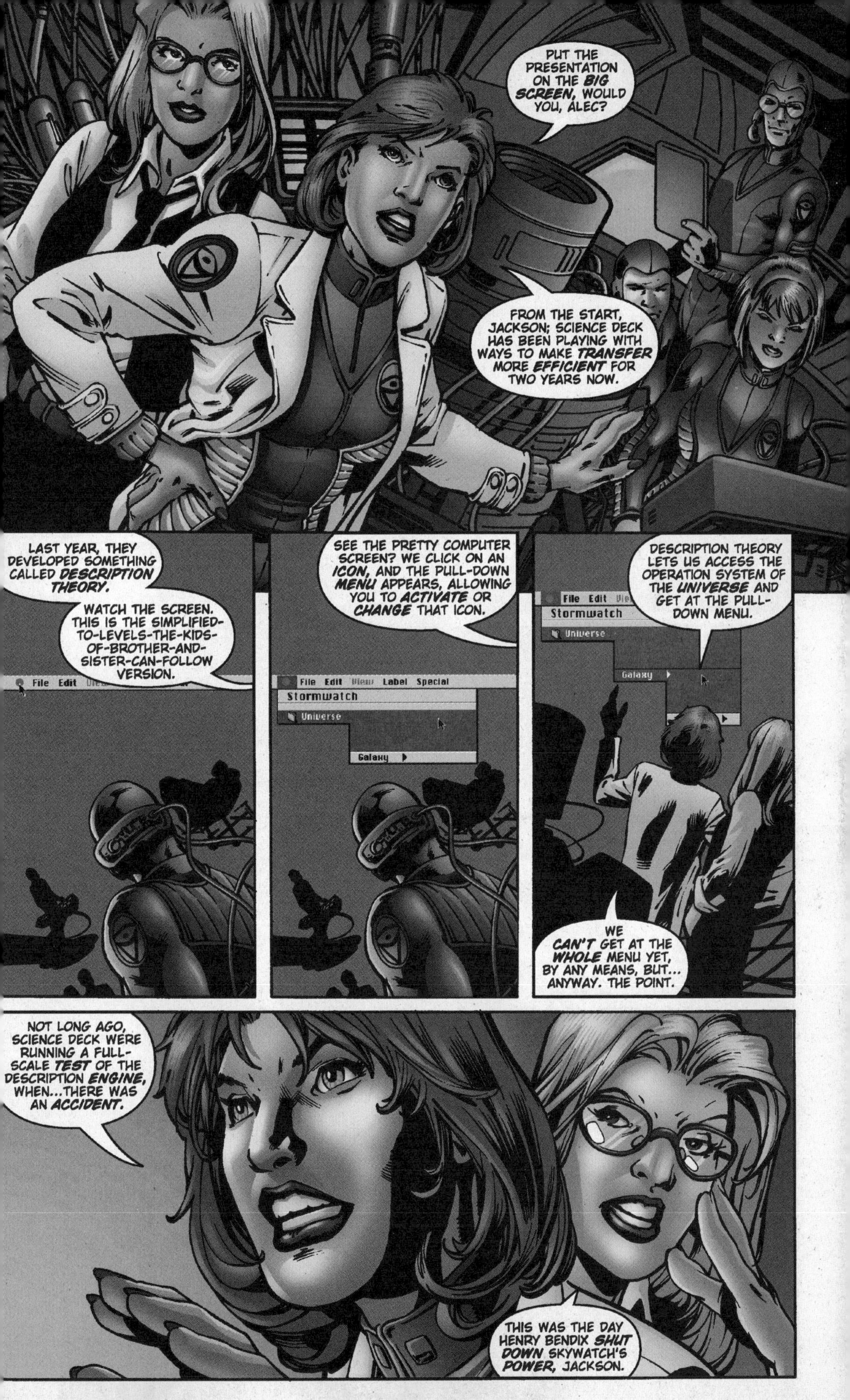
PUT THE PRESENTATION ON THE BIG SCREEN, WOULD YOU, ALEC?
FROM THE START, JACKSON; SCIENCE DECK HAS BEEN PLAYING WITH WAYS TO MAKE TRANSFER MORE EFFICIENT FOR TWO YEARS NOW.
LAST YEAR, THEY DEVELOPED SOMETHING CALLED DESCRIPTION THEORY.
WATCH THE SCREEN. THIS IS THE SIMPLIFIED-TO-LEVELS-THE-KIDS-OF-BROTHER-AND-SISTER-CAN-FOLLOW VERSION.
File Edit
SEE THE PRETTY COMPUTER SCREEN? WE CLICK ON AN ICON, AND THE PULL-DOWN MENU APPEARS, ALLOWING YOU TO ACTIVATE OR CHANGE THAT ICON.
File Edit View Label Special
Stormwatch
Universe
Galaxy
DESCRIPTION THEORY LETS US ACCESS THE OPERATION SYSTEM OF THE UNIVERSE AND GET AT THE PULL-DOWN MENU.
File Edit
Stormwatch
Universe
Galaxy
WE CAN'T GET AT THE WHOLE MENU YET, BY ANY MEANS, BUT... ANYWAY. THE POINT.
NOT LONG AGO, SCIENCE DECK WERE RUNNING A FULL-SCALE TEST OF THE DESCRIPTION ENGINE, WHEN...THERE WAS AN ACCIDENT.
THIS WAS THE DAY HENRY BENDIX SHUT DOWN SKYWATCH'S POWER, JACKSON.

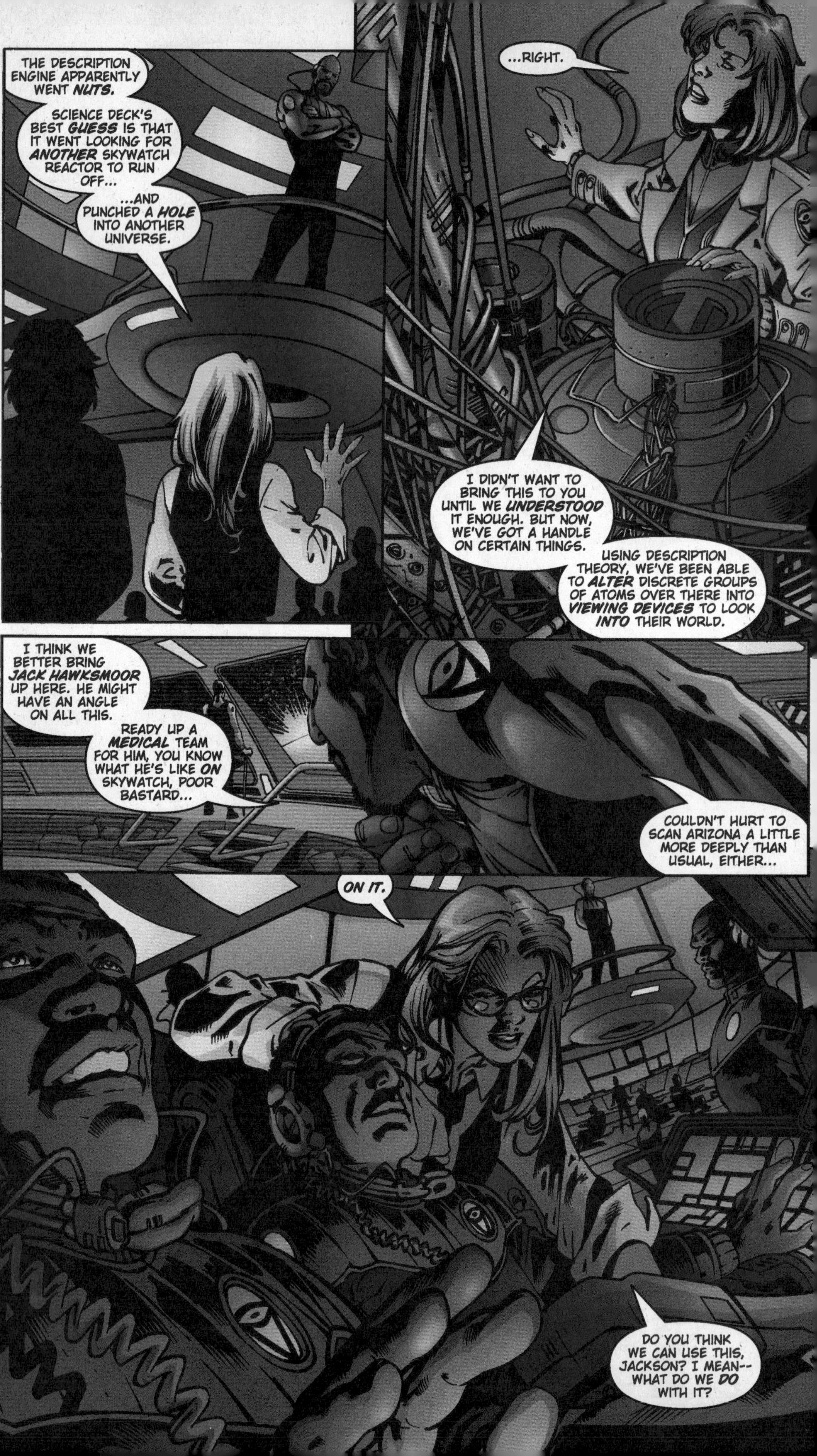
THE DESCRIPTION ENGINE APPARENTLY WENT NUTS.
SCIENCE DECK'S BEST GUESS IS THAT IT WENT LOOKING FOR ANOTHER SKYWATCH REACTOR TO RUN OFF...
...AND PUNCHED A HOLE INTO ANOTHER UNIVERSE.
...RIGHT.
I DIDN'T WANT TO BRING THIS TO YOU UNTIL WE UNDERSTOOD IT ENOUGH. BUT NOW, WE'VE GOT A HANDLE ON CERTAIN THINGS.
USING DESCRIPTION THEORY, WE'VE BEEN ABLE TO ALTER DISCRETE GROUPS OF ATOMS OVER THERE INTO VIEWING DEVICES TO LOOK INTO THEIR WORLD.
I THINK WE BETTER BRING JACK HAWKSMOOR UP HERE. HE MIGHT HAVE AN ANGLE ON ALL THIS.
READY UP A MEDICAL TEAM FOR HIM, YOU KNOW WHAT HE'S LIKE ON SKYWATCH, POOR BASTARD...
COULDN'T HURT TO SCAN ARIZONA A LITTLE MORE DEEPLY THAN USUAL, EITHER...
ON IT.
DO YOU THINK WE CAN USE THIS, JACKSON? I MEAN-- WHAT DO WE DO WITH IT?

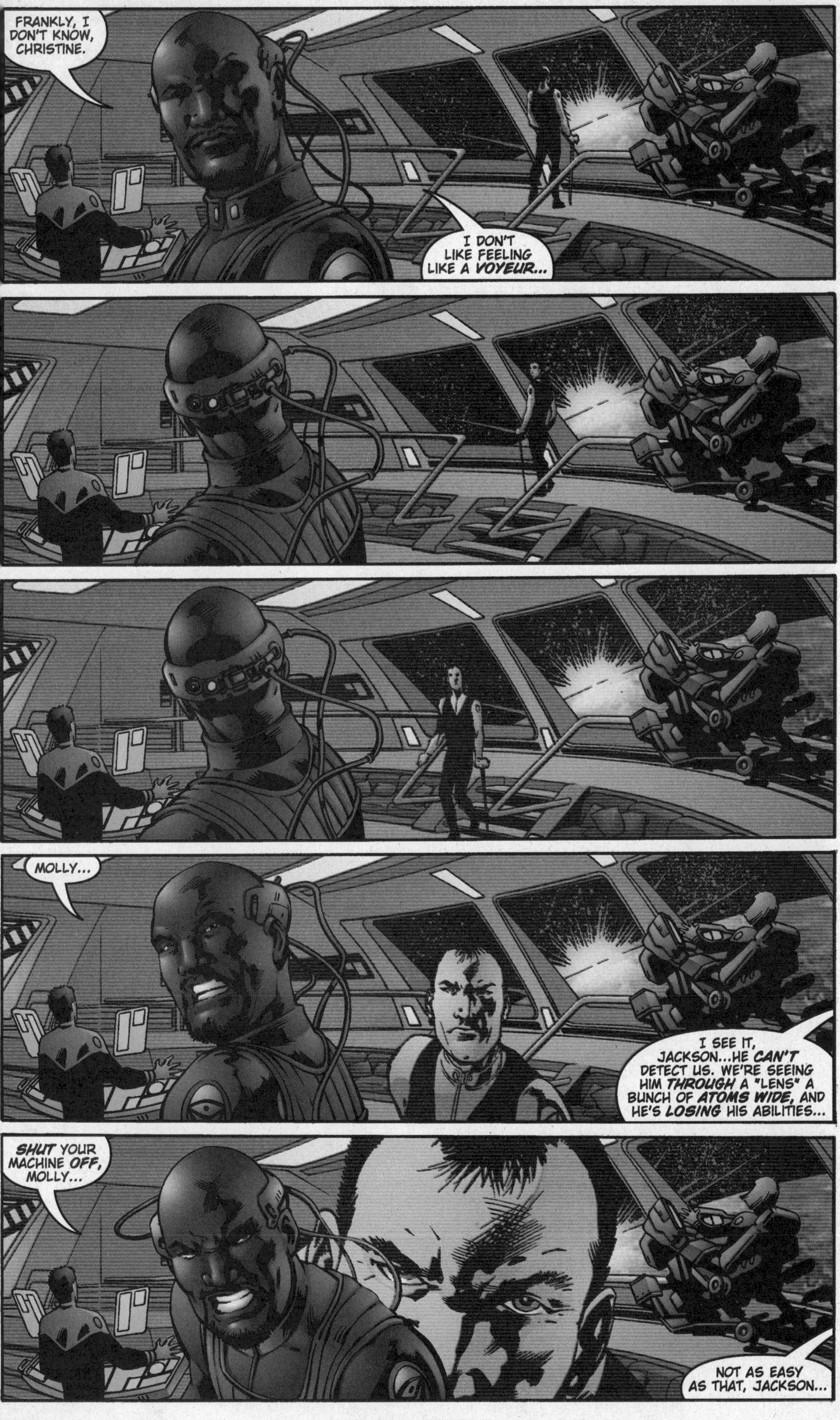
FRANKLY, I DON'T KNOW, CHRISTINE.
I DON'T LIKE FEELING LIKE A VOYEUR...
MOLLY...
I SEE IT, JACKSON...HE CAN'T DETECT US. WE'RE SEEING HIM THROUGH A "LENS" A BUNCH OF ATOMS WIDE, AND HE'S LOSING HIS ABILITIES...
SHUT YOUR MACHINE OFF, MOLLY...
NOT AS EASY AS THAT, JACKSON...

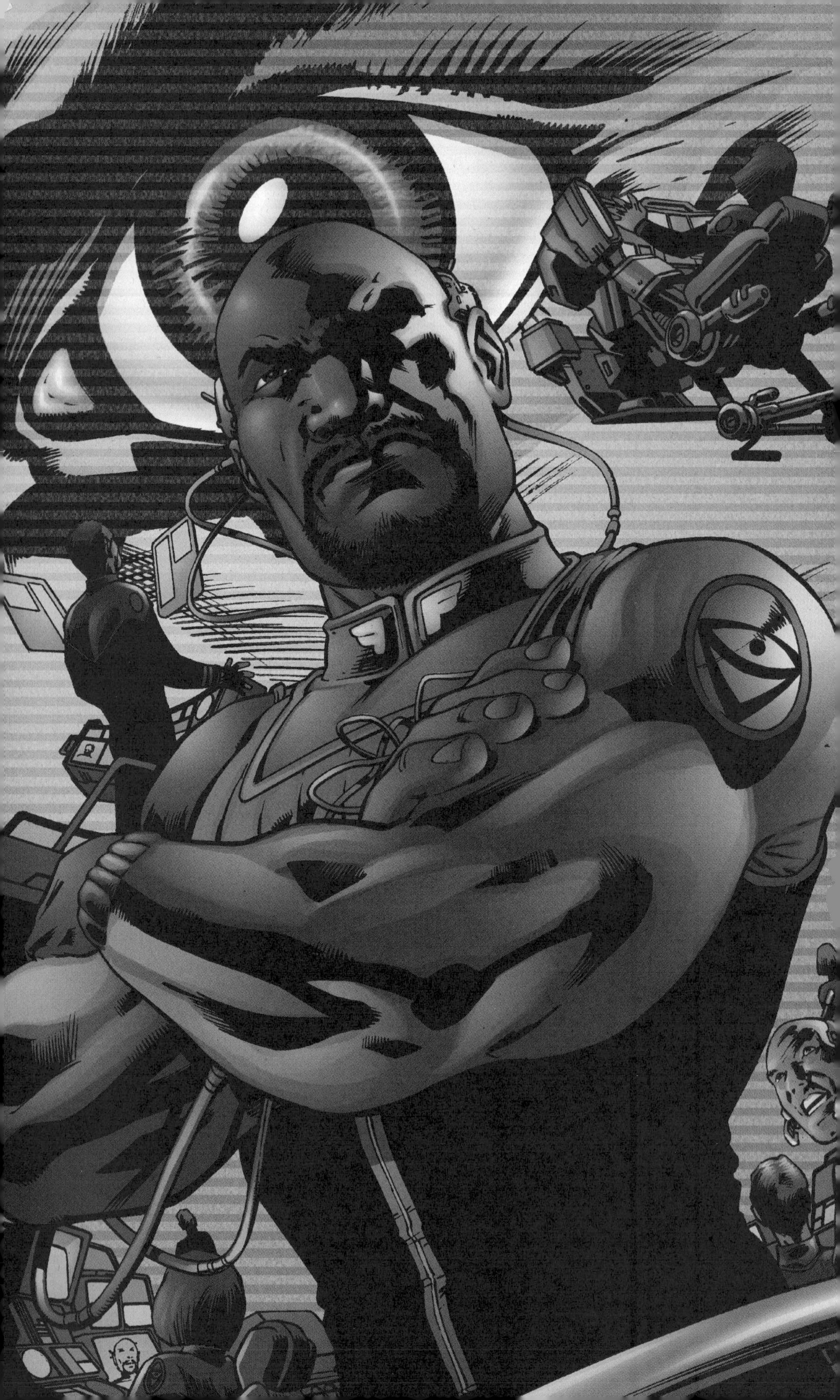

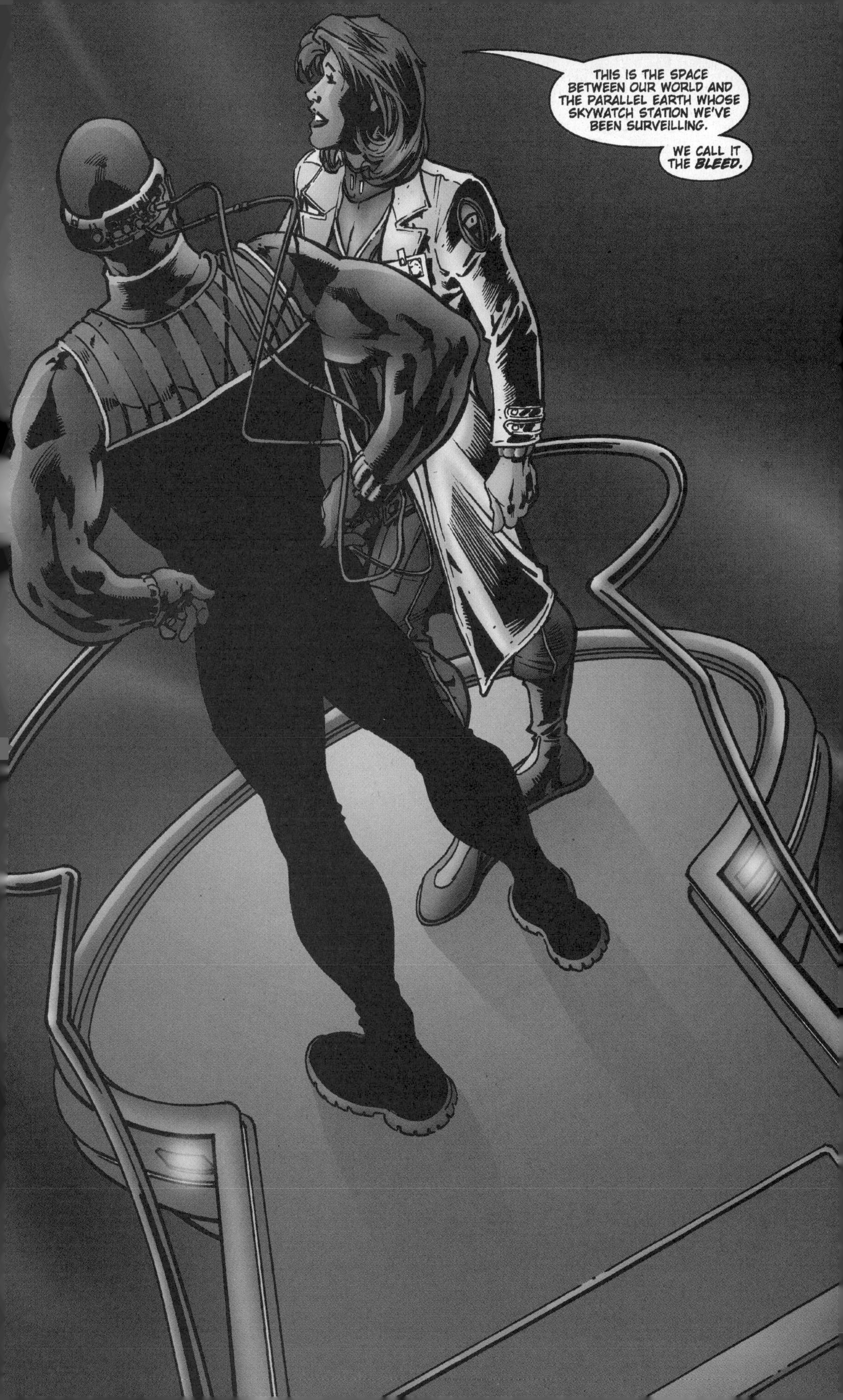
THIS IS THE SPACE BETWEEN OUR WORLD AND THE PARALLEL EARTH WHOSE SKYWATCH STATION WE'VE BEEN SURVEILLING.
WE CALL IT THE *BLEED.*

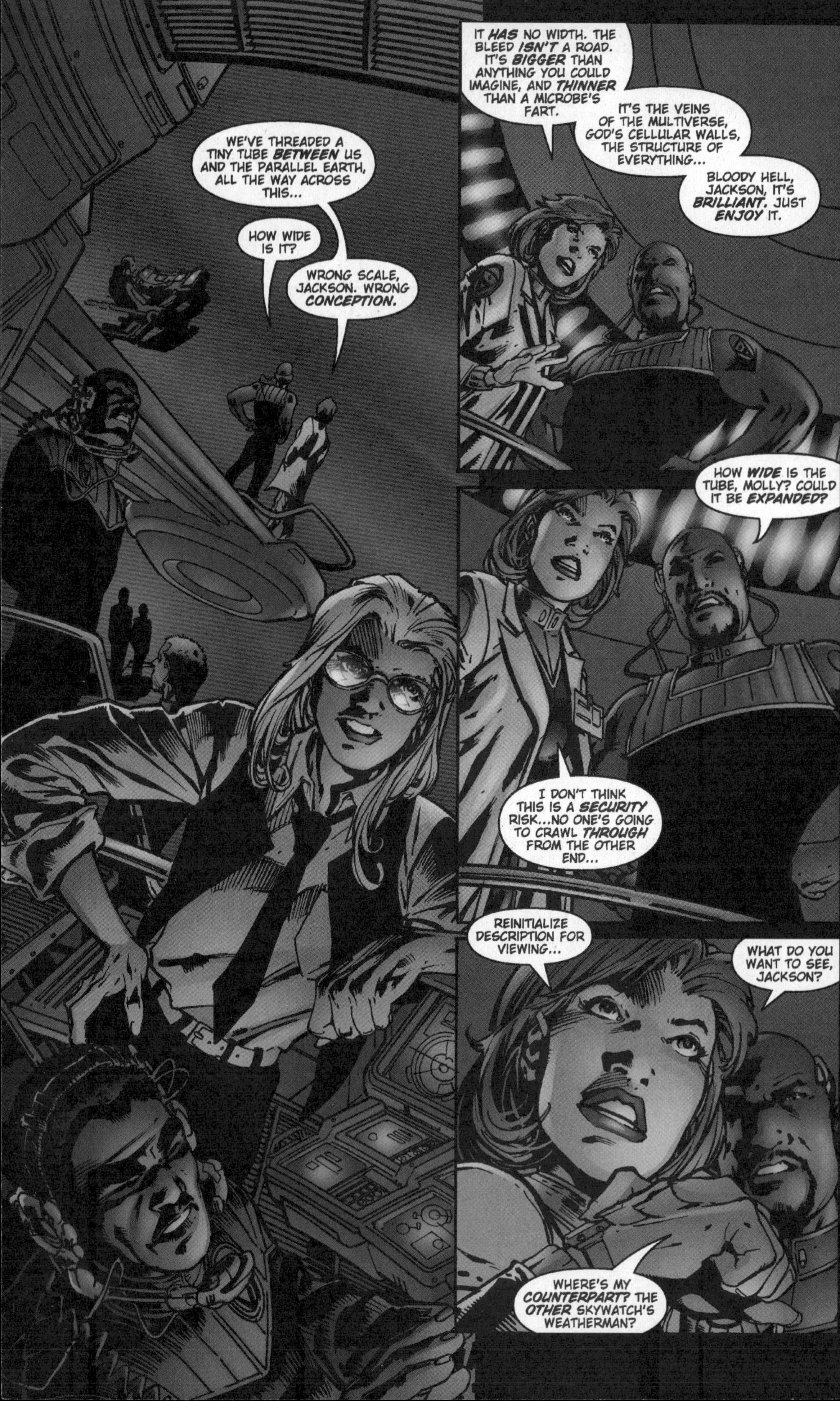

WE'VE THREADED A TINY TUBE BETWEEN US AND THE PARALLEL EARTH, ALL THE WAY ACROSS THIS...
HOW WIDE IS IT?
WRONG SCALE, JACKSON. WRONG CONCEPTION.
IT HAS NO WIDTH. THE BLEED ISN'T A ROAD. IT'S BIGGER THAN ANYTHING YOU COULD IMAGINE, AND THINNER THAN A MICROBE'S FART.
IT'S THE VEINS OF THE MULTIVERSE, GOD'S CELLULAR WALLS, THE STRUCTURE OF EVERYTHING...
BLOODY HELL, JACKSON, IT'S BRILLIANT. JUST ENJOY IT.
HOW WIDE IS THE TUBE, MOLLY? COULD IT BE EXPANDED?
I DON'T THINK THIS IS A SECURITY RISK...NO ONE'S GOING TO CRAWL THROUGH FROM THE OTHER END...
REINITIALIZE DESCRIPTION FOR VIEWING...
WHAT DO YOU WANT TO SEE, JACKSON?
WHERE'S MY COUNTERPART? THE OTHER SKYWATCH'S WEATHERMAN?

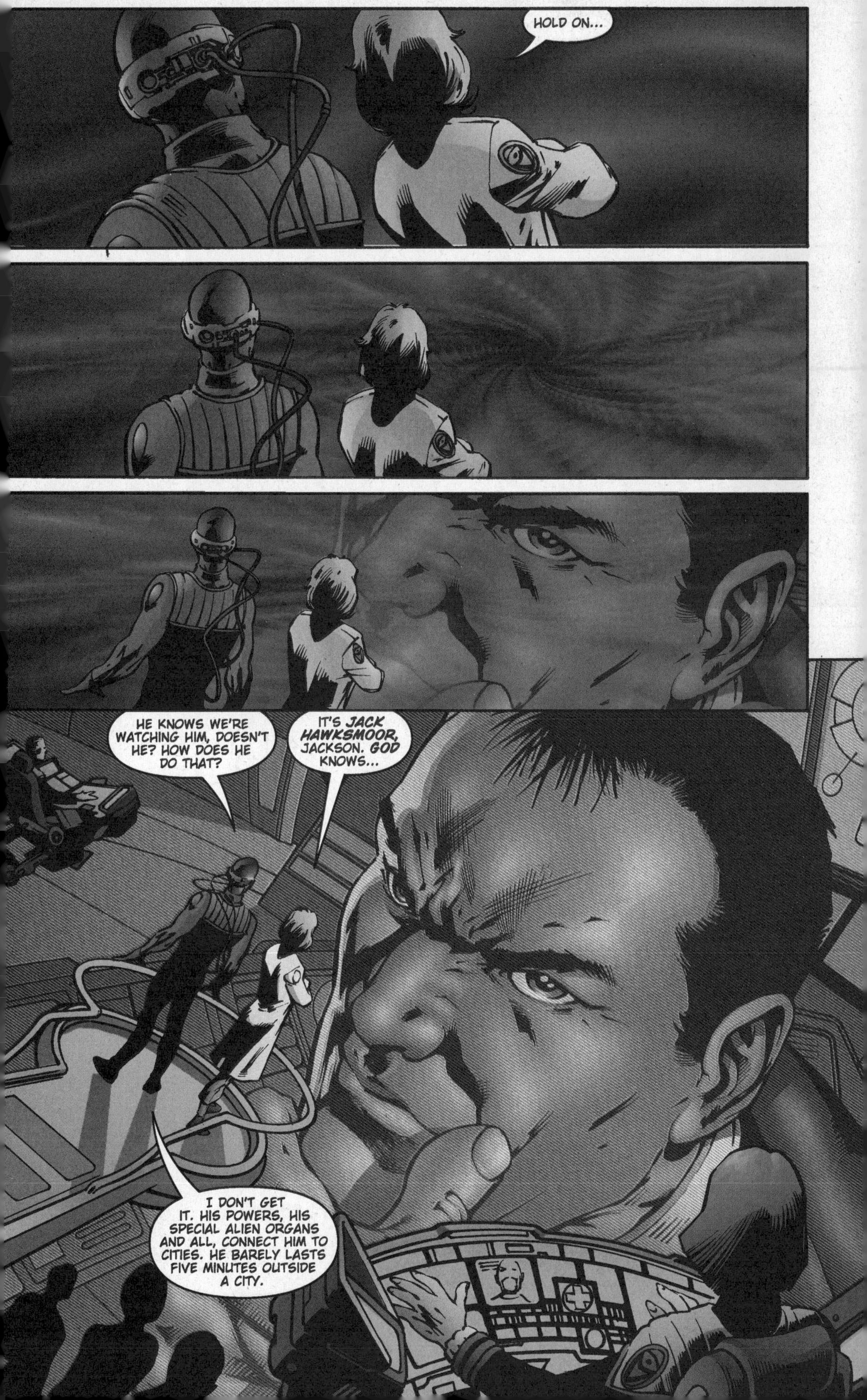
HOLD ON...
HE KNOWS WE'RE WATCHING HIM, DOESN'T HE? HOW DOES HE DO THAT?
IT'S JACK HAWKSMOOR, JACKSON. GOD KNOWS...
I DON'T GET IT. HIS POWERS, HIS SPECIAL ALIEN ORGANS AND ALL, CONNECT HIM TO CITIES. HE BARELY LASTS FIVE MINUTES OUTSIDE A CITY.

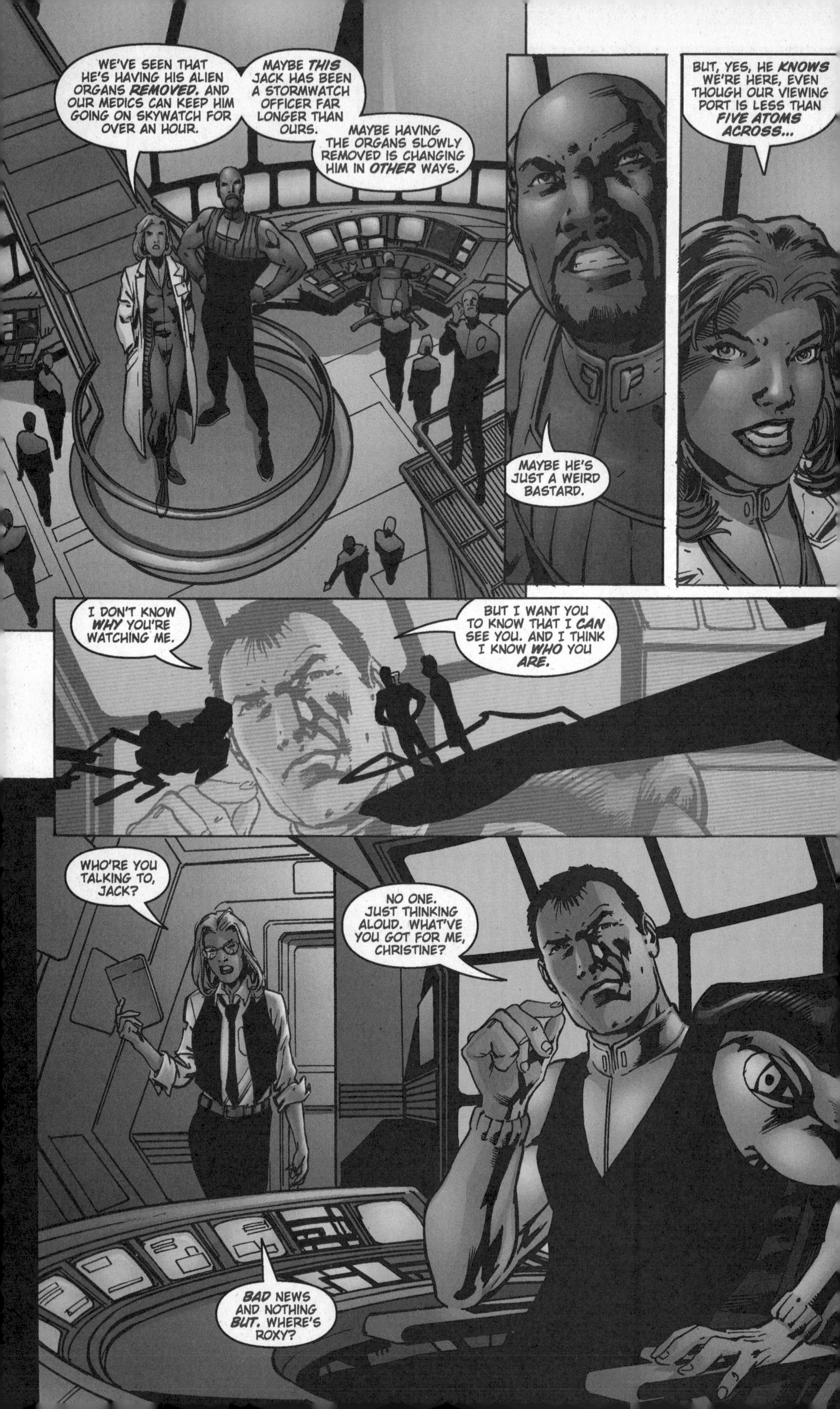
WE'VE SEEN THAT HE'S HAVING HIS ALIEN ORGANS REMOVED. AND OUR MEDICS CAN KEEP HIM GOING ON SKYWATCH FOR OVER AN HOUR.
MAYBE THIS JACK HAS BEEN A STORMWATCH OFFICER FAR LONGER THAN OURS.
MAYBE HAVING THE ORGANS SLOWLY REMOVED IS CHANGING HIM IN OTHER WAYS.
MAYBE HE'S JUST A WEIRD BASTARD.
BUT, YES, HE KNOWS WE'RE HERE, EVEN THOUGH OUR VIEWING PORT IS LESS THAN FIVE ATOMS ACROSS...
I DON'T KNOW WHY YOU'RE WATCHING ME.
BUT I WANT YOU TO KNOW THAT I CAN SEE YOU. AND I THINK I KNOW WHO YOU ARE.
WHO'RE YOU TALKING TO, JACK?
NO ONE. JUST THINKING ALOUD. WHAT'VE YOU GOT FOR ME, CHRISTINE?
BAD NEWS AND NOTHING BUT. WHERE'S ROXY?

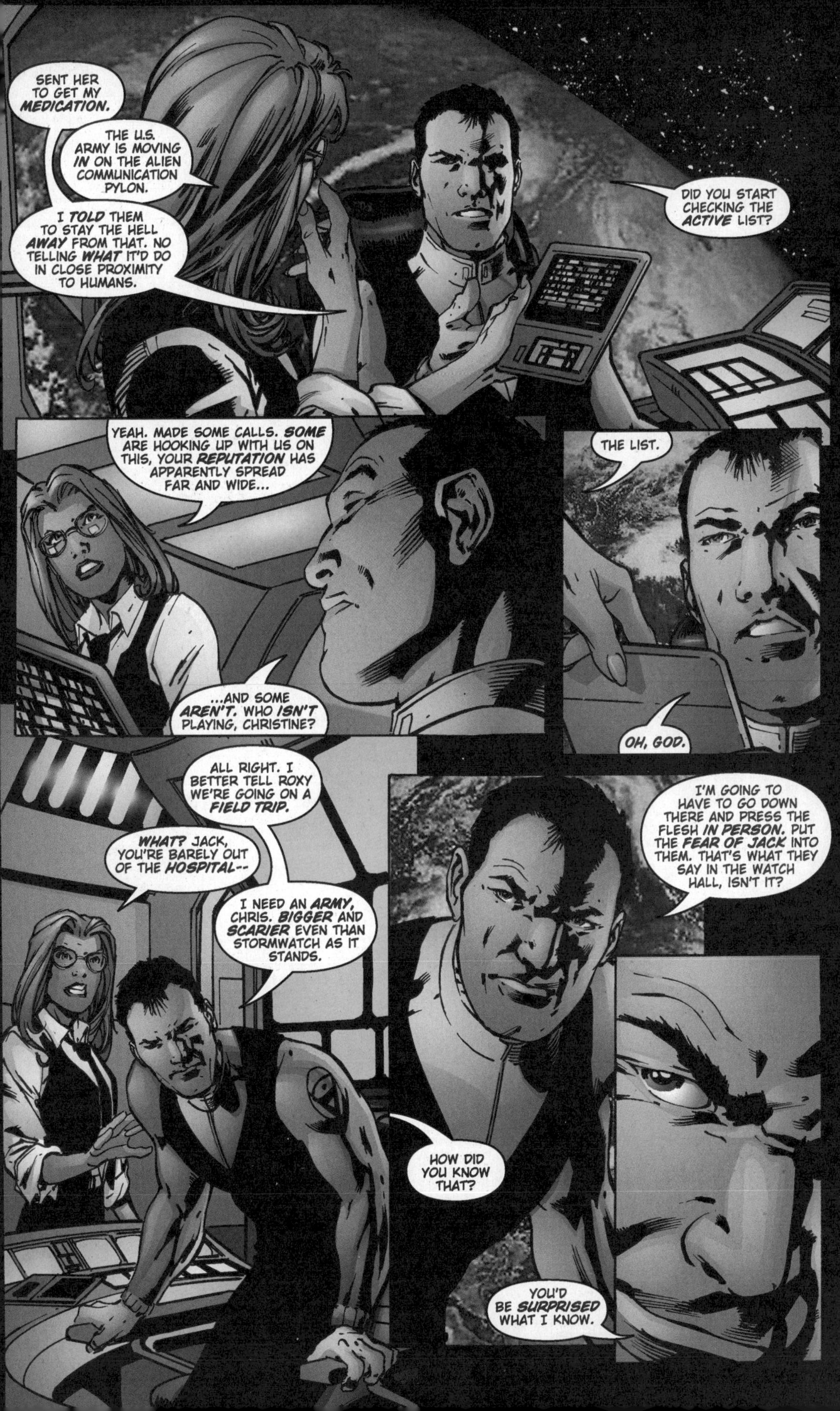
SENT HER TO GET MY MEDICATION.
THE U.S. ARMY IS MOVING IN ON THE ALIEN COMMUNICATION PYLON.
I TOLD THEM TO STAY THE HELL AWAY FROM THAT. NO TELLING WHAT IT'D DO IN CLOSE PROXIMITY TO HUMANS.
DID YOU START CHECKING THE ACTIVE LIST?
YEAH. MADE SOME CALLS. SOME ARE HOOKING UP WITH US ON THIS, YOUR REPUTATION HAS APPARENTLY SPREAD FAR AND WIDE...
...AND SOME AREN'T. WHO ISN'T PLAYING, CHRISTINE?
THE LIST.
OH, GOD.
ALL RIGHT. I BETTER TELL ROXY WE'RE GOING ON A FIELD TRIP.
WHAT? JACK, YOU'RE BARELY OUT OF THE HOSPITAL--
I NEED AN ARMY, CHRIS. BIGGER AND SCARIER EVEN THAN STORMWATCH AS IT STANDS.
I'M GOING TO HAVE TO GO DOWN THERE AND PRESS THE FLESH IN PERSON. PUT THE FEAR OF JACK INTO THEM. THAT'S WHAT THEY SAY IN THE WATCH HALL, ISN'T IT?
HOW DID YOU KNOW THAT?
YOU'D BE SURPRISED WHAT I KNOW.

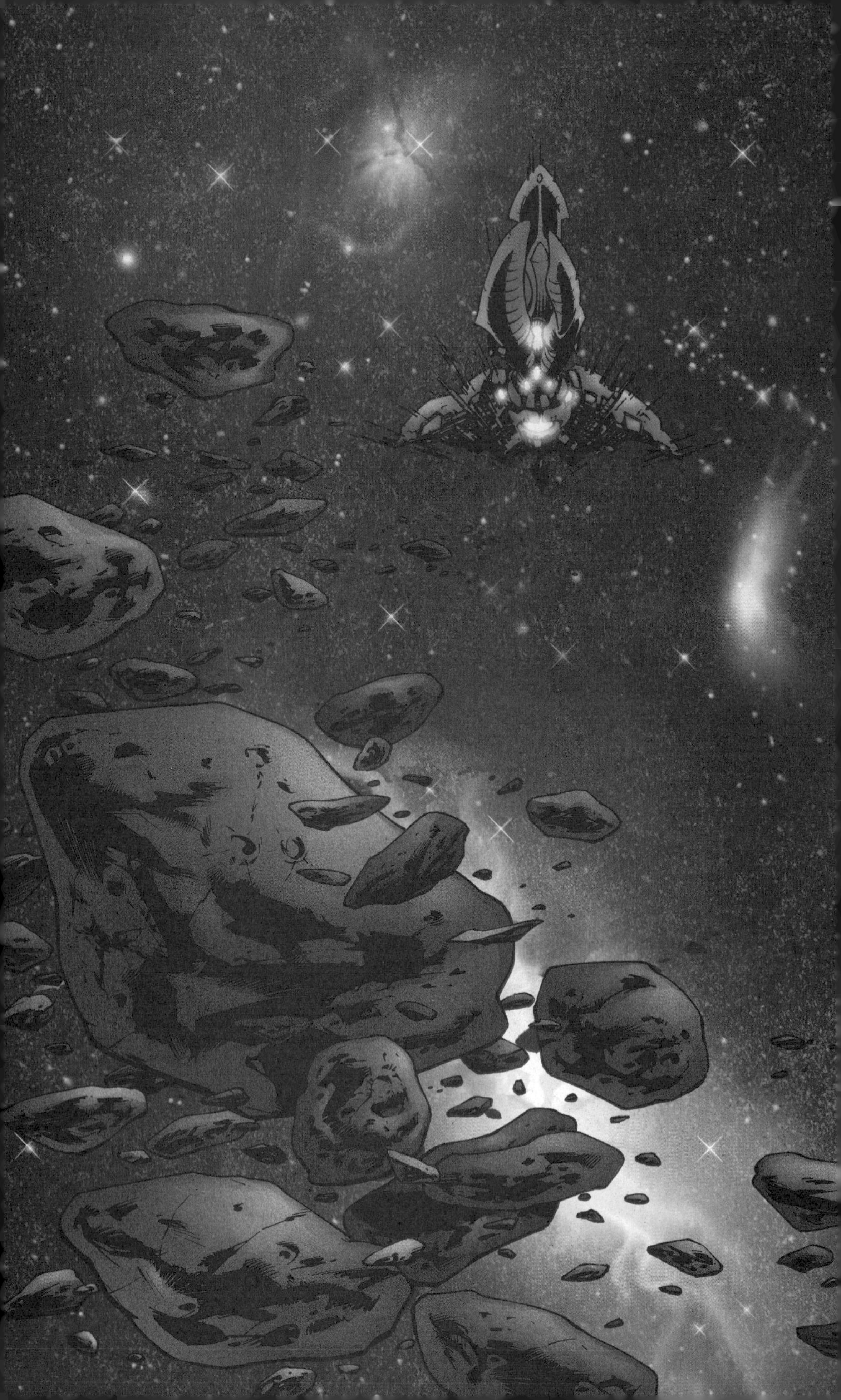

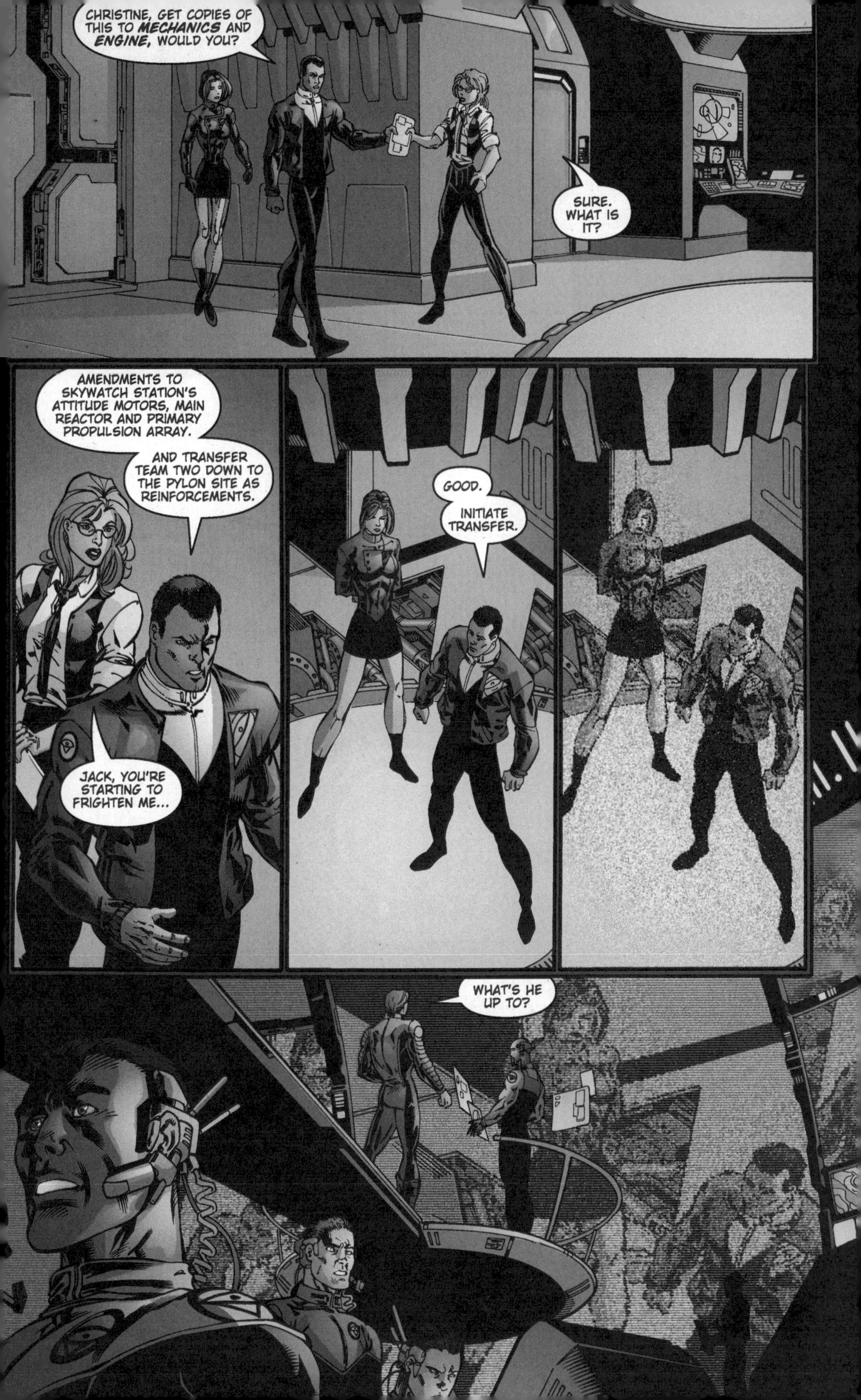
CHRISTINE, GET COPIES OF THIS TO MECHANICS AND ENGINE, WOULD YOU?
SURE. WHAT IS IT?
AMENDMENTS TO SKYWATCH STATION'S ATTITUDE MOTORS, MAIN REACTOR AND PRIMARY PROPULSION ARRAY.
AND TRANSFER TEAM TWO DOWN TO THE PYLON SITE AS REINFORCEMENTS.
JACK, YOU'RE STARTING TO FRIGHTEN ME...
GOOD.
INITIATE TRANSFER.
WHAT'S HE UP TO?

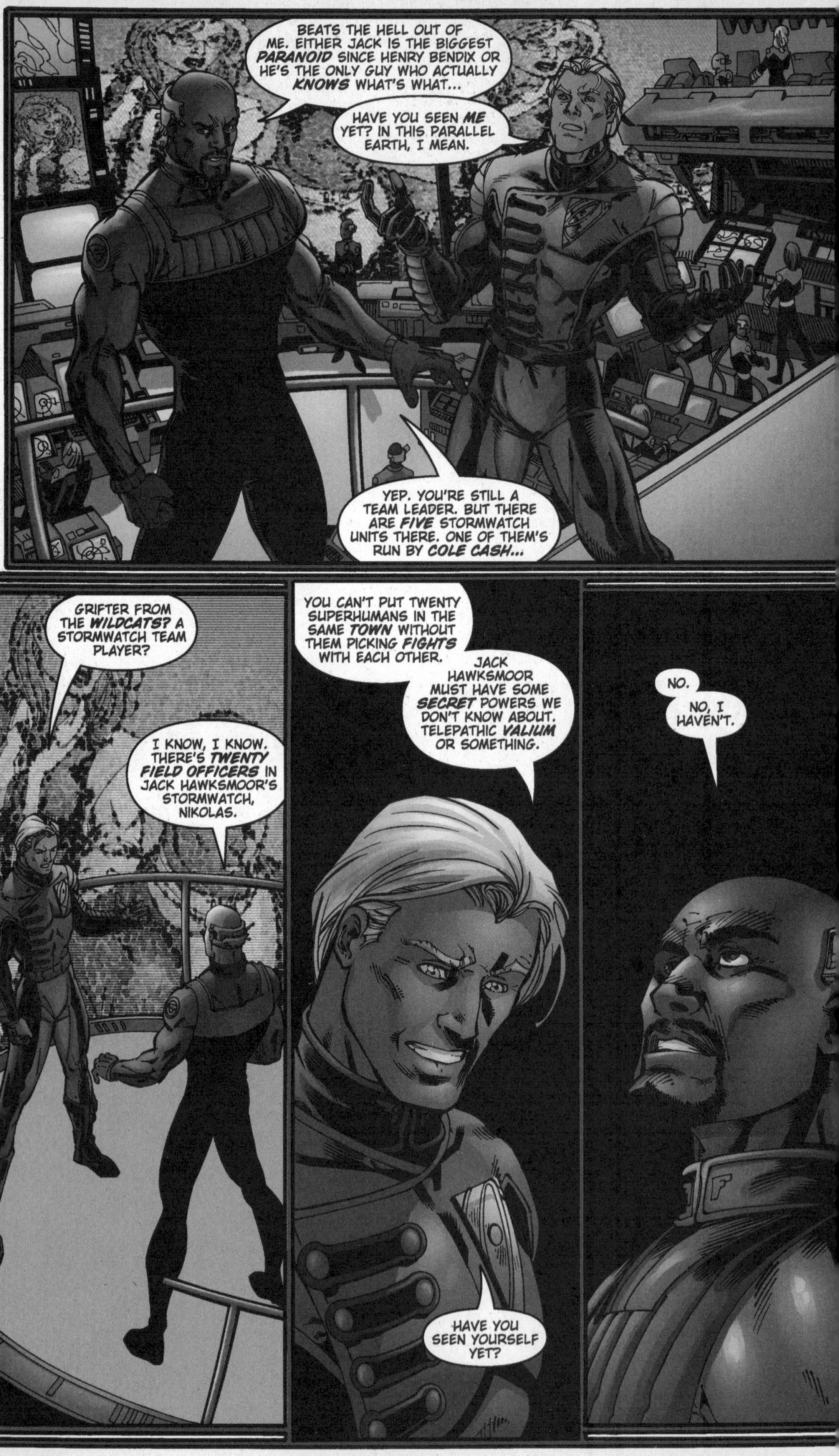
BEATS THE HELL OUT OF ME. EITHER JACK IS THE BIGGEST PARANOID SINCE HENRY BENDIX OR HE'S THE ONLY GUY WHO ACTUALLY KNOWS WHAT'S WHAT...
HAVE YOU SEEN ME YET? IN THIS PARALLEL EARTH, I MEAN.
YEP. YOU'RE STILL A TEAM LEADER. BUT THERE ARE FIVE STORMWATCH UNITS THERE. ONE OF THEM'S RUN BY COLE CASH...
GRIFTER FROM THE WILDCATS? A STORMWATCH TEAM PLAYER?
I KNOW, I KNOW. THERE'S TWENTY FIELD OFFICERS IN JACK HAWKSMOOR'S STORMWATCH, NIKOLAS.
YOU CAN'T PUT TWENTY SUPERHUMANS IN THE SAME TOWN WITHOUT THEM PICKING FIGHTS WITH EACH OTHER.
JACK HAWKSMOOR MUST HAVE SOME SECRET POWERS WE DON'T KNOW ABOUT. TELEPATHIC VALIUM OR SOMETHING.
HAVE YOU SEEN YOURSELF YET?
NO.
NO, I HAVEN'T.

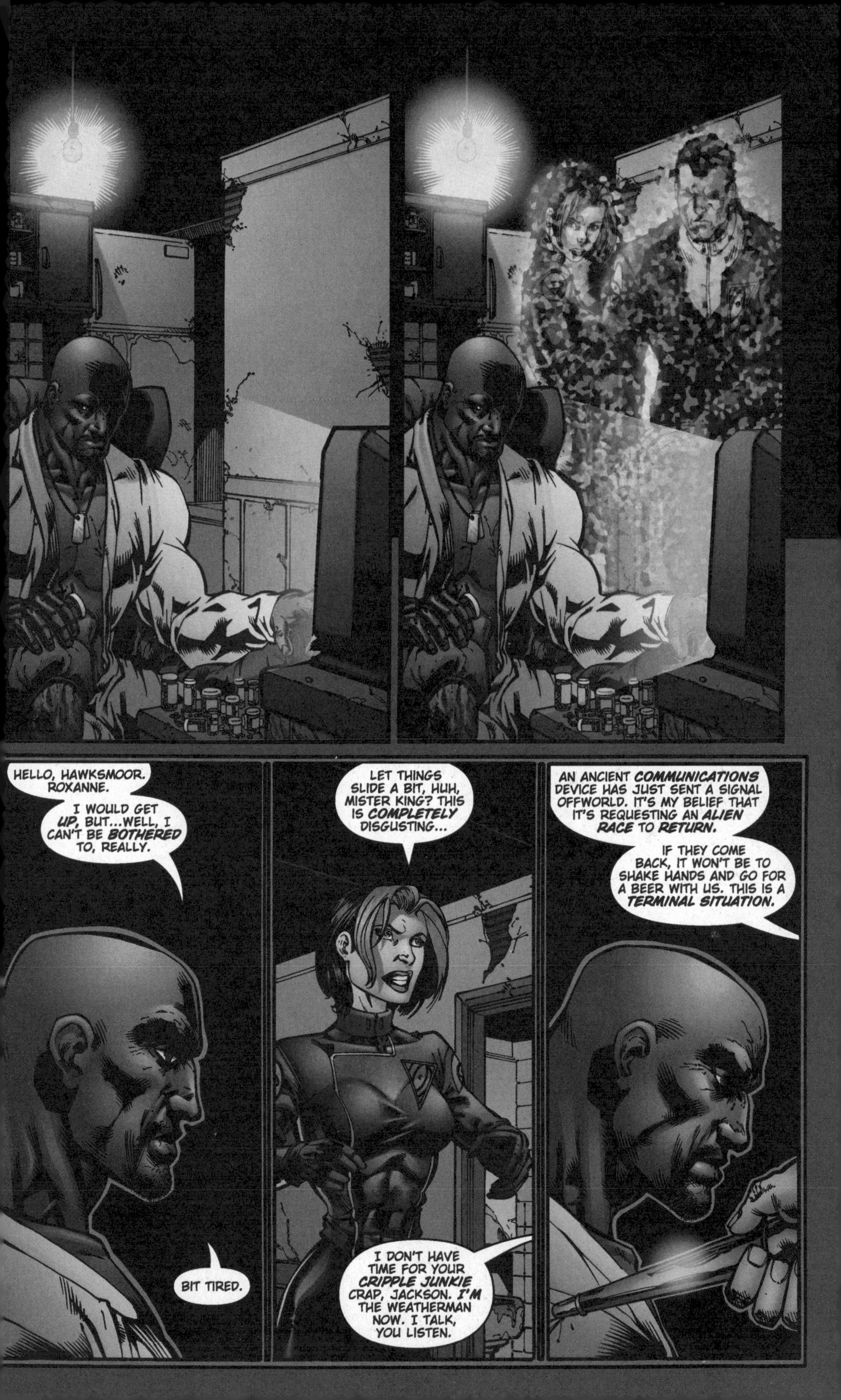
HELLO, HAWKSMOOR. ROXANNE.
I WOULD GET UP, BUT...WELL, I CAN'T BE BOTHERED TO, REALLY.
BIT TIRED.
LET THINGS SLIDE A BIT, HUH, MISTER KING? THIS IS COMPLETELY DISGUSTING...
I DON'T HAVE TIME FOR YOUR CRIPPLE JUNKIE CRAP, JACKSON. I'M THE WEATHERMAN NOW. I TALK, YOU LISTEN.
AN ANCIENT COMMUNICATIONS DEVICE HAS JUST SENT A SIGNAL OFFWORLD. IT'S MY BELIEF THAT IT'S REQUESTING AN ALIEN RACE TO RETURN.
IF THEY COME BACK, IT WON'T BE TO SHAKE HANDS AND GO FOR A BEER WITH US. THIS IS A TERMINAL SITUATION.

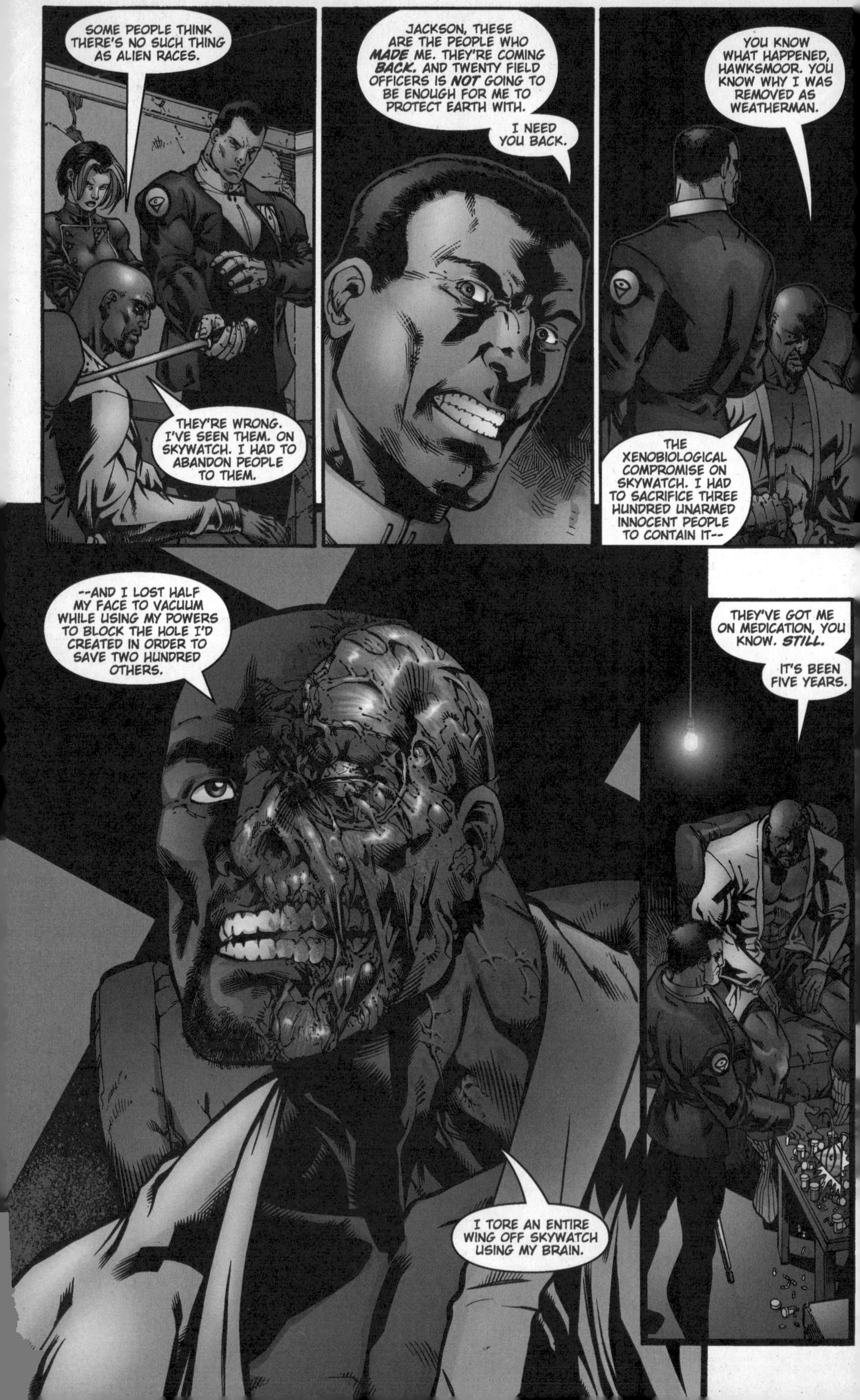
SOME PEOPLE THINK THERE'S NO SUCH THING AS ALIEN RACES.
THEY'RE WRONG. I'VE SEEN THEM. ON SKYWATCH. I HAD TO ABANDON PEOPLE TO THEM.
JACKSON, THESE ARE THE PEOPLE WHO MADE ME. THEY'RE COMING BACK. AND TWENTY FIELD OFFICERS IS NOT GOING TO BE ENOUGH FOR ME TO PROTECT EARTH WITH.
I NEED YOU BACK.
YOU KNOW WHAT HAPPENED, HAWKSMOOR. YOU KNOW WHY I WAS REMOVED AS WEATHERMAN.
THE XENOBIOLOGICAL COMPROMISE ON SKYWATCH. I HAD TO SACRIFICE THREE HUNDRED UNARMED INNOCENT PEOPLE TO CONTAIN IT--
--AND I LOST HALF MY FACE TO VACUUM WHILE USING MY POWERS TO BLOCK THE HOLE I'D CREATED IN ORDER TO SAVE TWO HUNDRED OTHERS.
I TORE AN ENTIRE WING OFF SKYWATCH USING MY BRAIN.
THEY'VE GOT ME ON MEDICATION, YOU KNOW. STILL.
IT'S BEEN FIVE YEARS.

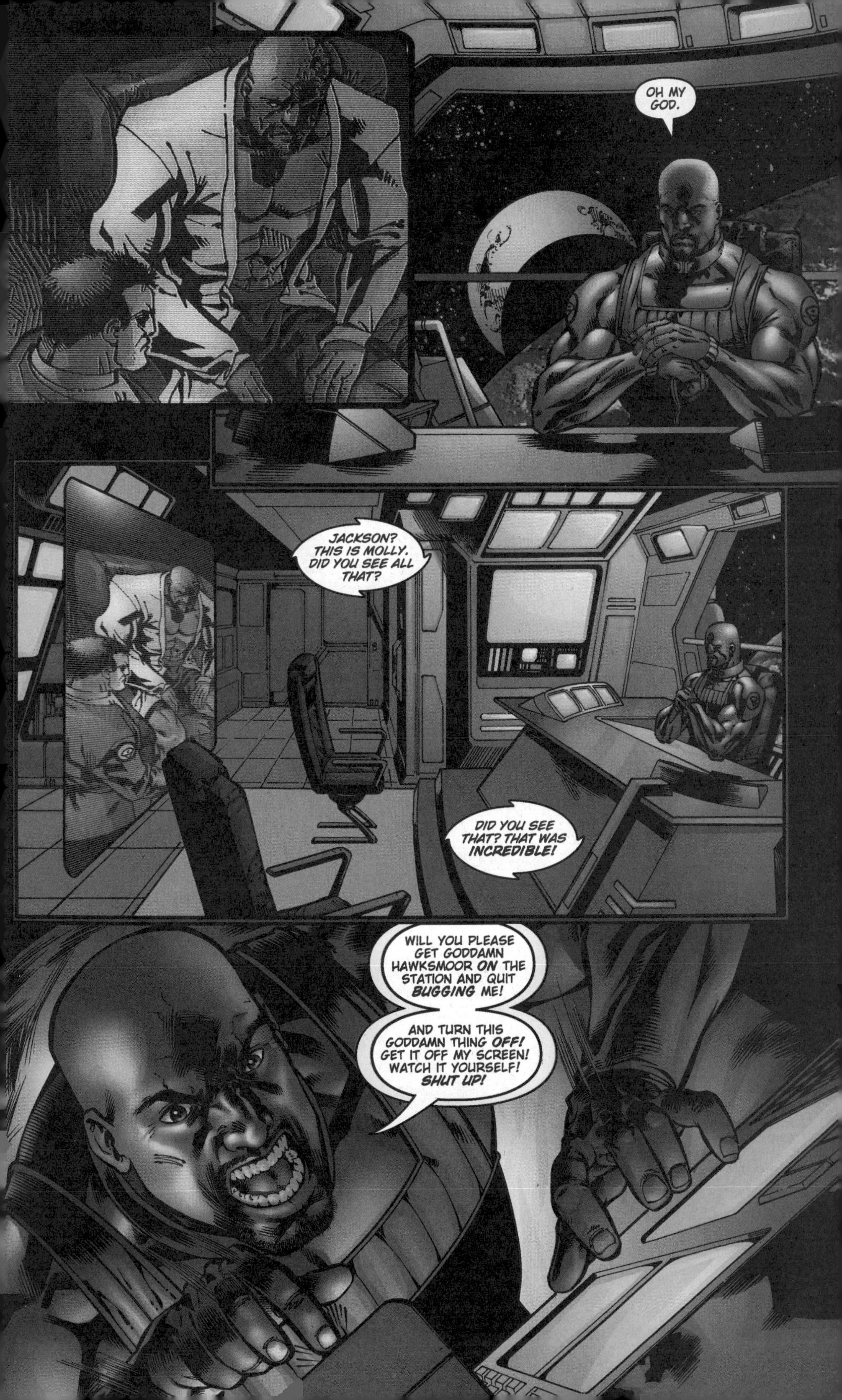
OH MY GOD.
JACKSON? THIS IS MOLLY. DID YOU SEE ALL THAT?
DID YOU SEE THAT? THAT WAS INCREDIBLE!
WILL YOU PLEASE GET GODDAMN HAWKSMOOR ON THE STATION AND QUIT BUGGING ME!
AND TURN THIS GODDAMN THING OFF! GET IT OFF MY SCREEN! WATCH IT YOURSELF! SHUT UP!

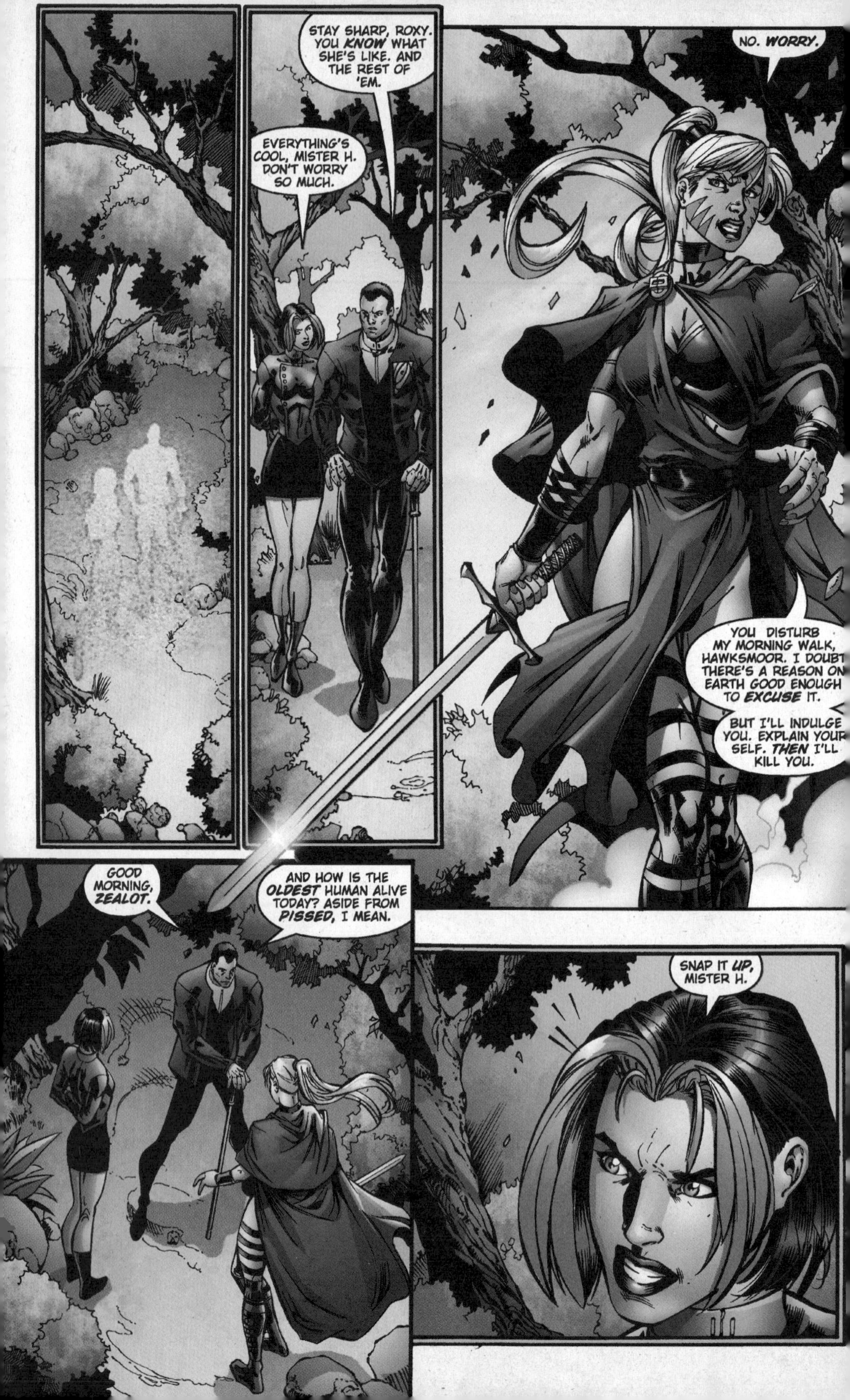

STAY SHARP, ROXY. YOU KNOW WHAT SHE'S LIKE. AND THE REST OF 'EM.
EVERYTHING'S COOL, MISTER H. DON'T WORRY SO MUCH.
NO. WORRY.
YOU DISTURB MY MORNING WALK, HAWKSMOOR. I DOUBT THERE'S A REASON ON EARTH GOOD ENOUGH TO EXCUSE IT.
BUT I'LL INDULGE YOU. EXPLAIN YOURSELF. THEN I'LL KILL YOU.
GOOD MORNING, ZEALOT.
AND HOW IS THE OLDEST HUMAN ALIVE TODAY? ASIDE FROM PISSED, I MEAN.
SNAP IT UP, MISTER H.

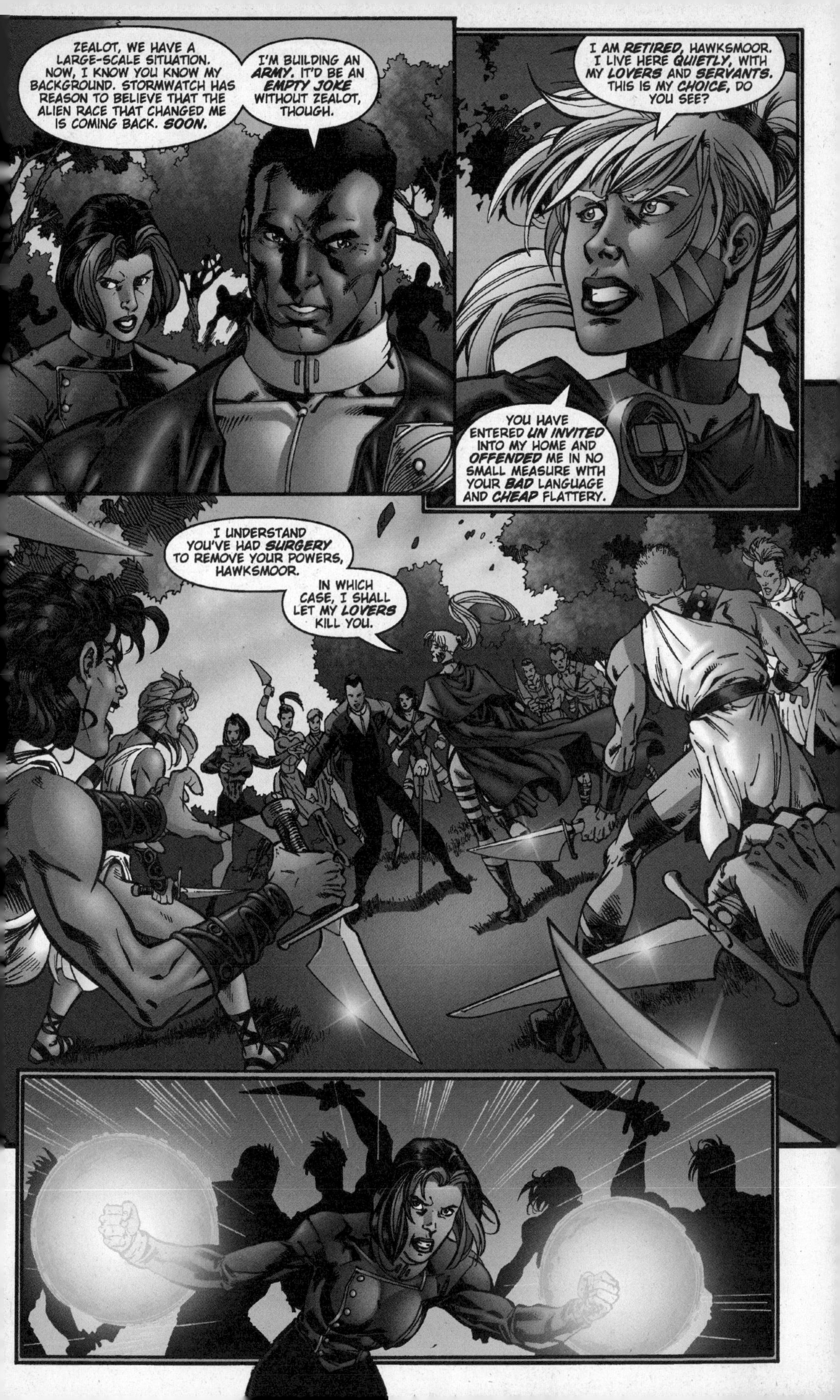
ZEALOT, WE HAVE A LARGE-SCALE SITUATION. NOW, I KNOW YOU KNOW MY BACKGROUND. STORMWATCH HAS REASON TO BELIEVE THAT THE ALIEN RACE THAT CHANGED ME IS COMING BACK. SOON.
I'M BUILDING AN ARMY. IT'D BE AN EMPTY JOKE WITHOUT ZEALOT, THOUGH.
I AM RETIRED, HAWKSMOOR. I LIVE HERE QUIETLY, WITH MY LOVERS AND SERVANTS. THIS IS MY CHOICE, DO YOU SEE?
YOU HAVE ENTERED UN INVITED INTO MY HOME AND OFFENDED ME IN NO SMALL MEASURE WITH YOUR BAD LANGUAGE AND CHEAP FLATTERY.
I UNDERSTAND YOU'VE HAD SURGERY TO REMOVE YOUR POWERS, HAWKSMOOR.
IN WHICH CASE, I SHALL LET MY LOVERS KILL YOU.

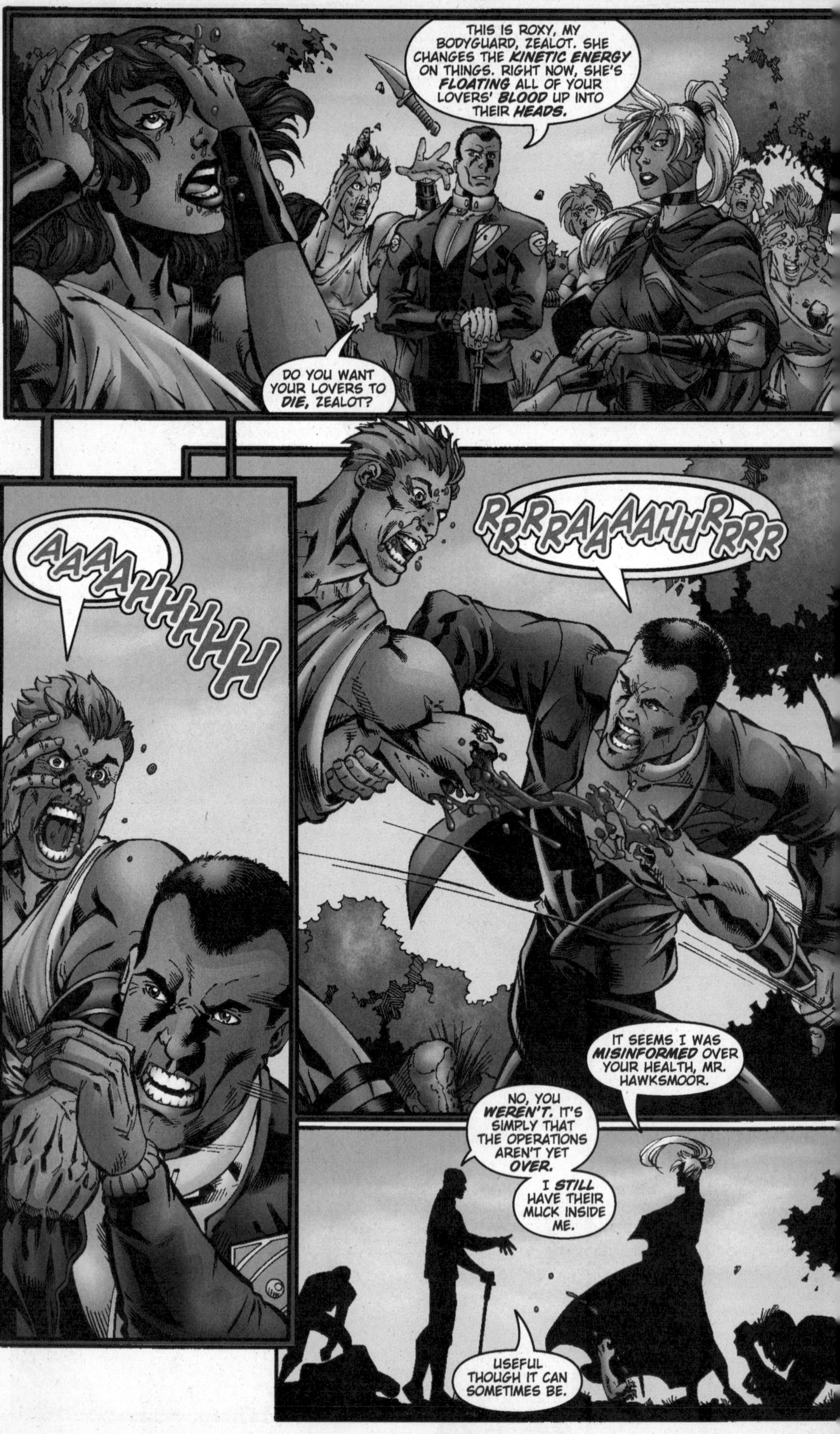

THIS IS ROXY, MY BODYGUARD, ZEALOT. SHE CHANGES THE *KINETIC ENERGY* ON THINGS. RIGHT NOW, SHE'S *FLOATING* ALL OF YOUR LOVERS' *BLOOD* UP INTO THEIR *HEADS*.
DO YOU WANT YOUR LOVERS TO *DIE*, ZEALOT?
AAAAHHHHHH
RRRRAAAAAHHRRRR
IT SEEMS I WAS *MISINFORMED* OVER YOUR HEALTH, MR. HAWKSMOOR.
NO, YOU *WEREN'T.* IT'S SIMPLY THAT THE OPERATIONS AREN'T YET *OVER.*
I *STILL* HAVE THEIR MUCK INSIDE ME.
USEFUL THOUGH IT CAN SOMETIMES BE.

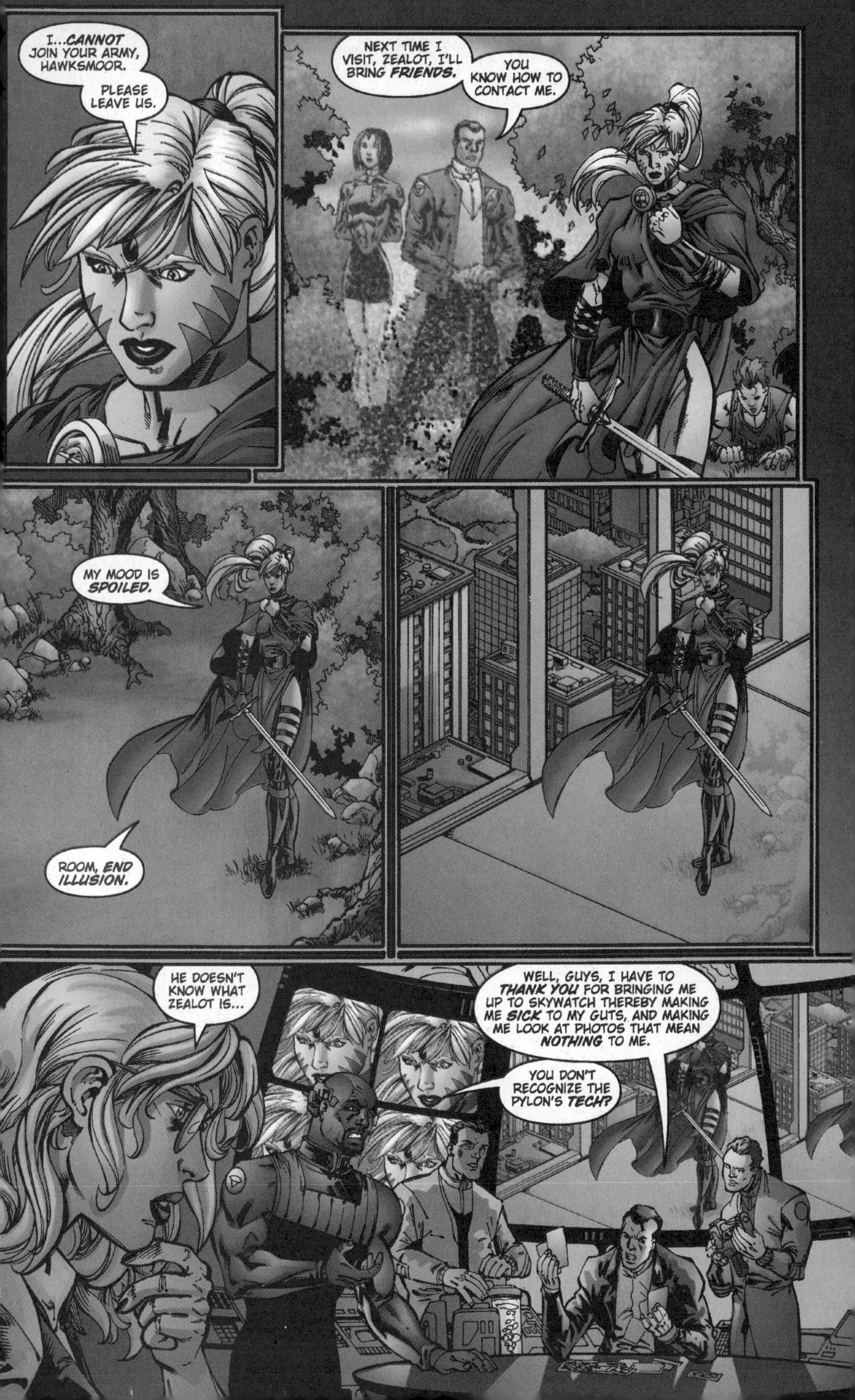
I...CANNOT JOIN YOUR ARMY, HAWKSMOOR.
PLEASE LEAVE US.
NEXT TIME I VISIT, ZEALOT, I'LL BRING FRIENDS.
YOU KNOW HOW TO CONTACT ME.
MY MOOD IS SPOILED.
ROOM, END ILLUSION.
HE DOESN'T KNOW WHAT ZEALOT IS...
WELL, GUYS, I HAVE TO THANK YOU FOR BRINGING ME UP TO SKYWATCH THEREBY MAKING ME SICK TO MY GUTS, AND MAKING ME LOOK AT PHOTOS THAT MEAN NOTHING TO ME.
YOU DON'T RECOGNIZE THE PYLON'S TECH?

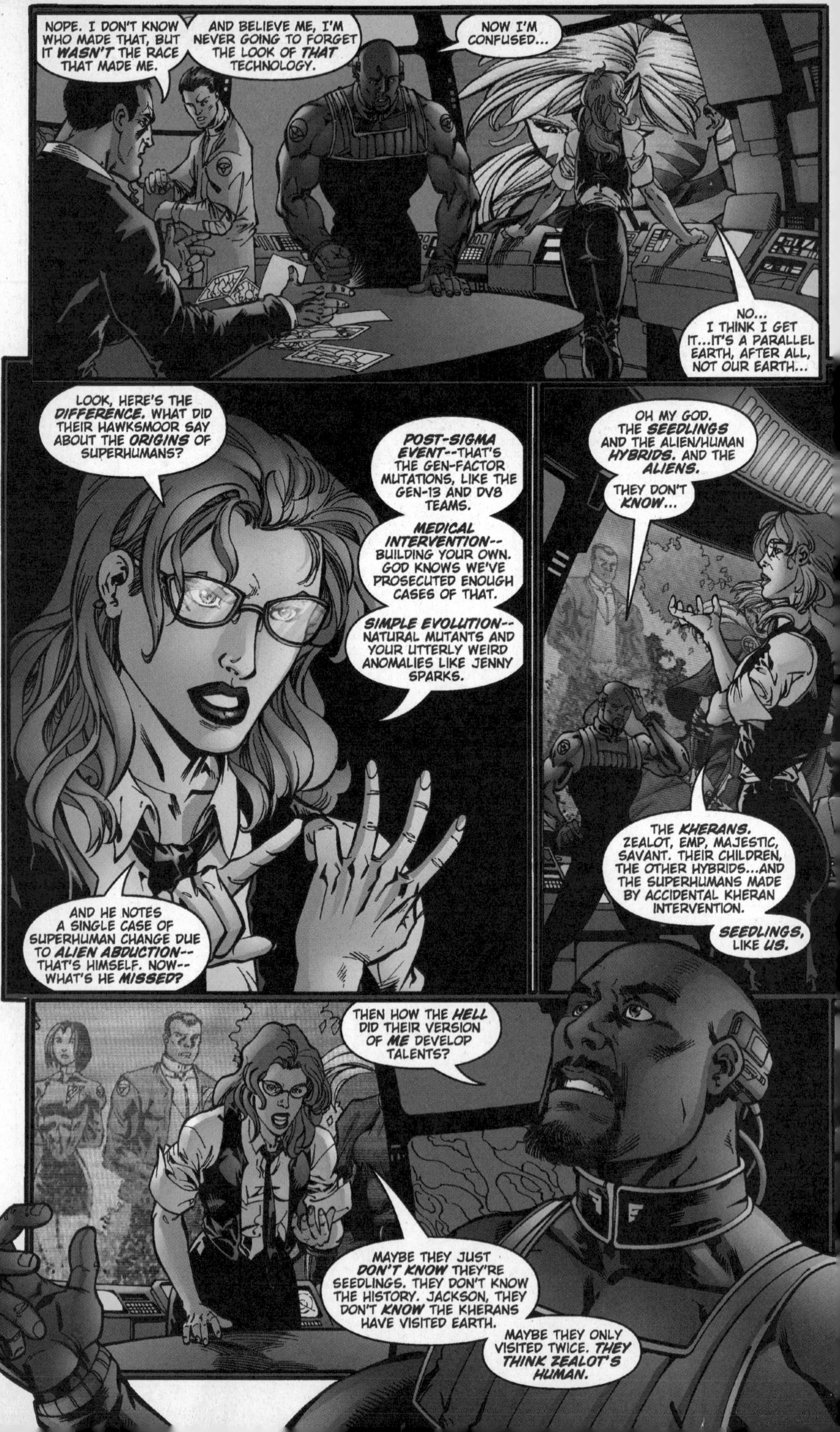
NOPE. I DON'T KNOW WHO MADE THAT, BUT IT WASN'T THE RACE THAT MADE ME.
AND BELIEVE ME, I'M NEVER GOING TO FORGET THE LOOK OF THAT TECHNOLOGY.
NOW I'M CONFUSED...
NO... I THINK I GET IT...IT'S A PARALLEL EARTH, AFTER ALL, NOT OUR EARTH...
LOOK, HERE'S THE DIFFERENCE. WHAT DID THEIR HAWKSMOOR SAY ABOUT THE ORIGINS OF SUPERHUMANS?
POST-SIGMA EVENT--THAT'S THE GEN-FACTOR MUTATIONS, LIKE THE GEN-13 AND DV8 TEAMS.
MEDICAL INTERVENTION--BUILDING YOUR OWN. GOD KNOWS WE'VE PROSECUTED ENOUGH CASES OF THAT.
SIMPLE EVOLUTION--NATURAL MUTANTS AND YOUR UTTERLY WEIRD ANOMALIES LIKE JENNY SPARKS.
AND HE NOTES A SINGLE CASE OF SUPERHUMAN CHANGE DUE TO ALIEN ABDUCTION--THAT'S HIMSELF. NOW--WHAT'S HE MISSED?
OH MY GOD. THE SEEDLINGS AND THE ALIEN/HUMAN HYBRIDS. AND THE ALIENS.
THEY DON'T KNOW...
THE KHERANS. ZEALOT, EMP, MAJESTIC, SAVANT. THEIR CHILDREN, THE OTHER HYBRIDS...AND THE SUPERHUMANS MADE BY ACCIDENTAL KHERAN INTERVENTION.
SEEDLINGS, LIKE US.
THEN HOW THE HELL DID THEIR VERSION OF ME DEVELOP TALENTS?
MAYBE THEY JUST DON'T KNOW THEY'RE SEEDLINGS. THEY DON'T KNOW THE HISTORY. JACKSON, THEY DON'T KNOW THE KHERANS HAVE VISITED EARTH.
MAYBE THEY ONLY VISITED TWICE. THEY THINK ZEALOT'S HUMAN.

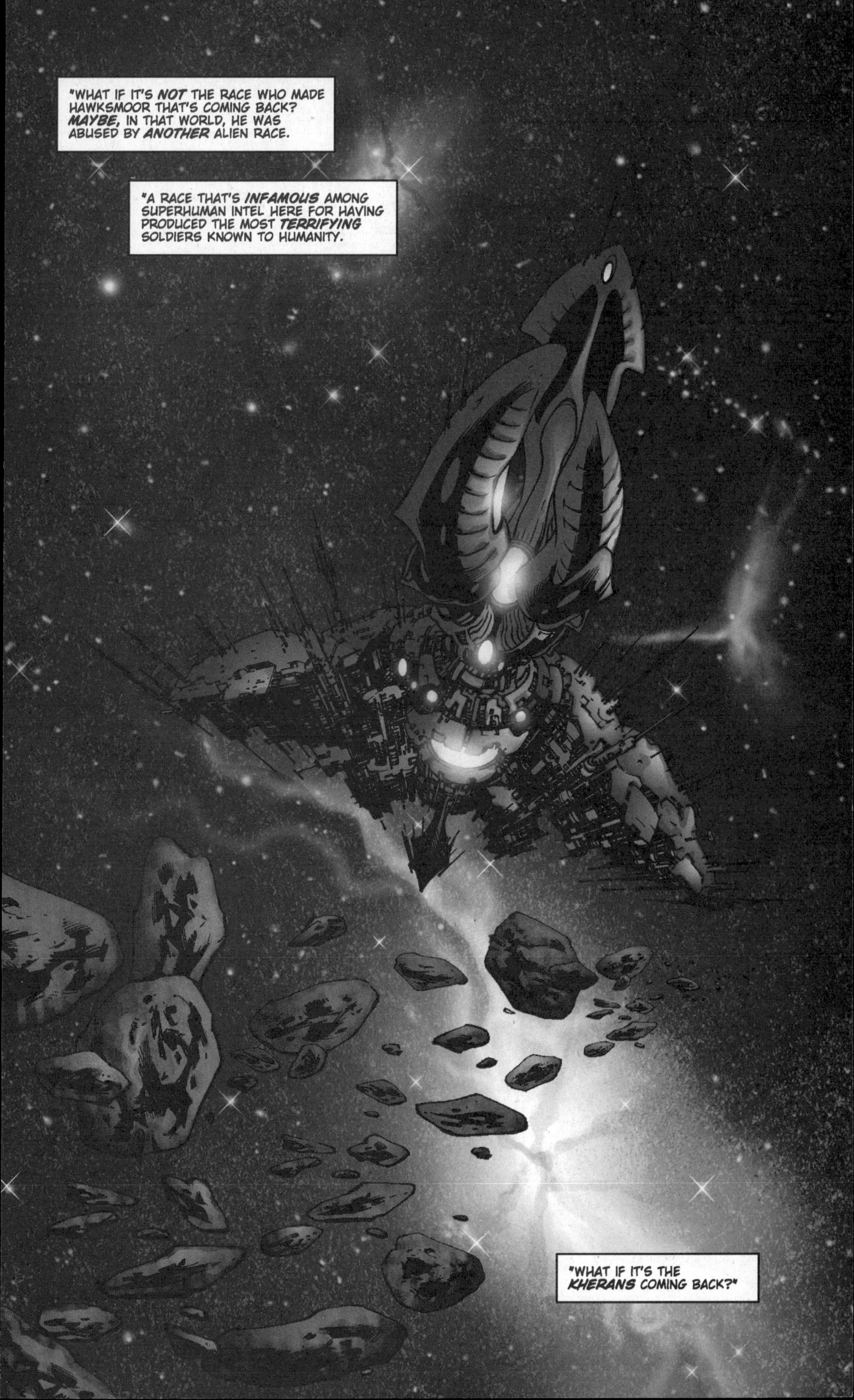
"WHAT IF IT'S NOT THE RACE WHO MADE HAWKSMOOR THAT'S COMING BACK? MAYBE, IN THAT WORLD, HE WAS ABUSED BY ANOTHER ALIEN RACE.
"A RACE THAT'S INFAMOUS AMONG SUPERHUMAN INTEL HERE FOR HAVING PRODUCED THE MOST TERRIFYING SOLDIERS KNOWN TO HUMANITY.
"WHAT IF IT'S THE KHERANS COMING BACK?"

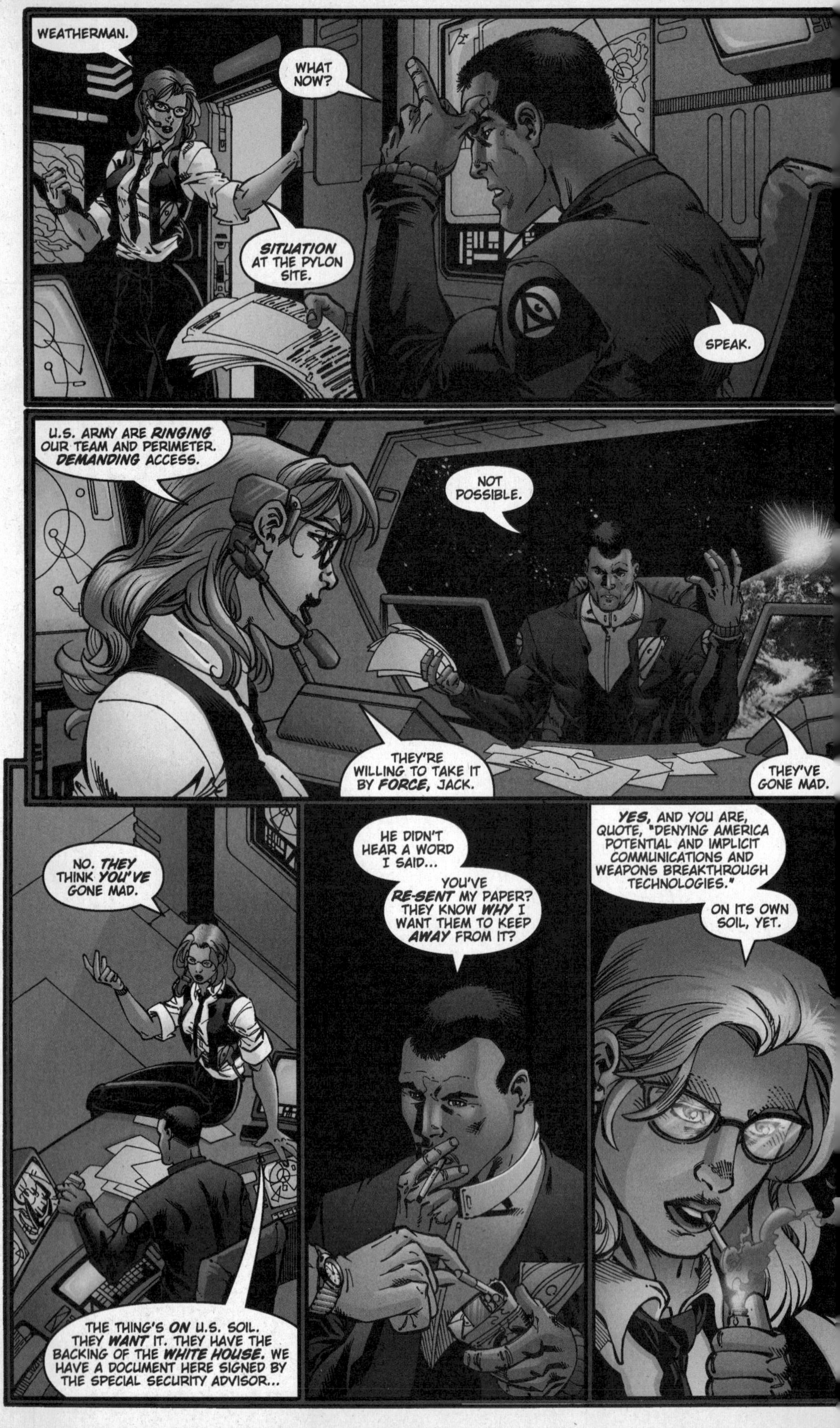
WEATHERMAN.
WHAT NOW?
SITUATION AT THE PYLON SITE.
SPEAK.
U.S. ARMY ARE RINGING OUR TEAM AND PERIMETER. DEMANDING ACCESS.
NOT POSSIBLE.
THEY'RE WILLING TO TAKE IT BY FORCE, JACK.
THEY'VE GONE MAD.
NO. THEY THINK YOU'VE GONE MAD.
THE THING'S ON U.S. SOIL. THEY WANT IT. THEY HAVE THE BACKING OF THE WHITE HOUSE. WE HAVE A DOCUMENT HERE SIGNED BY THE SPECIAL SECURITY ADVISOR...
HE DIDN'T HEAR A WORD I SAID...
YOU'VE RE-SENT MY PAPER? THEY KNOW WHY I WANT THEM TO KEEP AWAY FROM IT?
YES, AND YOU ARE, QUOTE, "DENYING AMERICA POTENTIAL AND IMPLICIT COMMUNICATIONS AND WEAPONS BREAKTHROUGH TECHNOLOGIES."
ON ITS OWN SOIL, YET.

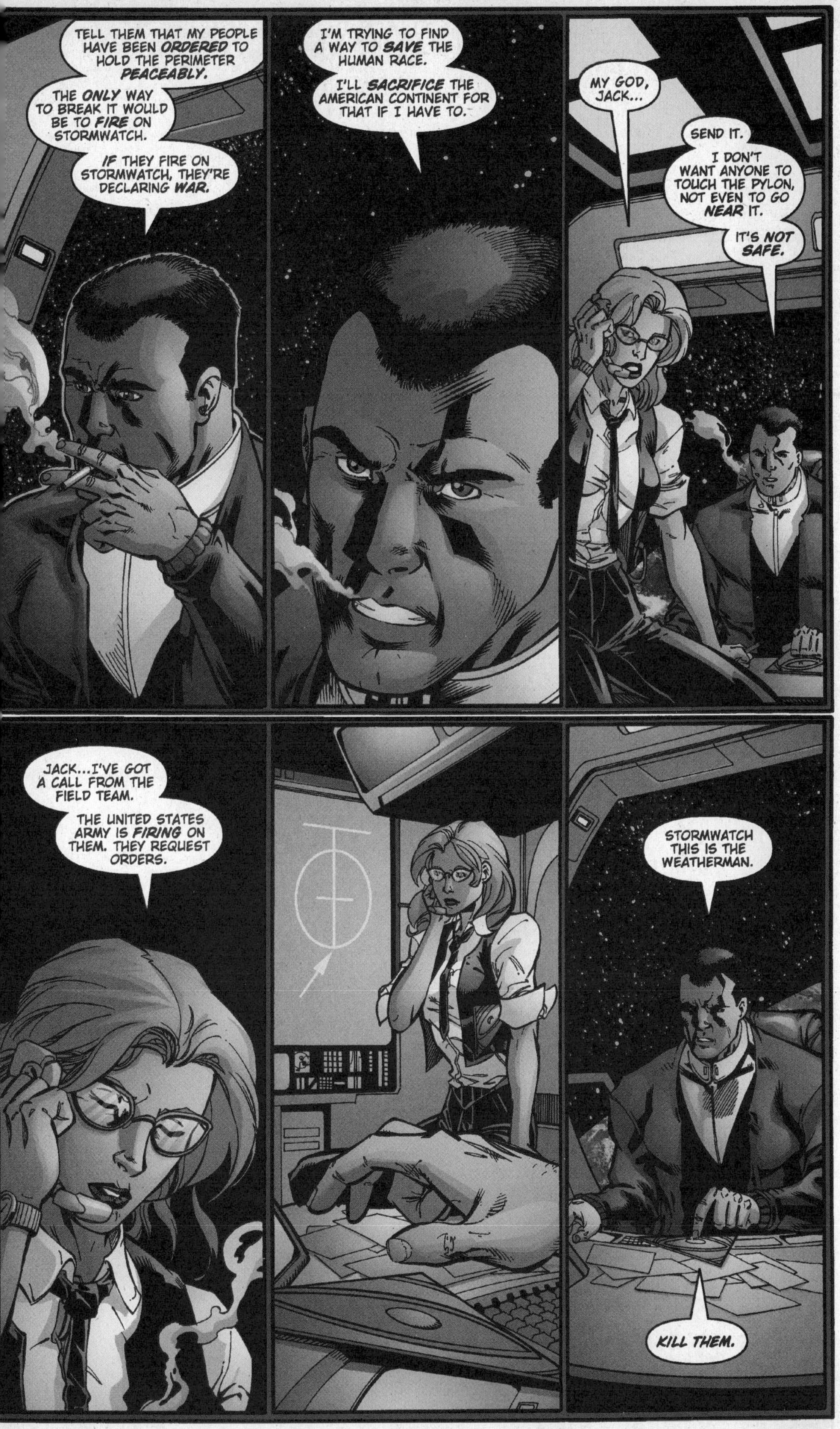
TELL THEM THAT MY PEOPLE HAVE BEEN *ORDERED* TO HOLD THE PERIMETER *PEACEABLY.*
THE *ONLY* WAY TO BREAK IT WOULD BE TO *FIRE* ON STORMWATCH.
IF THEY FIRE ON STORMWATCH, THEY'RE DECLARING *WAR.*
I'M TRYING TO FIND A WAY TO *SAVE* THE HUMAN RACE.
I'LL *SACRIFICE* THE AMERICAN CONTINENT FOR THAT IF I HAVE TO.
MY GOD, JACK...
SEND IT.
I DON'T WANT ANYONE TO TOUCH THE PYLON, NOT EVEN TO GO *NEAR* IT.
IT'S *NOT SAFE.*
JACK...I'VE GOT A CALL FROM THE FIELD TEAM.
THE UNITED STATES ARMY IS *FIRING* ON THEM. THEY REQUEST ORDERS.
STORMWATCH THIS IS THE WEATHERMAN.
KILL THEM.

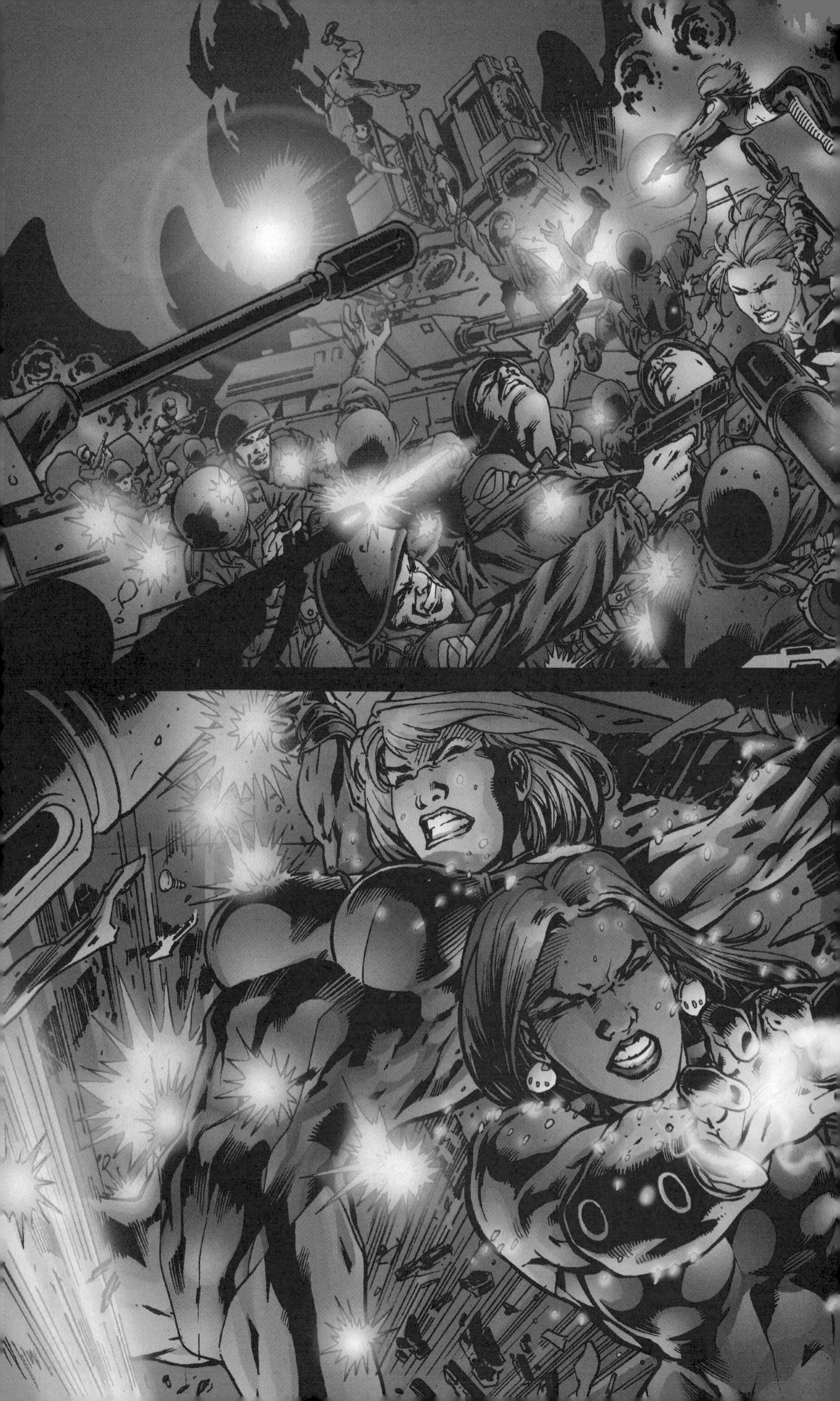

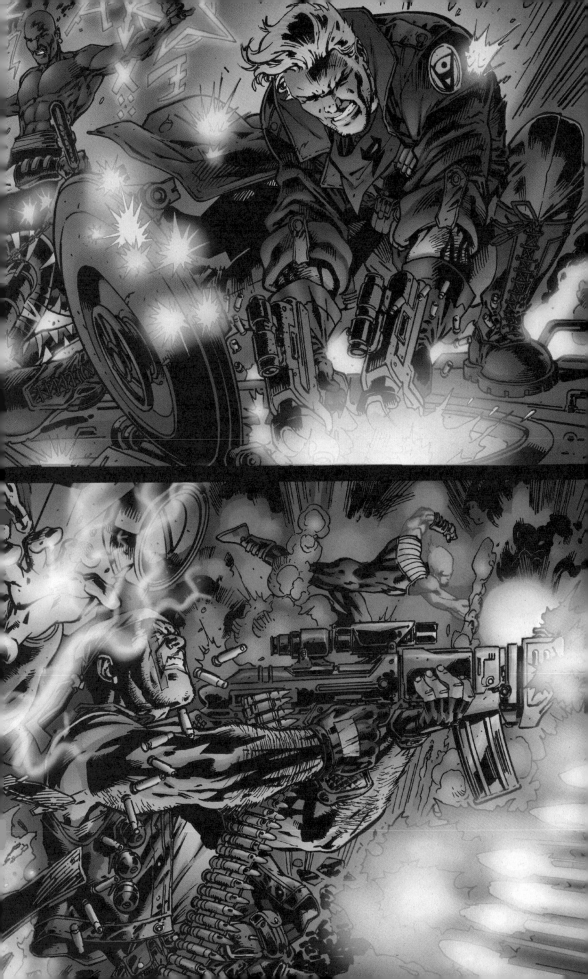

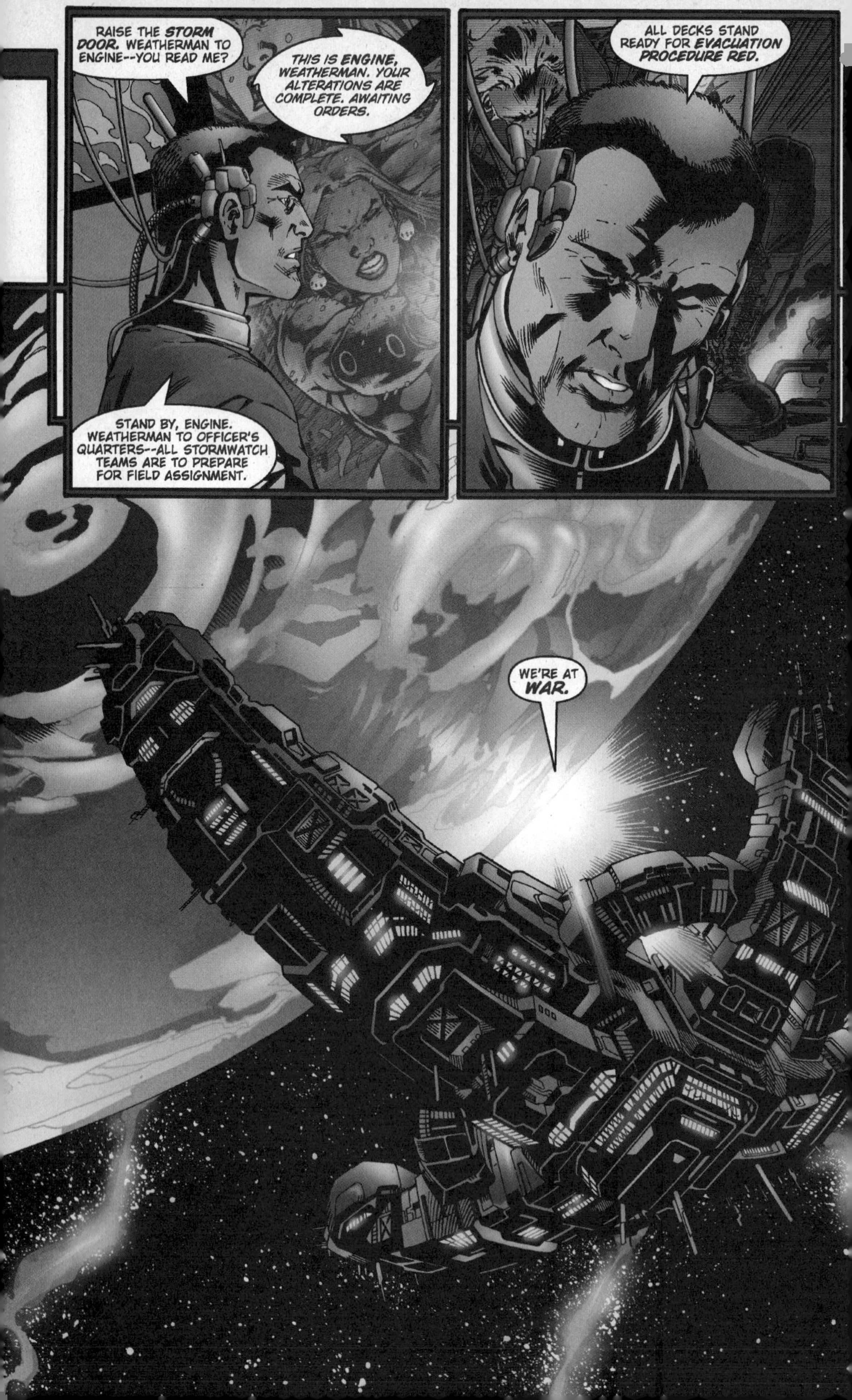
RAISE THE STORM DOOR. WEATHERMAN TO ENGINE--YOU READ ME?
THIS IS ENGINE, WEATHERMAN. YOUR ALTERATIONS ARE COMPLETE. AWAITING ORDERS.
STAND BY, ENGINE. WEATHERMAN TO OFFICER'S QUARTERS--ALL STORMWATCH TEAMS ARE TO PREPARE FOR FIELD ASSIGNMENT.
ALL DECKS STAND READY FOR EVACUATION PROCEDURE RED.
WE'RE AT WAR.

FROM THE LOG OF
JACK HAWKSMOOR,
WEATHERMAN:

*MY GOD. I'VE HAD TO GO TO **WAR** WITH AMERICA, JUST TO SAVE THE REST OF YOU...*

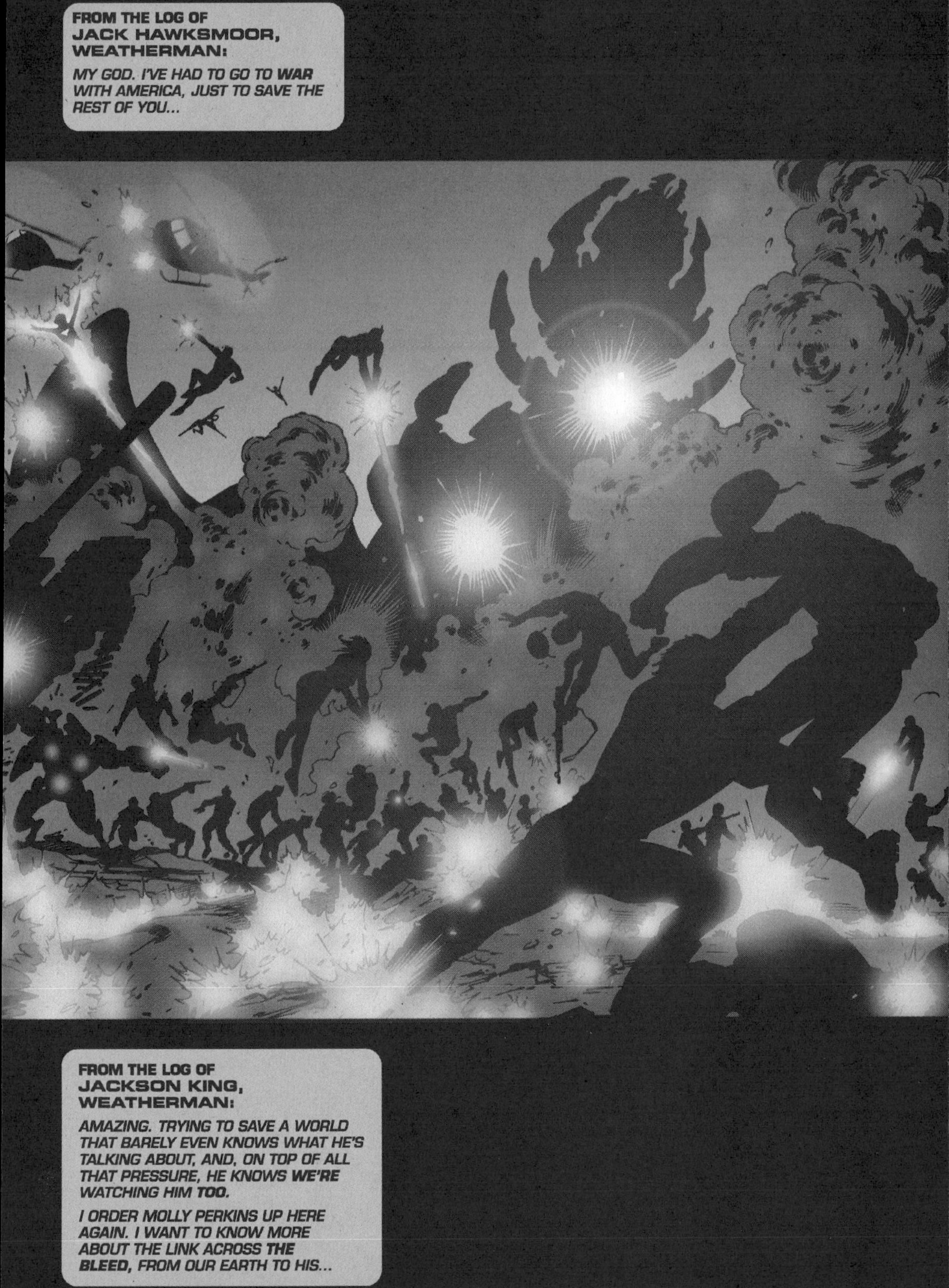

FROM THE LOG OF
JACKSON KING,
WEATHERMAN:

*AMAZING. TRYING TO SAVE A WORLD THAT BARELY EVEN KNOWS WHAT HE'S TALKING ABOUT, AND, ON TOP OF ALL THAT PRESSURE, HE KNOWS **WE'RE** WATCHING HIM **TOO**.*

*I ORDER MOLLY PERKINS UP HERE AGAIN. I WANT TO KNOW MORE ABOUT THE LINK ACROSS **THE BLEED**, FROM OUR EARTH TO HIS...*

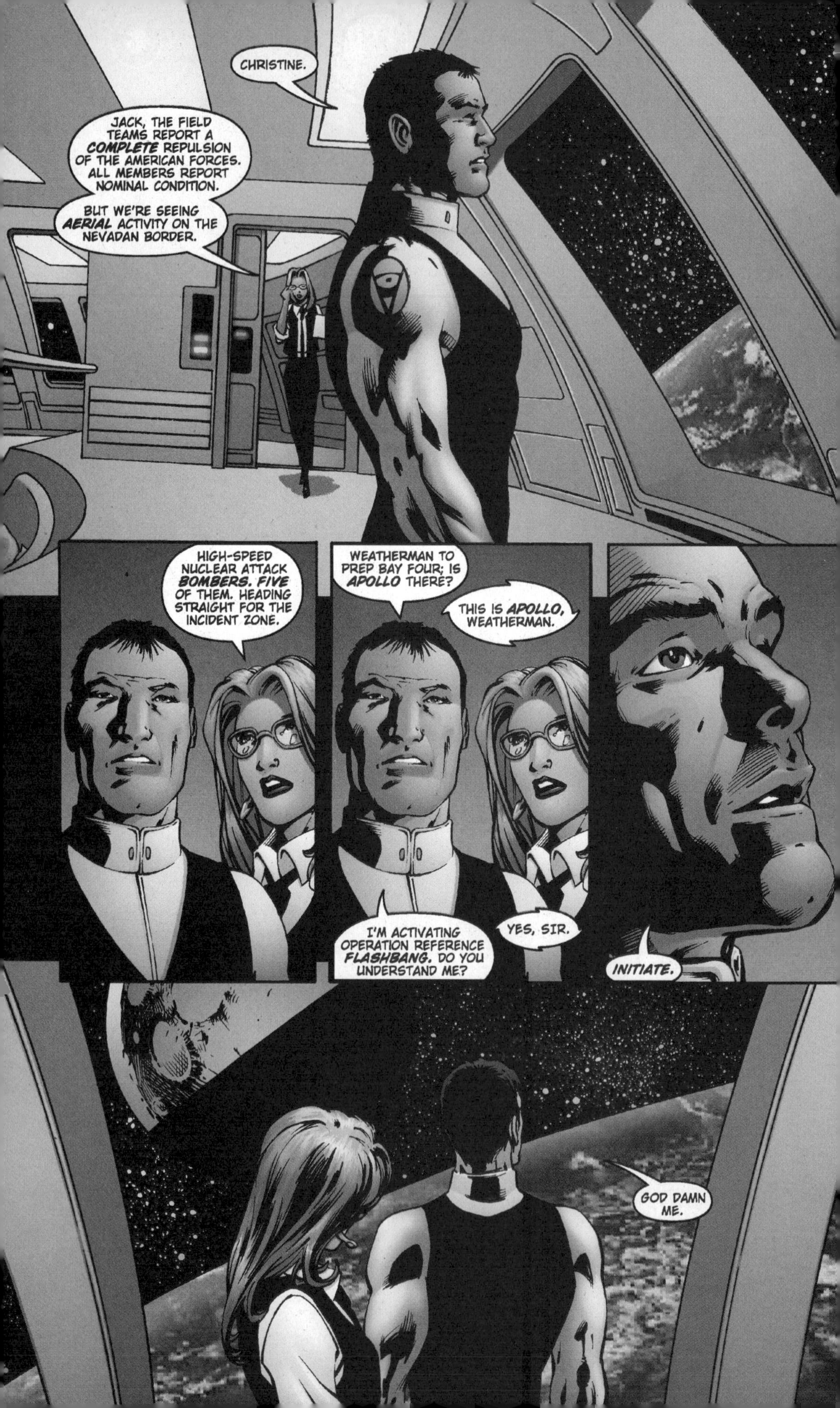
CHRISTINE.
JACK, THE FIELD TEAMS REPORT A COMPLETE REPULSION OF THE AMERICAN FORCES. ALL MEMBERS REPORT NOMINAL CONDITION.
BUT WE'RE SEEING AERIAL ACTIVITY ON THE NEVADAN BORDER.
HIGH-SPEED NUCLEAR ATTACK BOMBERS. FIVE OF THEM. HEADING STRAIGHT FOR THE INCIDENT ZONE.
WEATHERMAN TO PREP BAY FOUR; IS APOLLO THERE?
THIS IS APOLLO, WEATHERMAN.
I'M ACTIVATING OPERATION REFERENCE FLASHBANG. DO YOU UNDERSTAND ME?
YES, SIR.
INITIATE.
GOD DAMN ME.

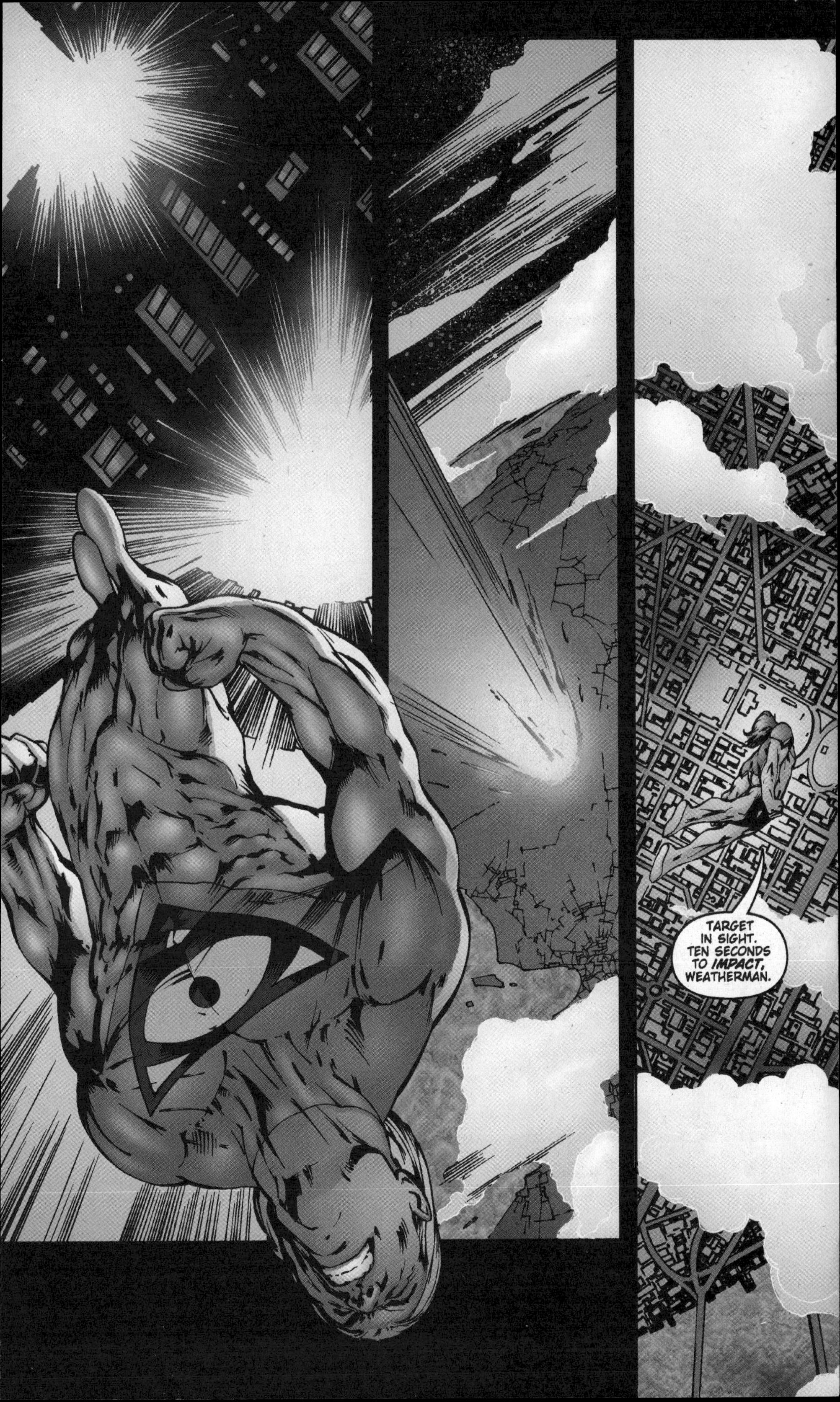
TARGET IN SIGHT. TEN SECONDS TO *IMPACT,* WEATHERMAN.

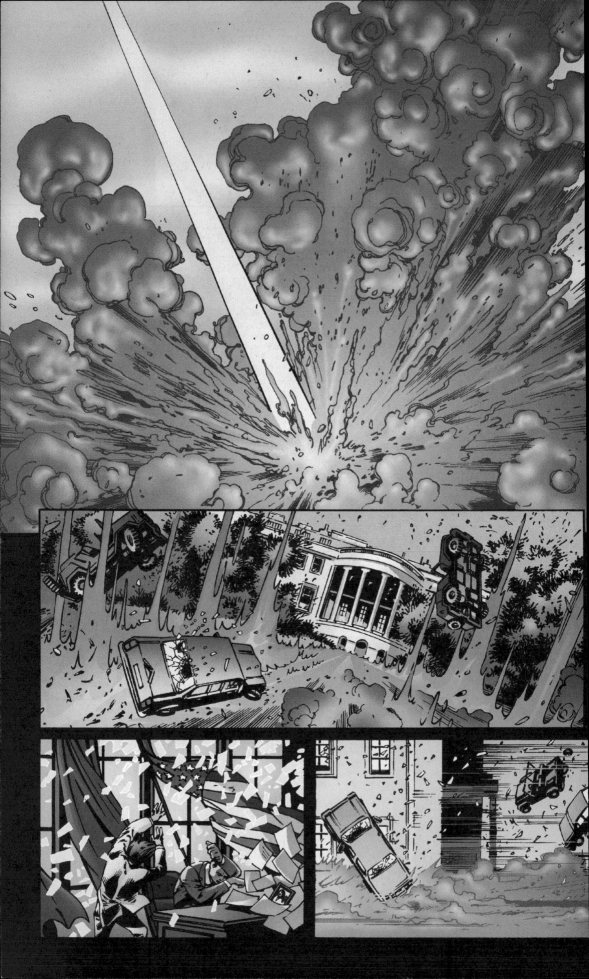

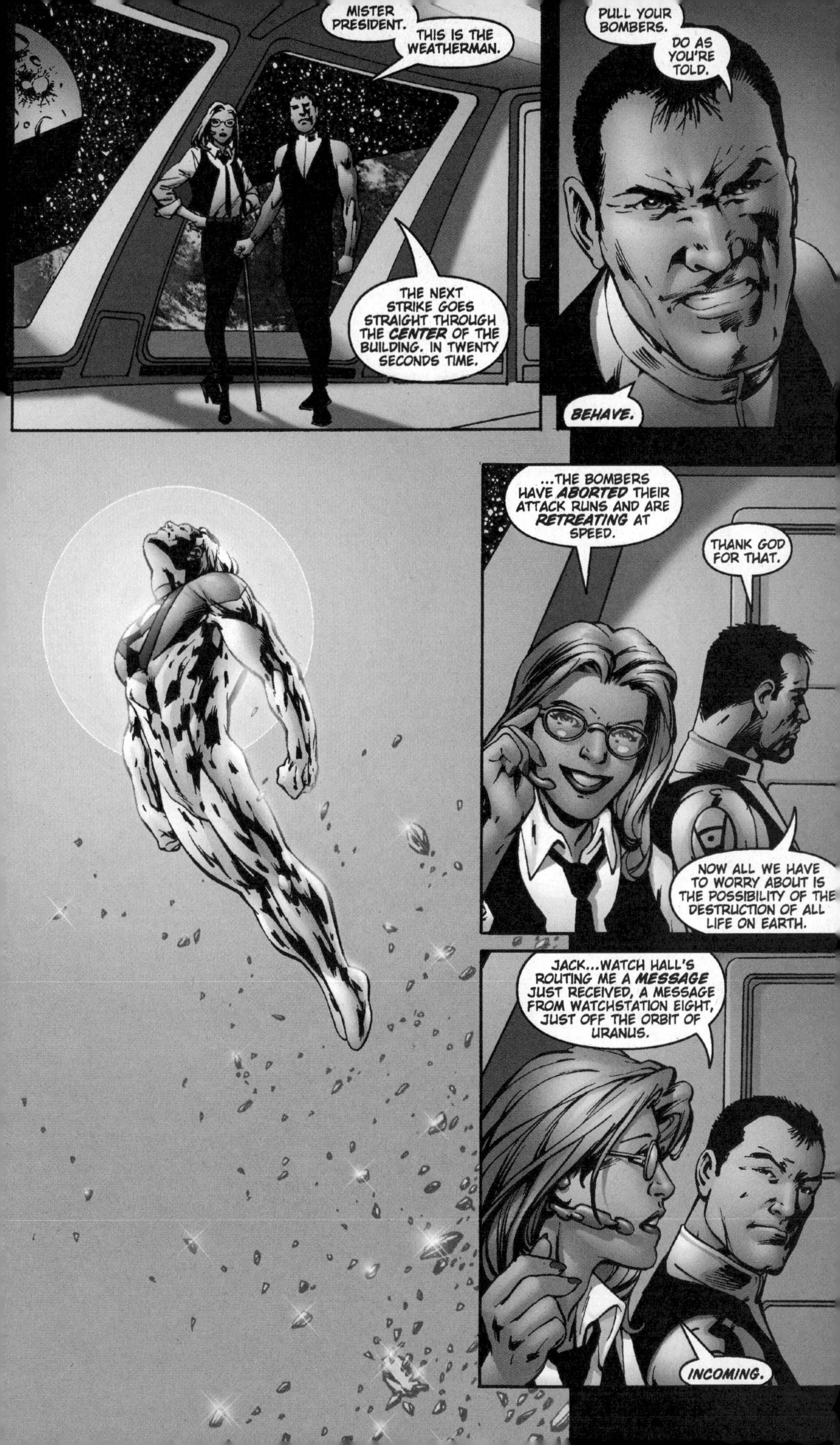
MISTER PRESIDENT.
THIS IS THE WEATHERMAN.
THE NEXT STRIKE GOES STRAIGHT THROUGH THE CENTER OF THE BUILDING. IN TWENTY SECONDS TIME.
PULL YOUR BOMBERS.
DO AS YOU'RE TOLD.
BEHAVE.
...THE BOMBERS HAVE ABORTED THEIR ATTACK RUNS AND ARE RETREATING AT SPEED.
THANK GOD FOR THAT.
NOW ALL WE HAVE TO WORRY ABOUT IS THE POSSIBILITY OF THE DESTRUCTION OF ALL LIFE ON EARTH.
JACK...WATCH HALL'S ROUTING ME A MESSAGE JUST RECEIVED, A MESSAGE FROM WATCHSTATION EIGHT, JUST OFF THE ORBIT OF URANUS.
INCOMING.

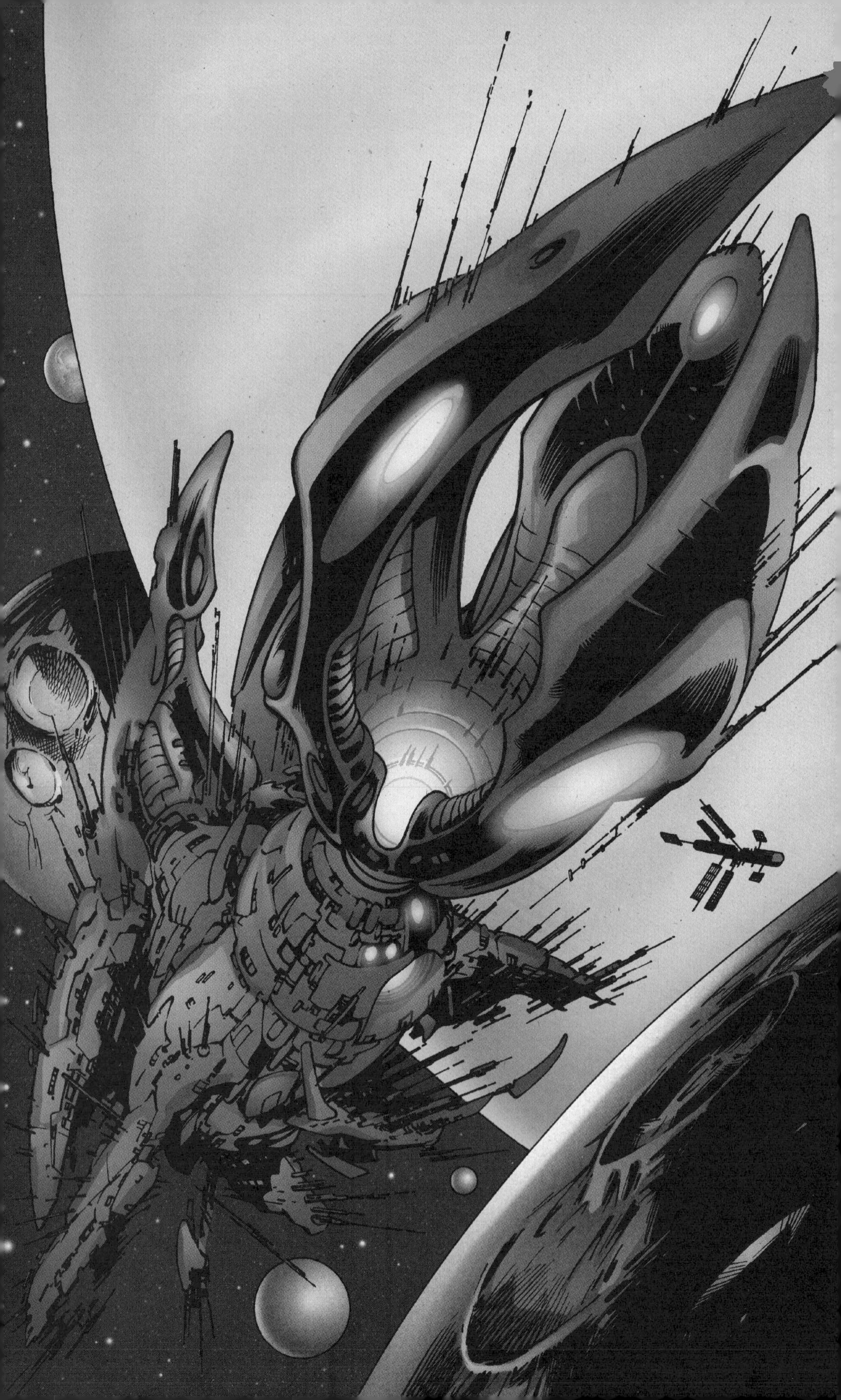

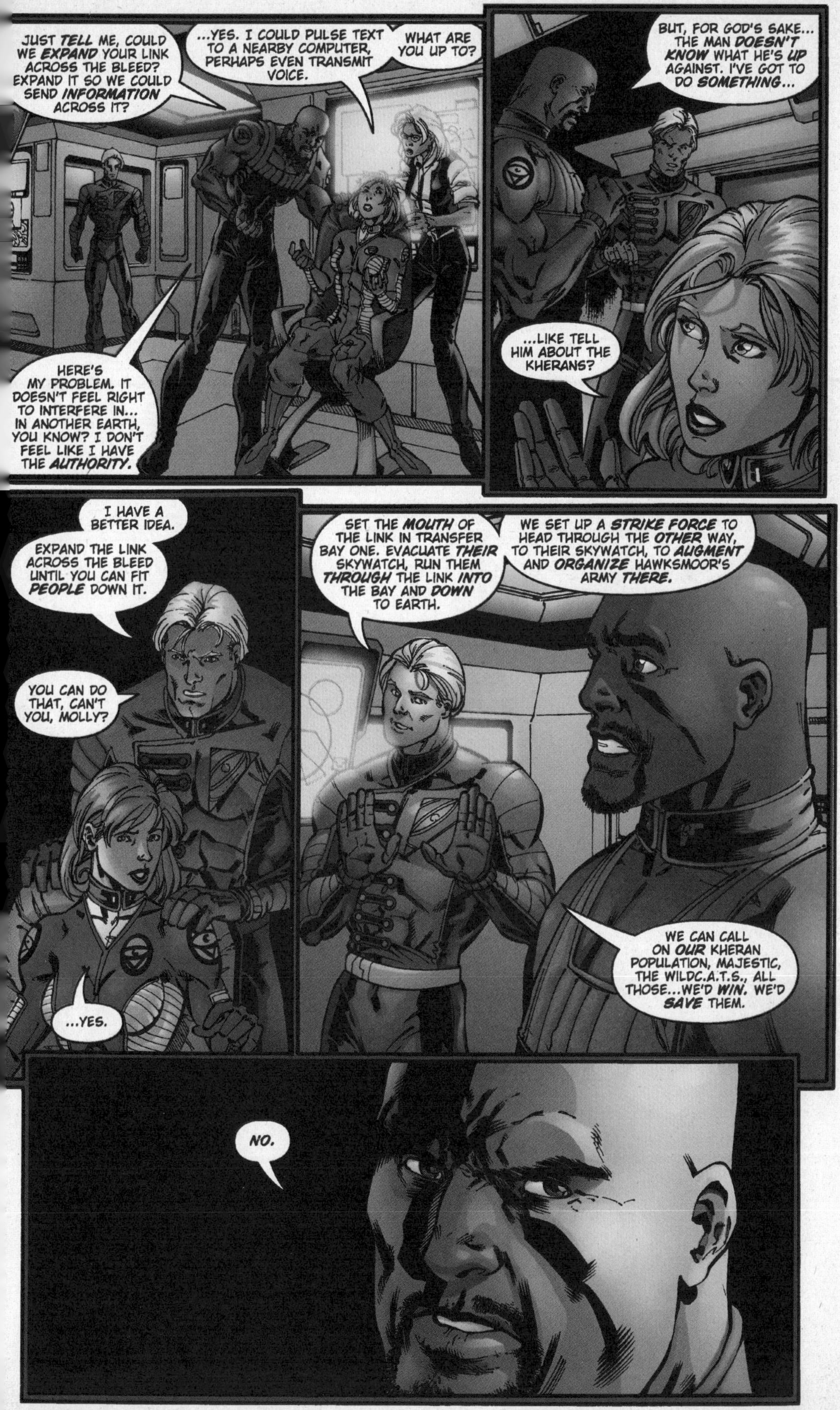
JUST TELL ME, COULD WE EXPAND YOUR LINK ACROSS THE BLEED? EXPAND IT SO WE COULD SEND INFORMATION ACROSS IT?
...YES. I COULD PULSE TEXT TO A NEARBY COMPUTER, PERHAPS EVEN TRANSMIT VOICE.
WHAT ARE YOU UP TO?
HERE'S MY PROBLEM. IT DOESN'T FEEL RIGHT TO INTERFERE IN... IN ANOTHER EARTH, YOU KNOW? I DON'T FEEL LIKE I HAVE THE AUTHORITY.
BUT, FOR GOD'S SAKE... THE MAN DOESN'T KNOW WHAT HE'S UP AGAINST. I'VE GOT TO DO SOMETHING...
...LIKE TELL HIM ABOUT THE KHERANS?
I HAVE A BETTER IDEA.
EXPAND THE LINK ACROSS THE BLEED UNTIL YOU CAN FIT PEOPLE DOWN IT.
YOU CAN DO THAT, CAN'T YOU, MOLLY?
...YES.
SET THE MOUTH OF THE LINK IN TRANSFER BAY ONE. EVACUATE THEIR SKYWATCH, RUN THEM THROUGH THE LINK INTO THE BAY AND DOWN TO EARTH.
WE SET UP A STRIKE FORCE TO HEAD THROUGH THE OTHER WAY, TO THEIR SKYWATCH, TO AUGMENT AND ORGANIZE HAWKSMOOR'S ARMY THERE.
WE CAN CALL ON OUR KHERAN POPULATION, MAJESTIC, THE WILDC.A.T.S., ALL THOSE...WE'D WIN. WE'D SAVE THEM.
NO.

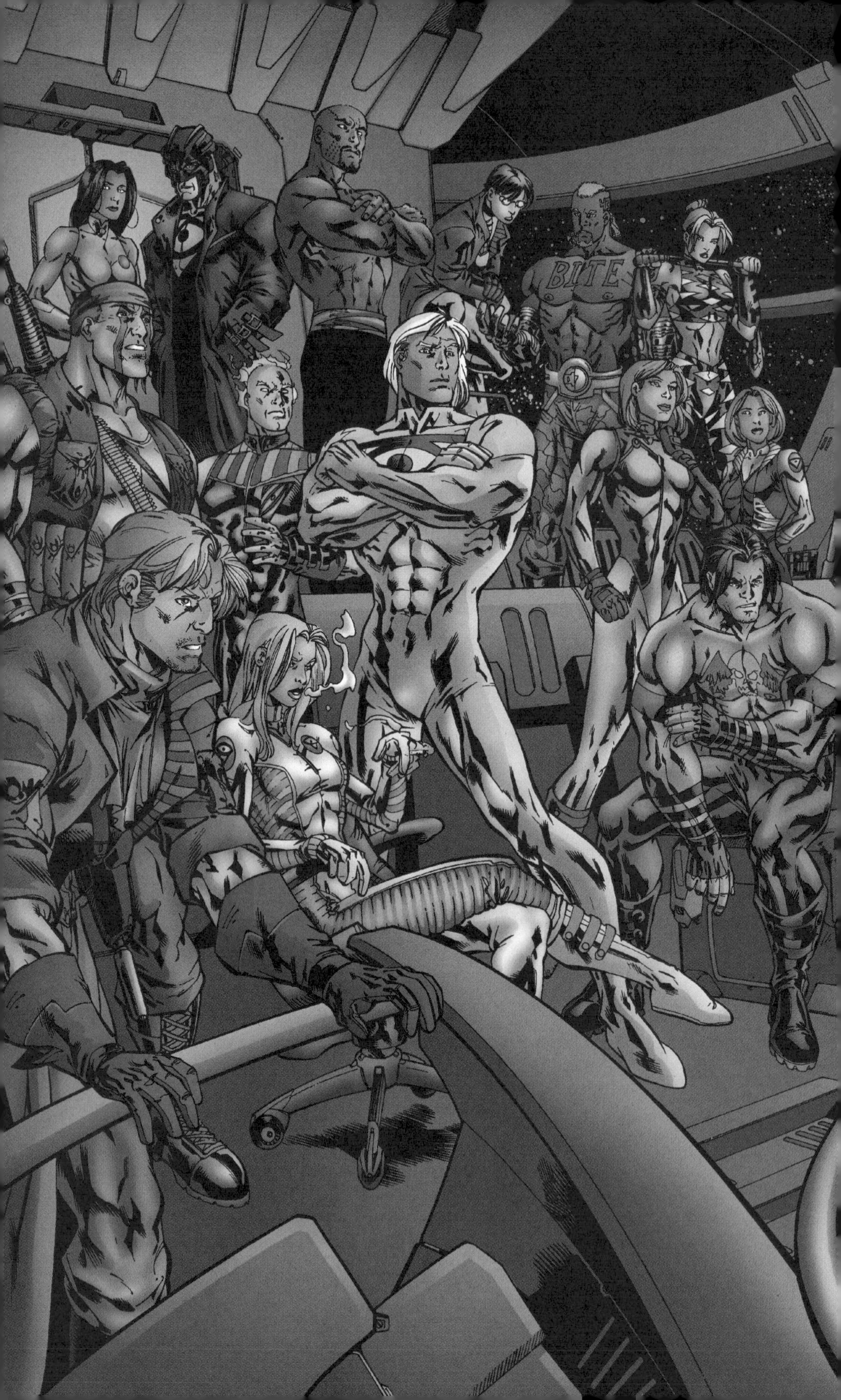
BITE

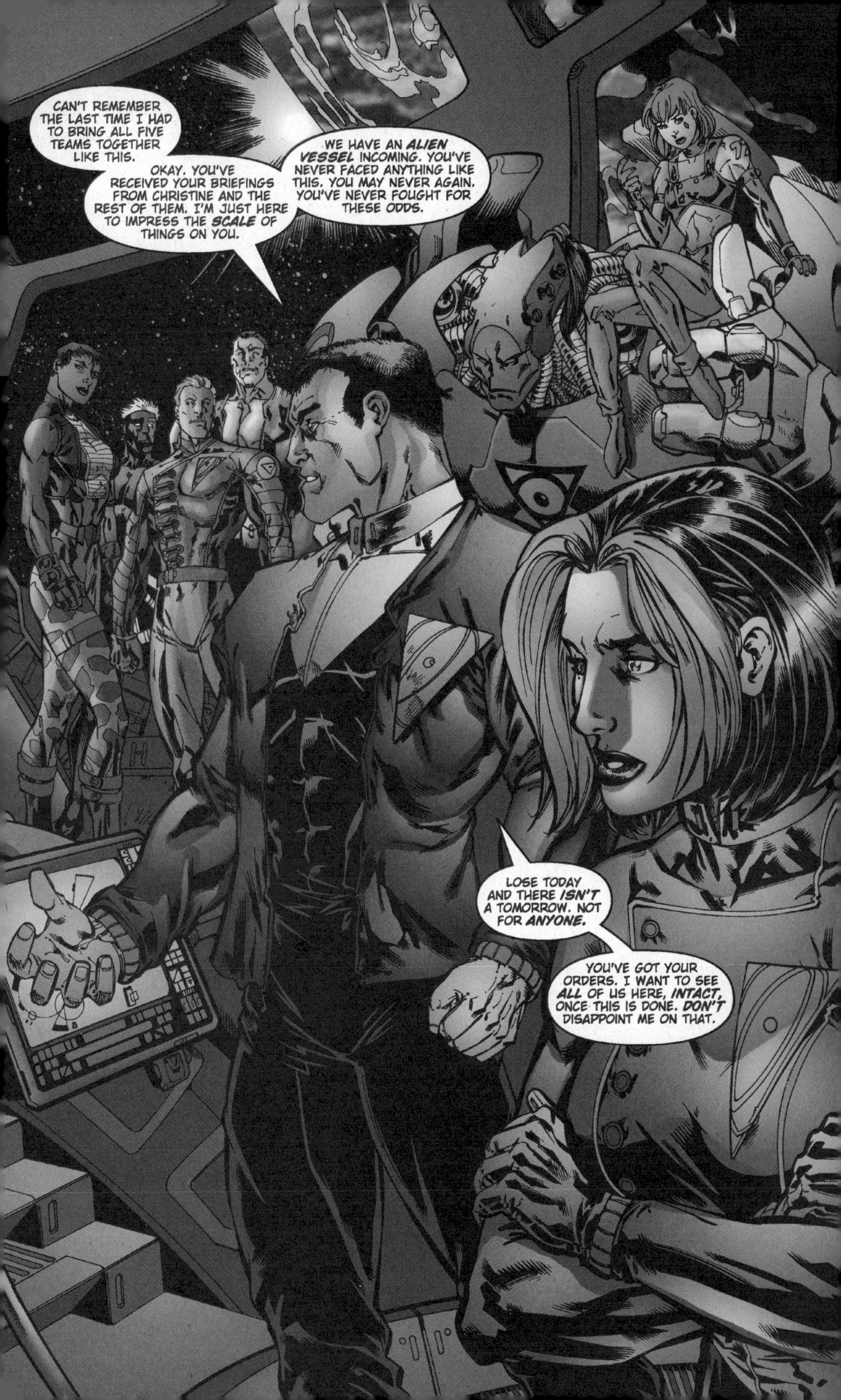
CAN'T REMEMBER THE LAST TIME I HAD TO BRING ALL FIVE TEAMS TOGETHER LIKE THIS.
OKAY. YOU'VE RECEIVED YOUR BRIEFINGS FROM CHRISTINE AND THE REST OF THEM. I'M JUST HERE TO IMPRESS THE *SCALE* OF THINGS ON YOU.
WE HAVE AN *ALIEN VESSEL* INCOMING. YOU'VE NEVER FACED ANYTHING LIKE THIS. YOU MAY NEVER AGAIN. YOU'VE NEVER FOUGHT FOR THESE *ODDS*.
LOSE TODAY AND THERE *ISN'T* A TOMORROW. NOT FOR *ANYONE*.
YOU'VE GOT YOUR ORDERS. I WANT TO SEE *ALL* OF US HERE, *INTACT*, ONCE THIS IS DONE. *DON'T* DISAPPOINT ME ON THAT.

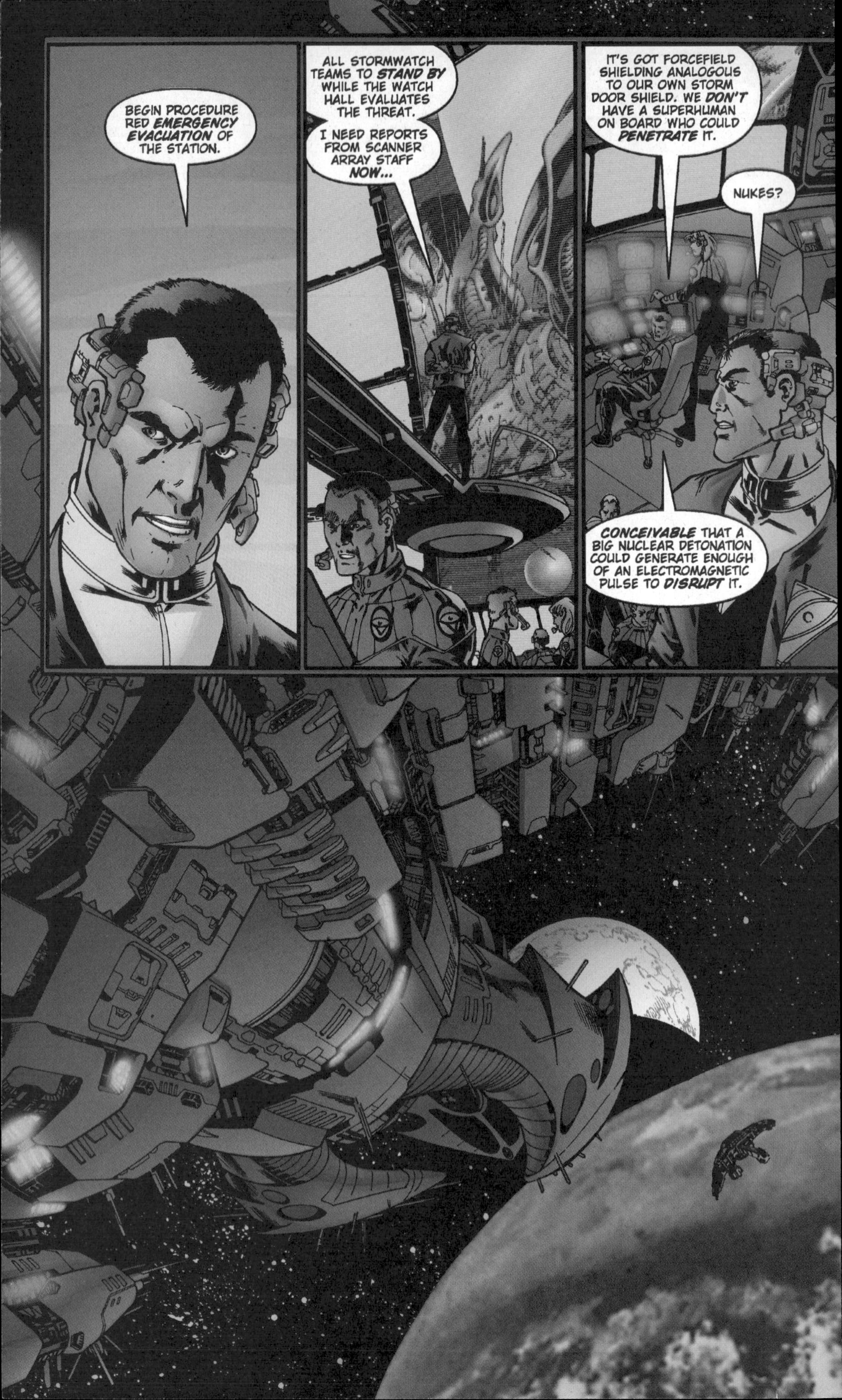
BEGIN PROCEDURE RED EMERGENCY EVACUATION OF THE STATION.
ALL STORMWATCH TEAMS TO STAND BY WHILE THE WATCH HALL EVALUATES THE THREAT.
I NEED REPORTS FROM SCANNER ARRAY STAFF NOW...
IT'S GOT FORCEFIELD SHIELDING ANALOGOUS TO OUR OWN STORM DOOR SHIELD. WE DON'T HAVE A SUPERHUMAN ON BOARD WHO COULD PENETRATE IT.
NUKES?
CONCEIVABLE THAT A BIG NUCLEAR DETONATION COULD GENERATE ENOUGH OF AN ELECTROMAGNETIC PULSE TO DISRUPT IT.

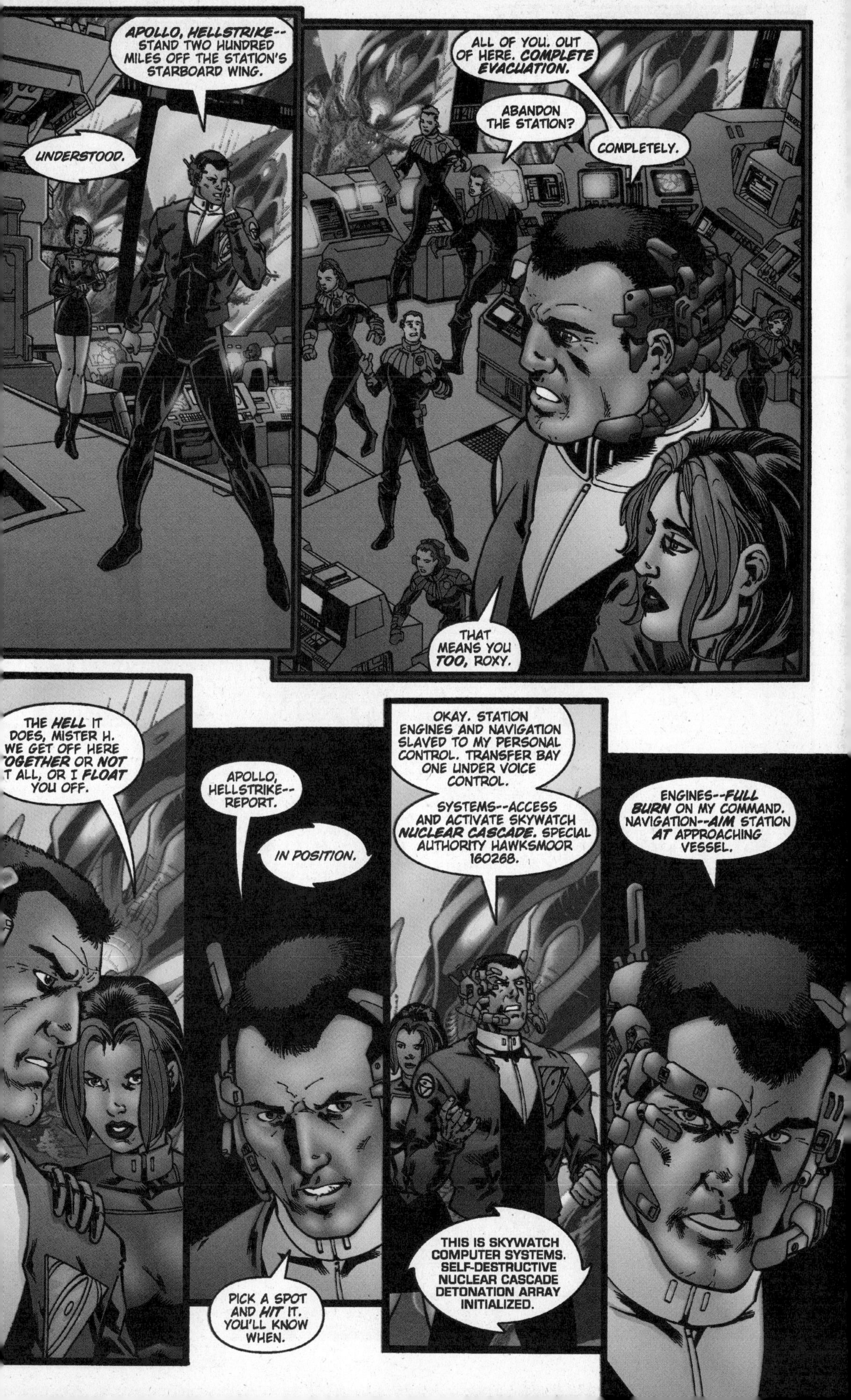

APOLLO, HELLSTRIKE-- STAND TWO HUNDRED MILES OFF THE STATION'S STARBOARD WING.
UNDERSTOOD.
ALL OF YOU. OUT OF HERE. COMPLETE EVACUATION.
ABANDON THE STATION?
COMPLETELY.
THAT MEANS YOU TOO, ROXY.
THE HELL IT DOES, MISTER H. WE GET OFF HERE TOGETHER OR NOT AT ALL, OR I FLOAT YOU OFF.
APOLLO, HELLSTRIKE-- REPORT.
IN POSITION.
PICK A SPOT AND HIT IT. YOU'LL KNOW WHEN.
OKAY. STATION ENGINES AND NAVIGATION SLAVED TO MY PERSONAL CONTROL. TRANSFER BAY ONE UNDER VOICE CONTROL.
SYSTEMS--ACCESS AND ACTIVATE SKYWATCH NUCLEAR CASCADE. SPECIAL AUTHORITY HAWKSMOOR 160268.
THIS IS SKYWATCH COMPUTER SYSTEMS. SELF-DESTRUCTIVE NUCLEAR CASCADE DETONATION ARRAY INITIALIZED.
ENGINES--FULL BURN ON MY COMMAND. NAVIGATION--AIM STATION AT APPROACHING VESSEL.

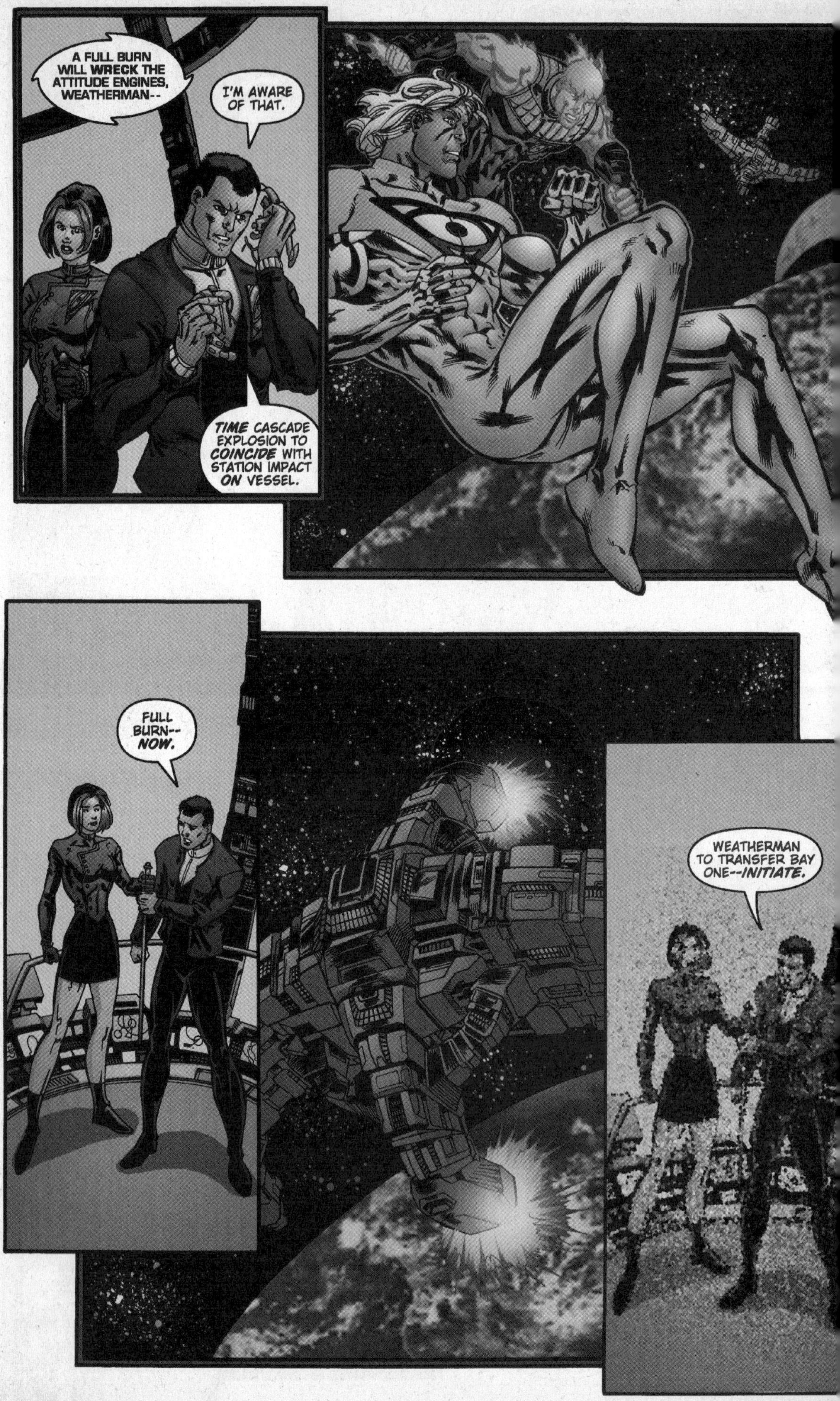
A FULL BURN WILL WRECK THE ATTITUDE ENGINES, WEATHERMAN--
I'M AWARE OF THAT.
TIME CASCADE EXPLOSION TO COINCIDE WITH STATION IMPACT ON VESSEL.
FULL BURN-- NOW.
WEATHERMAN TO TRANSFER BAY ONE--INITIATE.

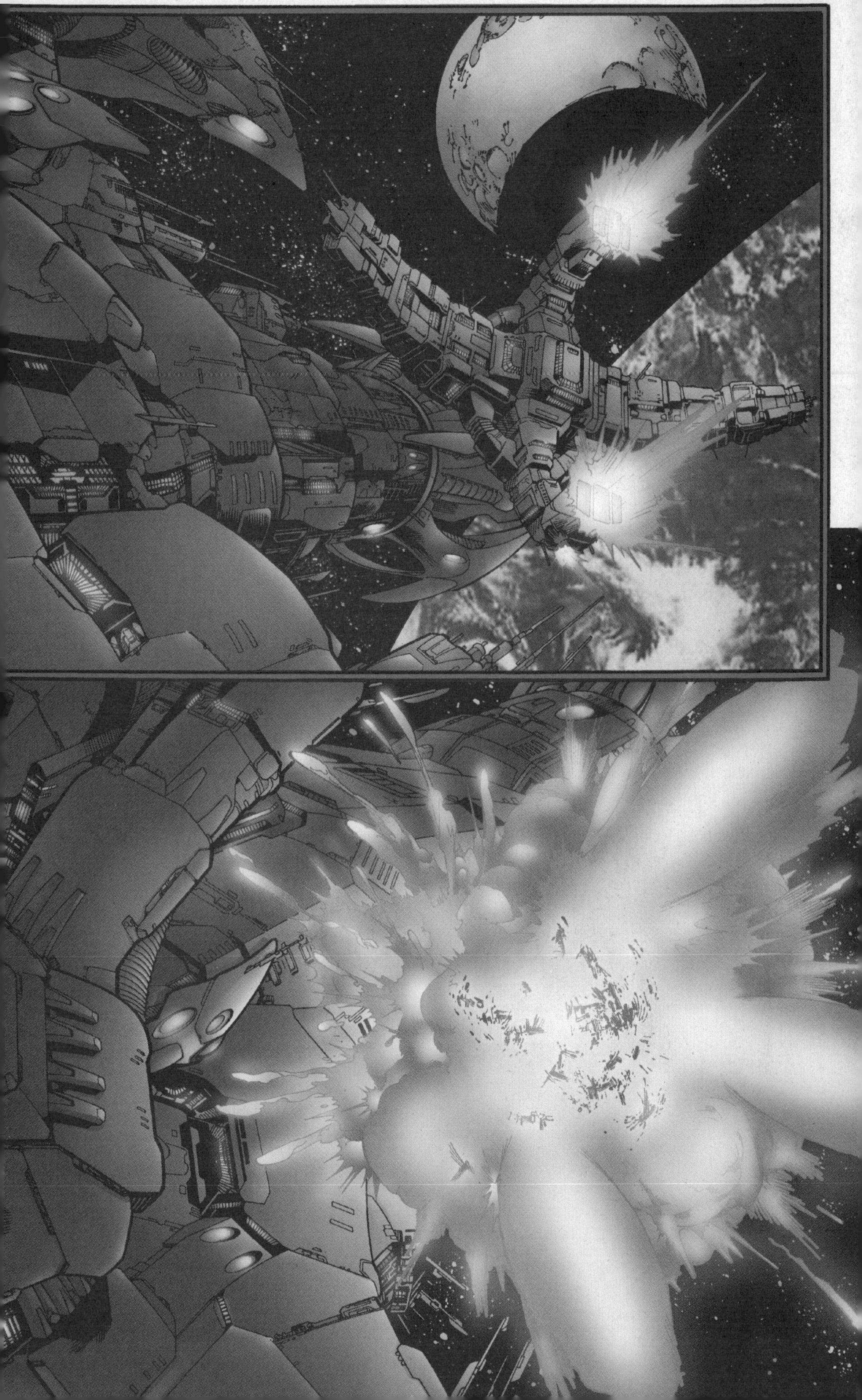

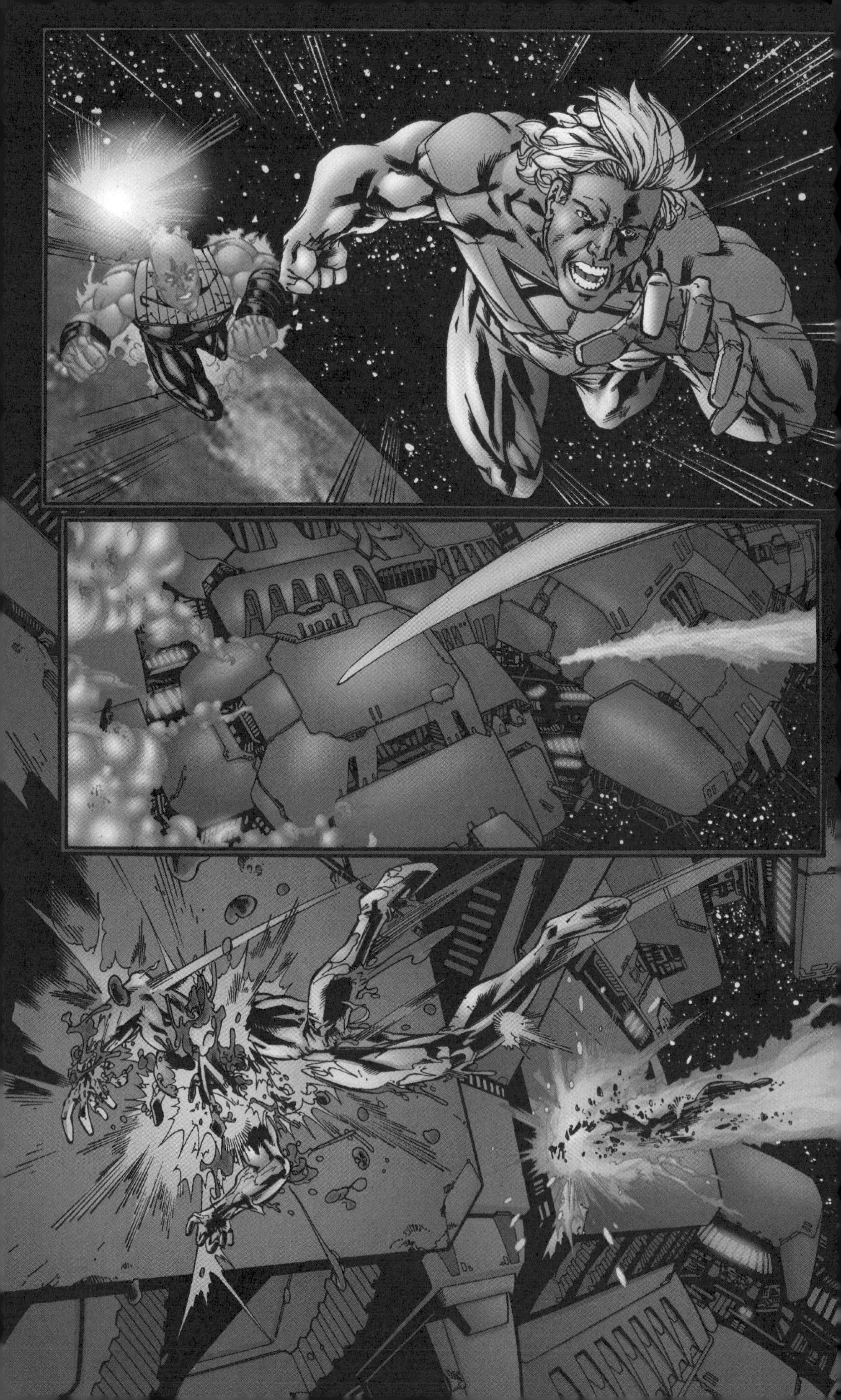

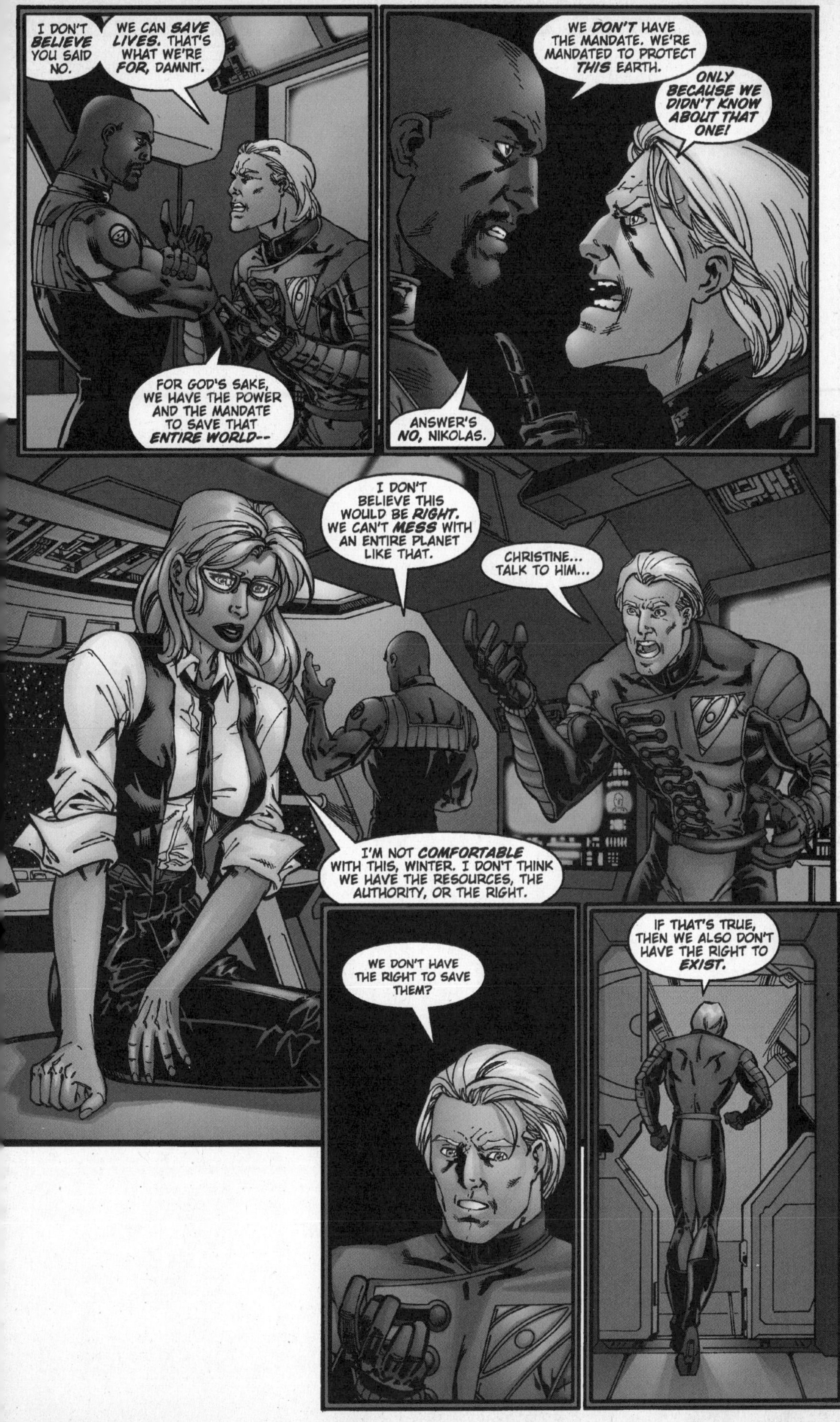
I DON'T BELIEVE YOU SAID NO.
WE CAN SAVE LIVES. THAT'S WHAT WE'RE FOR, DAMNIT.
FOR GOD'S SAKE, WE HAVE THE POWER AND THE MANDATE TO SAVE THAT ENTIRE WORLD--
WE DON'T HAVE THE MANDATE. WE'RE MANDATED TO PROTECT THIS EARTH.
ONLY BECAUSE WE DIDN'T KNOW ABOUT THAT ONE!
ANSWER'S NO, NIKOLAS.
I DON'T BELIEVE THIS WOULD BE RIGHT. WE CAN'T MESS WITH AN ENTIRE PLANET LIKE THAT.
CHRISTINE... TALK TO HIM...
I'M NOT COMFORTABLE WITH THIS, WINTER. I DON'T THINK WE HAVE THE RESOURCES, THE AUTHORITY, OR THE RIGHT.
WE DON'T HAVE THE RIGHT TO SAVE THEM?
IF THAT'S TRUE, THEN WE ALSO DON'T HAVE THE RIGHT TO EXIST.

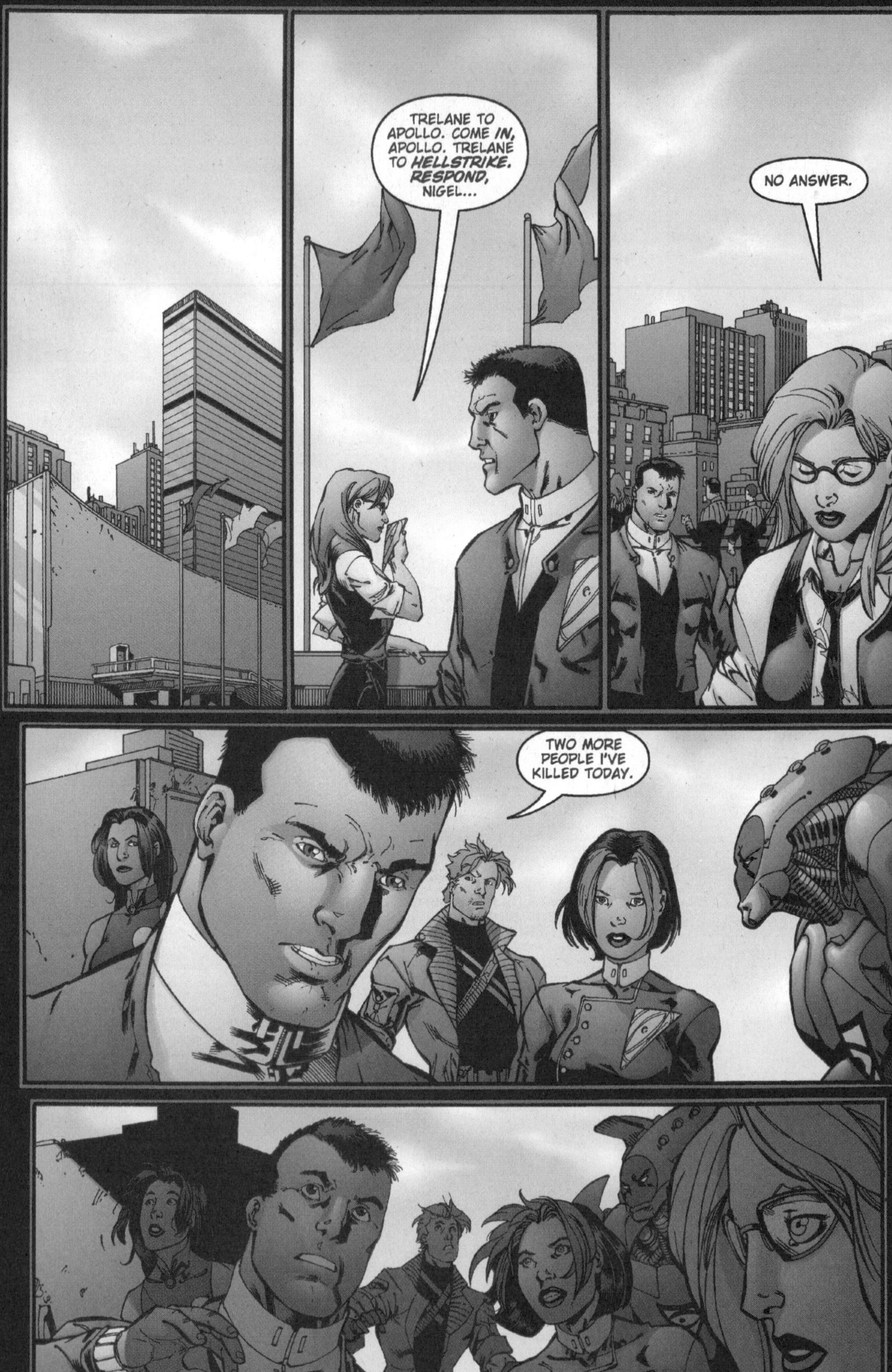
TRELANE TO APOLLO. COME IN, APOLLO. TRELANE TO HELLSTRIKE. RESPOND, NIGEL...
NO ANSWER.
TWO MORE PEOPLE I'VE KILLED TODAY.

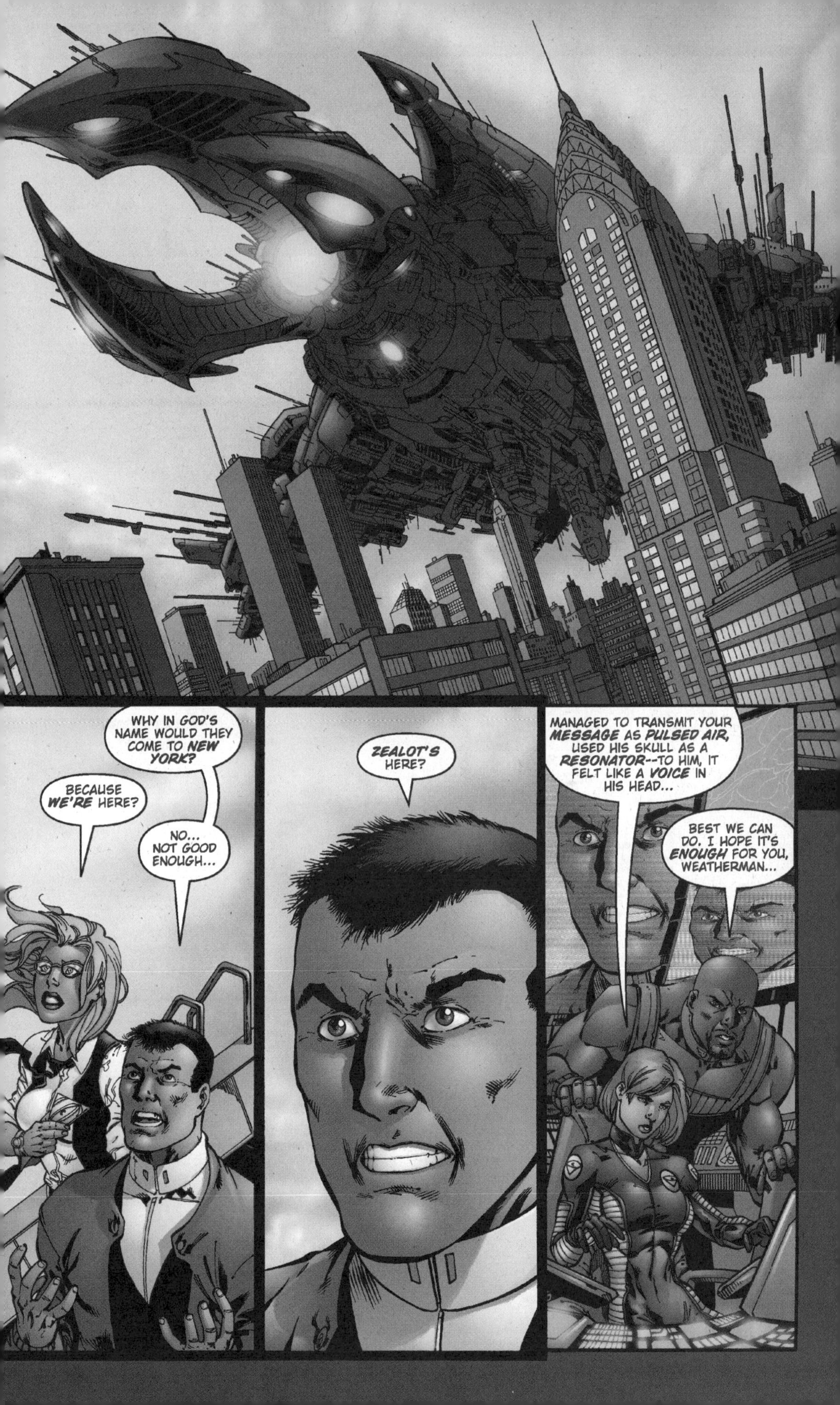
WHY IN GOD'S NAME WOULD THEY COME TO NEW YORK?
BECAUSE WE'RE HERE?
NO... NOT GOOD ENOUGH...
ZEALOT'S HERE?
MANAGED TO TRANSMIT YOUR MESSAGE AS PULSED AIR, USED HIS SKULL AS A RESONATOR--TO HIM, IT FELT LIKE A VOICE IN HIS HEAD...
BEST WE CAN DO. I HOPE IT'S ENOUGH FOR YOU, WEATHERMAN...

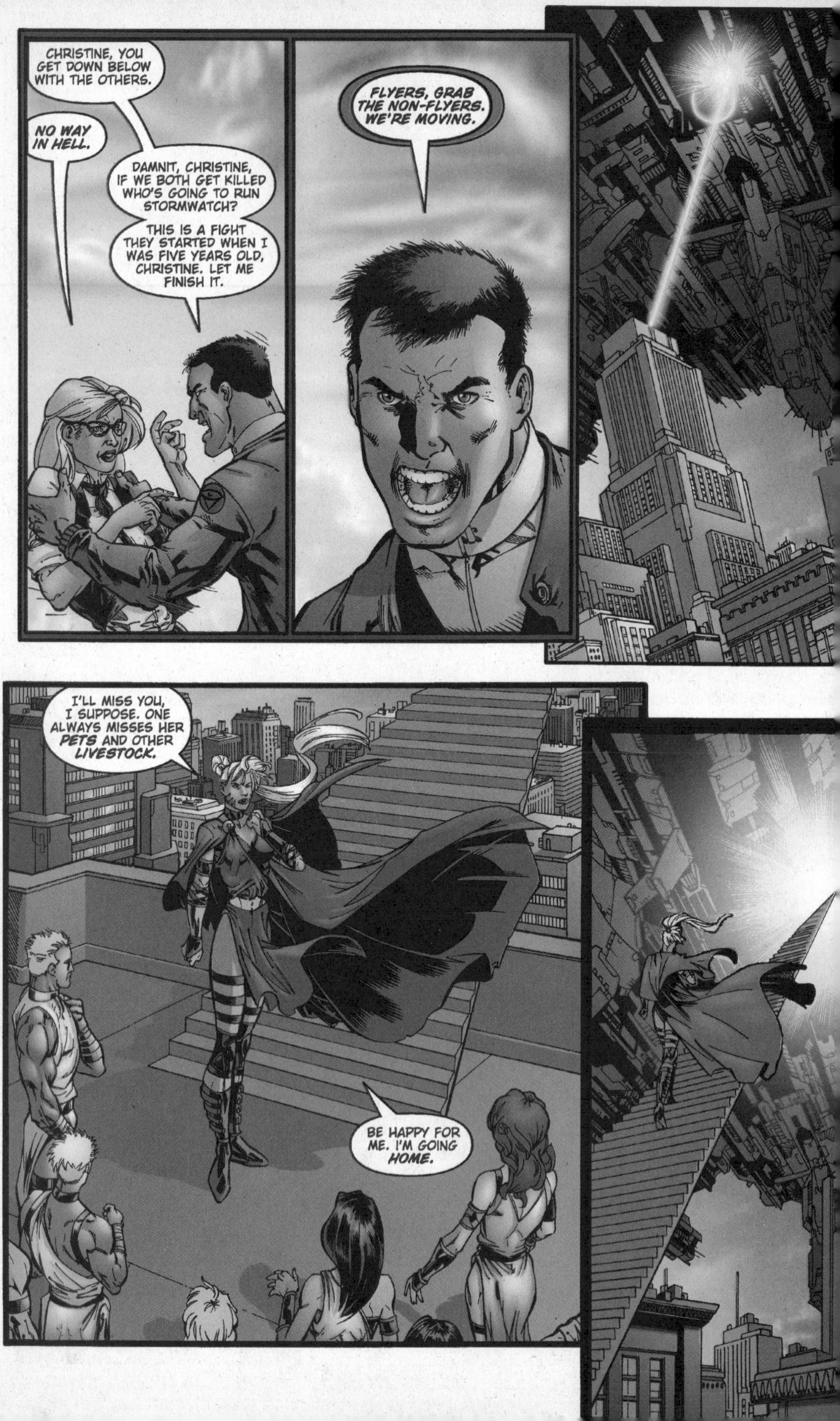
CHRISTINE, YOU GET DOWN BELOW WITH THE OTHERS.
NO WAY IN HELL.
DAMNIT, CHRISTINE, IF WE BOTH GET KILLED WHO'S GOING TO RUN STORMWATCH?
THIS IS A FIGHT THEY STARTED WHEN I WAS FIVE YEARS OLD, CHRISTINE. LET ME FINISH IT.
FLYERS, GRAB THE NON-FLYERS. WE'RE MOVING.
I'LL MISS YOU, I SUPPOSE. ONE ALWAYS MISSES HER PETS AND OTHER LIVESTOCK.
BE HAPPY FOR ME. I'M GOING HOME.

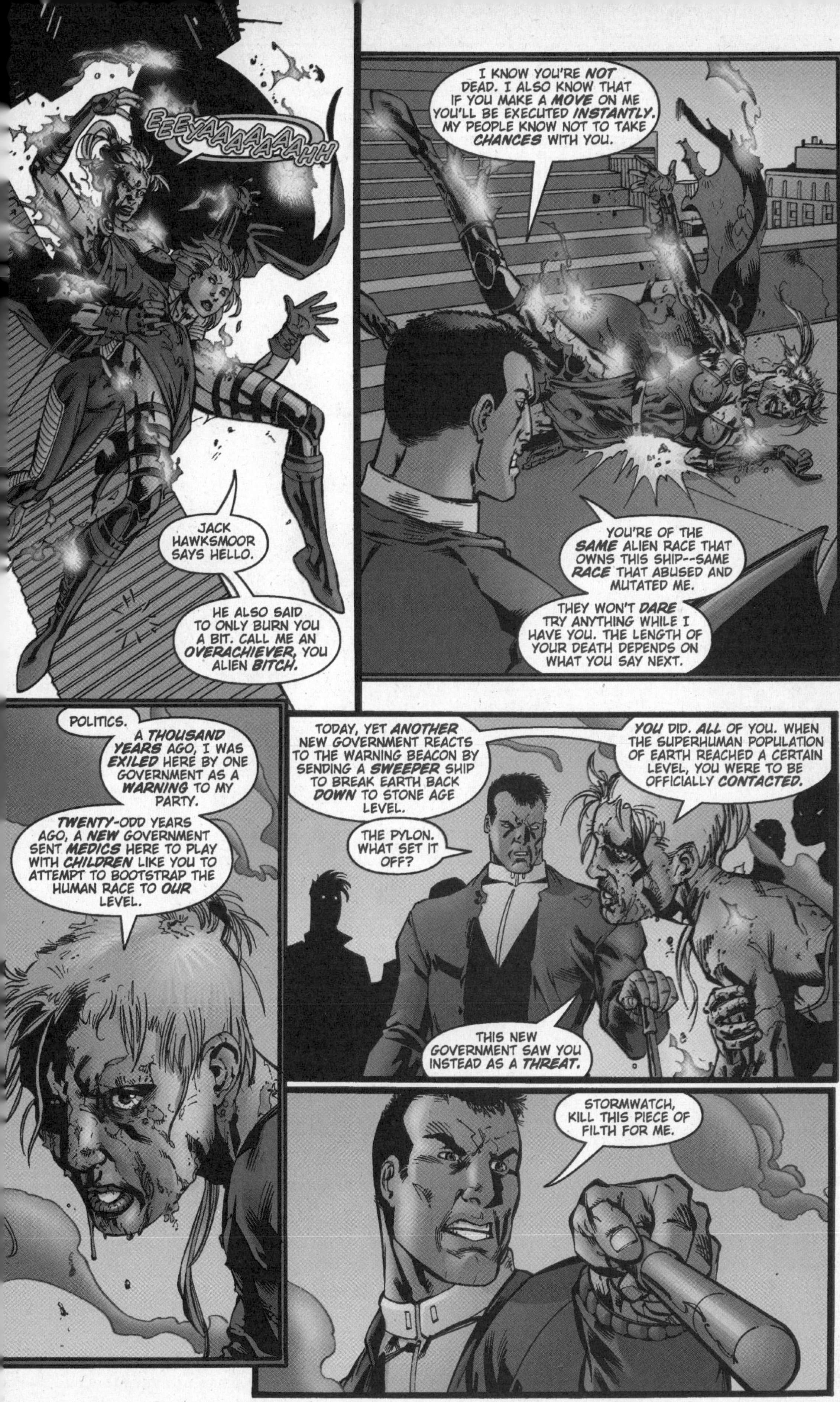
EEEYAAAAAAAHH
JACK HAWKSMOOR SAYS HELLO.
HE ALSO SAID TO ONLY BURN YOU A BIT. CALL ME AN OVERACHIEVER, YOU ALIEN BITCH.
I KNOW YOU'RE NOT DEAD. I ALSO KNOW THAT IF YOU MAKE A MOVE ON ME YOU'LL BE EXECUTED INSTANTLY. MY PEOPLE KNOW NOT TO TAKE CHANCES WITH YOU.
YOU'RE OF THE SAME ALIEN RACE THAT OWNS THIS SHIP--SAME RACE THAT ABUSED AND MUTATED ME.
THEY WON'T DARE TRY ANYTHING WHILE I HAVE YOU. THE LENGTH OF YOUR DEATH DEPENDS ON WHAT YOU SAY NEXT.
POLITICS.
A THOUSAND YEARS AGO, I WAS EXILED HERE BY ONE GOVERNMENT AS A WARNING TO MY PARTY.
TWENTY-ODD YEARS AGO, A NEW GOVERNMENT SENT MEDICS HERE TO PLAY WITH CHILDREN LIKE YOU TO ATTEMPT TO BOOTSTRAP THE HUMAN RACE TO OUR LEVEL.
TODAY, YET ANOTHER NEW GOVERNMENT REACTS TO THE WARNING BEACON BY SENDING A SWEEPER SHIP TO BREAK EARTH BACK DOWN TO STONE AGE LEVEL.
THE PYLON. WHAT SET IT OFF?
YOU DID. ALL OF YOU. WHEN THE SUPERHUMAN POPULATION OF EARTH REACHED A CERTAIN LEVEL, YOU WERE TO BE OFFICIALLY CONTACTED.
THIS NEW GOVERNMENT SAW YOU INSTEAD AS A THREAT.
STORMWATCH, KILL THIS PIECE OF FILTH FOR ME.

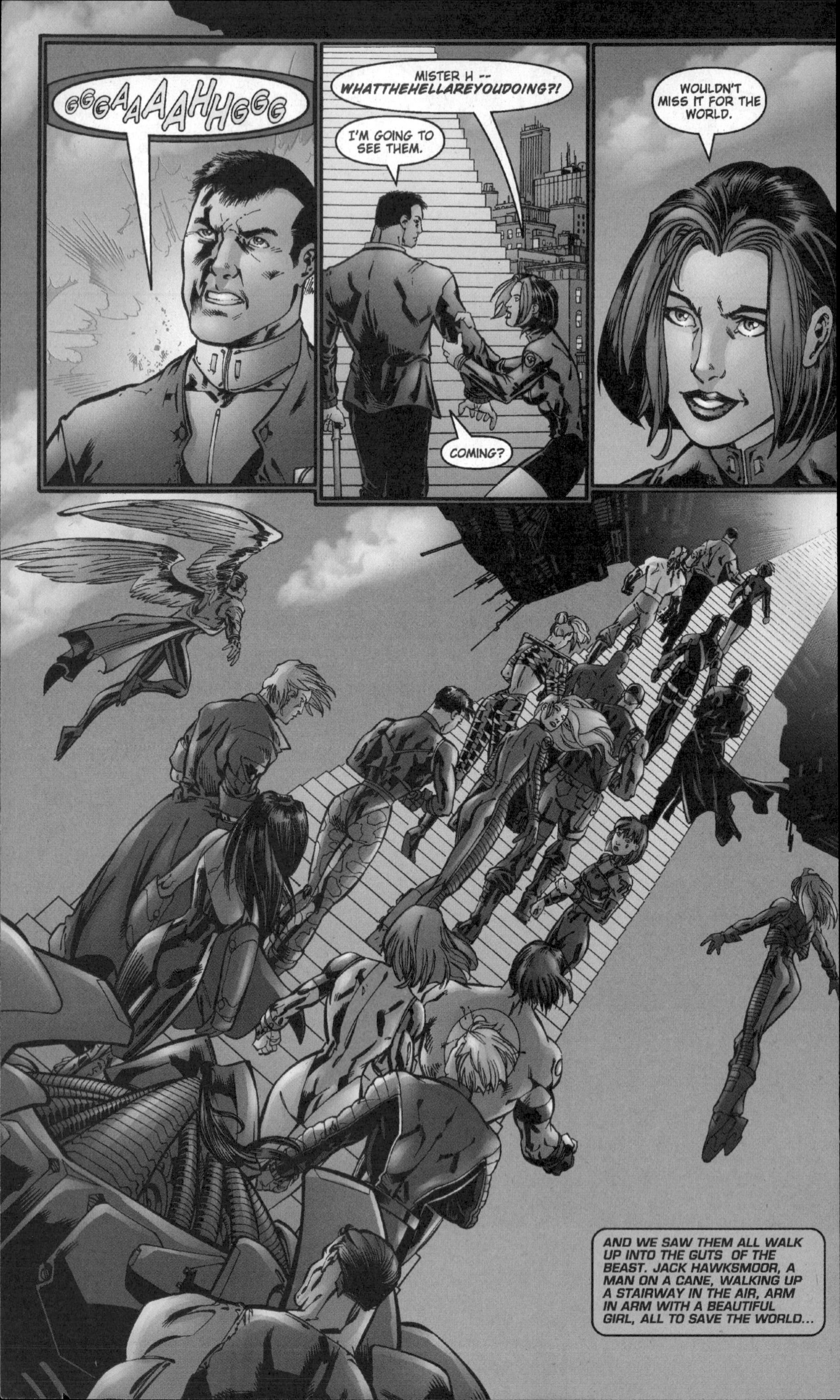

GGGAAAAHHGGG
MISTER H -- WHATTHEHELLAREYOUDOING?!
I'M GOING TO SEE THEM.
COMING?
WOULDN'T MISS IT FOR THE WORLD.
AND WE SAW THEM ALL WALK UP INTO THE GUTS OF THE BEAST. JACK HAWKSMOOR, A MAN ON A CANE, WALKING UP A STAIRWAY IN THE AIR, ARM IN ARM WITH A BEAUTIFUL GIRL, ALL TO SAVE THE WORLD...

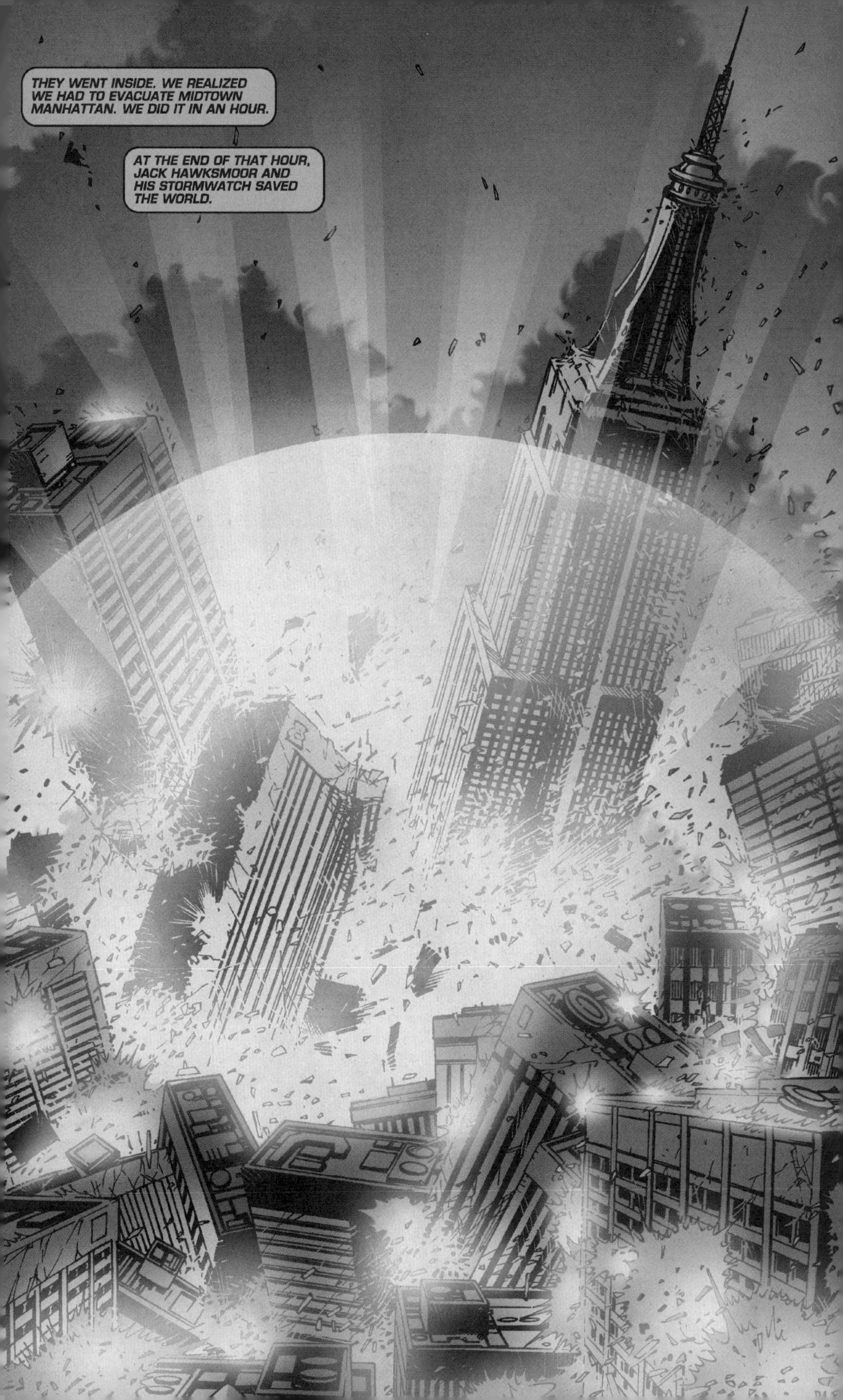
THEY WENT INSIDE. WE REALIZED WE HAD TO EVACUATE MIDTOWN MANHATTAN. WE DID IT IN AN HOUR.
AT THE END OF THAT HOUR, JACK HAWKSMOOR AND HIS STORMWATCH SAVED THE WORLD.

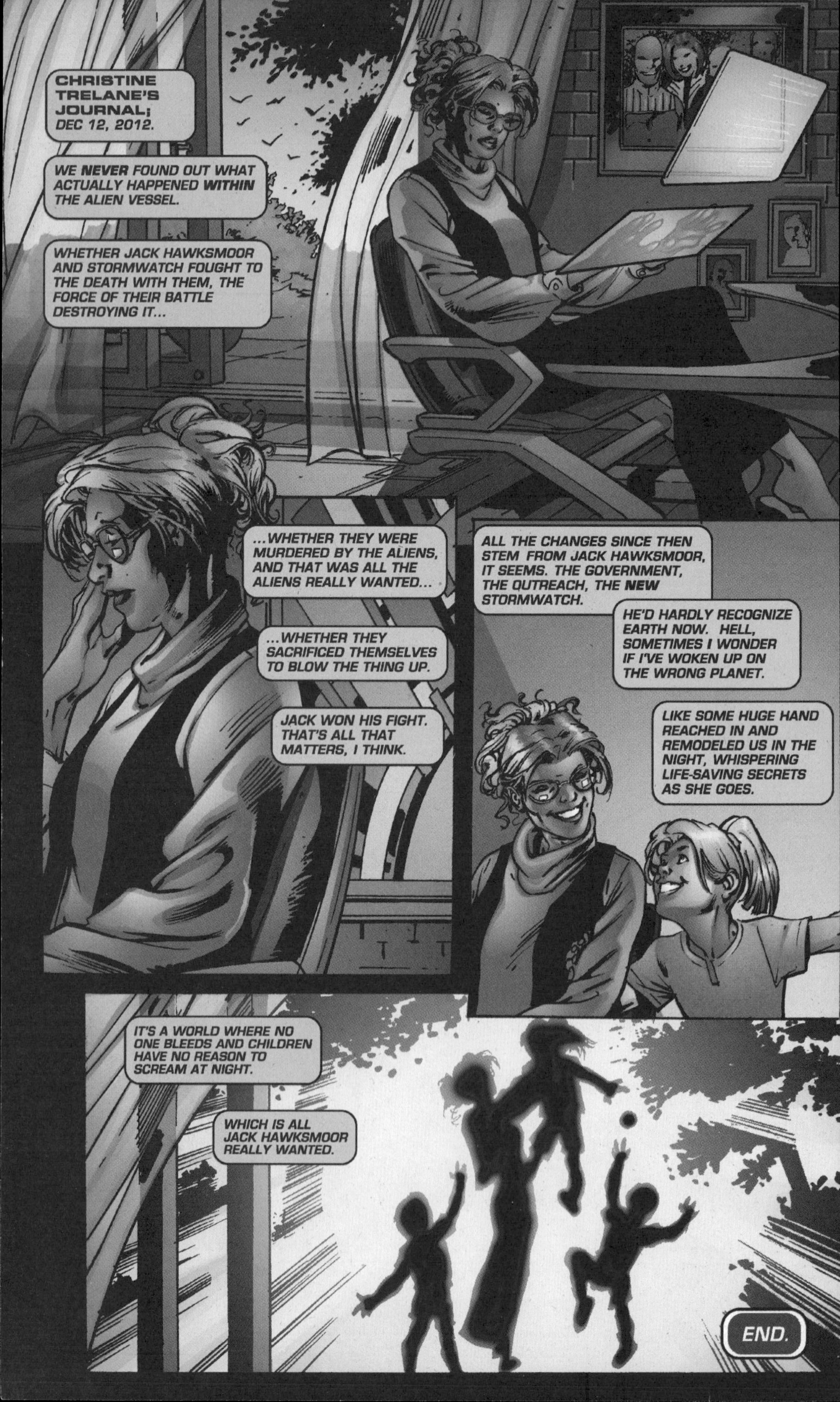
CHRISTINE TRELANE'S JOURNAL; DEC 12, 2012.
WE NEVER FOUND OUT WHAT ACTUALLY HAPPENED WITHIN THE ALIEN VESSEL.
WHETHER JACK HAWKSMOOR AND STORMWATCH FOUGHT TO THE DEATH WITH THEM, THE FORCE OF THEIR BATTLE DESTROYING IT...
...WHETHER THEY WERE MURDERED BY THE ALIENS, AND THAT WAS ALL THE ALIENS REALLY WANTED...
...WHETHER THEY SACRIFICED THEMSELVES TO BLOW THE THING UP.
JACK WON HIS FIGHT. THAT'S ALL THAT MATTERS, I THINK.
ALL THE CHANGES SINCE THEN STEM FROM JACK HAWKSMOOR, IT SEEMS. THE GOVERNMENT, THE OUTREACH, THE NEW STORMWATCH.
HE'D HARDLY RECOGNIZE EARTH NOW. HELL, SOMETIMES I WONDER IF I'VE WOKEN UP ON THE WRONG PLANET.
LIKE SOME HUGE HAND REACHED IN AND REMODELED US IN THE NIGHT, WHISPERING LIFE-SAVING SECRETS AS SHE GOES.
IT'S A WORLD WHERE NO ONE BLEEDS AND CHILDREN HAVE NO REASON TO SCREAM AT NIGHT.
WHICH IS ALL JACK HAWKSMOOR REALLY WANTED.
END.

COVERS

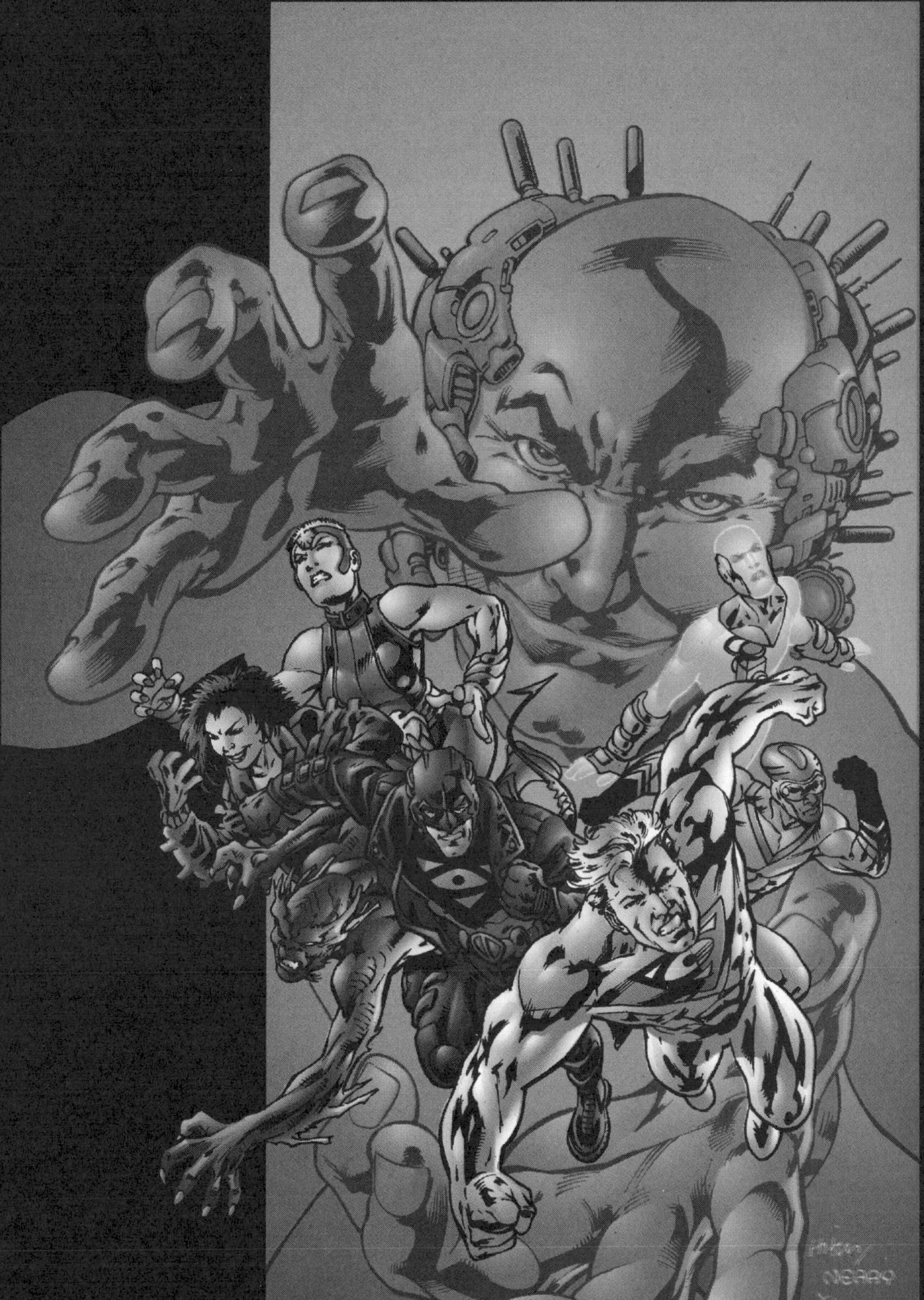

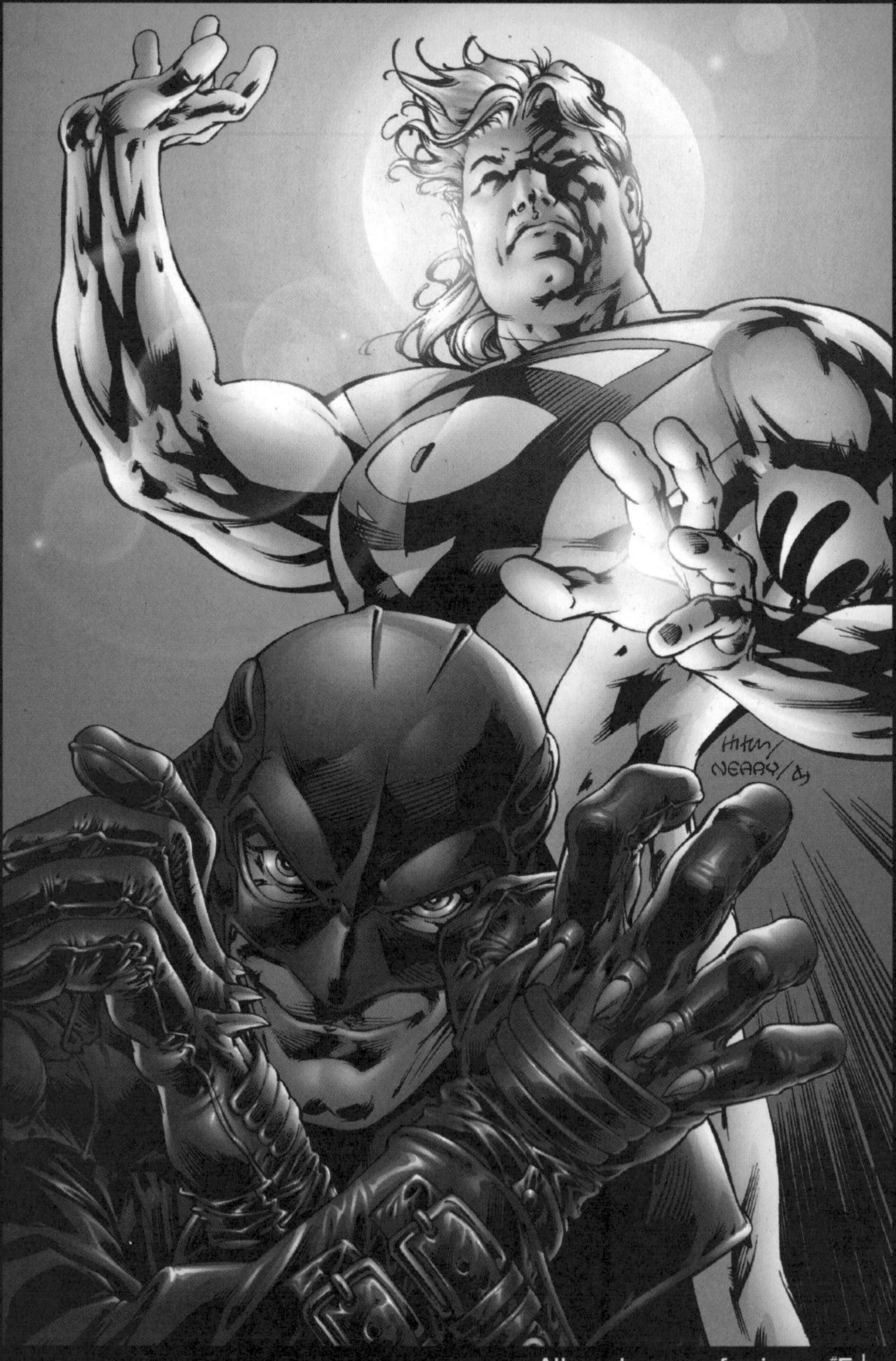

Alternate cover for issue #5

COVERS

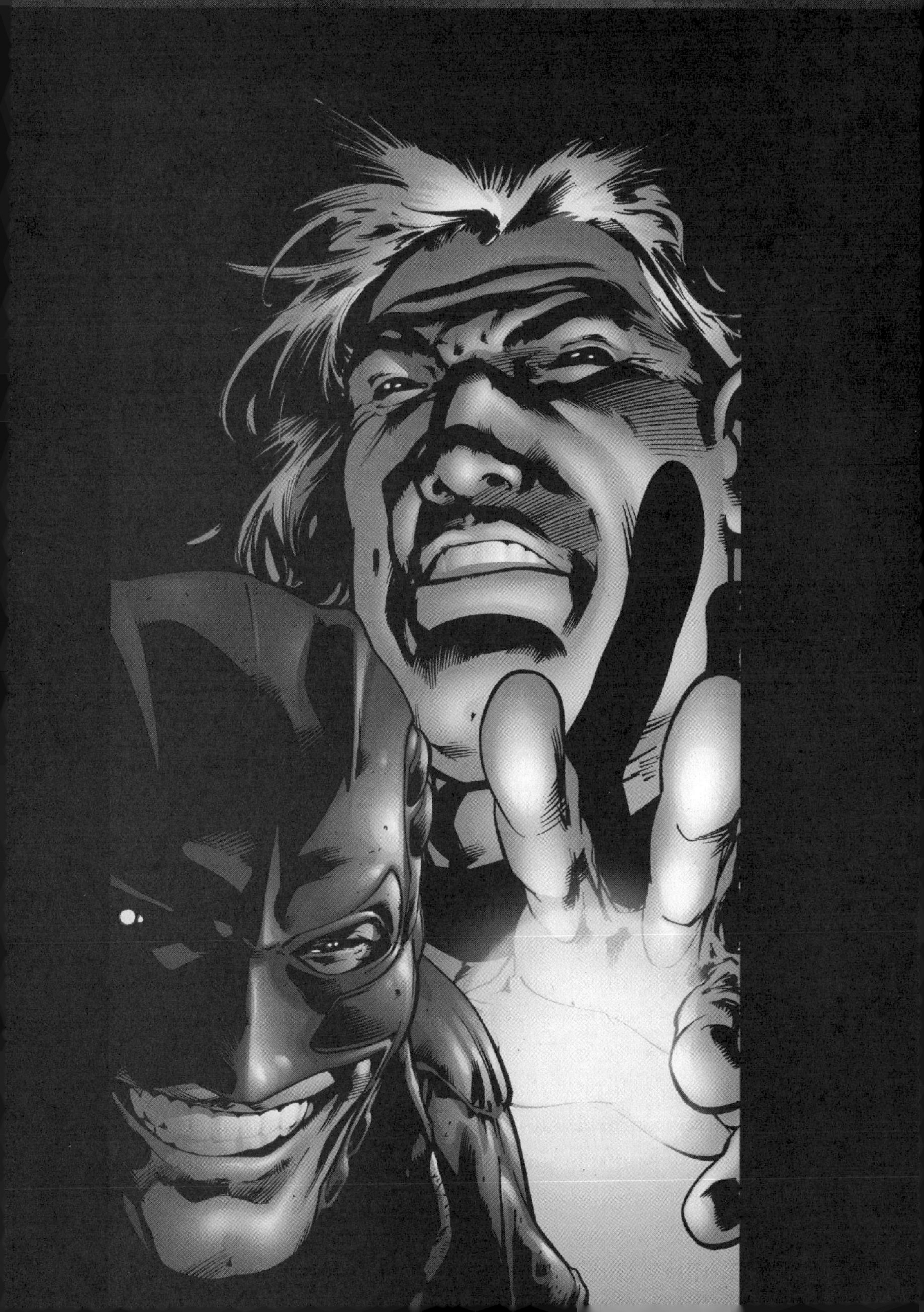

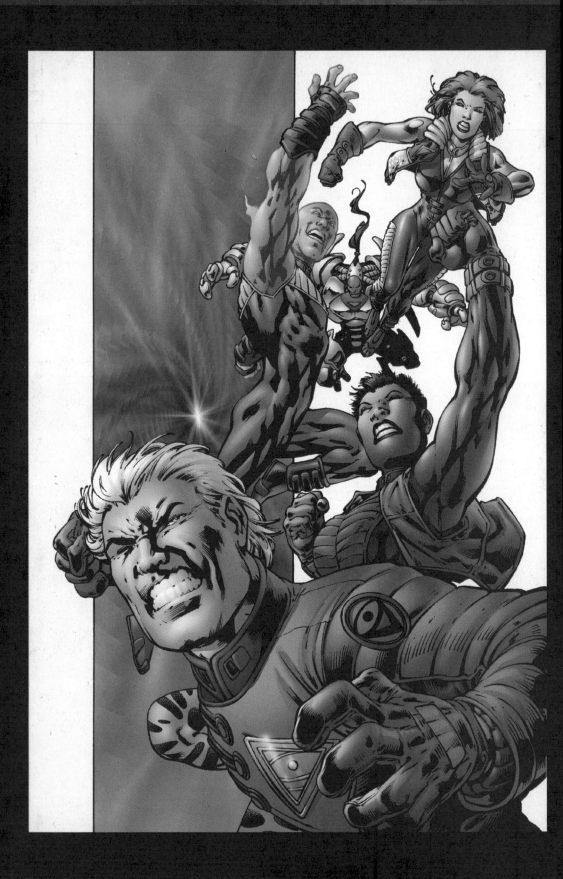

COVERS

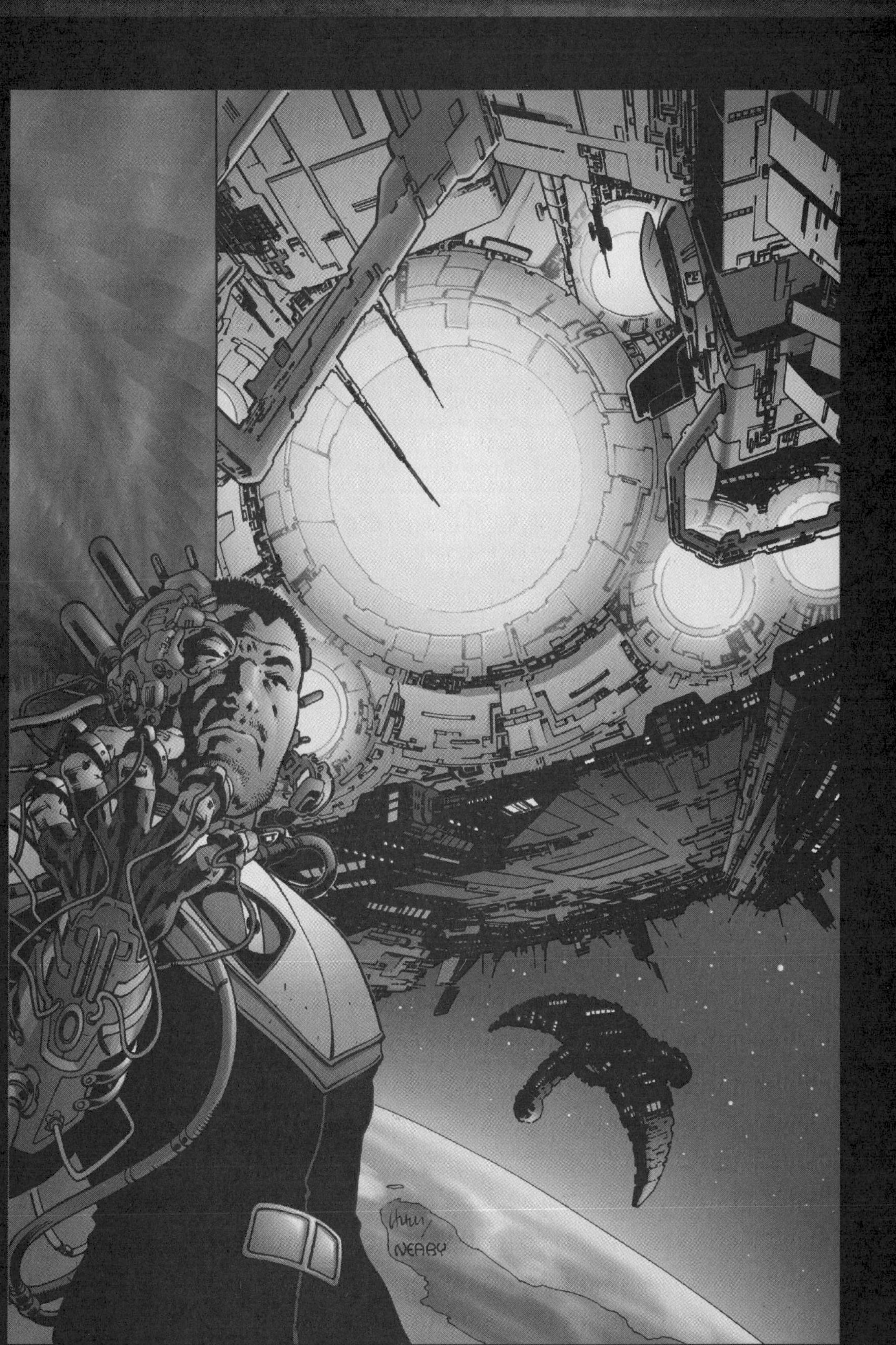
NEARY

Look for these other great books from WildStorm and DC:

COLLECTIONS

Crimson: Loyalty & Loss
Augustyn/Ramos/Hope

Crimson: Heaven & Earth
Augustyn/Ramos/Hope

Deathblow: Sinners and Saints
Choi/Lee/Sale/Scott

Danger Girl:
The Dangerous Collection #1-3
Hartnell/Campbell/Garner

Divine Right:
Collected Edition #1-3
Lee/Williams

Gen¹³
Choi/Lee/Campbell/Garner

Gen¹³: #13 ABC
Choi/Lee/Campbell/Garner

Gen¹³: Bootleg Vol. 1
Various writers and artists

Gen¹³: Grunge the Movie
Warren

Gen¹³: I Love New York
Arcudi/Frank/Smith

Gen¹³: Interactive Plus
Various writers and artists

Gen¹³: Starting Over
Choi/Lee/Campbell/Garner

Gen¹³: We'll Take Manhattan
Lobdell/Benes/Sibal

Kurt Busiek's Astro City:
Life in the Big City
Busiek/Anderson

Kurt Busiek's Astro City:
Confession
Busiek/Anderson/Blyberg

Kurt Busiek's Astro City:
Family Album
Busiek/Anderson/Blyberg

Kurt Busiek's Astro City:
Tarnished Angel
Busiek/Anderson/Blyberg

Leave It to Chance:
Shaman's Rain
Robinson/Smith

Leave It to Chance:
Trick or Threat
Robinson/Smith/Freeman

Resident Evil Collection One
Various writers and artists

Voodoo: Dancing in the Dark
Moore/Lopez/Rio/Various

Wetworks: Rebirth
Portacio/Choi/Williams

StormWatch: Lightning Strikes
Ellis/Raney/Lee/Elliott/Williams

StormWatch: Change or Die
Ellis/Raney/Jimenez

StormWatch: Force of Nature
Ellis/Hitch/Neary

WildC.A.T.s: Gang War
Moore/Various

WildC.A.T.s: Gathering of Eagles
Claremont/Lee/Williams

WildC.A.T.s: Homecoming
Moore/Various

WildC.A.T.s/X-Men
Various writers and artists

Wildcats: Street Smart
Lobdell/Charest/Friend

WildStorm Rising
Windsor-Smith/Various

OTHER COLLECTIONS
OF INTEREST

Art of Chiodo
Chiodo

The Batman Adventures:
Mad Love
Dini/Timm

Batman:
The Dark Knight Returns
Miller/Janson/Varley

Batman: Faces
Wagner

Batman: The Killing Joke
Moore/Bolland/Higgins

Batman: Year One
Miller/Mazzucchelli/Lewis

Camelot 3000
Barr/Bolland

The Golden Age
Robinson/Smith

Green Lantern: Emerald Knight
Marz/Dixon/Banks/Various

Green Lantern: Fear Itself
Marz/Parker

JLA: New World Order
Morrison/Porter/Dell

JLA: Rock of Ages
Morrison/Porter/Dell/Various

JLA: Year One
Waid/Augustyn/Kitson

JLA/ WildC.A.T.s
Morrison/Semeiks/Conrad

Justice League of America:
The Nail
Davis/Farmer

Kingdom Come
Waid/Ross

Ronin
Miller

Starman: Sins of the Father
Robinson/Harris/
Von Grawbadger

Starman: Night and Day
Robinson/Harris/
Von Grawbadger

Starman: Times Past
Harris/Jimenez/Weeks/Various

Starman: A Wicked Inclination
Robinson/Harris/
Von Grawbadger/Various

Watchmen
Moore/Gibbons

For the nearest comics shop carrying collected editions and monthly titles from DC Comics call 1-888-COMIC BOOK.